BORDER BRIDE

"Will you expect me to obey your every command without question?" Janet asked.

"I should be able to expect that," he said, but the amusement her words stirred revealed itself in his tone, and he knew she heard it.

Her eyebrows shot upward. "I do not believe that even the Scottish marriage rite made me your slave, sir."

"You promised to obey me."

"Aye, and I will when your commands are reasonable."

He sighed. "Jenny, lass, I have admitted being thoughtless. I know that in fairness I ought to have taken time to hear what you had to say before sending you away, both before I left for Kielbeck and later, before I sent you to your room. But do not take that to mean I will debate my every command with you, for I will not. If you insist on defying me, you will invite grief, so from now on, if you decide to ignore an order of my giving, be prepared to suffer the consequences. I promise you, I am not always as understanding as I am trying to be now. Our marriage is young, and I want it to grow strong. Thus, I am willing to compromise—but only a bit, lass. You will not usurp my position as master of Broadhaugh."

This time, when her hand touched his thigh, he knew she did it deliberately. His body did not know the difference, though. It leapt in response.

She said softly, "Hold me close, Quinton. I want you to make love to me."

He did not hesitate, and if there was any question about who won the final point, he did not care. . . .

Books by Amanda Scott

BORDER FIRE
HIGHLAND SPIRITS
DANGEROUS LADY
HIGHLAND TREASURE
HIGHLAND SECRETS
HIGHLAND FLING
DANGEROUS ANGELS
DANGEROUS GAMES
THE BAWDY BRIDE
DANGEROUS ILLUSIONS

Published by Zebra Books

BORDER FIRE

Amanda Scott

Zebra Books
Kensington Publishing Corp.

http://www.zebrabooks.com

ZEBRA BOOKS are published by

Kensington Publishing Corp.
850 Third Avenue
New York, NY 10022

First Printing: April, 2000
10   9   8   7   6   5   4

Printed in the United States of America

Dedicated to my cousin
Nancy J Fulsom,
who shares my genetic love for
tales of the Scottish Border,
in the hope that she will enjoy this one.

AUTHOR'S NOTE

The correct pronunciation of Buccleuch is "Buck-loo," with the accent on the second syllable.

Chapter 1

"Now Liddisdale has ridden a raid,
but I wat they had better stayed at hame."

The Borders
February 1596

Tattered skirts of mist shadowed the high, gibbous moon as the raiders approached the dark hamlet of Haggbeck in the shadow of England's Cheviot Hills. A thin, crisp layer of snow covered the ground, and there were thirty riders; but their ponies' hooves were nimble and quick, and made little noise for so many.

At a sign from their leader, a group of ten led by Ally the Bastard circled toward the common lands to collect the cattle, sheep, and horses. The main party continued into the hamlet.

The band of reivers had traveled through the night following intricate byways known to few but their leader. He was a man, legend said, who could find his way to hell and back through smoke-filled Limbo and pitch-black Purgatory. The secret haunts of Liddesdale were his refuge, the Cheviot Hills and Tynedale forests his hunting grounds, the Debatable Lands and Bewcastle Waste his playing fields.

Other men respected him as a leader of excellent head, believing his skill for penetrating the darkest night or the thickest mist unmatched by any other of his time. He knew his ground to an inch, and he had an uncanny knack for evading the watchers that the English Queen had set to guard her border.

Those watchers presented a formidable barrier, for from Solway to Berwick, from October to mid-March, by day or by night, the entire frontier remained under watch. Local English nobility and gentry bore responsibility for arming and horsing their men, as well as for inspecting the watches they set over every hilltop, ford, and dale, to guard every conceivable passage over their marches.

In times past, English wardens had sentenced to death any man who failed to resist Scottish raiders, and English landowners were still under strict orders to enforce the rules. But over the years those rules had relaxed, and nowadays English watchers who failed to raise a hue and cry against thieves faced no more than being held liable for the goods stolen during their watch.

Twice already that night, the Scottish leader had waved his men to lurking places while watchers passed within yards of them. Unfortunately, one could not count upon the Queen's guardians to be in the same places each time. Pairs or larger groups of them patrolled together, moving from dale to ford to hilltop and back, ready to catch any careless reiver who showed himself.

The Scottish side had its guards, too, of course, and beacons on hilltops and tower roofs set to give fiery warning of English raids. However, unless a powerful lord commanded otherwise, the Scots tended to be less organized than their English counterparts, relying on other means to warn of attack or to protect against one.

In any event, that night the raiders known the length and breadth of the Borders as Rabbie's Bairns reached their target easily. They had chosen Haggbeck in simple retaliation for an earlier English raid on the Liddesdale holdings of Curst Eckie

Crosier. Curst Eckie wanted his cattle back, and if the raiders could collect more, and a few horses or sheep to boot, so much the better.

The leader raised his hand again as the riders neared the hamlet center.

"No sign of anyone waking," he murmured to the big man riding beside him with the vicious, long-handled, curved-bladed weapon known as a Jeddart or Jedburgh ax slung over one muscular shoulder.

"Nay, Rabbie," the man replied. "They be lazy creatures, these English."

"Keep your voice down, Hob. They say all Grahams sleep with an ear to the wind, and we are deep in Graham territory. The river Lyne and Brackengill Castle lie just over that hill to the south of us."

"Aye, sure, I'll keep mum," Hob the Mouse said in a deep, rumbling mutter. "D'ye ken where be the house with iron gratings to its windows, Rab? Curst Eckie said he heard tell of such, and I promised him we'd find it and carry them home."

"Does Curst Eckie covet iron bars for his cottage windows?" Laughter filled the leader's voice.

"Aye, sure, and me, as well. Ye can laugh, Rabbie, but Curst Eckie and me, we'll ha' the last laugh. Once we've got iron fixed to our windows, won't no thievin' Englishmen climb in through them, ye'll see."

"Until some thievin' Englishman steals them back again," the leader retorted with a chuckle. "If you must have them, you'll most likely find them on the biggest house, there in the village center."

One of the riders raised a trumpet, and seeing his gesture, the leader nodded. The man put the horn to his lips, and its clarion call rang through the night. In moments the hamlet was awake. Screams mingled with the shouts of angry men.

The raiders charged the cottages, some dismounting to round up women and children while others dealt with their menfolk. Scuffles broke out right and left as half-dressed men rushed out with swords drawn to defend families and property. The clash of steel on steel soon joined with feminine shrieks and the cries of children startled awake. Over all, the trumpet's martial notes rang out with eerie clarity.

Signing to the hornsman to stay near, the leader watched closely for a telltale glint of moonlight off an enemy pistol or sword, and listened for the familiar twang of bowstrings or any other unusual sound in the night above the din of the skirmishing. He held his sword at the ready in one hand and a pistol in the other.

The screams of the women and children did not disturb him, for he knew his men would not seriously harm or molest any female or bairn. Only one follower of his had ever done such a thing, and the leader had summarily hanged him from the first tree they had come upon after eluding pursuit, as a warning to the others that he would see his orders obeyed.

Huge Hob the Mouse had found his iron gratings, and while others held cottagers at bay with pistols and lances, he and another man liberated the grates by the simplest of methods. They ripped them off the windows with their bare hands.

As they did so, a young rider called Sym's Davy came galloping through the hamlet, shouting, "Rabbie, there's riders coming from the south!"

"How many?"

"Thirty, maybe forty!"

"Has Ally the Bastard gathered the beasts?"

"Aye, sure, about thirty kine and as many horses, but there be sheep, too, Rabbie, and the riders be coming gey fast."

"Can they see Ally and his lads yet?"

"Nay, for they're ahind the hill, yonder east."

"Then ride like the devil, lad, and tell Ally to split his men, half to ride ahead with the cattle and horses, the others to drive the sheep. Tell them I said to abandon the sheep if they must but to get the horses and cattle to Liddesdale."

"Aye, sure, they can scatter the sheep ahind 'em to slow

them what follow," Sym's Davy said, grinning. "What of these lads here, then?"

"They'll ride with me. We'll draw the pursuers after us to cover your retreat. Off you go now." Gesturing to his hornsman, he shouted, "Blow them away, Jed. We're off at speed."

The response came in a blast of notes from the trumpet, sounding retreat. The raiders who were engaged in fisticuffs, swordplay, and other such exercises broke off their activities at once. Those who had dismounted leapt to their saddles with whatever booty they had stolen from the cottagers, and in moments the little band was away, the hornsman riding behind his leader, blowing merrily as he rode. The trumpet's notes taunted and teased the Englishmen to follow if they dared.

Hoofbeats thundered through the dale. Looking back, the leader smiled to see that his tactic had drawn the pursuers straight through the hamlet after them. The group following was large enough to make it unlikely that others had turned off to seek out more of his reivers in the rugged landscape. Knowing the hills and glens as he did, he could afford to let them keep his party in sight long enough to draw them well away west of the others. When they had ridden far enough to be sure that Ally the Bastard, Curst Eckie, and the others had got the animals safely on their way to Liddesdale, they could easily lose their pursuers.

Exhilarated by victory, he shouted, "We'll have moonlight again, lads!"

Laughter and cheers greeted his slogan, echoing the trumpet's notes. Deciding minutes later that they had ridden far enough west of the hamlet, he looked back again. They had entered a winding, narrow glen, and he knew the head of it was not far off. The pursuers had neither gained on them nor fallen behind.

The sides of the glen were moderately steep and covered with bracken, shrubbery, drifts of snow, and thickets of birch and beech trees. He knew that whoever led the pursuit would expect him to ride up the gradual slope to the glen's head, rather than attempt a more difficult route. Waiting only until a bend briefly hid them from view, he wrenched his pony's head to the right.

Liddel Water lay but two miles beyond the hill. What snow remained on the open patches of ground was thin and rutted, and so would not instantly reveal their tracks; and thickets would cover them long enough to reach the hilltop if their ponies were swift. Jed the Horn rode on up the glen, knowing from experience exactly what his master expected of him. With luck, their pursuers would continue to chase trumpet notes long enough for the rest of them to make it over the hill. As for the hornsman's own safety, it was comparatively easy for one rider to find a lurking hole and elude pursuit.

The plan worked perfectly. As the riders reached the hilltop, they heard drumming hoofbeats below. Exchanging delighted grins in the pale moonlight, they let the ponies pick their own way down the other side.

Hob the Mouse moved up alongside the leader. "That be one in the eye for the English, I'm thinking."

"Aye, it is," the leader said with a chuckle. " 'Tis a fine braw night, Hob. Good fresh air, a compliant moon, and a good stretch of the wit make life mighty fine for a man of adventure."

"Profitable, too," Hob said with a laugh. "Curst Eckie and me, we've got grating enough for both his cot and mine."

"Whisst," Rabbie commanded as they approached a shadowy, shrub-crowned hillock. "Can that be— Ambush!" he cried, realizing that the shadows at the hillock's top were not shrubs but mounted men. He wheeled his pony toward a cleft worn into the hillside by a rivulet, but before he had ridden ten feet, he saw above him a screen of lances and more steel-bonneted men. Grimly, he drew rein.

"Dinna turn aside, Rabbie," a man shouted behind him. "There canna be but ten o' the villains!"

"Nay, lads," he said loudly enough for his voice to carry to the silent ambushers. "In five years I ha' lost only three men—four if ye count the hanging—and I'm no going to lose any tonight unless God Himself ordains it. They outnumber us, and they've cut us off on two sides. There are lances ahead."

"Faith, they'll clap us all in irons!"

"Not us." Lowering his voice, he said, "Hob, lead the lads back the way we came till you reach that pond shaped like a birch leaf. Do you remember it?"

"Aye, but will ye no go with us, then, Rab?"

"No. When you reach that pond, cut over the lower of the two hills you'll see ahead of you. Kershopefoot Forest begins just the other side of it. Ride north and keep to the forest's cover till you reach Kershope Burn. You can cross into Scotland easily there, and make for home through Liddesdale."

"Aye, sure, but which of the lads will ye tak' wi' ye?"

"None of them. We can't expect that ruse to work twice in a night, especially against so many. They'd just split and follow us. If there is anything that might keep them together, though, it'll be the chance to capture Rabbie Redcloak."

In dismay, Hob said, "Ye'll no just ride bang up to them, laddie!"

"Not I. I mean to lead them a merry chase, but first I must be certain they know what a prize they'll catch if they're quick enough."

"But, Rabbie," Hob protested, "what if they send just a few after ye and the rest after us? They'll see in a trice that ye're nobbut one man."

He grinned. "Aye, but they think that one has the strength and skill of a wizard, and they'll believe that the rest of you are trying to draw them away from me. They'll not think for a moment that it's the other way about, not when they see this in the moonlight," he added, pulling off the dark, furry, hooded cloak he wore over his padded leather jack and breeks, and flipping it so its red silk lining showed.

"But if they catch ye—"

"Then I shall employ my gifts of gentle persuasion to good advantage until you and the lads come to rescue me. If the worst occurs, I shall simply await the next Truce Day and win free by ransom.''

''Aye, if Himself will agree to pay one,'' Hob said doubtfully.

''Never fear. I shall talk my way out of trouble long before we need worry about that.''

''Aye, well, ye've a tongue on ye could wheedle a duck off a tarn, 'tis true.''

''It is, so go now,'' the leader said. ''They've only waited this long to see what we will do. They won't wait much longer.'' Raising an arm, he shouted, ''Ride, lads! We'll have moonlight again!''

Still waving, he wheeled his pony toward the head of the glen, urging it to a canter. When he believed that both groups of ambushers could see his figure clearly and must realize that his men had not followed him, he pulled back on the reins till the horse reared and wheeled again, making his cloak billow wide and free. As it did, the misty clouds screening the moon parted to illuminate the cloak's fiery red color. Spurring his pony hard, he rode up the slope to his left, opposite the waiting lancers. Keeping well clear of the ambushers on his right at the head of the glen, he charged back into the heart of Graham country.

After only a moment's hesitation, both sets of riders galloped after him, shouting their excitement at having deduced the identity of the most notorious reiver on either side of the Border.

Certain that he could elude them easily whenever he chose to do so, he let them keep him in sight. He knew that the sturdy border pony he rode had miles of distance left in it, and exhilaration surged through him, filling him with energy.

The mist was clearing overhead, which was both a boon and a worry—boon in that he could easily see his way, worry in that his pursuers could see him just as plainly. Twists and turns appeared throughout the rugged, hilly landscape, but he knew them all. His agile brain had been sorting and sifting the best routes for escape from the instant he had seen the first ambushers.

He wasted no thought on the identity of those who pursued him. Since he was deep in Graham country, it was likely that at least some were Grahams, but the area nearby on both sides of the Border was littered with members of that unholy tribe, which was as likely to fight its own as to fight men of other loyalties.

Reaching the top of a hill, he glanced back and saw that several riders had narrowed the distance. Two were within bowshot, so he dared not linger.

Suddenly, from behind, a trumpet sounded. For an instant he thought it was Jed the Horn, but the notes played soon told him that it was not. Then, to his shock, a second horn answered, and a third—one from ahead, the other to his left, and both much too close for comfort. If he did not take care, he warned himself, they would surround him. The moonlight no longer felt friendly.

A dog bayed, then another, and another.

He urged his pony away from the sounds. Only one direction beckoned now. He turned toward the Mote of Liddel, where the river Esk joined Liddel Water a few miles to the northeast. From that point, for a short distance, the Liddel formed the line between Scotland and England. Spurring his pony, he realized that his sole remaining hope lay in the valiant beast's nimble speed.

Cresting a hill a short time later, he saw moonlight glinting on black water in the distance and knew it to be the Liddel. Minutes more and, barring accident, he would cross into Scotland.

They could follow, of course—and legally—by declaring a "hot trod" and informing the first person they met on the other side that they were in pursuit of a dastardly reiver. They could even demand that the warden of the Scottish west and middle marches help capture him. He smiled at the thought, but the smile vanished when he realized that the moonlight glinted not only on water but also on steel. Horsemen moved to line the water's edge. He was trapped.

Resigned, he reined his pony to a walk, hoping that his men and their hard-earned booty had not fallen into what now looked like a singularly well-organized trap involving upwards of a hundred men and—from the veritable chorus of baying behind him— an equal number of sleuth hounds. Amused by the thought of Hob the Mouse's chagrin should he and Curst Eckie Crosier lose their precious iron grates before they had mounted them to their windows, it occurred to him that if his men had eluded capture he might use those gratings to help bargain for his freedom.

Some twenty yards from the line of armed horsemen, with others closing in behind him, he drew his pony to a halt, murmuring, "Come and get me, lads. Power lies with the one who makes the other move first."

He would have to resort next to his second famous gift, that eloquent tongue that supposedly could wheedle a duck from a tarn or an eagle from its aerie. He hoped the gift would live up to the legend. If it failed him, his captors would keep him locked up until the next Truce Day, and then he would have to face his own people with a bill of grievance hanging over him. There was a certain amount of irony in that situation, but he would nonetheless do everything he could to avoid it.

The horsemen at the water's edge remained where they were—almost, he thought, as if they feared he might yet escape if even one of them should move.

He waited patiently and with dignity until the riders he heard approaching from behind him had stopped. Horses whuffled and snorted, and trappings clinked and rattled, but for a long, tense moment no one spoke. He knew their leader waited for him to move, and the knowledge amused him. It was a game, after all, and every man in the Borders knew its rules.

Remembering at least one incident when a captor had shot a captive in the back with an arrow from close range, he felt a tremor between his shoulder blades. He did not think the men who had captured Rabbie Redcloak would dare do such a thing, however. They would thereby succeed only in making Rabbie a martyr whose ghost would roam the Borders for years to come. No Englishman would want to effect such an outcome.

The silence stretched taut, and he sensed the men in front of him growing impatient. Their leader must have sensed the same, for he spoke at last.

"Rabbie Redcloak, I hereby order your arrest for leading forays against the Queen's subjects; for driving off herds of cattle, horses, and sheep; for slaying innocent people and stealing their goods; and for kidnapping subjects of the queen and holding them illegally whilst demanding ransom for their release."

"All that?" He turned without haste, searching the shadowy faces for the one who had spoken, as he added lightly, "Indeed, 'tis a litany of offenses, albeit a false one. Who, if I may mak' so bold as to ask ye, has the honor to be my captor?"

"Sir Hugh Graham of Brackengill, deputy warden of the English west march, has that honor, you God-forsaken scoundrel. Scize him, lads! 'Ware arms!'"

The next few moments might have proved ignominious had it not been for the captive's great dignity. The men who surged toward him, clearly expecting him to resist, stopped and glanced uncertainly at one another when he calmly held out his hands, wrists together, waiting to be tied.

As they removed his sword, pistol, and dagger, one said, "Do we leave him on his horse, Sir Hugh?"

"Aye, I'm in a hurry to reach my bed, lads, so we'll let him ride."

Hearing amusement in his tone, the captive stiffened.

"Bind him facedown across his saddle," Sir Hugh said. "Cover all but his devil's face with that damned red cloak, so the world can see what we've captured."

Stoically, their captive allowed them to obey that humiliating order, keeping his countenance and calm through sheer force of will. They passed ropes beneath the pony's belly to tie his wrists to his ankles, stretching his body over the saddle. Only when the faithful beast shifted and shied in protest of unfamiliar hands beneath its belly did he speak, saying quietly, "Stand easy, lad."

He felt the animal shudder, but it calmed, and he drew a deep breath in an attempt to calm himself. When the leader called for them to ride, though, humiliation became of less concern than the pain caused by the ungainly position.

His padded jack protected his chest and stomach, and his leather breeches protected his nether parts, but the men who had tied him had stretched him tight and the bindings hurt. They had not bothered to remove his steel bonnet or to bind his stirrups, and the stirrup near his head began bouncing about when the rider leading the pony urged it to a trot. The metal stirrup rang torturously against the captive's helmet and threatened his face if he looked forward or back. The one on the other side smacked his calves and thighs, reminding him of a day in his boyhood when his mother had taken a beech-tree switch to them for some long-forgotten sin. He hoped he did not face a long journey. In the mood Sir Hugh was in, he would not put it past the man to make him ride facedown all the way to Carlisle.

In fact, they had ridden for less than an hour when he saw castle walls loom ahead. Although his awkward position let him see less of the landscape than usual, he knew that they had reached Brackengill, Sir Hugh's home. Remembering that Sir Hugh served as a deputy to Lord Scrope, warden of the English west march and keeper of the royal castle of Carlisle, he decided that Sir Hugh intended to house him overnight before delivering him to Scrope.

They rode through tall, wide-open gates into a torchlit courtyard, and before the gates had shut behind them, the captive noted that the number of men escorting him had decreased significantly.

"Bring him."

Sir Hugh's curt command resulted in the captive being quickly cut loose and pulled off the pony to stand precariously on weakened, pain-ridden legs between two of the armed men. They dragged him willy-nilly into a low-roofed, dark building that looked and smelled like a stable. It was cold. His host, he decided sardonically, would not be housing him with any degree of comfort.

His wrists were still bound, and his fingers and hands had grown numb. His entire body ached as if it had been racked.

Torches burst into flame and cast a flickering red-orange light over the scene. His senses had not misled him. They were inside a stable, and some half-dozen men stood around him, their shadowy faces reflecting the reddish glow. Involuntarily the captive thought of hellfire.

Ruthlessly banishing the comparison from his mind, he forced himself to stand erect and face his captor. Somewhat to his surprise, he regarded Sir Hugh almost eye-to-eye. That was no common occurrence, for with the exception of Hob the Mouse, he usually looked down upon his fellows.

Sir Hugh took off his own steel bonnet, revealing a thick mass of curly red hair. Hanging the bonnet on a stall post, he pushed one beefy hand through his curls and scratched his head. His neatly trimmed beard glimmered red in the torchlight. His eyes glinted like cold gray steel.

The captive inhaled deeply, then in a voice heavy with the Scottish Borderers' accent, he said, "I'd be gey willing to mak' a fair bargain over this wee misunderstanding betwixt us."

"You are in no position to make any bargain," Sir Hugh snapped. "Your race is run, Rabbie Redcloak."

" 'Tis true ye caught me fair, sir," he said, "but I canna think what grievance ye mean to claim agin me."

"Theft, for one, you scoundrel!"

"Ah, but I dinna carry any stolen goods, as ye must ken the noo."

"You are a thieving murderer!"

"Yet there be no man, lass, or bairn wha' can claim to ha' suffered harm at my hands this nicht, sir."

"Mayhap that is so tonight, but it is of no—"

"Moreover," the captive interjected swiftly, "I might could just put a wee finger on certain articles that ha' gone missing over the past month or twa gin ye give me cause to act in a generous manner toward ye, sir.''

"I do not doubt that," Sir Hugh said grimly. "Has it not occurred to you yet to wonder just how it is that you find yourself in this predicament tonight?''

Since he had been wondering that very thing from the instant he realized that a considerable force of men had driven him into a trap and surrounded him, he said simply, ''Aye, I canna deny ye've whetted me curiosity considerably on that point.''

"We knew you would strike at Haggbeck," Sir Hugh said smugly.

The captive said nothing, knowing Sir Hugh wanted him to suspect betrayal by one of his own. Refusing to rise to the bait, he waited patiently for him to go on.

"I knew you'd not be able to resist retaliating after we raided the Crosiers in Liddesdale. On that occasion my men purposely claimed to ride from Haggbeck.''

"I see. 'Twas a wee trap ye set, then.''

"Aye, and I've had plump watches out patrolling every night since," Sir Hugh said. "Their sole mission was to capture you and put an end to the absurd notion that you are some sort of invincible Border legend.''

"Aye, sure, and it seems to have been a grand effort, indeed, sir, but to what purpose? Ye still ha' no evidence to support a simple bill of grievance.''

"I have your presence here on the English side," Sir Hugh snapped.

"There is that," Rabbie admitted generously. "However, men on both sides o' the line frequently cross over to drink in a tavern or attend a horse race. Moreover, and if I dinna mistake the matter, the place where ye captured me lies in Debatable Land. So even that evidence is like to result in a clearing o' the bill.''

"There is no longer any Debatable Land," Sir Hugh said, ignoring the rider. "Not on this side, at least. The Scotch Dike put an end to it years ago.''

"Aye, so our twa governments would ha' us believe," he replied. "Border folk still believe strongly in it, though, and so ye will see come Truce Day."

"We need not concern ourselves with Truce Day," Sir Hugh said.

"Ah, that's fine, then—just a wee misunderstanding amongst friends."

"There is no misunderstanding, either. Your days of thieving and creating chaos in the Borders have ended."

"Aye, sure, if ye say so. We can mak' any agreement ye like."

"I say so because it is true. Moreover, if you are thinking that your thieving Bairns will discover where you are and raid this castle to release you, you can think again. None but my most trusted men know where you are now, nor will they. As we speak, a heavily armed party is riding on to Carlisle. If anyone managed to track us tonight, they will assume that you went with that party and will not dare to attack one so large and heavily armed. And, by tomorrow, they will think it too late to do anything for you."

The prisoner remained silent, although there was much he would have liked to say. Sir Hugh was wrong to think the Borders' magical lines of communication would not eventually reveal his whereabouts to his Bairns. Within days at most, they would learn exactly where he was and would plan their rescue accordingly. If he were not free within a sennight, he would be much surprised.

With grim formality, Sir Hugh said, "Lord Scrope is away, but as deputy warden, I act for him. In that capacity, I hereby sentence you, Rabbie Redcloak, to be housed for a week's time in a dungeon here at Brackengill to contemplate your sins and make your peace with God Almighty. At the end of that time, I shall erect a gallows and hang you by the neck until you are dead. Take him below, lads."

Despite the hellish glow of the torchlight, the prisoner felt an icy chill.

Chapter 2

"And Fairly Fair your heart wou'd cheer,
As she stands in your sight."

Bewcastle Waste, the English West March

The little valley lay winter bleak under a thinning layer of snow. Its only sign of life was a faint spiral of smoke wafting from a gray stone longhouse next to a half-frozen burn running through its center. Like other such houses, this one consisted of a stable and byre at one end and the family dwelling at the other. Carelessly, as if in defiance of the wintry chill, doors to both stable and byre stood open, as did the door to the house end. The only other structures on the farm were a dry-stone sheep pen and a ramshackle stone-walled barn. From the top of the low hill that formed the valley's south side, bare stones and the gray slate roofs of the buildings looked like ash smudges on the sparkling snow.

A lone rider rode down the hill on a sleek gray gelding with a black mane and tail. The rider was small and slight of build, with long, straight, silver-blond hair blowing free, and she wore an enveloping gray cloak that nearly matched the color of her horse. She rode astride, using a cross-saddle, in the practical fashion that on all but the most formal occasions Border women had favored for the past hundred years. She rode fast enough for many to call her reckless, but unlike most women, she rode skillfully, as if she were part of her horse.

Ahead, at the farm, she saw chickens and geese, but no dog, no larger animals, no children—indeed, no people at all. The chickens and geese scattered noisily when she rode into the yard.

Dismounting, she patted the gelding affectionately and tied its reins to the railed gate of the sheep pen. Then, tucking her riding whip into her girdle next to the small dagger she carried there—where other women carried pomander balls or mirrors—she deftly plaited her long, fine hair into a more civilized knot at the nape of her neck. As she did so, a childish female voice wafted to her ears.

"Andrew, put down that pistol afore ye hurt someone!"

"I'll *not* put it down, and ye canna make me. I'm goin' to shoot me a damned Scots reiver!"

Without haste, the rider untied one of her bundles from the saddle and walked toward the family end of the house while the argument continued inside.

"Och, ye heathenish bairn, our mam's goin' to wash your mouth with soap an ye say such wicked things. And what would the vicar say? What about that, eh?"

"Won't say nothing an ye dinna tell him. B'ain't none o' his business who I shoot. I might shoot you, Nancy Tattlemouth. Then what would ye do?"

Reaching the threshold, the rider swiftly surveyed the dimly lighted scene inside, then said sternly, "Andrew, put down that weapon at once, and come here to me. Nancy, pick wee John up off the floor before he crawls into the fire, and Peter, you go outside, please, and fetch the other bundle off my saddle."

The children froze at the sound of her voice. Even the baby crawling toward the open fireplace paused and looked over its shoulder.

"Mistress Janet!" Three voices spoke as one.

"Aye, and I am shocked to hear you quarreling so. Do as I bid you, Andrew, unless you want to feel my riding whip across your backside."

In the middle of the room, the defiant little boy was still pointing a wheel-lock pistol at his sister, who was not much older than he was. Lowering the weapon, he looked warily at the whip Janet Graham had tucked into her girdle.

"Did you hear me?" she asked.

"Aye, I did."

"Then come here."

"Will ye beat me?"

"You deserve it," Janet said, holding out her hand for the pistol.

Meeting her gaze, the boy said, "Me da said females didn't ought to touch guns. 'Damned dangerous to let 'em,' he said, 'cause they're skeered of 'em."

"Do I look scared, Andrew?"

"Mistress Janet's not skeered o' nothing," the little girl declared, putting her fists on her skinny hips and jutting her chin toward her brother.

"Thank you, Nancy," Janet said without looking away from the pistol, "but I am speaking to Andrew now. Pick up wee John and wipe the soot off his hands."

"Aye, mistress." The little girl scooped up the baby with practiced ease and bore him to the washstand.

Janet's palm remained outstretched, waiting.

Slowly, his reluctance plain, the boy handed her the long-barreled pistol.

Examining it with competent ease, she said, "Luckily for you, Andrew, the mechanism is not wound, but I doubt you knew that when you pointed it at Nancy."

His thin lips twisted, but whether his annoyance stemmed from his knowledge or the lack of it Janet did not know, nor did she care.

Putting the pistol on top of the only cupboard and setting her bundle on the nearby table, she turned back to Andrew and said, "Come here to me now, and mind your manners. Where's your mam?"

After a pause during which the boy took a single short step toward her but offered no reply, his sister said, "Our mam's gone up the dale to fetch the sheep."

"Why did not you and Peter do that for her, Andrew? You are both quite old enough to tend sheep."

Again it was his sister who replied, saying, "Our mam said there was reivers about 'twixt here and Brackengill, mistress. Even though Sir Hugh caught some of 'em in the night, she said it wasna safe today for the lads to fetch the sheep."

"Ye need not tell Mistress Janet what Sir Hugh's about doing," Andrew said scornfully. "He's her ain brother, is he no? Likely she'll know what he's about."

"Mind your manners like she said," his sister said loftily, "or I'm telling our mam ye was rude and that Mistress Janet took our da's pistol from ye."

"Tattle-mouth."

"That will do," Janet said. She was grateful to know where Hugh had gone during the night. His consistent refusal to explain his actions irritated her, and that irritation stirred as she spoke. Her tone brought a flush to Andrew's cheeks.

"Where d'ye want this, Mistress Janet?" Peter stood in the doorway, holding the bundle he had fetched for her. He was both younger and smaller than Andrew.

Smiling, she thanked the little boy and said, "Put it on the table, laddie, but first shut that door. You are wasting the fire, you lot, by letting all the heat out."

When Peter had shut the door, she added, "You and Nancy can open both bundles and put the things away. I've brought you bread and some scones from our bakehouse, and a gingerbread man for each of you, although I'm thinking that I may have to take Andrew's man back and feed it to Jemmy Whiskers, since Andrew's got a demon in him today."

"Ye'll no feed my man to your cat!"

Nancy and Peter rushed to open both bundles, and with

delight in her voice the little girl exclaimed, "Ye've brought us blaeberry jam!"

"I have," Janet said, "and some other things for your mam and for the new bairn when it arrives. If you slice the bread thin, you can make a jammy piece for each of you and save your gingerbread men for your dinner. Whilst you are doing that, Nancy, Peter can watch wee John. Andrew is going to come outside with me for a talk." Putting a hand on the oldest boy's shoulder, she urged him to the door.

He did not resist. Outside he said, "Ye wouldna really give me gingerbread man to your cat, would ye, Mistress Janet?"

"That depends on you. Will you wave a pistol about like that again?"

"Me da did it," Andrew muttered stubbornly.

Janet kept her opinion of Andrew's father, Jock Graham, to herself. "He was a full-grown man," she said. "You are not."

"Well, I willna do it again an it vexes ye," he said. "Can I have me gingerbread man now?"

"If you eat it now, you will not have any at dinner."

"But ye will not give it to the cat."

"No," she said, "but if I ever see you waving a weapon around like that again, my laddie, I'll skelp you good myself."

"Aye, I believe ye would."

"I would, and you cannot kill any Scotsmen till you're grown, either."

"Them damned Scots reivers killed me da, did they not?"

"Aye, but your da was raiding at the time," Janet reminded him.

"Our lot ha' become like slaves t' the damned Scots," the little boy declared, clearly repeating words he had heard from his father's lips. "If we ride agin 'em after they've stolen from us, 'tis no more than they deserve, the filthy heathen."

"Aye, perhaps, but the Scots think the same of us, you see. Your father was in Liddesdale when he was killed, and Liddesdale lies in Scotland."

"I ken that," the boy muttered scornfully. "He were with Sir Hugh, getting back on them what stole our kine."

Janet sighed. "They always, all of them, say they are getting back, lad. Still and all, someone must have organized the first raid, you know."

"The bluidy Scots, that's who. Well, we've got one of them now, and that's a reet good thing, I'm thinking."

"Who's got one?"

"Sir Hugh, that's who. He's captured Rabbie Redcloak, and I wish I'd been with him when he done it. That's why I were waving yon pistol about. I dinna ken how to shoot it, but I mean to learn, and when next Sir Hugh goes—"

"Hugh caught Rabbie Redcloak?"

"Aye, *and* he's goin' to hang the filthy bastard, too."

Knowing that word of any major event in the Borders flew through the air as if by magic, Janet did not waste her breath asking the boy how he knew about the capture, nor did she question the accuracy of his information. She did feel obliged, however, to point out one obvious error in his report.

"He cannot hang him, Andrew. That is against the law. He must first claim a grievance against him at the next Truce Day with the Scots. Until then, he must give him into Warden Lord Scrope's keeping at Carlisle Castle."

"He's going to hang him," Andrew said flatly. "He said so, himself."

Janet had a tender spot in her heart for the four fatherless children. Serious, capable Nancy reminded her of the child she had wanted to be. Peter's merry smile and uncomplicated manners stirred a nearly envious affection, and wee John with his gurgles and secret sounds made her yearn for a child of her own. But she liked naughty Andrew best. Of them all he was the one most like the real Janet, the Janet who remained after her polite, submissive facade had fallen away. Andrew longed as much as she did to control the unmanageable world that enfolded them. Against all odds the fatherless boy strove to

protect his family, firing up like a banty cock when adults or—
worse—other children laughed at his determination.

Janet knew how he felt and did her best to avoid treating
him like a child. Thus, in response to his insistence that Sir
Hugh would hang the infamous reiver, she tempered her words,
saying only that she would see about that.

In truth, his certainty discomfited her, for she knew her
brother well, and she could not deny that he was wholly capable
of making and carrying out such a threat. The only thing that
might stop him was Queen Elizabeth's oft-repeated demand
for peace in the Borders. Elizabeth would not thank any deputy
march warden for stirring up more unrest, and Hugh must know
that hanging the most notorious reiver on either side of the line
would likely result in mayhem.

Leaving the children to stow away their treats, Janet went
outside, took a shepherd's crook from the byre to use as a
walking stick, and followed the twisting burn up into the nearby
hills, keeping watch for their mother. Snow crunched underfoot,
and she slipped more than once, but she was as competent
afoot as she was on a horse. Half an hour later, she saw Jock's
Meggie, as the children's mother was known, following a strag-
gling herd of sheep down the little valley. Meggie's swollen
belly preceded her, and her gait looked awkward and ungainly.

Janet hurried to meet her, forcing a path between the slow-
moving sheep with the crook. "Meggie," she scolded as soon
as she was within earshot, "you should not have come off
away up here all alone like this. What if the babe should come?
What would you do?"

"Sit me down and have it out, I expect," Jock's Meggie
said with a smile. "I could not let the bairns fetch them, Mistress
Janet, not with reivers about. They say they got away with
every cow, horse, and sheep at Haggbeck in the night; but Sir
Hugh, bless him, set a trap and caught that dreadful Rabbie
Redcloak at last."

"So Andrew told me."

"They say that devilish Scot's killed more than a hundred

good Englishmen, mistress, and likely my Jock amongst them. It'll be a boon to us all an Sir Hugh hangs him high.''

Taking the lead and wielding her crook expertly to encourage stragglers and wanderers to keep with the flock, Janet said, "So you also heard that Sir Hugh means to hang the reiver, did you?''

''Aye, 'twas Small-Neck Tailor told me, and he had it straight from one o' Sir Hugh's men-at-arms. Said he'll hang him within the sennight, did Small-Neck.''

''Indeed.'' Janet's thoughts raced. She could not let Hugh do something so egregious, because once men of property flouted the laws of the Borders, they might as well have none. Already, many called the Borderers lawless and unruly—worse things, too. It was Hugh's duty to improve the situation, not to make it worse. It was fine that he had caught the villain, but she would have to make him see reason before he hanged him. She would have to persuade him to take his captive to Carlisle Castle to await the next Truce Day, when he could file a proper bill of complaint against him. Once Hugh got his judgment, then he could hang the reiver.

An hour later, having helped Meggie pen her sheep, Janet mounted the gray gelding and started for home, her agile mind sifting ways to deal with her brother. By the time she reached Brackengill she had considered and rejected a number of plans and knew only what she had known from the start, that first she must manage to bring up the subject without pitching him into one of his infamous tantrums.

Riding through the gateway into the bailey, she looked around for signs of anything unusual and saw none. Men-at-arms were everywhere, but that was as it should be. Five were casting dice in a corner. A pair of others wrestled in the center amidst a small group of onlookers. As she rode past them, a lad ran out of the stable to help her dismount and to take her horse.

Still alert for the slightest indication that the castle held a notorious prisoner, she strolled to the well near the kitchen entrance and dipped water from the bucket on the stand. Drinking from the dipper, she continued her examination, and decided that if Hugh was holding such a prisoner on the premises, he certainly had done all he could to conceal the fact.

Tucking her whip under her arm and pulling off her gloves, she went inside through the main entrance and up the spiral stone stairway to the great hall. Stepping over the threshold, she sniffed automatically. In the same instant that she decided the rushes needed changing, she swiftly scanned the chamber to be certain that her brother was presently its sole occupant.

Sir Hugh Graham sat in his armchair at the big oak high table near the far end, writing in his ledger. Near his feet, two dogs scuffled, snarling, and behind him a fire roared in one of the two enormous fireplaces that faced each other from the ends of the hall. He did not look up.

A lackey came to take Janet's cloak, gloves, and whip. Dismissing him, she moved past her brother to warm her hands at the fire.

Hugh looked up then with a frown. "Where the devil have you been?"

"Visiting Jock's Meggie and others, as I do every Thursday, Hugh. We bake on Wednesday, and I take our extra baked goods to those who need them on Thursday. I have done so for years, and every week you ask the same question."

"You've no business riding out alone," he growled. "I tell you that every week, too, my lass, but you never heed me. One day, some heathenish Scot is going to abduct you, and when he does, I hope you won't expect me to rescue you."

"I shan't, Hugh. I believe you'd warn him to have a care, though."

"Aye, of your sharp tongue." Grudgingly, he smiled at her. "Truly, Janet, you should take one of the lads with you—a groom, a lackey, the kitchen boy. I do not care who it is, so long as he carries a weapon of some sort."

"I've got my dagger, Hugh. I never go out without it."

"Much good it would do you if you were attacked. A wench

against a strong man is no contest, as you've found out to your cost more than once.''

She did not reply, for it was true, and it was not a subject that would grow more agreeable with discussion. Sir Hugh, like most men she knew, was quick to violence, and his response to any confrontation was to exploit his physical superiority. He was more likely to knock a man down than to reason with him, and a woman, too. As a result, Janet chose her battles with him carefully.

Now she said casually, ''I heard that reivers struck Haggbeck last night.''

''Aye, they did.''

''One of the lads said you caught some of them.''

''Aye, well, we caught one.'' His gray eyes gleamed, but he said no more.

''Only one?''

The gleam turned to flint. ''In this instance, one is enough.''

''Indeed, sir, and how is that? I should think that the people of Haggbeck would prefer you to catch them all and save their livestock a trip across the line.''

''The one we caught will save more than their livestock. We captured Rabbie Redcloak. What do you think of that, eh?'' Smug triumph underscored his words.

''Well done, Hugh. Lord Scrope will be so pleased that I warrant he will write the queen and tell her how grateful she should be. Did you ride to Carlisle last night, then? You must have ridden swiftly to go so far and yet return so soon.''

''I did not ride to Carlisle.''

''Ah, then you trusted one of your land sergeants to deliver him to his lordship. That surprises me, but I do not question your judgment in such matters.''

''He's in the dungeon,'' Sir Hugh said curtly, ''and in the dungeon he'll stay.''

''*Our* dungeon? But surely you must take him to Carlisle, Hugh.''

''Nonsense. My dungeon here is as stout as any at Carlisle

and will be all the stouter for the fact that his Bairns do not know where to find him."

"But, Hugh—"

"That's enough, Janet," he said implacably. "Rabbie Redcloak has led more raids into Cumbria, Redesdale, and Tynedale than any other six of those damned Scotch villains. The sooner he meets his Maker the better it will be for all of us. I aim to hang the bastard at first light Wednesday morning."

Thinking of young Andrew and deciding that men sounded much the same at nine or ninety, she said, "Hugh, you have sworn to uphold the law."

"Aye, so?"

"Border law is clear on such matters, sir. When you capture a man from the other side, you must offer him for ransom until you can present a bill of griev—"

"You know nothing about it," he snapped. "Go tend to your woman's work."

"But I do know," she said calmly. "What your tutors did not teach me along with reading and writing, you taught me yourself, Hugh. You explained about wardens' meetings, and less than a fortnight ago you were complaining because Sir Walter Scott of Buccleuch had refused to agree to the site Lord Scrope suggested for the next one. You blamed Buccleuch for delaying it, but then you and Scrope refused to accept the site he suggested, or was it the date? I do not recall precisely, but Truce Days originally were supposed to occur once a month, were they not? Mayhap the reason they now occur only a few times a year is because you men can never agree when or where to hold one."

"Don't you have household duties to attend?"

"Aye, I do, but I want to understand this because I am a Graham, sir, just as you are. When one Graham breaks the law, men call us all lawbreakers."

Surging to his feet so hastily that he overturned his chair, he leaned across the table and roared, "Hold your tongue, woman! You speak of affairs that do not concern you."

"But they do," she insisted. "We must never forget that the Scottish Grahams are a broken clan, Hugh. It is they and men like them who have kept the Debatable Land a haven for lawlessness. Though we strive constantly to separate ourselves from those Grahams, 'tis only by the greatest good fortune that Thomas Scrope likes you well enough to have named you his deputy."

" 'Tis men's business to deal with reivers," he snapped, ignoring, as was his custom, a point that he did not wish to debate. "It is your business to tend the kitchen, or your needle-work or tatting, or whatever the devil it is that you women find to eat up your time. You ought to be married by now, Janet, but will any man have you? No, because you cannot keep a civil tongue in your head. You dare to look every man in the eye as if you too were a man. What you need, lass, is a good beating, and if you do not take yourself off at once, that is what you will get."

He meant it, and she knew that she dared not press him further. Bobbing a curtsy, she said, "I will go, sir, for I had no wish to infuriate you, but I do think it is unfair that you men make all the rules and simply expect us women to obey them."

"Well, at least you know how it should be," he muttered. "You might put that knowledge to use, lass, and behave as a well-brought-up young woman should. Now, go," he said, adding, "I doubt that my prisoner would thank you for your interest. Doubtless he feels sorry enough for himself by now without your pity."

Although the prisoner was not one who wasted time in self-pity, when the door at the top of the stone steps had slammed shut, the blackness enveloping him had seemed absolute, even terrifying. He had been unable to see anything, and his other senses seemed to have shut down along with his sight. He knew he was locked in an underground cell behind a stout, iron-

barred door, with a crude stone bench at the back. The state
of its stone floor told him his host had imprisoned others there
before him and was not a man anyone would praise for his
housekeeping. That he had been right to expect a lack of comfort
gave him no satisfaction, however, and when the blackness
enveloped him, the shock of its totality was petrifying.

Time seemed to have stopped, and in that moment, that
unnaturally lengthening and expanding, timeless moment, his
imagination had conjured up a swirling, bottomless pit that
surrounded him. He felt as if he stood on a pinnacle of stone
no bigger around than his own two feet. He had always thought
them huge, but suddenly, in that pitch-blackness, they seemed
unnaturally small and growing smaller by the minute. He felt
dizzy and terrified that he might fall, a terror not mitigated in the
least by his vague awareness that it was wholly unreasonable.

Mockingly, as the terror began to ease, he recalled his surrender, remembering his brazen attitude and the way he had taunted
Sir Hugh. He remembered smiling at the thought of his own
laird's fury at having to ransom him at the next Truce Day.
His belief then in the safety of his name, in the protection that
his position as a legendary leader of men would provide him,
seemed in the sudden, oppressive blackness of his lonely cell
like pointless arrogance.

In his mind he could still hear the echo of Sir Hugh's
departing words. No Truce Day, no ransom, no removal to
Carlisle Castle to await a meeting of the wardens and the redress
of grievances. Before then his greatest worry had been the
knowledge that he would have to stand before Buccleuch, to
see his fury and know that later he would have to deal with
that fury face-to-face. Buccleuch was no man to cross, certainly
no man to infuriate; but with the thought of death by hanging
swirling around him like that bottomless pit, facing Buccleuch
suddenly represented safety and nothing more.

A scrabbling sound startled him from his shock, abruptly
diverting his thoughts. He knew that starving rats could devour
a prisoner, and instinctively he drew his cloak protectively

around him. That sudden movement and the feel of the thick, silk-lined fur steadied him. His knees still felt as though he would be wise not to trust them, but solid good sense told him that there was no pit, that the dizziness he still experienced was merely a disorienting result of the sudden blackness.

Drawing a deep breath, ignoring the dry ache in his throat and his bladder's sudden, nearly overwhelming demand for relief, he reached out with his right hand and took one careful step at a time until it touched stone. It was not far, because the cell was small. Feeling along the wall, he found a corner, then the bench.

Though gratified by the small accomplishment, he knew he would not sleep until he had relieved his bladder. Stooping, using the wall to guide him and hoping that his fingertips would not encounter alien fur or sharp little teeth before he found the bucket he was certain must be there, he groped around until he found it.

Carefully relieving himself, he replaced the bucket and groped his way back to the bench, where he wrapped himself in his thick, hooded cloak and lay down. His thigh-length leather jack contained steel plating, and was not generally meant to sleep in, but it would help keep him warm and thus it was bearable. Using the hood to pillow his head, he slept.

When next he opened his eyes, he was astonished to see light. Not much light, to be sure, but enough to discern the bars of his cell. Getting up, aware that his body ached from his unforgiving couch, he walked stiffly to the bars and looked up the steep stairway.

The light's source proved to be a narrow crack beneath the door, and he decided that it must be sunlight. It faded to darkness and then showed light again for some time before a pair of guards finally came to empty his slops bucket and to give him a small jug of water.

Sunlight flooded the stairway and cell when they opened the upper door, making him wince at its brightness. Then one aimed a cocked pistol at him and ordered him to stand back while the other opened the barred door to exchange the bucket for the jug and an empty bucket. Aside from the gruff order, neither had spoken, nor did they return before the thin line of light faded again and returned.

Judging by that light, it was the third morning since his arrival, which meant that it was Saturday. He had slept sporadically, for his stomach growled constantly, and he had drunk sparingly of his water. Knowing that it would not last much longer, even so, he wondered if Sir Hugh Graham meant to reduce him to a thirst-crazed skeleton before hanging him on Wednesday.

Chapter 3

"Great love they bare to Fairly Fair
Their sister soft and dear. . . ."

Janet bided her time, employing subtle rather than direct means to learn where the prisoner was housed and trying to disguise her quest as part and parcel of her usual duties. Her brother had said "the dungeon," but Brackengill featured more than one such disagreeable lodging.

One was an oubliette, the grated opening to which lay in the center of a small flagstone courtyard on the south side of the keep. No one guarded it. However, no guard was necessary, because the grate had a cunning lock, the hole itself was nearly twenty feet deep, and its stone walls dripped with slime even in winter.

She visited the courtyard, but peering down the hole, she could see only blackness. No voice responded when she called down to ask if anyone was there. Hardly proof that no one was, she knew, since the prisoner might be unconscious or too weak to reply. Still, the likelihood was small.

She next visited the cellars beneath the castle kitchen but

found no guard there either, and no prisoner. That left the most likely spot, the oldest dungeon in the castle, deep beneath the stable's stone floor; however, that one was also the least accessible, since it lay in an area that she rarely frequented. She doubted that her brother's men would allow her to see the prisoner, let alone visit him, if she simply asked them to do so. Nor were they likely to let the slightest display of curiosity pass without telling Hugh that she had expressed unnatural interest in his prisoner.

Therefore she waited patiently until Saturday morning, when Sir Hugh rode out early with a party of his men. As usual, he did not inform her of his destination or tell her when he meant to return, but experience assured her that he would not do so for at least three or four hours. Thus, the coast would remain clear long enough to confirm her suspicion and perhaps even to gain a look at the captive.

Accordingly, she went to the kitchen and asked a kitchen maid to prepare a tray with two mugs of ale and generous helpings of sliced bread and ham. Carrying the tray to the stable, Janet approached the entrance to the dungeon steps, where a man-at-arms stood guard. His expression brightened, and he smiled at her.

"Good morning, Mistress Janet. I tell ye that tray be mighty welcome."

She smiled. "I brought just the two mugs, Geordie, so I hope you are the only one presently standing guard over our captive. Sir Hugh did not tell me how many guards he'd set when he asked me to provide a meal for the villain."

"The tray's for him?" The guard sounded both surprised and disappointed.

"Aye, it is," Janet said, instilling her voice with weary resignation underscored by a touch of anger. "Sir Hugh wants him to suffer, he said, but he does not want the man to grow too weak to appreciate his punishment."

The guard's eyes gleamed with humor. "Aye, that sounds

like the master, that does. I'll take it on down to him, then."
He held out his hands.

Janet had expected this, however, and she shook her head,
smiling. "Nay, Geordie. In truth, I want a look at the rogue.
You can take the time to enjoy your ale whilst I whisk this
down to him. He is locked up behind bars, is he not?"

"Aye, but—"

"Then he cannot harm me, and I may never again have a
chance to see a fellow so dastardly and dangerous that Sir Hugh
means to hang him without trial. First help yourself to some
bread and ham, and then open that door for me."

"But, mistress, I—"

"Open the door, Geordie," she said firmly, looking him in
the eye.

"Aye, mistress." Snatching a handful of meat and a thick
slice of bread, he unlocked the door, leaving it ajar so that she
would have light. "Have a care now."

"Aye, I will." She descended cautiously because her body
blocked most of the light, making it difficult to see the uneven
steps below. At the bottom, iron bars glinted. When she reached
them, she said quietly, "Are you awake?"

The reply came instantly. "I am, indeed, but 'tis as mucky
as a morass in here, and it isna fit for a man of taste, let alone
for entertaining feminine company."

His deep voice surprised her, for although it bore the familiar
and, to her ear, easily detectable accent of the Scottish side of
the line, it had a musical lilt that she found particularly pleasant.
He did not sound at all like the rogue she had imagined.

"Are you hungry?"

"Art mad, lass? Of course, I am hungry. These villains
havena fed me in nigh onto three days. Nor ha' I bathed or
brushed these rags o' mine. I'd eat the rats, but they are all the
company I've had, and eating them would seem uncivil."

She shivered. "Are there truly rats in there with you?"

"Aye, of course, there are. I'd no be surprised if they ha'
fleas, too. Take care the wee creatures dinna run up your skirts."

She kept listening after he fell silent, and she heard nothing. "I do not believe you," she said. "I do not hear any rats."

"Likely they're trained no to speak when a lass is present," he said amiably. "To what do I owe the pleasure of your visit to this filthy hole?"

"I've brought food, that's all."

"It is enough. Must I perform a service before I receive it?"

Suppressing an unexpected bubble of amusement, she said, "Forgive me. I am not versed in the correct way to serve dungeon meals. I did promise not to put myself in danger, however, so I must trust you to take things politely from my tray."

"I'd never harm a lass, and certainly never one so bonny as yourself, sweetheart. Where did ye learn to speak so prettily?"

He spoke rather prettily himself, she thought as she balanced the tray with one hand. Holding the mug of ale toward him with the other, she said, "Do not be impertinent, sir. Will you take this mug politely, or shall I just set it on the floor?"

"For the love of heaven, lass, dinna set it down! The rats would have it in a trice. I promise I'll no harm ye. Just hand it gently through the bars."

He stepped forward then, and she saw him for the first time, albeit only as a figure of shadows. Still, she could see that beneath his shaggy beard his face was that of a young man, and even in the dim light his eyes seemed expressive. She could not discern their color, but she did detect a glint of humor.

Carefully she handed the mug through the bars, and when his fingers touched hers, their warmth surprised her. They looked ordinary, yet there was something about their touch that stirred unfamiliar feelings. It was, she told herself, nothing more than the thrill of touching a notorious outlaw. Nonetheless, it was all she could do to keep her hand steady until he took the mug.

The tray tilted on her other hand, and she reached swiftly to steady it. Hoping that he had not noticed her nervousness, she held out the tray and said, "I have ham and bread, sir, if—" She broke off, realizing that it was the second time she had called him "sir." She would not make more of the error by speaking of it, though. Doubtless he had taken her for a castle servant, rather better spoken than most, but still a servant. He would not think it odd that she called him so.

"Hold it nearer, lassie. My mouth fair waters at the smell of that ham. 'Tis cruel to hold it so temptingly where I canna reach it."

"Forgive me," she said. "I told you, I have not done this before."

"And I asked before, lass, why ye're doing it now. Ye dinna belong in this filthy place, and I doubt that Sir Hugh ordered this. He'd rather I starve."

"Aye, he would," she agreed. "I thought you should eat, though."

"Well, I'm grateful, but if he catches you doing this, what will he do?"

"I don't know," she replied, ignoring a shiver. "My coming here is not without risk, however. Sir Hugh is not always kind to . . . to his servants."

"You are no servant, lass."

She had begun to enjoy the role that she had created for herself, but his words stopped her cold. "How do you know that? I mean, what makes you think—" She stopped when he laughed. Laughter was wholly out of place in that hole, yet his was so infectious that she nearly joined him before she realized that the upper door was still open and Geordie would hear them. "Please, stop laughing," she begged urgently. "If Geordie hears . . ."

"So the guard up there thinks that Sir Hugh sent you, does he?"

"Aye, he does."

"Who are you, lass?" His voice took on a distinct note of command.

She hesitated but then decided that his knowing would change nothing. Geordie would tell Hugh that she had visited him, and whatever happened then would be her own fault and no one else's.

"My name is Janet Graham," she said.

"And in a land that's littered with Grahams, Janet Graham is . . ."

Again she hesitated.

He did not speak. In the silence she could hear him chewing.

"I am Sir Hugh's sister," she said at last.

"Holy Mary," he exclaimed, choking. "Have you gone quite mad?"

"I did not expect to be holding conversation with you," she pointed out. "I thought only to bring food to a hungry prisoner."

"The prisoner is grateful, mistress," he said. "He hopes, however, that Sir Hugh does not hang us both with the same rope."

"He might want to, I suppose," she admitted, "but he would not dare. We have powerful friends who would strongly protest. Do you want the rest of this?"

"I do, but then you take yourself off, and do not come back."

Again her amusement bubbled forth. "Do you dare give me orders, reiver?"

"Aye," he said, moving near the bars to take the rest of the ham and bread from her tray. "You need someone to tell you what to do, lass, for plainly you have no sense of self-preservation. Sir Hugh Graham is a hard man."

"I must take the mug when I go," she said evenly.

He nodded, swallowed what was left, and held out the mug, saying, "I am truly grateful, lass, but I meant what I said. Do not attempt to do this again."

Reaching for the mug, she encountered his fingers again, and when she tried to take it, they wrapped around hers. His grasp was firm but gentle, and when her gaze met his, she found it hard to look away. Slowly, he drew her nearer.

A footstep scraped above, and Geordie called, "Mistress Janet, you'd best hurry along. Someone will be coming soon to take my place."

"Go, lass," the prisoner said, releasing her and stepping back, "and know that you go with my thanks."

Again, she could see no more than his shadowy figure at the back of the cell.

Dangling the mug by its handle and carrying the tray in the same hand, she went slowly back up the uneven stairs, her thoughts frozen, her body overheated.

The prisoner watched her go, thinking that she was a brave but foolish woman to have defied her brother so. Doubtless Sir Hugh would soon learn what she had done and would punish her. He hoped the man would not be too harsh. She had done a kindness, nothing more, and no lass should suffer for a kind heart.

Thinking of what she had risked, he sat on his stone bench and ate the last of his small meal more slowly, savoring every bite. His benefactress deserved no less.

Janet returned the tray and both mugs to the kitchen, stopping long enough to tell Sheila and Matty, two of the kitchen maids, that Sir Hugh would expect his dinner at the usual time.

"If he dines at home, that is," she added with a smile. "Of course, if he does not return by noon, he still will expect hot food soon after he does return."

"We know that, Mistress Janet," plump Sheila said with a smile.

"Yes, I know you do," she said, "but Sir Hugh's temper being what it is, one naturally wants to make certain that he will not be displeased."

"Aye, mistress," Sheila agreed, nodding fervently.

Turning to Matty, Janet said, "The rushes in the hall must be changed. Gather some lads to clear the old ones out straightaway, and set others to carry fresh ones in from the long garret. We've still got rosemary drying in the ceiling rack, and a few other herbs as well, that you can mix in with the rushes. Also, pray ask one of the lads to replace the threshold onto the stairway. Ned Rowan stumbled over it yester-eve and broke off a considerable chunk. We shall soon have rushes scattered up and down the stairs, and someone is bound to slip.''

"Aye, mistress, I'll see to it," Matty said.

Busying herself with household chores, Janet tried to keep her mind off the man in the dungeon, but as the morning progressed, her imagination kept presenting her with tantalizing images of him. Fascination vied with anger over his plight, and since her temper was nearly as volatile as Sir Hugh's, whenever she thought she heard a sound that might herald his return, she hurried to look out the nearest window that gave a view onto the bailey. Soon her patience was spent.

When noon arrived without any sign of him or his party, she ordered dinner put back an hour, declaring that they would dine then whether Sir Hugh and his men had arrived or not. While she waited, she attacked her mending, but although she tried to think of things other than the hapless prisoner, she still could not. Surely, she thought, the entire English Border west of the Cheviots must have heard by now that Hugh had captured Rabbie Redcloak and meant to hang him without trial.

Even Thomas Lord Scrope must have learned of Hugh's intent. Scrope lived miles away in Carlisle, where he served as keeper of its great castle when he was not in London serving as Cumberland's Member of Parliament. He might be away now, she knew, although Hugh had received messages from him not long since, complaining that the Scots—meaning Buccleuch of Hermitage, of course—had refused to agree to his latest suggested site or date for the next wardens' meeting.

The thought of Truce Day was not helpful, for her imagination presented her at once with a mental list of Border lords on both sides of the line who would learn what Hugh had done. When she considered their likely reactions, her anger with her brother increased.

She did not waste time worrying about what the Scots would

say, although it galled her to know they would be right to
protest. Nor did she worry much about English lords who lived
near Brackengill. Most of them, particularly Sir Edward Nixon
of Bewcastle, had suffered serious losses to Scottish reivers,
and several were friendly to the English Grahams—presently,
at all events. Therefore, chances were good that they would
support Hugh's actions, perhaps even to the point of hanging
the reiver. After all, it would not be as if they had done it
themselves.

Lord Medford of Bellingham was a high stickler, however.
He and his forebears had done much to create the *leges marchi-
arum*, or "march laws," that ruled the Borders, so he would
not look kindly upon any man who broke them.

Unfortunately for Hugh, most lords of the English middle
march—and Hargrave, Loder, and Sawkeld from the west
march—allied themselves more closely with Medford than with
Scrope or Hugh himself, or with any other Graham. Those
men, she knew, would strenuously oppose his actions. Indeed,
Hargrave was a Bell, and the English Bells were feuding with
the Grahams, who had been feuding with the Scottish Bells for
nearly a decade. It was all very complicated, as Hugh should
know, and those who might stand with him one moment could
turn against him the next. She had to make him see reason.

He and his men returned at last a few minutes before one,
and by then she was fairly spoiling for a fight. Although servants
had long since set up the trestle tables, and everyone in the
castle had already waited an hour past the usual time, she felt
only mild annoyance when he ordered them to put dinner back
another half hour. She knew that he wanted time to change
into attire more comfortable than the metal-plated leather jack,
steel helmet, and other protective accouterments that he wore
whenever he rode outside the castle walls.

Nevertheless, when he entered the hall at last, she was pacing
the floor, stirring the fresh rushes and filling the air with the
scent of rosemary and herbs.

Without speaking, he strode to the fireplace near the high

table and stretched out his hands to warm them. The noise of others entering the hall after him forced her to walk nearer to make herself heard.

"Good afternoon," she said, keeping her voice calm, knowing that she would get farther with kind words than with sharp ones. "Did your business prosper?"

"Aye," he said without looking at her. "Shot a brace of grouse, too. I had a lad give them to Sheila to hang. We can have them for dinner one day soon."

"It is early yet for grouse," she said.

"Aye."

"Hugh, I—"

"My men and I are hungry, Janet, and they are ready to serve the food." He offered his arm. "Come, let us not keep everyone waiting."

Glancing toward the lower tables to see that his men had gathered around them and were waiting to sit, she put a hand on his forearm and went with him to the high table. As soon as they sat down, servants with baskets scurried from man to man handing out stale bread for trenchers, and the others took their seats. Hugh said a brief grace, and a servant set a huge platter of sliced ham before him.

Although she sat beside him, the near silence of men and women eating their dinner made it difficult to mention his captive with any degree of casualness. There was still much for everyone to do before day's end, and everyone ate hastily, not in the more leisurely way that they would later eat their supper.

The latter meal, though smaller, was the social time of day at Brackengill, just as it was in most Border households. Laughter and conversation would reign then, and someone would play music. Now the feeling was companionable rather than cheerful. The fires roared, and odors of burning wood, roasted meat, and warm ale mixed with the sweet herbal scents from the new-laid rushes.

Although Sir Hugh owned considerable land and collected

a respectable income for a Border lord, his household did not
operate on a grand scale. What money he was able to lay his
hands on went into improving Brackengill, and over the years
since he had attained his majority, he had done much. He
had replaced the wooden stockade walls with stone, and had
expanded the family living quarters, encouraging his sister to
make them as comfortable as she could.

They lived well compared to many, but even when he enter-
tained company for dinner, there was no butler to prepare knives
for the carver or to slice the bread before it came to the table.
Generally, everyone used trenchers rather than plates—except,
of course, when important visitors dined with them. In such
an event, no lord who owned plates of any sort would use bread
for trenchers unless unusual circumstances such as the arrival
of a sudden and unexpectedly large number of guests required
him to do so.

Fresh bread came to Sir Hugh's table in small, individual
loaves that diners could break at will. Janet swiftly scanned
the basket that the servant set before him, looking for any
loaves that were too brown or that still had oven grit on them.
She did not want him to find reason today to complain about
the food.

At the trestle tables, the bread frequently was several days
older and each person scraped his own. When leftover loaves
grew too hard to break easily, the kitchen maids would cut
them in half for use as trenchers.

When Hugh reached for the salt, Janet held her breath. Until
the days grew warmer, there was always risk that it would
cake. It was Sheila's job to make certain that the top of the
container did not touch its contents and discolor them, and that
the salt remained fine, white, and dry. Still, one could never
be certain.

Apparently finding the salt satisfactory, Sir Hugh called for
ale from his personal supply, and a pewter goblet was quickly
filled for him. Watching him rip a roasted chicken to pieces

while she toyed with her own food, Janet noted with satisfaction that, despite the wait, the skin was crisp the way he liked it.

Although it was frequently the habit in large households for dogs to wander through the hall at will, begging and fighting each other for scraps and other choice bits that the men threw to them, no dogs attended meals at Brackengill. Once Janet had learned how much easier it was to keep the hall floor presentable without them, she had banished them from mealtimes.

The minutes marched by, but finding no easy way to bring up the subject of the captive while they ate, she waited, responding when Hugh spoke to her but content to let him speak with Ned Rowan and another of his sergeants who sat with them. Not until the servants began to clear away the food and everyone else began to return to their duties did she say, "I would speak privately with you, brother."

"Now?" he demanded, frowning at her. "I have much to do, lass."

The frown did not auger well for their discussion, but Janet pressed on, keeping her tone even as she said, "I want to discuss your prisoner again, sir."

"There is no point in that," he snapped, adding more moderately. "You tend the household well, lass. I noticed the fresh rushes, and I know that it is no mean achievement to keep a household fresh at this time of year. I know, too, that I have you to thank for having my dinner when I want it, for looking after the linens and such, and keeping the servants contented, even cheerful. However," he added sternly, "do not think that your expertise in household matters qualifies you to meddle in those that are of no concern to you."

"Your honor *is* my concern," she insisted, fighting to keep from raising her voice. "What touches your honor touches mine."

"My honor! What the devil do you think you are talking about?" He made no attempt now to keep his voice down.

Suppressing a wince, she managed to keep from looking around the room to see if others were watching them. Though many of the men had gone, she knew that those who lingered, and the servants, could hear everything he said to her.

"Please, Hugh, do not shout."

"I have been in the saddle all morning, Janet, and since I am to take supper with Nixon tonight at Bewcastle, I'll spend much of this afternoon in the saddle, as well. I've neither time nor patience to deal with your woman's whining now."

"Then when, sir? If you hang the man without a trial, you will anger all our friends and allies who believe in the laws of the Borders. You could even lose your position as deputy warden."

"Nonsense. Scrope wants to be rid of that devil Redcloak as much as I do, and so do many others hereabouts—Sir Edward Nixon, for one."

"Aye, but what of Medford? He will demand your head, Hugh, or at least that you pay a fine for evading proper procedures. Hanging a man without trial may even be murder in his eyes—aye, and in God's eyes, too!"

"Don't be daft," he snapped, signing to a passing lad to fetch him more ale.

Janet bit her lower lip to keep from snapping back at him. Waiting until the servant had gone away again, she said with forced calm, "Hugh, I beg of you, consider carefully what you do. You are a man of your word, are you not?"

"Aye, when it suits my purpose. What of it?"

"You prevaricate, sir. I know you well, and I know that when you give a man your solemn word, you keep it. It is a badge of honor with you."

"I will not debate my decision with you, Janet. It is not seemly for a man to debate such matters with a woman."

"Are not laws made because men agree to their making, and then swear an oath to uphold them?"

"No one on our side of the line intended for the law to protect scoundrels like Redcloak, who steal from us."

"Pray, do not attempt to clothe your anger in pious respectability, sir. We have just agreed that I know you well. It is not the thieving that angers you, for you have led thieving raids into Scotland yourself, and so has nearly every other man of property on this side of the line. Our lot is no more law-abiding than the Scots.''

"We only seek redress for wrongs done to us," he growled.

"Now you sound like a sanctimonious prig," she retorted impatiently. "You know as well as I do that men on both sides say that very same thing whenever they raid. The excuse is as ancient as the behavior."

"They steal our horses, and we take them back; that's all."

"That is not all. Men, women, and children are killed in raids on both sides. Raiding destroys lives and property, Hugh." Aware that her voice had risen, she looked guiltily around the hall to see that three of Hugh's men and the two lads dismantling the trestle tables were still there.

Following her glance, Sir Hugh said grimly, "Hold your tongue. Thank God it is men who decide these matters, not women."

"Women would have better sense," she retorted. "We would not expect others to obey laws that we ourselves flout. How can you break a law that you have sworn an oath to uphold, Hugh?"

"I have sworn to serve my queen and the warden of the west march," Hugh said. "That God-forsaken reiver in my dungeon is one of the most scurrilous thieves in the Borders, and he deserves to hang."

"Then let them declare his sentence at the next Truce Day."

"A Scottish jury would hear our complaint against him, not an English one," he reminded her. "Even though we would select its members, do you think that such a jury would ever order Rabbie Redcloak hanged? He is a legend to them, lass, a man they greatly admire. They would probably reward him."

"But—"

"We have sent bills against him before," Hugh went on impatiently, "and he and his supporters have ignored them. More times than not the Scots insist that he does not exist. Well, I have proved that he does, but if any Scotsman demands to know how we dared to hang him, I shall simply refer to their own insistence that there is no such person, and that will be that.''

''Hugh, you can achieve the same end by holding him until the wardens' meeting in the legal manner, and presenting him for trial. No one can deny his existence after you present him to them in person.''

''That's enough, Janet. I don't want to hear another word out of you on the subject. Do you understand me?'' His voice had risen again.

Before she could answer, a man spoke from the threshold. ''Beggin' your pardon, Sir Hugh, but will ye be wanting a full company to ride to Bewcastle?''

''Aye, I will,'' Hugh said, scraping back his chair and getting to his feet, clearly having decided that his discussion with his sister was over.

Drawing breath to steady herself, Janet said boldly, ''If you insist on going forward with this mad plan, Hugh, I shall have no recourse other than to let Thomas Scrope know what you mean to do.''

He glowered at her. ''Damnation, lass, who do you think will take such a message if I forbid it?''

''I don't know,'' she replied honestly. ''If I must go myself, though, I will.''

''By God, you will not defy me further in this!'' he bellowed.

Her own anger quickly igniting, she stood to face him, wishing she were taller so that she could look him eye to eye. Grimly, she said, ''I do not count it defiance, Hugh. Scrope must support me in this. He will not want it known throughout the Borders that he allows his deputies to defy the law when it suits them to do so, or that they will hang men without trial.''

He leaned closer, his fury plain. ''You will go nowhere but to your bedchamber, my lass, and you will stay there until I give you leave to come out again. Do you hear me?''

''Hugh, you are mad! If you hang him, you will be fortunate to survive him by a sennight, for when his people learn of it, they will demand your life in return for his. What will you do if King James of Scotland demands your arrest?''

"I'll tell Jamie what I tell you," he snarled. "I caught the man red-handed and it is my right to hang him!''

"But Hugh—''

"No more!" he roared. "Go to your room!''

Taking an involuntary step backward, she said nonetheless firmly, "I will find a way to stop you, Hugh. I may be sorry for it, but—''

Her words ended in a cry when he slapped her, nearly knocking her off her feet. She managed to remain upright only by the merest good fortune. Pressing a cool hand against her flaming cheek, she straightened. Aware of their audience, augmented now with faces peeping through doorways, she looked him in the eye and said, "Do you seek to silence me with violence, sir? I think our people will not support you in this instance. Indeed, I believe that once it becomes widely known that you mean to hang your Scottish reiver on Wednesday—''

"I no longer mean to hang him on Wednesday," he said evenly.

His grim demeanor made her breath catch in her throat, but she managed to reply just as evenly, "I hope that means that I have made you see reason, sir.''

"Rabbie Redcloak will hang at sunrise tomorrow," he declared. Looking at the man near the doorway, he said, "Do you hear me, Ned? I want a gallows built for that scoundrel, and I want it built before I return from Bewcastle. See to it!''

"Hugh, please.''

Menacingly, he put his face close to hers again and growled, "If you do not go to your room, you will feel my hand on your backside next, lass.''

Unable to believe that she had failed so miserably, Janet hesitated, but when he straightened and reached for her, her courage vanished and she fled.

Chapter 4

"Herself would watch you all the day
Her maids watch all the night. . . ."

Fighting tears of helpless fury, Janet went straight to her bedchamber, only to meet the kitchen maid, Sheila, on the landing outside her door. Pulling herself together as she had done many times in the past under similar circumstances, Janet said quietly, "What is it?"

"Beg pardon, Mistress Janet, but Matty would know where ye will eat your supper when it's time, bein' Sir Hugh has said he means to sup at Bewcastle."

"Godamercy, I've only just eaten my dinner." Realizing that the maid was attempting to assure her that, despite Hugh's orders, they would somehow provide her with her supper, she smiled ruefully and said, "Someone can bring some warm bread and milk to me here, Sheila. I doubt that I shall want anything more."

The girl nodded, her eyes still fixed on Janet's face. Her sympathetic expression made it clear that she wanted to say more.

Janet returned the look directly, and the maid's gaze dropped. "I'll tell Matty," she said, bobbing a curtsy.

Janet knew that Sheila was concerned about her and had wanted to say as much but that the maid knew it was not her place to do so. Although grateful for the kindness, Janet was even more grateful that Sheila had held her tongue, because overt sympathy would only have made her feel worse than she already did. She was glad, too, that the exchange had helped her recover her composure. Her stomach still felt as if it contained a pair of wrestling shrews, and her eyes still burned from tears she had neither shed nor quite managed to suppress, but she was quickly regaining her customary composure.

Entering her bedchamber and shutting the door, she looked at the cold, well-swept hearth and debated whether to light a fire, knowing that she would soon have to send someone to fetch more wood if she did. Generally, a servant would not light a fire in this room until after supper, giving it just enough time to lose its chill before Janet prepared to retire. The stone chamber was chilly—nay, ice cold—now, but she had no wish to see anyone else until she could be certain that she had herself under control again.

Hugh could stir her emotions like no one else. He enjoyed wielding power over her. Indeed, he probably enjoyed it the more knowing that she resented his male authority to order her about. She knew that if her parents had lived, her attitude might be different, and that she might even accept her lot the way other women did. She could not know one way or another, however, for her parents had not survived her early childhood. She barely remembered them. What she remembered most was their voices—one soft, the other booming loud like Hugh's.

Remembering that booming voice now, she decided that she probably had answered her own question. Hugh was his father's son, after all. The late Sir Harold Graham probably would have beaten any rebellious daughter into proper submission to her God-ordained lot in life. That Hugh had not been able to do it was no evidence that Sir Harold must also have failed. Her mother's portrait over one of the hall fireplaces depicted a pale, pretty woman with downcast eyes. That should be proof enough of Sir Harold's domineering ways. She could not imagine allowing anyone to paint her own portrait to display such waxen meekness.

Since glass was prohibitively expensive, the only window in the chamber was unglazed. Nevertheless, its shutters stood open to the wintry outside air in order to admit light. Walking across the stone floor to look out, she stared at the gathering gloom. The wall below formed part of the castle's curtain wall, joining with the new stone wall of the stockade that Hugh had finished the previous year. Windows on the floors below were no more than arrow slits, but the one where she stood was nearly two feet wide and arched gracefully at the top. She felt the cold, standing there, but the wonderful view calmed her as it always did.

The sun was low in the sky, but the days were growing steadily longer. To the east, still aglow in the waning light, the landscape formed a patchwork of sun-gilded, snow-dappled farmland set against rolling hills, dotted with isolated farms and hamlets with stone- or slate-roofed cottages. Narrow stone bridges crossed fast-running becks that divided vast, snowy fields punctured from below by coarse dark grass and by the reeds and rushes of scattered bogs.

Moaning, ever-present wind blew out of the west, sculpting the trees into queer, surrealistic shapes. In the distance she saw a shepherd striding across a field with his flock, and as always, watching his dogs work the sheep stirred a brief fascination. They darted, dropped low, then darted again, moving the muddy sheep as quickly as they would go, driving them from whatever pasturage they had managed to find to the shelter of their pens. The sheep were reluctant, but the dogs urged them on, needing to get them to safety before the increasing chill turned wet ground to treacherous ice. It occurred to her then that ice would force Hugh to travel more slowly than usual when he returned from Bewcastle late that night.

Gray and white predominated everywhere she looked, but soon spring would visit the Borders again, and wildflowers would paint the rolling landscape with color. Rabbie Redcloak would never see the flowers, though. He would be dead.

She rubbed her hands together, suddenly aware of their icy chill; but rubbing did no good, for the chill had spread to the rest of her. Remembering the way the reiver had made her feel, the way her body had warmed to his lightest touch, she wondered what it would be like to have him touch more than just her fingertips.

Unfamiliar, surprisingly erotic feelings stirred deep within her, in places that she had not known could stir so.

Looking over her shoulder, fearing that such wantonness might somehow reveal itself to a watcher, she saw only the cold, empty bedchamber. She had known that she was alone, of course, and had looked only because her guilt at such wicked thoughts had momentarily overwhelmed common sense. In the way of such things, however, the moment she reassured herself of her solitude, memories of Rabbie Redcloak swept back— warming, then chilling, then warming her again, as if blocks of ice floated on the hot blood coursing through her veins.

Only too easily could she imagine herself alone with him again. Only too easily could she recall the radiant warmth of his hand, the way his deep, melodious voice had touched her soul, and the memory stirred feelings and fantasies that she had never before experienced but which she instantly recognized as wicked, or at least carnal. She remembered the way his fingers had caught hers, the way he had drawn her nearer before Geordie's voice broke the spell. She knew from the way the reiver had touched her that she had stirred something in him, too. Could men be wanton?

That he would live only until sunrise made her want to cry, and her sorrow made her wish she could touch him just once more before he died.

* * *

In his cell, the prisoner had decided from what little he had seen of Janet Graham that she was a bonny lass but a bit of a fool. Remembering the touch of her slim fingers when she had given him the mug and taken it back again gave him some pleasure in his otherwise dismal solitude, though. He hoped again that if Sir Hugh had learned of his sister's bold defiance, he had not been too harsh with her.

The reiver had spent most of the time since her visit thinking about her, giving his imagination free rein so long as it pictured him with her and did not dwell on images of a gallows rope. He found it easy to close his eyes and imagine himself with her. He could imagine her in his bed at home. He could imagine stroking her smooth skin—surely, it was smooth and unblemished, rosy and clean. He wondered what color her eyes were. They would be blue, he decided, a soft, true blue.

She was proud, and he liked proud women.

The door at the top of the stone steps crashed open, shattering his reverie. The flood of fading daylight from outside seemed as bright as the noonday sun. He heard the unmistakable sounds of hammers, hammering nails into wood.

"Ye hear that, ye thievin' reiver?" The guard's voice echoed down the stairs, reverberating off the stone walls, a roar of sound in the hitherto oppressive silence. "That's your gallows they're a-building, reiver. What do ye think o' that?"

The door crashed shut again, and again blackness closed around him.

Scratching sounds at her door sometime later diverted Janet's thoughts to more practical matters. She did not bother to command the visitor to enter, for she knew that to do so would be useless. No servant's hand caused the noise. She went to open the door, then stood back to let Jemmy Whiskers enter.

The small orange cat strolled in, tail high in its usual stately, silent fashion, as if its size and weight were ten times greater than the reality. Studiously ignoring her, the cat padded to the hearth, where it halted and gazed at the cold stones for a long, silent moment. Then, glancing over a shoulder, it made a brief inquiring noise.

"Very well, I will light the fire," Janet said, shutting the door and going to fetch the tinderbox. "I have had more important matters to think about, and it will not grow warm straightaway. If you are cold, you may jump onto the bed."

She had passed the intervening time aimlessly, her mind seeming unable to grasp any thought and hold it. Her fury with Hugh proving pointless, she had tried to think of her duties, of tasks that remained undone or that should be accomplished in the days ahead. But, although the minutes passed, they did not pass with any speed. She was not a sedentary creature by habit, and the time that had crept by had shown her that long periods spent so would surely drive any sane person mad. That thought had led her inevitably to think of the prisoner again.

Kneeling to light the fire, she coaxed it patiently, aware of the cat's intense supervision. When it was well started, she closed the shutters and drew forward a small, low bench of the sort known as a cracket. Sitting, she watched the flames, letting her thoughts take what course they chose. When the cat jumped onto the cracket beside her, she touched its head, stroking lightly.

Jemmy Whiskers purred, turning his face up into her palm and pushing against it. She stroked under his chin with a fingertip, glad of his company as her thoughts lingered on the tall, broad-shouldered man in the dark dungeon cell.

She could not doubt that Hugh would keep his word. Though he did not always believe himself bound by rules others had made, he did pride himself on being true to his word when he had given it. It shocked her, therefore, that he could so easily disdain a law that he had sworn to uphold. How dared he reduce a solemn oath to a mere quibble!

Border laws had been hammered out over the centuries to protect everyone on both sides of the line. Although the clans had occupied much the same land over that time as they did now, the line itself had changed numerous times. Even Brackengill had once been on the Scottish side—as had all of Cumberland—as part of the kingdom of Strathclyde. Four long centuries had passed since then, and throughout that time men had labored to produce the laws under which all Borderers now lived. For Hugh to ignore one of the most powerful of them was a measure of his fury with Rabbie Redcloak and his Bairns.

She wondered again what Scrope would think of Hugh's decision to hang the reiver; however, since she could think of no way to bring the matter to his attention and stir him to act before the horrid deed was done, she rejected that line of thought as unproductive. She wondered next if anyone nearer than Carlisle could change Hugh's mind, but soon discarded that thought, as well. If she could not persuade Hugh to do the right thing, no one could. Nothing could save the reiver now.

Unless . . .

She looked thoughtfully at Jemmy Whiskers. "Could I possibly do it alone?"

The little cat's eyelids had been drooping, but they opened in response to her voice. Taking her words as an invitation, Jemmy murmured sleepily and climbed into her lap, nudging her hand with his head, encouraging her to go on stroking him.

She complied, finding it possible at last to bring order to her thoughts. He would need a horse—preferably his own if she could identify it and provide it for him—and he would need food, in case he had to hide out for a time before he could get safely across the line. He would also need to know the safest route to take. First, however, he would have to get free of the dungeon, free of the guards, free of Hugh.

It occurred to her that by now someone might have told Hugh about her visit to the prisoner's cell. He clearly had not learned of it before their discussion in the hall, but it was only a matter of time before he did. If he had learned of it, she would know soon enough, and she would have no chance to get near the dungeon.

He had been in a hurry to get to Bewcastle, though, and she doubted that he would have concerned himself with his captive before leaving. She did not think that Geordie would have volunteered the news of her visit, in any event. Someone else would have had to do so, and most of the men liked Geordie and would have been reluctant to subject him to a tongue-lashing or worse. If Hugh had not known before leaving, she had at least a small chance of success, for he would not return until late. She had to make the attempt.

Providing the reiver with his own horse was possible if she could identify it, and the food would present little difficulty, since there was plenty left over from dinner to provide supper for the household and still leave some for him to take with him. The great problem was the guard at the dungeon entrance and anyone else who might still be awake in the stable or the bailey at an hour suited for whatever plan she decided to attempt. The middle of the night would be best insofar as the castle was concerned, for all but the rampart guards would be asleep then; however, Hugh and his men might return by midnight, and anyone moving about after that would look suspicious. She would have to act sooner.

She did not think the guards on the ramparts would try to stop a lone rider leaving by the postern gate before midnight. They would assume that the men below knew him and had approved of his leaving. In any case, she could think of no way to incapacitate the men on the walls, nor could she justify putting the entire castle at risk of attack to save Rabbie Redcloak. Besides, Hugh would kill her if he came home to learn that she had somehow disabled all of his guards.

The cat murmured, annoyed because she had stopped stroking.

"I have things to do, Jemmy Whiskers." She set the cat down and went to open a shutter and look out. The landscape was dark, and there was no moon yet. "It's freezing," she said to the cat. "I shall need my warmest cloak."

Collecting a heavy, dark wool, fur-lined cloak from the wardrobe, she draped it over her shoulders, leaving the hood down while she searched for gloves. Rejecting patens in favor of heavy boots that would give her more freedom of movement, she left the bedchamber, letting the door swing to behind her. Then she had to open it again when the cat loudly protested being left behind.

Crossing to the service stair, she hurried down to the kitchen with Jemmy Whiskers darting ahead of her. The cat ran into the kitchen, but Janet paused just outside to listen. Only female voices sounded within, so she peeped round the doorway to reassure herself that the sole occupants of the chamber were the two maidservants, Sheila and Matty, busy preparing supper for the household. The sight made her realize that her hastily conceived plan required adjustment.

"Matty," she said briskly as she entered, "I am going to walk outside for a few minutes to get some exercise before I eat my supper."

The two maids exchanged a glance that told her they knew that Hugh had ordered her to keep to her room. However, Matty said only, " 'Tis like ice out there, mistress. Ye'll catch your death."

"You know better than that," Janet said, smiling. "However, if it is truly so cold out tonight, perhaps the men would enjoy a toddy later to warm them. I will think about that whilst I walk. You go ahead and serve the household when you are ready. You can serve mine upstairs after you have finished eating your own."

"Very well, mistress," Matty said, nodding.

Janet left through the kitchen door, walking briskly, her way lighted by the warm glow of torches set into brackets on the wall. The cold was even sharper than she had expected, for a breeze eddied in the bailey, making the torches waver and flicker. The area was sheltered from the winds that seemed always to blow, albeit not so sheltered as her bedchamber, which faced to the east, and neither was as cold as the open moors would be. She hoped that Hugh had allowed Rabbie Redcloak to retain his signature cloak. If he had not, the man would freeze. Perhaps she should take him one of Hugh's, just in case.

She frequently walked around the bailey for exercise before supper, so the men paid her little heed. They would be gathering in the hall soon for their meal, and that, she knew, was the thought uppermost in their minds. As she walked toward the stable, she saw that many of them were already moving toward the main entrance, leaving behind only those who guarded the walls.

When she saw the stable lads join the others, she walked into the stable, noting that one of the younger men stood guard outside the door leading to the dungeon. She saw him look at her, and raised a hand in greeting.

Inside the stable, the lads had extinguished the torches while they had their supper, but radiance from those outside provided light enough for her purpose. She walked slowly from stall to stall, recognizing many of the animals by location and size. Her own gray gelding pushed its muzzle against her shoulder, and she wished that she had a sugar lump or carrot to give it. She would bring it something special next time to atone for the oversight.

At the end of the row of stalls, she found what she sought. The pony there was larger than the others, and remembering the height of the captive and the breadth of his shoulders, she knew it must belong to him. Hugh would appreciate its size, for he was also a large man. The horse snorted, and she wondered if it were uncut but dismissed the thought even as it formed. A stallion would smell the mare two stalls down even when she was not in heat. The horse stood calmly and so was doubtless a gelding.

Leaving the stable, she bade the dungeon guard a good evening. "Have you just begun your watch, or do you near the end of it?"

"Nearing the end, mistress," Small Neck Tailor said. "Yaro's Wat will take my place when he's eaten his supper. Then I'll get mine. I'll be glad to get it, too, I can tell ye."

"I'm sure you will," she said. "There is plenty of the ham from dinner left over, and I saw Matty slicing cheese, so I am sure you will get plenty."

He smiled, clearly looking forward to the ham and cheese, and she hurried back to the kitchen entrance. She had seen no sign that anyone outside remembered that she was in disgrace with Hugh. Not that the men were any more likely than Sheila or Matty to speak of that disgrace or to order her back to her bedchamber. Still, she would have much more difficulty putting any plan into action if the men believed that Hugh would punish anyone who obeyed a command of her giving.

Back in the kitchen, she found only Sheila, putting food on a tray.

"I'm nearly ready to take your supper up, mistress."

"Good," Janet said. "Bring some of that sliced ham and cheese, too, will you, and maybe a manchet loaf or two. My walk has stirred an appetite, after all."

"Aye, mistress, gladly."

Upstairs, Janet waited until the maid had brought her tray, fetched wood for the fire, and gone away again. Then, hurrying to Hugh's room, certain that his man would linger in the hall, she found a thick woolen cloak in his wardrobe and carried it back to her room. There she drank her milk and ate some of the bread but put the ham, cheese, and the rest of the bread into a drawstring bag for the reiver.

She sat comfortably by the fire with Jemmy Whiskers curled in her lap for an hour or so until Sheila returned to take away the tray. While the maid was in the room, Janet exerted herself to look like a woman about to prepare for bed, and after that, time passed slowly, but it passed. At last, setting down the cat, she got her cloak and Hugh's and, draping the former inside the latter, swung both over her shoulders. Their combined weight was enough to make her grateful that she did not often do such a thing.

Tying the drawstring bag to her girdle beneath the cloaks, she pulled on her gloves and hurried down to the kitchen.

Chapter 5

"I never yet lodged in a hostelrie
But I paid my lawing before I gaed."

Matty and Sheila were banking the great kitchen fire, and Janet's entrance startled both of them.

Smiling, she said, "Before you and Sheila retire, Matty, I think we should take toddies out to the guards in the bailey. It is a very cold night, and I do not want them making excuses to slip inside rather than stay at their posts where they belong. Fetch some cider, please, and pour it into the pot on the hob. We'll use the poker to hurry the heating, so set it in the coals now to get hot. Sheila, do you know where Sir Hugh keeps his brandy?"

"Aye, mistress," the girl said, her eyes widening, "but we're no allowed—"

"Never mind, I'll fetch it," Janet said. "The men are due a treat, but you are quite right to remind me that he does not like the servants to touch his spirits. I do not want his wrath to fall upon you for this instead of on me. Fetch out a half-dozen chopins. That should be enough, I'd think."

"Aye, mistress. Are ye sure, then, about the brandy?"

"You just heat the cider," Janet said, hurrying from the kitchen to Hugh's small private chamber near the hall, where she knew he kept his French brandy in a wooden chest. She could hear the men in the hall laughing and talking, and someone playing a lute. They were settling down for the night, and since most of them slept in the hall, they would not disturb her.

She knelt beside the chest to open it. It was not locked, for Hugh believed—and with good reason—that no one would dare take anything from it. Since she wanted to make the toddies sufficiently potent to dull the guards' alertness long enough to serve her purpose, she was tempted to take three bottles; but she decided that Matty and Sheila would balk at such a blatant misuse of their master's brandy. The cider was potent even without the added brandy, and on such a cold night the men had doubtless drunk a good deal of ale with their supper. She settled for two.

Carrying the bottles back to the kitchen, she opened them and poured their contents into the pot of warming cider.

"Mistress Janet!" Matty was scandalized. "Sir Hugh never said to give those men all that brandy to drink."

Janet winked at her. "Sir Hugh annoyed me today, Matty. This will serve as excellent punishment for him, and the men will be glad of its warmth."

"That cider's strong by itself, mistress," Matty said, exchanging a look with Sheila. "With brandy added, 'tis more like to put them to sleep, I vow."

Sheila frowned. "The master will be gey wroth wi' ye, mistress."

Suppressing a shiver at how wroth her brother would be, Janet managed to say lightly, "He has been wroth with me before, and I expect that he will be again, but the men out there are cold. If they spend all their time stamping their feet to warm themselves, or slip indoors to seek warmth, they will not guard us well. I believe that if we do them a kindness, they will exert themselves more, and with reivers about, perhaps thinking about rescuing their leader . . ." She shrugged, letting their imaginations fill in the rest.

Matty said, "Sir Hugh's new wall is stout, mistress. No heathenish reivers will get through it."

Sheila did not look as confident, but since neither woman offered more argument, Janet was satisfied. In other circumstances she might have taken the opportunity to explain Matty's error, but presently it suited her plan to let them both think scornfully of raiders, and to believe that with the guards even half-awake, Rabbie's Bairns could never breach the castle's stone walls.

When the cider was hot, she told Sheila to finish banking the fire and then to take herself off to bed.

"Matty can help me carry the toddies out to the men," she said.

"I'll help her, mistress. Ye oughtn't to go out again on such a cold night."

"Don't be daft," Janet said. "I'm dressed more warmly than either you or Matty. Moreover, there must be no doubt in Sir Hugh's mind that this was my doing, so the men must see me. Now tend the fire as I bade you, Sheila, so that Matty can go to bed as soon as we have finished."

Sheila obeyed, so Janet picked up the chopins and followed Matty to the kitchen door.

Holding the pot in one hand, the maid opened the door with the other. Three stone steps led up to the torchlit bailey, where Janet saw with relief that Yaro's Wat had taken Small Neck Tailor's place at the dungeon entrance. She knew that the men followed no particular schedule, and she had feared that Geordie might have decided to stand guard in place of the smaller, slighter Wat. Geordie had a head for spirits that was the envy of many a Graham, and his presence might well have spoiled her hastily conceived plan.

The only other men in sight were a stable lad mucking out stalls and a guard by the postern gate, who would doubtless remain to admit Hugh and his men on their return. The main gates generally remained closed and barred after dark.

Matty said firmly, "I'll serve the three men on the wall first, mistress. Climbing them steps should keep me from freezing whilst I'm about it. I only hope I dinna drop the pot. My fingers be like icicles in this cold."

"I'll hold the pot whilst you fill three chopins," Janet said. "You tell them they can each have the one tote but no more. Sir Hugh must not find them drunk when he comes home."

Matty grimaced, but she made no objection when Janet took the pot from her and held it while she dipped each chopin to fill it.

Janet said casually, "I'll serve the three down here."

"But, mistress, 'tis enough that ye're here. Ye should not be serving—"

"Don't argue. The sooner we do this and get back inside, the sooner you will be warm again. I am wearing a heavy cloak and I do not mind the cold, but you are not dressed warmly enough to linger. Now go."

Matty obeyed with barely concealed gratitude, and Janet went first to the man by the postern gate, dipping him up a full chopin of the potent brew and assuring him that it would warm him through. He accepted it gratefully.

Filling another for the lad mucking out stalls, she took it into the stable, which now was aglow with torchlight. As she offered him the toddy, she said, "I do not think I know that large beast in the last stall."

" 'Tis the reiver's pony, mistress," the lad said, leaning his rake against a wall and taking the chopin she held out. "I thank ye. 'Tis cold, the night."

"Aye," she said, still eyeing the magnificent horse. "I warrant Sir Hugh will like having that one. I'd like it myself."

"That b'ain't no lady's horse, Mistress Janet. Scottish Border ponies be but half-trained beasts at best. Sir Hugh said he'll soon teach this one manners, though."

That settled the matter as far as Janet was concerned. Moreover, if the reiver rode away on his own pony, Hugh could not charge him with another horse theft.

Offering the lad a refill, she made sure that she still had plenty for Yaro's Wat, and strolled outside to the dungeon door. "I hope you don't have to stand here all night, Wat," she said. "It's perishing cold out here."

Taking the mug she held out to him, he sipped, then looked at her curiously. "Strong stuff this be, mistress."

"Aye," she said, grinning at him. "I thought you'd be glad of it."

"I am that. Warms me right through, it does."

"Good. *Will* you have to stand here all night?"

"Only till two. Then Geordie said he'd take my place till dawn."

"Why do I not leave the pot, then?" Janet suggested. "The cider will not stay hot, but mayhap you will think of a way to warm some for him."

"An there be any left," Wat said, chuckling, "we'll find a way, I warrant."

Satisfied, Janet turned away to find Matty hurrying toward her. "Dinna leave that pot with him, Mistress Janet. Cook will be beside herself an she finds it missing, come morning. Both Sheila and me will be in for it then."

"Pour the rest into the loose pail from the well then," Janet said. "Someone will be glad to finish off the cider, and we must not waste it."

"Aye," Matty said doubtfully, but she knew better than to dispute Janet's decision in front of Yaro's Wat. Fetching the pail, she poured the cider into it, then set it down by the grinning Wat and walked with Janet back to the kitchen entrance. There, however, she said anxiously, "Mistress Janet, them lads ought not to be drinking their fill of that stuff. They'll be ape drunk or worse within the hour."

"Hush, Matty. This is my affair, and if Sir Hugh finds out, he will know exactly whom to blame for it. If you are wise, you will not mention to anyone that you had anything to do with it. The men will not betray you, I assure you. Indeed, they most likely will say nothing at all about the cider, so unless we suffer some horrid mischance, Sir Hugh need never learn what happened to it.''

''Very well, mistress, I'll warn that Sheila to keep her mouth shut. Got a tongue on her like a beggar's clapper, she does, but I trow she'll listen to me. Still and all, ye're up to summat, and I dinna like to think what Sir Hugh will do when he finds out what ye've done.''

''No one else will suffer for it, Matty,'' Janet said. ''If I must, I shall tell him I drank his stupid brandy myself.''

''Ye'll never!''

''I shall if I must. I'll bid you good night now,'' she added before the woman could think of anything more to say on the subject. ''I am not ready to go upstairs yet. I think I will take another turn round the bailey.''

Matty sighed but said only, ''Good night then, mistress. Dinna forget to bar the kitchen door when ye come in.''

Waiting in the shadows just outside the door until she could be sure that Matty had gone to bed and the kitchen was empty, Janet went back to the fireplace and lifted the heavy poker from its hook. Holding it under her two cloaks, she counted slowly to three thousand, then went back outside. The stable was dark, and only the two torches flanking the main gate remained alight. By their ambient glow she could see Yaro's Wat, his head tilted back as he finished off what was left in his chopin. She wondered if any remained in the pail at his feet.

Waiting till she feared that her feet had begun to freeze, she walked out of the shadows at last, as certain as she could be that the men on the wall had taken cover from the cold. Even if they had not, she thought they would be watching more carefully for Hugh's return than they would for activity inside the bailey. She would have been happier had Wat gone to sleep, but she trusted to her imagination and his brandy-weakened senses to get her inside the dungeon.

She had walked close enough to be surprised that he did not

greet her before she realized that, although he leaned upright against the wall, his eyes were shut. If he had not fallen asleep standing up, he was as near that state as made no difference.

Quickly, she slipped past him and had put her hand on the latch before she remembered that, before, he had had to unlock the door for her. Gently she tried to lift the latch, but it did not move. Frustrated, she peered more closely at Wat. He did not move. For the benefit of anyone who might be watching, she nodded, hoping it would look as if they were talking. Then, keeping her back to the bailey and the opposite wall, she slipped a hand gently inside his coat and unhooked from his belt the ring with its two keys. Her hands shook, and she could barely breathe. She was certain that he would waken at any moment and demand that she give back his keys.

Unlocking the door, she slipped inside and quickly pushed the door shut behind her. Blackness enveloped her, and she felt dizzy, knowing that the steep stairs fell away before her like a yawning chasm. Carefully gathering her skirts in the same gloved hand that gripped the poker she had taken from the kitchen, she placed the other, with Wat's keys, against the wall to steady herself while she felt for the next step. Knowing she would ruin all if she fell, she made her way with maddening slowness, one step at a time, to the bottom. Not a sound came from the cell.

"It's just me," she whispered.

"I can see that," he said.

"You can see?"

"Aye, after a fashion, but keep your voice down. When one spends one's days and nights in pitch black, one's eyes adjust to the slightest light, and you did open the door, after all. I cannot see much now, and I saw only a cloaked devil before you spoke. What are you doing here, lass? I told you not to come again."

"I've come to let you out."

"You *must* be the devil then."

"Don't blaspheme," she said sternly. "I've brought you

food, and I know where your horse is. Nearly everyone in the castle is asleep, but there are guards above, and two of the lads sleep in the stable, so you must go carefully, and very quietly. I'll help you sneak out through the postern gate. Then you must make for Liddel Water. I'll tell you exactly how—''

''Lass, no one knows better than I do how to find the Liddel, or which route is the best and safest to take me there, but what about you?''

She leaned the poker against the wall. ''What do you mean?''

''I mean,'' he said patiently, ''what do you risk by freeing me?''

''You need not concern yourself with that,'' she said impatiently as she felt with her fingers and the key for the keyhole in the iron-barred door.

''You should not do this,'' he said. ''It would be enough if you could just get word to my Bairns. They are a canny lot and may well learn where I am in time to do something before your brother hangs me on Wednesday. But since he said that none but his most trusted men know I am here—''

''Hugh is not going to wait until Wednesday,'' she said. ''He means to hang you at sunrise. They have already built the gallows.''

''The guard very kindly told me that they were building them, but I took that to mean that your brother intended to be prepared for the day in case we had a storm. Surely, though, you are mistaken about his intent to hang me tomorrow. By my calculation, tomorrow is Sunday. Would he hang a man on the Sabbath?''

Grimly, she retorted, ''Do you want to wager your life that he will not?''

He was silent. The only sound was the rattle of the keys as she continued to search for the keyhole.

''What's that sound?''

''I've got Wat's key ring. I'm just not sure which key is the right one.''

"Good lass. Give it to me, though, before you drop it. It could take a week to find it amidst the muck on the floor."

Just the thought of what might lie beneath her feet—something she had not thought about before—was enough to make her hand him the keys. His fingers brushed hers, sending a wave of warmth through her. Then, after a rattle of metal against metal, she felt the door open toward her.

He was free.

She felt suddenly vulnerable. What if he really was as bad as they had said he was? What if he just strangled her and left her lying in the muck on the floor? Two strong hands found her shoulders, surprising a squeak of protest from her.

"Be silent," he muttered. "You'll have the guard down on us."

"He's drunk, I think," she murmured back, aware only of the warm hands grasping her shoulders. "He was slumped against the wall when I approached, and he did not even look at me when I took his keys from his belt."

"Your brother should have more reliable guards."

"I gave them all cider laced with brandy," she said. "We must not dawdle, though. Hugh took his supper at Bewcastle, but he may well return before midnight, and it must be getting on for ten now. As cold as it is, I am counting on icy tracks to slow him, but ice will slow you, as well, of course."

"What will he do to you?" he asked again.

She shivered. "We must not think about that. Have you still got your cloak, or did they take it from you?"

"I've got it," he said. "It is all that's kept me from freezing down here, for all that it must be warmer here than it is outside."

"I brought one of Hugh's in case you needed it," she said. "I'm wearing it over my own."

"You think of everything, lassie, but you still seem to lack that sense of self-preservation we discussed the last time we met. Now, tell me what your brother will do to you when he finds what you've done. And do not lie to me!"

"Who will tell him that I did anything?" she countered. "No one saw me."

He was silent for a time. Then, musingly, he said, "If a man I had set to guard a captive fell into a drunken stupor and let him escape, I would hang him at cockcrow—sooner if I already had a gallows built and a noose prepared."

She had not thought of that. The image his words created made her feel sick.

"Ah, well," he said, "we won't think about that now. Doubtless by morning you will think of a way to prevent it. You seem to have a fertile imagination."

"Aye," she said doubtfully. Then, fearing that he would worry if she did not persuade him that she could handle Hugh, she said more firmly, "I will think of something. Hugh is not so difficult to manage if one but knows the way of it."

"He beats his servants, though."

"How would you know that?"

"You told me. Remember?"

She did not remember putting it like that, exactly, but she shrugged. "I have managed Hugh for twenty years, sir. I can manage him now." Hearing her voice falter, she added hastily, "We should hurry."

"Aye, we should," he agreed. "Let me lead the way, since doubtless I can see better than you can. You hold my hand and mind your skirts."

She let him take her hand before she remembered the poker. "I brought a weapon in case you need it," she said. "It's here somewhere." Feeling along the wall, she found the poker and handed it to him.

"I'd prefer to have a sword, but this will do," he said with a touch of laughter in his voice. "I can see that you make an able assistant. Come quickly now."

Following him up the stairs was easier than she had thought it would be. As they neared the top she could even make out the steps. He opened the door without hesitation, although he did so slowly, peering out before he opened it all the way.

"The postern gate is there at the end of the stable," she murmured. "Your pony is tied in the last stall."

He did not reply. Glancing around the bailey, he stepped outside, still holding her hand. But once outside the door, he released her and gave her a gentle push toward the stable.

Hurrying ahead of him, Janet listened anxiously for a cry of alarm from the ramparts or elsewhere, but none came. If any guard still watched the postern, he was as stuporous as Wat.

Hearing no sound behind her, she looked back when she reached the stable entrance to see that he was farther back than she had thought. He closed the distance with a few quick strides, however, moving with eerie silence, and she led the way into the stable. When they were halfway along the row of stalls, she was surprised to hear him give a low-pitched whistle. Hearing no response, she turned to say curiously, "Is he not yours, then?"

"Aye, he is. I did not want him to greet me, however, and we must pray that none of the others proves too friendly. My bold fellow's a canny one, he is."

Something caught at Janet's hem, startling her. She tried to pull her skirt free, but whatever it was that had caught it tugged back. Then she heard a low-pitched, warbling "meow."

The reiver muttered, "What the devil?"

"It's Jemmy Whiskers," she said, scooping up the little cat and cuddling it. Jemmy began to purr loudly.

"He's a damned nuisance. Set him down."

"I can't. He'll wail if I ignore him, and someone will hear him. I won't let him give you away, though. I'll just hold him."

He made a sound like a growl but did not argue, and soon she heard the familiar sounds of leather and harness.

"Are you saddling him?" She had not expected him to take the time to do so.

"Aye, the saddle's right here on the stall rail, and 'tis a fine one. I dinna want to leave it. Did ye say you've brought two cloaks with you?"

"Aye, but I do not think either would serve well as a saddle blanket."

He chuckled, and a moment later, he stepped back. Only then did she realize that the torches flanking the gate had gone out. Only starlight lit the bailey now.

"Come," he murmured.

"Won't they hear his shoes on the bailey cobblestones?"

"Bless you, lass, most Scottish ponies wear no shoes unless reivers shoe them backwards to lead their followers astray. My lad moves as silently as the wee cat, and he's near as deft in his movements, too," he added proudly.

Still carrying Jemmy Whiskers, grateful for the warmth of his small body, Janet followed as the reiver led the pony out of the stable, staying close to its wall and then to the curtain wall as they moved toward the postern gate. As they neared it, a snore startled them both. The guard lay curled across the gateway.

"Damnation," the reiver muttered. "I'll have to use the poker after all."

The lad was young, Janet knew, and would have to face Hugh. As she tried to decide whether it would be better for him to face his master with a broken head or a whole one, the reiver murmured against her ear, "Does it open outward or in?"

"Out," she said.

"As it should," he said. " 'Tis more secure against intruders that way, a gate is. Not a sound now, lass. Not so much as a whisper."

She could barely see what he was doing, but he leaned away from her, and a moment later the gate swung open. To her amazement, the pony stepped daintily over the recumbent body, and the guard did not stir.

"Lift your skirts as you step over him," the reiver said, breathing the words just loudly enough for her to hear.

"I needn't do so," she whispered. "If you will just push

the gate shut, the latch and bar will fall back into place. It cannot be opened from outside.''

''Pushing it shut will make too much noise,'' he said. ''You'll have to draw it toward you and shut it gently, and you cannot do that from where you are.''

''But he's too close! I'll step on him.''

''No, you won't. There's room enough on this side of him to stand whilst you close and bar the gate, and you won't have to put the damned cat down to do it.''

It was hard to believe that she would fit, but since he could see better than she could from where he was, she decided to trust his judgment. It was difficult to manage both the cat and her skirts, but she gathered everything up that she could hold and carefully stepped over the guard. No sooner had she done so, however, than two strong hands grabbed her arms and pulled her close. Thinking he meant to kiss her, and hesitating to fight him, she kept silent just long enough to realize that he had eased the gate shut with his foot. She heard the latch click into place.

Horrified, she said, ''I can't get back in now without waking someone!''

''I hoped that was the case,'' he said. ''You are not going back, lass.''

''Not going back? Of course, I am. I must! Hugh will kill me!'' Fighting to keep her voice down, she nonetheless expected at any moment to hear a clamor erupt on the other side of the gate.

''I'm afraid he *will* kill you,'' the reiver said. ''That's why I'm doing this.''

''Doing what?''

''Abducting you, lass. I confess, though, I did not count on taking the cat.''

Chapter 6

"My ladye's kindly care you'd prove,
Who ne'er kenn'd deadly hate."

"You cannot take me with you," Janet protested, turning her back to the stiff, icy wind and clutching the two cloaks around herself and the little cat.

"I'd have to be a knave to leave you here," he retorted. "What is the least that your brother would do to you for betraying him like this?"

"He would not dare harm me," she muttered.

"Since for safety's sake you must speak low, I cannot pretend to know for certain that you are lying," he said, and although he, too, kept his voice low, she could detect wry amusement in his tone. "Nonetheless," he added, "your words do not persuade me."

She could not blame him. They weren't doing much to persuade her either, because she knew as well as he did that, under English law, aiding his escape constituted "high treason and felony." By helping him, she was not merely risking her brother's displeasure. She was risking her life.

Gently, his hands still on her arms, he said, "Shall I leave you here to face the consequences of your kindness to me, Mistress Janet Graham?"

She knew that he could feel the shudder that rippled through her body. Jemmy Whiskers felt it, too, for the little cat mewed. It made no attempt to free itself from her grasp, however. The mew was clearly just a comment.

Although the reiver did not press for an answer to his question, she knew that he must be impatient. Hugh and his men could return at any moment.

"I am not usually at such a loss for words," she said. "I own, though, you have put me in a dreadful position by shutting the gate."

"You put yourself in that position when you freed me, lass."

"Aye, that's true."

"Would you let that hapless guard hang rather than admit to your brother that you helped me? Not that your admission would help the guard, I'll wager."

She remained silent, unable to pretend that she would lie to Hugh.

"I thought as much," he said. "It is a pity that I did not think of all this before I saddled only the one horse."

She sighed. "I would have argued more fiercely with you inside the walls."

"Aye, I ken that fine." She heard the chuckle again in his voice.

"Do you dare to laugh at me, reiver?"

"Lassie, that I can laugh at anything just now is a good sign. We must go."

"You are right," she agreed. "We'll ford the river Lyne at the bottom of the hill. Then we should ride northeast to cross the Liddel at Kershopefoot Bridge."

"Something warns me that you're a managing sort of female, Janet Graham."

"Aye, perhaps," she agreed. "I have managed a large household for nearly eight years, you see, so it cannot be surprising that I have learned to be decisive.''

"I'd call it meddlesome, and we'll have a little less of it, if you please. We are not going to ride east or even north just yet. We'll follow the river west for a time instead, and then we'll make for the Scotch Dike.''

"But that's in the Debatable Land—''

"Aye, it is,'' he interjected. "I know what I'm doing, lass, and you'll help best now by being silent. We must—''

"But that area is dangerous!'' Thinking that she heard a sound from the east, and fearing that it might be Hugh, she turned to look as she added, "Moreover, it would be much quicker to—''

A hand clapped across her mouth, silencing her. In her ear, he said grimly, "You will be silent when I tell you to be silent. Both of our lives could depend upon it, and I am more experienced at this business of escaping the enemy than you are. Do you understand me?''

His tone made his point for him. She nodded.

"Good. Now, can I trust you to stand quietly whilst I mount, or must I put you up first and then try to swing up behind you? I warn you, my lad here is not accustomed to ladies' skirts or to cats, even wee ones.''

When he removed his hand from her mouth, she muttered, "I'll be quiet.''

"Excellent.'' On the word he was in the saddle, reaching a hand down to her. Somehow she managed to hold Jemmy Whiskers and her blowing skirts long enough to put a foot on his and let him swing her up to sit sideways before him.

"Will your pony be able to carry us both any distance like this?''

"Oh, aye. Now, hush. We'll ride alongside the wall so the lads above canna see us until we reach a point a wee bit nearer the trees by the river.''

"Surely you don't mean to gallop down this hill.''

"Stop trying to tell me what to do,'' he said. "Indeed, you

can stop your nattering altogether. If it were not for this ceaseless wind, they'd have heard us by now, drunk or sober.''

Knowing he was right, she kept quiet, and when at last he turned the bay away from the wall, she held her breath, expecting at any moment to hear shouts from above. None came, however, and she blessed the icy wind and Hugh's brandy.

The gelding padded quietly through the dark night. She could make out shapes of trees and bushes by starlight, and she knew that the moon would rise soon. With luck, they would be well away before Hugh and his men returned. Even as the thought crossed her mind, however, she glanced toward the west and stiffened at the sight of torches lighting the crest of the nearest hill.

"They're coming," she exclaimed. "Hurry!"

"We'll keep to a sensible pace," he replied calmly. "They cannot see us from where they are. The trees ahead make a black shadow that conceals us from anyone behind us. If we were riding along the horizon, they might see us, or if the moon should suddenly take it into its head to rise, they would. But the moon is on my side, lass. 'Tis a good Border moon that will pop out later to show us the way.''

"But they will be after us by then!"

"Not necessarily."

"Don't be a dolthead," she snapped. "Do you think that my brother will not raise the countryside to follow us when he learns of your escape?''

"Well, now, I warrant he would if he were to realize that I've gone, but if we are lucky, he won't learn any such thing before morning.''

"How can you say that? With Yaro's Wat in a stupor, and— Godamercy,'' she exclaimed when another thought struck her. "The keys! You left them in the cell door! Even if by some miracle Hugh should fail to notice that Wat—''

"Whisst now! Softly, lass. I did not leave the keys in the cell door.''

"Then you've still got them with you, and that's worse!

Hugh will hang Wat, and Wat is kind. He does not deserve such a horrid fate.''

''Then I am sorry if he will suffer for this,'' the reiver said. ''I warn you, though. You'd best never try to use any of my men in a like way, because if one of them ever drank himself into such a state that a wee lass was able to relieve him of his keys or his weapons, I'd hang him from the nearest tree.''

Janet winced, knowing that Hugh would do the same and would not need to seek a tree, thanks to the gallows already standing in the bailey. She would have given anything at that moment for the power to turn back the clock, to—

''If you are wishing that you had not done it, lass, I hope you will also remember that your brother meant to hang me at sunrise. I am grateful to you for my life and will do all possible to see that you come to no harm through helping me. That is why I do not have your Wat's keys. He has them.''

''What? But how—?''

''I kept them, and when I pushed you toward the stable, I took a moment to lock the dungeon door and put the ring back near his belt. The greatest likelihood is that when your brother returns, he and his men will make enough noise to wake the lad sleeping by the gate and to stir your Wat to life as well. If that occurs, they will none of them miss either of us until sunrise when Sir Hugh will seek me out to hang me. I also locked the cell door,'' he added with a chuckle.

''But why?''

''Think on it, lass. What will they think when they find both doors locked, the keys where they are supposed to be—indeed, everything as it is supposed to be?''

''They will think the devil flew away with you!''

''Aye, or that I'm Auld Clarty myself. In any case, it is bound to add to my legendary stature, don't you agree?''

His audacity amazed her. He had been within hours of meeting his Maker, and here he was instead, chuckling at a boyish prank. Hugh would certainly think that magic was involved, perhaps would even suspect that the devil had flown away with his prisoner—Her train of thought stopped abruptly, overtaken by another. "It is not just you that Hugh will think the devil flew away with," she said.

He chuckled again. "I wondered if that would occur to you."

"Holy Mary, preserve me," Janet muttered. "Do you really think he will believe the devil carried us off?"

"Well now, that depends."

"On what?"

"On whether you have ever before run away from home."

"I am not running away now," she protested.

"That depends on one's viewpoint, I suspect," he said. "However, I am reasonable enough to accept that as fact for the sake of the greater argument."

"You are making my head spin. What greater argument?"

"The devil. Remember him?"

"Aye, I do, and I am not at all certain that we ought to be discussing him so openly. Doubtless he hears every word we say."

"Oh, aye, but he and I are well acquainted, lass, and so long as you and I have right on our side, we need not fear him overmuch."

"Are you so certain then that we do have right on our side?"

"Aye, of course. We've saved me, have we not—for the moment, at least?"

"And are you certain that was the right thing for me to do?" she asked bitterly. When he chuckled again, she shook her head, feeling a need to clear it, then answered her own question. "Of course, you would think so. You must think me a dunce even to ask you such a question."

"Aye, it was a daft one to ask me. I cannot think of many things that a sensible man would consider more right than preserving his own life. I am certainly not ready to exchange mine for the great unknown beyond it."

They had reached the safety of the trees, and looking back, she saw Hugh's party approaching the postern gate. In the distance, she heard their shouts and then heard someone pounding on the postern gate with a sword hilt or some other heavy implement. Moments later, they disappeared inside.

Neither she nor the reiver said anything for several moments, and she knew that he was listening, just as she was, for sounds of imminent pursuit. When none came, she felt him relax.

Quietly she said, "It seems that your mischief worked its magic, reiver."

"So far," he said, "but we'll still ride for the dike, I think. If your brother misses us before morning, he will head for Kershopefoot Bridge, believing that we'd do as you suggested we should."

"I suppose he might, at that," she agreed with a sigh.

"He will. I did not mean that as criticism, however," he added. "I know that you meant only to set me on the most direct route, and I thank you for your kindness—indeed, for your many kindnesses. Is there any place away from Brackengill where your brother might believe you had gone this evening?"

The abrupt change of subject caught her by surprise. "Why?"

"Well, I was just thinking that you might not want to ride to Scotland with me, so if there is somewhere nearby where you might have gone to take supper with friends, just as he went to Bewcastle ..."

When he left the sentence unfinished, she sighed again. "Even if there were such a place, and people there who would agree to lie to Hugh to protect me, the fact of my having done such a thing without his leave would only infuriate him."

"He seems to infuriate with devilish ease," he said with audible annoyance.

"Most men do," she said. "Of course, I expect that you will tell me you are a man of mild temperament."

"Oh, aye. They do say that I am the placid one," he replied. "Of course, that's by comparison with my cousin, who is famous for his temper, so some might call that description a wee bit deceptive."

"What is your cousin's name?"

He chuckled. "Now, lass, do you think I am going to make you a gift of my particulars before we even cross the line? I am not such a fool."

"I do not think that I want to go to Scotland," she said, more to hear what he would say in reply than because she believed that he—placid or not—would give her much choice.

Nor did he. "You will go where I say, lassie. I am not an insensitive man, and I ken well that you will leave much behind. However, if we put our heads together, we may yet think of a way to get you home again and still keep that pretty head on your shoulders. Until we do think of such a way, however, you will bide with me."

"Bide with you? If you think for one minute, reiver, that you are going to—"

"Nay, I did not mean that as a threat, lass. Your honor is safe with me."

"I doubt that."

"Aye, well, you've the right to doubt, and in truth, since I've not yet seen you in full light, mayhap I did promise too lightly. We were speaking of the devil before, however. We ought to finish one subject before we begin another."

He seemed so calm, so certain that they were safe and that he could protect her, that his confidence was contagious. She felt herself relax.

Curiously, she said, "Are you saying that you do think Hugh will believe we have both been carried off by the devil?"

He chuckled again. "Nay, lassie, much as I'd like to believe it. Your brother is not a simpleton. He might waste a moment or two scratching his head, but once he learns that you are gone and that I have escaped, he will put the facts together and most likely arrive at the correct conclusion. All we have gained by my little trick is time, but time is ever a friendly ally. With luck we'll be across the line before he knows we're gone, which is more than I'd have expected."

"But what if he declares a hot trod? He has only to call out his men, tie a bit of burning turf to a lance, and ride across the border after us.''

''Aye, he might do that. For twenty-four hours he has the right to declare himself in hot pursuit of any escaped felon, even to cross the line and demand that the first citizen of Scotland he claps eyes on should go for the march warden, report that he's in pursuit, and demand his help. But I do not think that he will do that, or that it would avail him much if he did.''

''Why not?''

''Well, you see, he would first have to determine which march we entered.''

''But is not the Laird of Buccleuch acting warden for both the western and middle marches? I am certain that Hugh said he was.''

''Aye, and keeper of Liddesdale, as well; but the law is the law, and Sir Hugh cannot insist on searching two marches for us. Any road, Buccleuch is likely to tell him to go to the devil.''

''He cannot do that! By law he must honor a legitimate request.''

''Not if he claims that he does not know Rabbie Redcloak and doubts that he would find anyone in his marches or in all of Liddesdale who would admit to knowing any knave as scurrilous as your brother is like to describe me.''

Seated sideways as she was, Janet was able to look into his face, and her eyes had adjusted to the darkness enough so that she could make out his general features and shape, but she could not read his expression. She could still detect the ever-present note of amusement in his voice, however.

''I do not know how you can so easily mock the law,'' she said. ''Do you not fear hanging?''

''Bless you, lass, every man fears death, for we are but a moment away from it at any time. However, those who spend their living hours thinking of naught else waste their lives. I enjoy mine, and never more so than when I am risking death.''

''Men,'' she muttered.

"Aye, we're a sorry lot," he agreed.

"I do wish you would stop mocking everything I say."

"Then you must say something sensible," he said. "Do you really believe that all men are alike?"

"Not in every way," she said, "but in many ways. They like their comforts and expect women to provide them. They are brutal and cruel when it suits them to be and care not for what havoc their behavior wreaks in the lives of others. I have yet to meet one who is not selfish and stubborn and—"

"Enough," he said, laughing again. "I know I asked the question, but it seems to me that you have met a sorry lot of men. The ones I know are merry, even when they struggle to find food for their tables. They look after one another—aye, and after their families and friends, too. If they do expect their women to provide them with those comforts you mention, they generally appreciate them when they get them. Comfort of any sort is rare in their lives."

"Most of the men I know are either members of the gentry or their henchmen," she said. "When I think about them with their families, though, and not just talking amongst themselves, perhaps they are not so bad."

"You must have maidservants at Brackengill," he said. "Do your brother and his men treat them all badly?"

"No, for in the general way of things I do not allow them to. Of course, if Hugh loses his temper, there is not a great deal I can do to protect his target. Still, he does like a comfortable home, and over the years I have brought him to agree that our servants exert themselves more to make him comfortable if he treats them with some degree of courtesy. He takes pride in what he has achieved at Brackengill, and he knows that the comfort with which he has surrounded himself contributes a great deal to the impression that Brackengill makes on visitors."

"What else has he achieved then? I saw that he's got a strong stone wall, but the lodging he afforded to me was not what I would call splendid."

She suppressed a chuckle, not certain enough yet of his wry

humor to believe that he meant her to share it. "Hugh has spent years making Brackengill a home of which he can be proud," she said. "I do not know if you ever saw it as it was before, but when he inherited, the castle was no more than a pele tower surrounded by a wooden stockade. He inherited when he was twelve, but our uncle served as his guardian, and it was not until Hugh turned eighteen that Uncle allowed him to make any choices of his own. Once he could do so, however, he set about turning Brackengill into what it is today."

"Not without help, I'll wager."

"If you mean help from me, you cannot know much about nine-year-old girls. If I helped then, it was only by providing poorly embroidered cushions for the stone window seats. I have learned to help more since then, of course, for I organized the kitchens and have done much of the needlework. The arras cloth in the hall came from Belgium, of course, but—"

"I have not seen that," he said dryly. "Is it particularly good?"

"Oh, yes, magnificent," she said. "Don't think you can raid Brackengill to steal it, however. I doubt it would look as well on the walls of a reiver's cottage."

He chuckled again but did not deny that he had been contemplating such a thing. Hugging to herself what felt like a small victory, she wished that she could think she had sorted him out in her mind, but she could not. One moment he spoke with the broad accent of the Scottish Border, the next he sounded much as Hugh did. She decided that he had spent time with educated men and that, in her presence, he tried to ape their manner.

The gusting wind settled to a stiff breeze, and above its murmuring, Janet soon heard the gurgle of a nearby burn. Moments later she could make out the white froth of its rapids as they roiled over boulders and stones in its path.

She said, "I suppose you know exactly where we are."

"I've a fair notion," he said. "Every bit of water flowing west hereabouts flows into the Esk, you see, so once we find a place to cross this burn, we should be only a few miles from the dike. We'll cross the Esk just east of Netherby, where I know a ford. If your brother follows, he'll reach the line well east of that point. Doubtless you're sleepy," he added. "Why do you not rest for a time?"

"Have you tired of my conversation so quickly?"

"I have not, but there are any number of hamlets hereabouts, and now that the wind has fallen to a whisper, I think we should keep silent, lest someone hear us and come out to see who we are."

The warning was enough to silence her. They were still in Graham territory, and although any Grahams she encountered south of the line would be friendly to her, they would be likely to tell Hugh they had seen her. She did not intend to accept the reiver's invitation to nap, however, tempting though it was.

While they had talked, it had been possible to ignore their closeness to each other. Riding in silence made that more difficult. Her body touched his in too many places, and the motion of the horse constantly jostled them together. Moreover, of necessity his arms were around her, and his left one kept brushing her breast as he manipulated the reins. He did not carry a whip, so his right hand, behind her, was generally unoccupied, and she assumed that he rested it on his thigh as he rode. When he guided the pony to the edge of the burn and into the water a few moments later, he steadied her with that hand as if he feared she would fall.

On the other side, he held her while the pony lurched up the steep bank, and when they reached the flat, she felt almost sorry when he took his hand away.

Again the silence made her unnaturally aware of his nearness. She knew that she ought to be outraged that he was taking her away from the only home and family she had ever known, but she was grateful not to have to face Hugh and could think of little else beyond the reiver. She could hear him breathing, could feel the slightest movement of his left arm, and each of those movements stirred other sensations, deeper ones that made her feel wicked.

Just thinking of such wickedness conjured up a looming vision of Hugh, and the little shiver that followed momentarily expelled the wanton thoughts. Then the reiver shifted on the saddle. His right hand steadied her again, and feeling that hand on her arm sent new sensations tingling from one nerve ending to another, straight to the center of her body. The feelings warmed her and stirred thoughts that she knew she ought to pray to God for the strength to resist.

"Lean back against me, lassie," he murmured. "I willna bite."

His voice was seductively low-pitched. It seemed to vibrate through her, and she was too sleepy to muster more resistance. Her body felt like warm wax in his arms, as if it were molding itself against his. She obeyed his command without a thought of protesting.

He knew the instant she slept, because her weight settled against him. She was not heavy, and her body seemed to fit against his as if it had been created for the purpose. He wondered what had possessed him to make off with her as he had. Surely, it had been the most reckless thing he had done in a life filled with reckless deeds. He would never hear the end of it. Buccleuch would see to that if no one else did. Just the thought of his cousin's inevitable wrath stirred a prickling sensation along his spine. Surely even the hairs on the back of his neck stood erect.

She shifted—snuggling, seeking comfort—and when he moved his right hand and arm automatically to support her, he found his fingertips resting against the curve of her hip. A wave of her scent touched his nostrils, and his cousin's fierce image vanished in a trice as bodily instincts and reflexes banished thought of anything but Janet Graham. The scent of her, and the warmth emanating from her slender, curving body beneath the thick cloaks stirred other parts of him to life. The temptation to allow his fantasies a free rein was nearly irresistible.

A purring sound drifted to his ears, and for a moment, he thought the sound issued from the lass. When it continued steadily, rhythmically, he realized it came from the little cat she still held in the shelter of her arms beneath her two cloaks.

The sound reminded him of his folly. Bad enough that he had taken the wench, but he had taken the damned cat as well. Should anyone require proof that Mistress Janet Graham had unhinged him, the cat would provide it. He decided that when it came time to describe his escape, he would omit the cat. The legend of Rabbie Redcloak encompassed a host of audacious escapades, daring deeds, and admirable accomplishments—a number of which were even true—but he did not think the legend would benefit by adding his abduction of Jemmy Whiskers.

The lass did not stir until he began to descend the Esk's bank at the seldom-used crossing near Netherby. By then her head lay against his shoulder, and his right arm supported her body. Sleepily, she tilted her head back to look up at him.

"Where are we?" she murmured.

"Near the dike, about to cross the Esk. We'll make for Jess Armstrong's place. He's a broken man, but he keeps his mouth shut and I warrant he'll put us up for the day without making any fuss about it."

"For the day?"

"Aye, it's safer to lurk a bit, I think, since we'll have to make our way east and your brother will likely be searching for us soon. I want to put out a few ears to listen for news before I risk your bonny neck by riding farther."

"Where will we go?"

"To my place, I think, until I can decide what to do with you. There are Grahams on this side of the line, of course."

"Aye, but they are not friends of mine," she said.

He clicked his tongue. "Now, fighting within families is something I don't hold with," he said virtuously.

Sweetly she said, "Tell me again about this cousin of yours."

He chuckled. "Bless you, lass, we dinna fratch. Well, not as you mean, at all events. He will be wroth with me. I canna deny that, but 'tis only because I've put up your brother's back. It's his being a deputy warden, and all, that will put Wat in a stir. He has scruples, does Wat. He seldom shows them, but he does have them. Here now, hold on tight. This is probably the worst ford for twenty miles, and the water flows high and moves fast now that the thaw has begun."

She eyed the swiftly moving river warily. "Is it safe?"

"Oh, aye, my lad will make it. 'Ware the cat, though, because we might all get a wee bit damp, and that water's bound to be cold."

That proved to be an understatement, but Jemmy stayed dry; and not long after they reached the opposite bank, they came to a cottage and the reiver reined in.

Without dismounting, he shouted, "Jess!"

The door opened so quickly that Janet was sure the cottager had not been sleeping. Indeed, he seemed almost to have been awaiting their arrival. He hurried out, saying, "Dinna get down fra' the pony, Rab. Ye'll no be stayin'."

"Now, Jess," the reiver said calmly, "the lass is tired, and so am I. You may not have heard the news, but I ha' been imprisoned these three—"

"Och, do I no ken that? Still, Rab, ye're no t' stay here. Himself said ye're t' ride for Hermitage as fast as your pony's legs'll tak' ye. He'll meet ye there."

"Damnation," the reiver said. "We're for it now, lass, right enough."

Chapter 7

"With fairest words and reason strong,
Strave courteously in vain."

"I'm right sorry about this," the reiver said.

"But what's the hurry?" Janet asked. "Surely we can go inside and rest a bit."

"Believe me, I'd stay here if I could," he replied, "but I dare not."

"But you cannot take me to Hermitage! 'Tis the strongest fortress on the Scottish side of the line. 'Tis a prison, what's more."

"Aye, I ken fine that it is," he said. "Still, I must go there, lass. Even Rabbie Redcloak must obey orders from Himself."

"But the master of Hermitage is Buccleuch, and he's a terrible man! Hugh says that as warden of two marches and keeper of Liddesdale he wields his power like a fiery sword! Hugh says it is foolhardy for James to rest so much power in the hands of one man. He says that Buccleuch is nigh as powerful as the King himself."

"Aye, 'tis true," the reiver said with a sigh. "You can see

my dilemma, lass. I could leave you here, I suppose, although Jess might balk at the notion and you would not find his hospitality all that you might wish.''

Regarding the burly, unkempt Jess with disfavor, Janet barely managed to repress a shudder. ''You cannot leave me here,'' she said firmly. At least, she hoped she sounded firm and that no trace of the shudder had touched her voice. ''Since you made the decision to abduct me, Redcloak, you are stuck with me. I just hope Buccleuch believes you when you tell him that this madness was your idea and will not take me for a common doxy who somehow seduced you. Godamercy,'' she added when another thought struck, ''he might even decide to hold me for ransom!''

''Lassie, you've kept your wits about you thus far; dinna lose them now,'' the reiver said. ''I promise you, you've no cause to fear Buccleuch. He'll reserve his wrath for me. If I'm lucky, he'll just be glad to see that I am free. Jess,'' he added, ''d'ye ken aught o' Himself's mind when he said I were to make for Hermitage?''

Jess rolled his eyes. ''Hob the Mouse came here,'' he said. ''He tellt me that Himself be of a mind t' raise the Borders did he hear nowt afore Wednesday o' yer safe return or where them bastards was holding ye.''

''There, you see, lass? He's just been a wee bit worried about me.''

''He said,'' Jess added glumly, ''that he'd give ten pounds t' the man wha' tells him where he can find ye, so he can pin your ears back for ye himself.''

''Ah, I see,'' the reiver said. ''We'll be wasting no time then, and I'll see that you get the ten pounds, Jess.''

''I thank ye for that, Rabbie. Watch weel the noo. I've a sword and a pistol for ye, so ye willna lose your head to some deevilish thief.''

The reiver grinned at him. ''I thank ye for the weapons, Jess. I've felt naked without my own. Have you perchance got a bit of food to spare for us, as well?''

"Aye, my sister's inside puttin' up a bit for ye, and I've got a pony ye can tak' for the lass if ye like. Hold on a bit, and I'll fetch the lot out." He turned away, then turned back with a frown to say apologetically to Janet, "I must crave pardon, mistress, for I dinna possess a sidesaddle."

"I do not require one," she told him with a smile. "A simple cross-saddle will serve me well if you have one that I may use."

"I'm glad that you can ride astride, lass," the reiver said when Jess had gone to fetch the horse and saddle. "Many ladies do not, but I never thought to ask. If you'd required a sidesaddle, we'd have had to travel much more slowly, and as it is, it will take us the best part of the day to reach Hermitage. I've never yet understood how women can be comfortable riding sideways, any road."

"Women just have better balance than men, that's all," she replied sweetly.

Hugh would have scoffed, might even have snapped at her to hold her foolish tongue; but, to her surprise, the reiver grinned and said, "I never thought of that possibility. In truth, though, any saddle of Jess's is bound to be shabby, and not as comfortable as what you're used to. You might use that second cloak of yours to cushion it, and I'll be glad to put you up. You needn't worry that Jess will see more than he should. Your skirts are full enough to keep you decent."

"I am accustomed to riding astride," she said. "I have done so since childhood and sometimes even wear my brother's cast-off breeches beneath my skirts for extra comfort. I had no mother or father to tell me that I should not, you see, and Hugh was often away."

"I think I begin to see how you grew to be as you are," he said thoughtfully, "but we'll not discuss what I think of such an upbringing. At present I am just grateful that my own weary lad need carry the two of us no longer."

She did not know whether to be glad or sorry about that. She had rather enjoyed feeling his arms around her, and now that she could see his features clearly in the early gray dawn light, she saw that he was better looking than any reiver had a right to be.

He wore no helmet, and his shaggy hair and beard were darker than she had imagined them. His eyes were light brown or hazel. She would need more light to discern their exact color. When he walked, he did so with lithe, powerful grace, and in the saddle he sat tall and moved with his horse as if he had been born riding. She took care not to stare, however, having no wish to betray thoughts that were wholly inappropriate to their different stations in life.

When Jess returned leading a plump little gray mare, she made no objection when the reiver lifted her to its saddle. She required no assistance to arrange her skirts or her cloak, but she did not disdain his help when he held the reins while she did so and offered to fold Hugh's cloak to provide a cushion for Jemmy Whiskers.

The little mare did not seem to mind her skirts much, but the process tested its manners and the cat's patience. Remembering what the Brackengill stable lad had said about half-broken Scottish ponies, she wondered if the mare had been raised in England. Trading horses across the line was illegal, but that did not stop the practice. Nor did it stop the reivers from doing their own sort of horse-trading.

The sun was rising through a light mist as they rode over the first hill and beyond sight of the cottage. The day promised to be warmer than the previous one.

"How will you get the mare back to Jess?" Janet asked, breaking the silence.

The reiver shrugged. "One of my lads will see that she gets back to him," he said. A moment later, as he led the way down the other side of the hill, he added, "We'll head north for a bit. The Liddel flows as much from the north as from the east, you know, and it would not do for us to run into your brother and his men before we reach Hermitage.''

She nodded, although she had not really known which way the Liddel flowed. She had never been on the Scottish side of the line before, and she was a little surprised that it looked much the same as Cumberland. For some reason she had expected it to be different, but the hills bore the same melting patchwork of snow, and in many places, the same stiff brown grass poked through. In south-facing hollows, bits of green grass were starting to show, just as they were in similar hollows in England. Most seemed to have survived the freeze the night before, but it was still too early to count them as harbingers of spring on either side of the line.

The mist soon disappeared, leaving a bright blue sky, and the air, though crisp, held warmth that had been lacking for months. Janet knew, however, that the higher temperatures could vanish overnight and that more snow might blanket the hills before spring spread true warmth through the Borders.

Soon they came to the banks of a river as wide as the Esk.

"This cannot be the Esk," she said. "We crossed it again just before we arrived at Jess's cottage. We must be well to the east of it now.''

"Aye, that's right," he said. "We crossed the Esk near Langholm, where the horse races will be next month. Jess lives in Ewesdale, and this is Tarras Water. Tarrasdale is Scott country, so we're safe enough for a bit. We'll follow Tarras Water to the top of Pike Fell yonder. On the other side, we'll meet with Hermitage Water and follow it along down to the castle. That way, we'll avoid meeting your brother if he should decide to visit Buccleuch and present a demand for a hot trod. He'd follow the Liddel to Hermitage Water and follow it north to the castle.''

They rode in silence for a half hour after that before Janet noticed that the reiver kept glancing at her. His expression was unreadable, but for once she could discern no amusement. He seemed somehow to be measuring her.

"What?" She cocked her head. "Why do you keep looking at me as if my hair had turned green or I'd got a smudge on my nose?"

"Is that how you think I'm looking at you? I was only trying to judge whether you seemed able to ride all the way without stopping. You were awake most of the night, lass, and by my reckoning the morning is more than half gone."

"You were awake *all* night," she pointed out.

"Aye, but I'll warrant that I've had more rest than you have these past days."

She could say nothing to that. He had had much more time for resting.

"I'm not tired," she said. "You need not fear for my safety."

"This is wild country," he said. "We'll have no track to follow, only the water, and much of the time we will not be able to ride alongside it. There is too much shrubbery, and in places the terrain is unreliable."

She soon found that his description of the terrain was an understatement. The country was as rugged and bog-ridden as any she had ever seen. Cumberland, by comparison, was a gentle land. She hoped the gray mare was sure-footed.

Sir Hugh Graham did not discover that his prisoner had escaped until an hour after sunrise, because his man allowed him to oversleep. Since it had been unusually late when he got to bed, Hugh had not chided his servant. The prisoner certainly would not complain if his hanging was delayed.

Accordingly, Sir Hugh had broken his fast and attended to other morning duties before shouting for his men to prepare the reiver to meet his Maker.

Ten minutes later, Geordie rushed into the hall, white-faced and wide-eyed. "Master, he's vanished!"

Sir Hugh looked up from papers he had been reading at the hall table. "What the devil do you mean, 'he's vanished'?"

Geordie spread his hands helplessly. "He isna there, sir. The doors be locked, both of them, and I ha' the keys myself."

"Then he must be in the cell."

"Aye, that he must, but he isna there, I tell ye. 'Tis a witch's spell, most like, or one cast by Auld Clarty." Geordie made a hasty sign of the cross.

With difficulty Sir Hugh controlled his temper enough to say, "Search the castle, every inch of it. And if he got outside the walls, find out how he did so. And, Geordie," he added in a soft but menacing tone as the man turned to leave.

With visible reluctance Geordie turned back. "Aye, master?"

"If he has got away, I shall not waste his gallows. Whoever is responsible for this will hang, every man jack of them."

Sir Hugh got up to follow when Geordie hurried from the hall, but as he strode to the doorway, another thought struck and he shouted for a lackey. When one came running from the kitchen, Hugh said, "Has Mistress Janet arisen yet?"

"I dinna ken, master."

"Then find out, damn you!"

In minutes he learned that his sister was nowhere in the castle and that no one had seen her all morning. Within the hour he learned that the prisoner was likewise nowhere to be found.

"Shall I ha' the lads ready theirselves t' ride after him?" Geordie asked.

"And which way do you think they should ride?" Hugh asked curtly.

Geordie thought for a moment, then said, "North, sir?"

With a sigh, Hugh said, "Send parties to the usual places to ask if anyone chanced to see him. If you get word of the direction he took, we can organize a pursuit. Give them two hours. If you cannot get word of his direction, we shall ride to Hermitage and demand that the damned Scots find him and return him to us."

He did not tell the man that he suspected Janet had had a hand in the reiver's escape. If she had, she had committed march treason and there would be those who would demand her death. Angry as he was, he did not want that. He would bide his time, but he would lay hands on them both again, and when he did, he would see to it that they paid heavily for their mischief.

Janet had been following the reiver over rocky outcroppings and through boggy meadows for over an hour when he said casually, "For a lass, you ride as well as any I've seen."

The compliment caught her off guard. She knew that she was a competent horsewoman, even a skilled one, but Hugh was a man who favored criticism over compliments, and he could always find something to criticize.

With warmth in her cheeks she thanked him, glad that he was not looking directly at her, for she was certain that he would discern both her amazement and her delight. She did not think it wise to give a man like Redcloak the satisfaction of knowing how deeply his words had touched her.

They did not speak much after that, except when he pointed out certain signs now and again of his own men's passing. It fascinated her that he could tell who had crossed their path and which way the rider had gone, just from a few scratches in the dirt.

"Bless you, lass, it's how we communicate," he said. "If there's a raid, we cannot always wait for everyone to arrive at the meeting place, you see. So I leave my own sign for the stragglers, pointing the way."

Despite the signs they saw, they encountered no one, and although they pressed on without stopping more than necessary, the afternoon had advanced considerably when Janet caught her first glimpse of Hermitage Castle.

As big as it was, she thought she might have suspected its identity even had the reiver not said, "There it is, lassie, the strength of Liddesdale."

Eerie, bleak, and forbidding, even in slanting sunlight, the

rectangular castle loomed to the north of a thicket of trees
lining Hermitage Water. Set against the bleak brown and snow-
white moorland of Liddesdale, it was one of the largest castles
she had seen, but it had little in common with the fortress-
palaces that were springing up in northern England. Hermitage
was stark and, except for its enclosed, overhanging battlements
and iron grills over windows on the topmost level, it bore not
a touch of decoration, although the high flying arch linking
two corner towers at the north end was striking. To her right,
beyond the central block, she could see another tower and the
peak of yet another beyond it to the north. Built of squared,
close-fitting ashlar, its soft brown color suited the landscape.

She had heard much about the great Scottish stronghold, for
it was a royal and ancient seat. For many years it had belonged
to the notorious Stewart Earls of Bothwell. During their stewardship, Mary Queen of Scots had once ridden fifty miles to
Hermitage to be with her lover, the fourth earl, and had nearly
died of her adventure. The fifth and last Earl of Bothwell had
been a strong presence in the Borders, but it was not just his
Stewart name or his personal power that had made him so. It
had been his stewardship of the royal castle of Hermitage. That
stewardship, and its power, had passed from him to Sir Walter
Scott of Buccleuch, and she had heard it said more than once
that Buccleuch was an even more fearsome adversary than
Bothwell had ever been.

Janet saw that Redcloak was watching her. "It is a fierce-
looking place," she said, wetting suddenly dry lips. "Must we
truly go inside?"

"Aye, we must," he said, "but you will be safe, lassie. I
do not mean to hold you to ransom, nor would my laird allow
it. We'll think of a way to see you safe again even if it means
consigning you to Scrope's personal guardianship."

She wrinkled her nose. "I do not like Thomas Scrope or his
lady wife," she said. "They think only of gaming, the pair of
them, and their household is generally a shambles because he
cannot pay his debts."

He chuckled. "I've heard that said of him myself," he said. "Also that he is a coward. What do you hear of Hermitage?"

She shrugged. "That its present master is as fierce as his predecessor."

"Aye, that's true enough, but Buccleuch has an image to maintain, after all. I referred to the castle's history, though. Do you know aught of that?"

"I have heard tales," she admitted. "It is an important stronghold."

"If you are going to get on with folks hereabouts, it would be as well to know more than that. It has stood here more than three hundred and fifty years, after all. A chap called Sir Nicholas de Soules built it. They say he was the King's butler."

"Rather an isolated place to keep one's butler, I should think," she said dryly.

He chuckled. "Most likely he'd risen a bit before he built Hermitage. The English didn't much care for having so strong a castle right on the Border, however, so they fought over it, and it spent nearly as much time in the hands of your people as mine during its first hundred years. Then Sir William Douglas seized it. A ruthless man was Sir William. When the King failed to make him Sheriff of Teviotdale, he rectified the error by imprisoning the new sheriff at Hermitage and starving him to death. After that the King agreed to let Sir William take his place."

"If this discourse is intended to make me look forward to my visit, let me tell you that it falls short of the mark," Janet said tersely.

He chuckled again. "Dinna fash yourself, lass. All will be well, I promise you. Now, where was I?"

"Explaining rather more of the history of Hermitage than I wanted to hear," Janet retorted. "For that matter, how is it that you know so much about it?"

He shrugged. "It behooves one who answers to Buccleuch to know as much as he can about the man and his holdings. I do what I must, lass, that's all."

"Well, I do not know much about Buccleuch other than that he is a man whom many fear, so tell me more about him."

"Well, he is stepson to the fifth Earl of Bothwell."

"I have heard of Lord Bothwell," she said sagely.

He grinned at her. "Everyone has heard of Bothwell. The Earls of Bothwell owned Hermitage for more than a hundred years, but the fifth earl forfeited his lands two years ago when he went into exile, so he has lost Hermitage forever. He married Buccleuch's mother after Buccleuch's father died, and it now belongs to the Scotts, to Buccleuch."

"Because Bothwell is in exile?"

"Partly, but Buccleuch is also connected to many other powerful families, including the Douglas of Angus."

"Did Buccleuch have naught to do with his stepfather's crimes, then?"

The reiver shrugged, saying lightly, "I hope you know that that is not a topic of conversation in which to indulge with Buccleuch. It is enough to say that Jamie saw fit to pardon him for any wrongs he might have committed in his youth."

They were close enough now to see men on the battlements, indeed to see gun barrels poking through several of the gun holes.

"Are they aiming those guns at us?"

"Oh, aye, I suppose they are. The Crown has spent a fortune over the past forty years, installing artillery here. They put gun holes everywhere, as if they expect the place to be attacked with artillery."

"But surely it might be," she replied reasonably.

He shook his head. "Look around you, lass. What are the chances that anyone is going to drag heavy artillery into Liddesdale? Bringing in those guns that you see took them months and cost several lives. Fortunately, when one brainless dolt suggested building a road to make it easier, a brighter chap pointed out that the English would get more use out of such a road than we ever would."

"There are still arrow slits, too, I see."

"Aye, and while Hermitage is impervious to arrows, its attackers are far more likely to carry bows and arrows than heavy guns." As he spoke, he took off his cloak and turned it inside out, waving it over his head. "They recognize me now," he said when a banner waved wildly from the battlements.

Janet drew a deep breath as they neared the entrance. The walls towered above her, and it was all she could do to maintain her placid demeanor. Hermitage was a stronghold, not a residence. Although Buccleuch was married, there would be no women here. Of that she was certain, for maidservants had better sense than to seek work at all-male establishments. She did not know if that small fact had occurred to Redcloak, or if he would see that it could pose any problem.

He led the way, and by the time they reached the gate, two men-at-arms and a pair of lads had emerged to greet them.

"He's waiting above," one said, shooting a curious glance at Janet.

She was wondering how she was to dismount with grace and without losing Jemmy Whiskers, but Redcloak had already thought about that.

"Here, mistress," he said, tossing his reins to one of the lads and moving to her left. "Hand me the wee one first, and then I will lift you down."

Grateful for his assistance, she did not argue but handed him the small, warm cat. Jemmy stretched and yawned but made no objection when Redcloak handed him to an astonished man-at-arms.

Grinning at the fellow, Redcloak said, "Just hold him till the lady has dismounted and can take him back. And watch weel, man. He has sharp claws."

"Aye," the man grunted.

Redcloak returned, and by then Janet had managed to slip her right leg over the saddlebow. Again she was grateful for the mare's good manners, for the little beast stood as still as if she dealt with ladies and skirts every day. Redcloak lifted her down as if she weighed no more than the cat.

His hands were firm and warm at her waist, and when he set her on the ground, he drew her close enough for her breasts to touch his chest. That he did it on purpose was clear from the wicked glint of mischief in his eyes. For the first time since catching sight of the forbidding castle, she forgot about Buccleuch.

She remembered him quickly, however, when they entered the stronghold and she heard the heavy door bang shut behind them. They were in the southwest tower, in a dimly lighted chamber.

The reiver said to the lackey, "He is above, you say?"

"Aye, sir, in his private apartments."

"We'll find him, thank you, lad. This way, mistress," he added, taking Janet's elbow and urging her toward a spiral stairway off the corner of the chamber. "Just keep going up till I bid you stop," he said.

That the master's private apartments were near the top of the castle did not surprise her. They would be where he could enjoy the luxury of windows without worrying about invaders gaining entrance through them. At the next level, she saw through an arched doorway into a great central hall that filled most of the castle's central block. Doubtless it was the great hall and served the men-at-arms and servants for dining and sleeping. The laird would want private accommodations when his family visited, or for any entertaining that he might choose to do.

The southwest corner tower was clearly the finest of the four. She could tell from its warmth that the kitchens lay at its lowest level. The heat from their ovens would augment that of the fireplaces on the upper floors.

"There," Redcloak said when they reached the next level.

Janet turned and passed through a stone archway into a well-appointed hall nearly as large as the one below, with a hooded fireplace in one corner, carpets, arras hangings on the walls, cushioned benches at the long table, and several chairs, one of which had arms. Lighted by late afternoon sunlight through a narrow arched window opposite the stairway, the hall appeared presently to be unoccupied.

"Make yourself comfortable," Redcloak said as if it were his own home. "I'll find him."

Janet looked around. "Would there perhaps be . . ." She paused, wishing Hermitage had a hostess who would understand her predicament without words.

Redcloak grinned at her. "There is a closet just through that wee archway yonder. No one uses it but the laird and his chosen friends."

Hoping she would not find Buccleuch there, she left Jemmy Whiskers in the master's hall, went through the indicated archway, found the necessary, and quickly attended to her business. Returning to the hall, she found it still empty except for her cat. Picking him up, she sat gingerly on one of the cushioned benches, and as she was trying to decide if she wanted Redcloak and Buccleuch to join her or leave her in peace, she heard an unfamiliar masculine voice in the stairwell.

"So there you are! Who the devil is the wench you've brought with you?"

"Now, Wat—" She recognized Redcloak's voice.

The other retorted angrily, "Mind your tongue if you don't want to feel the flat of my sword across your back, you damned, impudent reprobate."

"If you think you can, my lad—"

"Christ's wounds, would you flout my authority? Scrofulous jackstraw! You deserve flogging. Why, at the very least, I should—"

"Mind your tongue," Redcloak interjected calmly. "The lady awaits us in your hall, and I'll warrant that she can hear everything we say."

"Sponge-wit, when I think what you deserve for this—"

"Then do not think about it. You are too young to die of an apoplexy."

A scowling, slender, dark-haired man who looked to be in

his early thirties strode briskly through the archway, and the energy crackling from him brought Janet instantly to her feet.

Redcloak said blandly, "Laird, may I present Mistress Janet Graham."

Still holding her cat, Janet curtsied low, knowing that she faced the Laird of Buccleuch.

"Graham? Graham!" he sputtered. "Christ's blood, Quin, tell me she is not kin to that damned, hasty-witted moldwarp at Brackengill!"

"Sir Hugh Graham is my brother," Janet said with dignity.

"You did not phrase that quite right, lass," Redcloak chided. "You must learn to say that Sir Hugh Graham has the honor to be your brother."

Buccleuch was staring at her in dismay. "Her brother! What madness is this, Quin? You've abducted a march warden's sister!"

"A deputy march warden," Redcloak said.

"Och, you fool! And him hot on your heels, no doubt."

Redcloak shrugged. "I've seen no sign of pursuit, but I cannot deny that I half expected to find him here with you."

"And what am I to tell him when he does come here? Have you thought of that, you pestiferous dolthead?"

"Aye, I have, and I decided that you can feign a great indignation—though you'll doubtless find that difficult—and deny knowing anyone by the name of Rabbie Redcloak."

"Aye, sure." Buccleuch looked speculatively at Janet, and she realized that he was seriously considering the suggestion. "I do not suppose," he said thoughtfully, "that you would support that declaration, would you, mistress?"

"I do not tell lies, sir," she said flatly.

Redcloak's eyebrows shot upward. "Never, lass?"

Feeling warmth flood her cheeks, Janet said to the master of Hermitage, "I will do naught a-purpose to bring disaster upon you or yours, sir. I cannot say that I have never told a falsehood, but neither can I pretend that I have ever lied to my brother when he has asked me a direct question. I do not believe I could do that.''

"I thank you for your honesty, mistress. Quin, by God, I should order you bound to the old oak and horsewhipped for this.''

A little to Janet's surprise, the reiver abstained from making another light rejoinder. Into the silence that followed the grimly uttered threat, she said, "Why do you call him Quin, sir? Is his name not Rabbie, then?''

"He has many names, mistress," Buccleuch said, casting another look of displeasure at the reiver.

"Including several that you bear," the reiver said quietly.

"I'll thank you to recall, however, that I am also your liege lord.''

"Aye, 'tis true, you are." The reiver made a profound leg and extended his right hand. "Shall I pledge this hand again? I am sorry that I let them take me, but at the time I thought it the best thing to do. I continued to think that right up until Sir Hugh Graham informed me that he meant to hang me without the benefit of a trial.''

"The devil he did!" Buccleuch exclaimed. "I wondered why that dimwitted pudding Scrope failed to send word of your arrival at Carlisle.''

"The reason is that Sir Hugh cast me into his dungeon at Brackengill. At first, he said that he would let me rot there till Wednesday, but the lass informed me last night that this morning's sunrise was to be my last.''

"Faith, but 'tis the Sabbath! Is that true, mistress?''

"To my shame, sir, it is," Janet said. "My brother was angry with . . . with this man. I do not know what to call him,'' she added in frustration.

"Do not trouble your head with trivialities," Buccleuch recommended. "Call him 'impudent knave' and 'varlet,' as I do.''

"Mind your manners, Wat," the reiver said. "If she believes you, Mistress Janet will think that she has risked her life to no good purpose. You will offend her sensibilities so—and mine, as well.''

"Risked her life! What's this? I assumed you'd abducted her out of pique.''

His expression of astonishment was so ludicrous that Janet bit her lower lip to keep from smiling and quickly lowered her gaze to the rich Turkey carpet.

"She set me free,'' the reiver said solemnly, "and if I do not mistake the matter, she thus committed march treason. Sir Hugh Graham might not wish her dead, but he will not thank her for her deeds. I could not leave her to face his fury.''

Buccleuch's next words wiped the half smile from Janet's lips.

"By God,'' he declared, "there is nothing else for it then. You'll just have to marry the wench.''

Chapter 8

"With him nae pleading might prevail . . ."

Janet stared at Buccleuch, wondering if he were daft.

Her tongue refused to move, and her body seemed to belong to someone else, for it did not feel as if it were connected to her. She did not want to speak as much as she wanted to scream that such a notion was madness. Her pulse was working overtime, however, for the sounds of its labor roared in her ears.

The colorfully rich trappings of the chamber seemed to spin around her as if she were in some strange dream and could not wake up because she could not stir a hand to pinch herself.

The reiver's deep voice brought her back to the moment with a thump when he said casually, "I do not think that I am of a mind to marry just yet."

Buccleuch snapped, "I don't care a pin for the set of your mind, sir. Consider the consequences if you do *not* marry her."

"Just think of the consequences if I do," the reiver said, still in that maddeningly mild tone. "The penalty for marrying across the line is death, Wat, or had you forgotten that small detail?"

"I have not forgotten anything, but it will be far easier for me to arrange a marriage than to protect you against the consequences of this crazy abduction. Christ, Quin, but you've put me in the devil of a fix! I must think on this. Get hence now, the pair of you, and leave me to it."

"And go where?" the reiver asked. "If I do not mistake the matter, you summoned me to Hermitage rather publicly, and Jess Armstrong has seen Mistress Graham in my company. I put no great faith in his discretion, so I think it likely that she will be safer under your protection than with me."

"She cannot stay here," Buccleuch retorted. "There are no other females on the premises, because Margaret and the bairns are at Branxholme. If you want to take Mistress Graham there— What the devil do *you* want?" This last question, although it had the effect of making Janet's head spin again, was directed to a lackey who had entered the hall hastily and without ceremony.

"Beggin' your pardon, laird," the lad said, "but there be a gentleman below demanding speech wi' ye. Calls hisself Sir Hugh Graham, he does."

Gasping, Janet swayed, but a firm hand caught her elbow, and the reiver said calmly, "Steady, lass."

Buccleuch made a sound that was so like a growl from one of her brother's dogs that Janet held Jemmy closer and nearly glanced around the hall for one.

The ensuing silence was brief. Then the master of Hermitage said grimly to the lackey, "Go back down and invite Sir Hugh to join me here. See that any men he has with him get ale and bread in the great hall and that someone provides his horses with water and grain. I shall not invite him to take supper with me."

"Aye, laird." The lad turned to leave but halted at a murmured command from his master.

"No one below mentioned my guests, did they?"

"Nay, laird, they ken better nor that."

"Excellent. See that they keep their tongues locked behind their teeth till Sir Hugh and his men have departed." When the lackey had gone, Buccleuch said, "The pair of you can go upstairs to my private apartments till I get shut of the man. You've no cause to fear harm here, mistress. He brought you thus far in safety, and betwixt us we'll see you safe out of this muddle."

"Thank you, sir. I pray that you will not tell my brother you have seen me."

"Have no fear o' that. Go now, and quickly."

To her surprise, the reiver said not a word but obeyed at once, urging her ahead of him into the stairwell. As she hurried to the next level, she kept expecting to hear him make one of his impudent remarks, but he did not.

The master's chamber proved to be as comfortably appointed as the hall below it; however, the fireplace boasted a carved mantel and occupied the center of the long wall. Thick, heavily embroidered bed curtains bore the same hunting and battle scenes that decorated the bedcover, and the carpet on the floor was another fine one. Other carpets covered several chests and coffers. Clearly, Buccleuch was a man of some wealth as well as great power.

"You need not move so far away," the reiver said as she walked toward an arched window recess with stone benches lining its three walls.

"I want to look out, to see where we are within the castle. I lost my sense of direction on that circular stairway."

"Well, do not show yourself in that window, lass. You never know who might be looking up here. It looks south over Hermitage Water and Liddesdale."

She hesitated, then decided she should listen to him. If Hugh truly suspected that Buccleuch sheltered her, he might leave men outside the castle for the sole purpose of keeping watch to see if she appeared at a window.

Still carrying her cat, she went to stand by the fireplace instead. It was tall enough so that if she were of a mind to do so she could walk inside it without doing more than bending her head a little. Not that she harbored such a wish. Critically, she noted that the hearth had not been swept recently. Indeed, it looked to her as if it had not been cleaned in some weeks. New fires had been laid on the ashes of the old. At Brackengill, she would not allow such untidiness.

The reiver remained silent, and conscious as she was of his presence, she could think of nothing to say to him. To declare that Buccleuch must be mad to think he could arrange a marriage between them would be a waste of breath and, under the circumstances, to announce that she had no intention of marrying a reiver seemed overly blunt and ungrateful besides.

Gratitude was an odd emotion, she decided, and fleeting, as well. That she had not had to face Hugh at the height of his fury with her was a godsend, but the reiver had clearly thought no farther than that moment. What had he intended to do with her after he got her to Scotland? The obvious answer did not seem to apply. Although the Laird of Hermitage had accused him of abducting her, Buccleuch had seemed to feel more put upon than angry, and he had promised to see her safe. It clearly had not occurred to him that the reiver might already have ravished her.

"What will become of me?" she asked bluntly.

"You will not suffer for helping me, lass. I promise you, I will see to that."

"You cannot think that I will marry you," she protested. "Not only would it be a dreadfully unsuitable union, but you would hang for it."

"Aye, perhaps."

"I cannot imagine how even a man as powerful as Buccleuch thinks he can prevent it. Once Hugh demands his aid, he is duty-bound to arrest you and to see that you present yourself for trial at the next Truce Day. And although Hugh believes a jury might excuse you for your crimes, abducting me is clear cause for them to hang you even if I were to testify that I went with you willingly. If you force me to marry you, no man could speak for you, least of all Buccleuch."

"Aye, I'm sure you have the right of it, lass, if that is what were to happen."

"Then, what will become of me?" she repeated.

"I do not know, but you will be safe because I have promised it and because Buccleuch has promised it. If the worst happens and he decides that he must send you back to Brackengill, he will force Sir Hugh to promise you safety first. Mayhap he will insist upon keeping you under his protection until he can make him give that promise before witnesses at the next Truce Day. Indeed, that may be an excellent scheme," he added with a twinkle. "With such an event pending, Scrope might actually agree to a suitable date and site before the turn of the century."

"I do not think the problem lies with Lord Scrope," Janet said gently.

"Do you not?"

"Nay, for all his faults, he is a man of honor."

"He is no more honorable than his father was before him," the reiver said flatly. "Scrope told some of his own men that he chooses to answer Buccleuch with delays, and so he does. It has become a pattern and practice for him."

"My brother says the delays are Buccleuch's doing. Hugh says Buccleuch snatches at any excuse to delay, that he blames the weather or some imagined breach of manners, or just declares that he does not like the suggested site. He said that of Sark, after all, and Sark has been an acceptable meeting site for years."

"Aye, but just now it is too close to Carlisle for our liking. The site should be nearer to Hermitage, more central, so that neither warden has to travel much farther than the other."

"That is just an excuse," Janet said scornfully.

"It is a good reason," he retorted. "Moreover, I do not believe that Buccleuch has ever blamed the weather. That is Scrope's favorite excuse, though. He does not like rain, he says, because he cannot see what everyone is doing and some-one might get up to mischief. He does not like snow because he gets too cold sitting at the grievance table and only a fool would try to move the proceedings indoors."

"Those sound like excellent reasons to me."

"Aye, well, them who get up to mischief do not need rain or snow to do it. And Scrope is the one who uses what Buccleuch calls beetle-witted legal niceties to avoid the meetings."

"There are always more grievances against the Scots than against the English," Janet said. "Why would Scrope delay?"

"Because he knows that half those English grievances come from men who should know better, men who have stolen from the Scots only to have the goods taken back. The Scots are not so quick to lay a grievance, because they know that chances are poor of getting their goods back in anything like a timely way—before their families starve to death, for example. Thus, they are more likely to take the matter into their own hands, to fetch their own goods back again."

"They should leave it to the law to decide who is right," Janet said.

"Aye, sure, but when the law is in the hands of men like Scrope, who delight in making a game of it, and who take wagers on the outcome, you cannot blame them too harshly, I think."

"Cannot blame you is what you mean, is it not?"

"Aye, lass, that it is. I'll not deny that I am one of them."

Another silence fell, and Janet realized that he had neatly avoided speaking of the threatened marriage. Not that it was a real threat, of course. Buccleuch, even with all his power, could not force her to marry a man she did not want. Only her brother could do that.

The thought of marrying the reiver stirred memories of the way he had made her feel when he touched her, and that errant memory stirred those feelings again. Ruthlessly suppressing them, she told herself that it did not matter how he made her feel. Janet Graham could not marry a common thief, and that was all there was to it. Even Buccleuch would see that. He must see that.

A shutter rattled, and she realized that the wind outside had increased again. When it carried to her ears the sounds of men shouting to one another, a frisson of fear shot through her. What if Hugh attacked Hermitage?

Surely, he could not be so daft. Even she knew the castle was impregnable. She had heard of its strength long before she had laid eyes upon it. Now, having seen its thick walls and mentally counted its men-at-arms—and doubling that number to account for those she had not seen—she told herself that Hugh would never be such a fool. He did not possess guns large enough to make a dent in Buccleuch's defenses, but she did not relax until the lackey who had brought them word of Hugh's arrival entered the bedchamber to say, "Himself wants ye below."

Half expecting to find her brother pacing the red-and-blue Turkey carpet in the master's hall, Janet entered with trepidation, but the only man awaiting them was Buccleuch.

"You're safe for now, mistress. He's gone. I warrant he'll return to England for the night, although doubtless he'll take shelter across the line and return in the morning to renew his search. Apparently, he believes that a reiver named Rabbie Redcloak has abducted his sister and means to hold her for ransom. He demanded my cooperation in laying the said Redcloak by the heels, and since I am honor-bound as warden to provide such cooperation, I sent ten of my men with him."

Behind Janet, the reiver chuckled and said, "I warrant he well nigh choked on his thanks for your assistance."

"He is a sad, ungrateful man, is Hugh Graham," Buccleuch said with humor glinting in his hazel eyes. "He said that my men would serve better by simply fetching the damned reiver to him. He implied that they know exactly where to lay hands upon this Redcloak. He even insinuated that I spoke less than the truth when I said that I did not believe such a man existed in all of Liddesdale."

"Surely he did not go so far as to call you a liar!" Janet exclaimed as she set Jemmy Whiskers down to explore.

"Nay, he knows better than to stir my temper here in my own den," Buccleuch said with a wolfish smile. "He said that I am sadly misinformed, and suggested that if the man were not a resident of Liddesdale, he might still be known to me, since I am native to upper Teviotdale. I said that, as far as I knew, no such man lived in upper Teviotdale either. I thought he would take me through each dale, one after the other, but he abstained from that useless exercise."

"He must be furious," Janet said, repressing a shiver. "What said he of me?"

"He said naught that any might count against you, mistress, but I'll wager he has a notion that you helped Quin escape. Still, he is a proud man, is Sir Hugh. He will not want others to know of it, and I think we can use his pride to our benefit."

"How so, sir?"

"I've promised to send word of your plight out and about Liddesdale and the surrounding area. I told him that many people will help search for you."

"Did he believe you?"

"It does not matter if he did," Buccleuch said. "I mean shortly to invent a rescue for you."

"Oh, sir, if you could do that, then I might truly return in safety. I doubt that Hugh would dare punish me too severely, for others would soon learn of it and would hold him accountable if they believed me the victim of an abduction."

"Aye, lass, that would be a good thing, I agree; but there is a wee hindrance."

"A hindrance?"

"Aye. According to your brother, however all this turns out, your reputation is shredded beyond repair. He said that no decent Englishman would offer for you, knowing that you'd spent a full night and more as a reiver's hostage. Even were he to have you tested and proven still to be a virgin—"

Janet gasped at the humiliating image these words produced.

" 'Tis sad, mistress," Buccleuch said, nodding sympathetically, "but they are his words, not mine. He evidently cares not a whit how much he might offend you."

"Nay, he would not," Janet said, "but even to have suggested submitting me to such humiliation. . . . It . . . it must not be thought of."

"It will not be," the reiver said grimly. "I promised that we would see you safe, lass, and so we will."

"Then you must agree to marry her forthwith," Buccleuch said gravely.

"Aye, well, as to that," the reiver replied with a grimace, "I—"

"Pray, sir, I must object," Janet interjected. "Legally, my brother might be able to force me to a marriage I do not want, but surely no one else can do so. At least, no one else can under English law," she added as the unwelcome thought struck her that the laws of Scotland might be different. Her stomach tightened painfully as she awaited Buccleuch's response.

He smiled, and to her surprise, the smile was both charming and sincere. "In Scotland," he said, "a lass generally obeys her family just as she would in England, but even her family cannot force her to wed against her will."

The pain in her stomach eased. "I am glad of that," she said.

Before she could say more, however, he added, "You are not answerable to me, lass, except insofar as you might wish to claim my protection. In that event, I'll expect you to obey my commands." Turning to the reiver, he said sternly, "This is your doing, so like it or not, you will accept the consequences. You bear an ancient and honorable name, and by God's grace and mine, you will do what you must."

"What name?" Looking in bewilderment from one man to the other, Janet said, "What does he mean, reiver? He does not speak to you as to a common vassal, nor do you behave like one. Indeed, you speak to him as if you were his equal. What is your surname? Just who are you?"

The reiver said evenly, "The rest of our conversation had

better be accomplished without the benefit of your presence, lass. Why do you not go—"

"Who are you?" Janet repeated, putting her hands on her hips. "Clearly, you are no ordinary cattle thief, or you would not speak as you do to the master of Hermitage." When he did not answer, she said grimly, "Tell me. Now!"

He looked at Buccleuch, who returned his look steadily, saying only, "Do you fear that she will unmask you?"

"I do not," the reiver said. Turning to Janet, he added with a rueful smile, "What I fear is finding myself on the receiving end of Mistress Graham's temper."

"You are there already," she said. "If you do not bring an end to this nonsense, you will speedily learn the extent of it. What is your family name, sir?"

Clearly as tired of the stalling as Janet was, Buccleuch said, "His surname is Scott, mistress, like my own. He is my cousin, and if my young son does not survive me, Quin will be my heir. If I die young, he will be the lad's guardian."

"By heaven, you should bring Margaret to Hermitage," the reiver said. "Her presence here it would resolve all—"

"She is not here, nor will I command her to come here," Buccleuch snapped. "You are going to marry Mistress Graham, Quin, so you had best stop cutting whids and tell her exactly who you are. We ken fine that your being my cousin may not sufficiently recommend you to her as a husband."

Janet did not feel that it would do any good to declare again that she would not marry the man no matter who he was, particularly now that Buccleuch had explained that Scottish law would support her refusal. She watched the erstwhile reiver, feeling no sympathy for his visible discomfort.

At last, facing her, he made a profound leg and said quietly, "Quinton Scott of Broadhaugh at your service, mistress."

"Broadhaugh? I do not know of such a place," she said. "Is it cottage, manor house, or one of the many pele towers I'm told litter the Scottish side of the line?"

He smiled, and her treacherous body responded instantly,

dismaying her and making it seem as if his words, when next he spoke, branded themselves on her mind. "Broadhaugh is my home, mistress. It is a house of peace, and if I have aught to say about it, it will remain a house of peace."

"It . . . it is a house, then," she said, fixing on the one word that seemed to answer her question.

Buccleuch said, "Broadhaugh is more correctly defined as a fortified manor house, mistress. 'Tis not so well fortified as Hermitage or Carlisle Castle, of course, but it sits high on a hill, and its defenses are adequate for its location."

Forcing herself to look at the laird so that she could regain her wits, she said, "Where is Broadhaugh exactly?"

"In Teviotdale," Quinton Scott said. "Not so much upper Teviotdale, mind you. Buccleuch did not lie to your brother, but he might have misled him a bit."

"I neither lied nor mislead him," Buccleuch said. "As far as I know there is no Rabbie Redcloak listed on any parish roll in *all* of Teviotdale."

Janet made the mistake then of looking back at Quinton Scott, and his gaze caught hers. The firelight reflected in his eyes made them look like molten gold, and she realized that she had never seen eyes quite that color before.

" 'Tis true there is no Redcloak," he murmured in response to Buccleuch, but his gaze still locked with Janet's. After a lingering pause, he added softly, "Well, lass? I do not know if we are suited to each other, but the laird commands it, so if you are agreeable, I would count it an honor to arrange a marriage between us."

The longer she looked into his eyes, the more her resistance crumbled. She felt now, however, that if she allowed herself to look away before he did, it would somehow be a sign of weakness. To her own ears, her voice sounded faint when she said, "My . . . my brother will never agree to such a marriage, sir. In any event, your connection to the laird and his power notwithstanding, the laws of both our countries forbid such a union."

"That's perfectly true, Wat," Quinton Scott said, still not looking away. "How do we overcome that law?"

" 'Tis the nature of wardens to mold the laws of our countries to suit the occasion," Buccleuch said with a shrug. "Let us order supper and discuss the matter. Have you a desire to retire for a short time before we eat, mistress?"

Quinton Scott smiled again, and Janet felt herself relax. As one, they turned to the Laird of Hermitage, and she said lightly, "I would like to refresh myself, sir, if one of you can provide me with a comb or brush."

"I can do that," he said, going to the stairwell and shouting for someone named Will.

Reluctant as she was to leave the two men alone to plot her future—or their version of her future—Janet nonetheless needed a few minutes to herself. Scooping up Jemmy Whiskers just as he settled down in front of the fire, she left the room.

"Fetch us ale, Will, when you've found Mistress Graham a hairbrush," Buccleuch called after the lad.

"How the devil do you mean to pull this off, Wat?" Quin demanded. "Hugh Graham will never agree to a marriage between his sister and me."

"Not if he knows that you're Rabbie Redcloak, he won't, but he gave me no reason to think that he harbors any such unfriendly suspicion."

"My identity is not a closely kept secret in Liddesdale," Quin pointed out. "Many on this side of the line know it. Although they do not talk openly, we have little reason to believe that no one on the other side knows it."

"Sometimes 'tis necessary to maintain a pretty fiction, however, and I'd not be surprised to find Sir Hugh Graham as willing as any other man to accept one if we can but show him one that will suit his purpose better than the truth."

"Why should he believe anything we tell him?"

"First, because a suitable marriage for the lass creates less scandal for him. He'll not want to admit that a common reiver carried off his sister from under his nose; but if he must, it will give him ease to add that a Scottish gentleman rescued her, killed the reiver, and fell passionately in love with her. We won't mention the wee cat,'' he added with a wry smile.

"Thank you for that small mercy, but I still cannot think much of the notion."

Ignoring the feeble protest, Buccleuch added, "If Sir Hugh agrees to the marriage, he can describe the events that led to it any way he likes. We'll have given him one version. If he rejects it, there are others. I trow he'll prefer any one of them to the pain of telling the truth, which is that his own sister helped his most important captive escape, then compounded her crime by running away with him."

"What exactly is our version to be, then?"

Indignantly, Buccleuch said, "Were you no listening, man? Sir Quinton Scott of Broadhaugh—that's you, lest you've forgotten—rescued Sir Hugh Graham's unfortunate sister—that's our bonny wee Janet abovestairs—from the wicked reiver. Having done so, Sir Quinton has expressed a strong willingness to wed with her."

"What is to keep Sir Hugh from scorning my offer? He can simply point out that the law forbids such a union and demand her return."

Thoughtfully, Buccleuch looked up at the paneled ceiling for a moment before he said, "I shall tell Sir Hugh we ken fine that you require his permission to marry her. I shall likewise say that we hope he will be generous enough to grant it; however, I shall also warn the pestiferous measle that we'll approach Scrope or even Elizabeth herself, if necessary. That will put it into his head that both Scrope and Elizabeth may well discover the truth if he does not take care to prevent it."

"Aye, I can see that he might think that way."

"He will. I've studied the man. He is Scrope's deputy, after all, and although I've not had to deal with him yet at a truce table, that may come to pass one day."

"Aye, but I have met him," Quin reminded him. "He is a hard man, Wat. I doubt he will be in any great hurry to grant the lass permission to marry anyone."

"He may want her to suffer, but that man thinks first of himself and his own interests," Buccleuch said firmly. "Next he considers Graham interests, and only after that does he reckon with England's interest or that of any other entity. I shall tell him that you believe in his sister's virtue but quite understand that even a breath of scandal would ruin her in England. I'll tell him, too, that we sympathize with him, because as men we know that scandal would deeply embarrass him, his family, and every one of his pestiferous English Grahams."

"Aye, that might dent his armor," Quin agreed, "but will he not know much about you, too, Cousin—enough to suspect your motives?"

"Aye, sure, but 'tis no secret now that Jamie and Elizabeth have both decided that peace in the Borders serves their political interests better than war. 'Tis my hope to procure that peace, or so I mean to tell Hugh Graham. I'll explain to him that if he can bring himself to agree to the marriage, it will serve— as such unions historically have served—to help assure the grand Union to come."

Quin grinned. " 'Tis a canny thought, my lad, letting him believe that his decision could bring peace to the Borders. It won't do any such thing, of course, because the damned English cannot keep themselves to themselves. They see Scots merely as vassals that must be subdued, but—"

"But it may serve long enough to secure Mistress Graham's safety and your own, Quin, and for the moment that will suffice. As to your folly in getting yourself caught, not to mention abducting the wench, I have more yet to say to you."

"I don't doubt it, but I'd as lief not hear it."

"You'll hear it anyway," his cousin said, his tone grim enough to stir prickles of uneasiness along Quin's spine.

He stood quietly for the next few moments, suppressing his resentment, while Buccleuch shredded his character and informed him that his behavior was about to undergo a sea change. "You'd best hope that Mistress Graham does not take it into her head to refuse this marriage, because if she does, you'll answer for your actions. I've warned you, time and again, that you were growing too reckless."

"Hold a minute," Quin said, his temper erupting at last. "You are as guilty as I am of recklessness, Wat. Worse! Your reputation for raiding far exceeds anything anyone credits Rabbie Redcloak with doing."

"Aye, 'tis so," Buccleuch agreed, "but I have the power to protect myself. Until you assume that power in my stead, Cousin, should you ever do so, you serve at my pleasure and Jamie's. Do you anger either of us, you will suffer for it." He held Quin's gaze for a long, uncomfortable moment before he added softly, "Have you aught more to say on the subject?"

Quin swallowed. Not only did his own fate hang on his reply but that of the Bairns, for without Buccleuch's support, they would all suffer. "I'll say no more," he said. "I must take responsibility for what I've done, and it is certainly my fault that Janet Graham left Brackengill in my company and is now here at Hermitage. If you believe that the only way now to protect her is for me to marry her, I will. I have said that already. But I owe much to the Bairns, too, Wat, and you know that I could not allow any of them to suffer merely to save myself."

"Marry the wench, Quin. What comes after that will come as God wills it, and in the end you must answer for your actions just as I must answer for mine."

"Aye, but first she must agree to the marriage," Quin reminded him, "and I have seen naught in that wench to make me think she will submit merely because we tell her she must. Her claws are nigh as sharp as her cat's."

Chapter 9

"Farewell, my dame, sae peerless gude,
And he took her by the hand ..."

On the stairway, Janet eavesdropped shamelessly. It had taken her only a few moments to tidy her hair in the laird's chamber, and she had started down the spiral stone stairs with Jemmy Whiskers in her arms when she realized that she could hear their voices. On tiptoe, she moved to the turn just before the landing outside the entrance to the master's hall, where she stopped to listen.

She heard much of Buccleuch's reprimand, and she knew that, earlier, he had not exaggerated for her benefit his displeasure with his kinsman. She could almost feel sorry for Quinton Scott. Buccleuch had a harsh temper and was skilled in the use of words to express it. She listened with respect, glad that Quinton Scott and not she was standing the brunt of it. Clearly, Buccleuch had faced a dilemma, for among other things, she heard him tell his cousin that he had pondered the wisdom of revealing Rabbie Redcloak's true identity in order to secure his release.

"And that would have worked only if you could have kept yourself from being hanged long enough for me to get word to Scrope and him to get word to Hugh Graham," she heard him snarl. "In truth, since I believed they'd house you at Carlisle to await the next wardens' meeting, you'd have been dead long before."

Hearing that, Janet grimaced and felt shame again that her brother had flouted the law. She could not fault Buccleuch for believing what he had. She wondered if she could trust Hugh to keep his part of the bargain if he did agree to let her marry Quinton Scott. That was, of course, if she agreed to marry him, and that was by no means as certain as Buccleuch had made it sound. The alternative, however, was not tempting, for if she went home, she would face both Hugh's wrath and social ostracism. Although she doubted that they would actually hang her for aiding a felon, no one would receive her after they learned she had spent a night in the company of any man who was neither her father nor her brother. Doubtless the same standard would hold true if she remained unmarried on the Scottish side of the line, assuming that Buccleuch would allow her to stay if she rejected his kinsman.

Her resolve weakened even more when she heard Quinton Scott claim full responsibility for her plight, because she knew that her predicament was not entirely his fault. Had she not decided in the first place to defy her brother's authority, she would not be in any predicament. On the other hand, she reminded herself, had that been the case, Quinton Scott would be dead.

Hearing Buccleuch command him again to marry her, she decided that she had better add her own voice to the conversation. A clatter of footsteps from below urged haste, for it could only be one of Buccleuch's men, and it was most likely the lackey, Will. She did not know whether whoever it was would come farther than the master's hall, but she did not want to be caught eavesdropping. Accordingly, she snatched up her skirt with her free hand and hurried down the few remaining steps to the hall, taking care to do some clattering of her own.

Above the sounds she made, she could hear Quinton Scott saying, "I tell you, Wat, the lass is not as likely to bow to your command as you think she is."

"She will not, sir," she said briskly as she entered. "I am not so submissive, nor will I become so now that I know Scottish law will support me if I refuse. I have no wish to marry a man who has so grossly deceived me, or one who engages in such nefarious activities as those in which Rabbie Redcloak engages."

Before Quinton Scott could reply, Buccleuch said, "Aye, well, we've work still to do, all of us. Ah, good, Will," he said on a heartier note, "you've brought our ale, lad! Will you take aught to drink, Mistress Graham, whilst they arrange the table for our supper?"

"No, thank you, sir," Janet replied, still watching Quinton Scott.

Obliquely, she saw Buccleuch wave the lackey away, and as he left, she became aware of others entering, bringing the wherewithal to set up for supper.

Buccleuch and Quinton Scott seemed to regard the newcomers as so much more furniture, but Janet's gaze automatically shifted to follow them at their work. Nature and habit stirred her to see how well they attended to their tasks.

Her distraction was fleeting, though, because Quinton Scott said gently, "I would remind you, mistress, that your brother engages in those same nefarious activities; even worse, he pretends to act for the English government when he does."

"Hugh has authority to act for the government," Janet said, raising her chin. "He is, I remind you, sir, deputy to our warden of the west march. When he acts in that capacity, he acts with all the authority of her majesty the Queen of England. You, however, possess no such authority. If King James backs your actions, I have not heard about it, nor has my brother."

"Your brother is—"

"Enough, Quin," Buccleuch snapped. "Cease your fratch-ing! You've given Hugh Graham the right to claim that you abducted his sister. 'Tis yourself who handed our bitterest ene-mies the means to bring our clan to its knees. If you mean to mend matters, you'll not do it by offending Mistress Graham or her pestiferous knave of a brother."

"But if she will have none of me—"

"Then you'll face the legal consequences of your escape and her abduction," Buccleuch declared. "I do not care if you do it as Rabbie Redcloak or as Sir Quinton Scott of Broad—"

"*Sir* Quinton!" Janet exclaimed, more outraged than ever.

"Aye, he is," Buccleuch said. "Jamie found himself in a good mood a few years back, at his queen's coronation, and knighted the both of us."

"You should be ashamed of yourself," Janet told Sir Quinton. "A man of high position to be playing such games— leading men into danger! It is one thing to do so in times of war, sir, but to do so now! I vow, I do not know what you deserve."

"Your brother is also a knight, mistress, albeit an English one. Still, if he possesses any honor, he protects his own people, and that is all I do. I support men who have suffered deprivation at English hands. I help them regain what is rightfully theirs, and I support the efforts of broken men—those who can claim no support from their kinsmen—to present their cases before the wardens or to do what is necessary to keep their wives and bairns from starving."

"You should trust the law to see to those things," Janet said stubbornly. "You are no better than Hugh, sir. If men like you do not support the law—if indeed, you flout it outright—how can you expect lesser men to obey it?"

"Aye, now that's an excellent question," Buccleuch said virtuously.

"Perhaps it is," Sir Quinton agreed, "but things being what they are, philosophical discussion gains us naught. We can scarcely resolve more abstract matters when our two sides cannot even agree on a site or date for a Truce Day.''

Buccleuch said testily, ''We do not need to resolve the problems of Truce Day now. 'Tis of greater import to settle the business of this marriage, Quin, and that remains your concern. I have said all that I mean to say.''

Janet said, ''You claim that my brother can force Sir Quinton to face legal consequences for abducting me, sir. Hugh might realize that Sir Quinton and Rabbie Redcloak are one and the same; however, I promise you that before I would allow him to demand his head, I would testify that Sir Quinton rescued me not only from Redcloak but from Hugh's wrath, as well. Many would believe me, too.''

''Mayhap they would, mistress,'' Buccleuch said, ''but no one here will ask such a thing of you. Much as I deplore your brother's interfering nature and his scurrilous intent to hang Quin without a proper trial, his present wrath is justified. You defied his authority, then compounded your sins by helping his prisoner escape. He or Scrope could order you hanged for march treason on that account alone. I doubt that either would, but I'll not take the chance. The pair of you will marry, or I'll withdraw my protection, and that's my last word on the subject. You need not decide now. I'll give you till we finish eating to make up your minds to it.''

Serving men arrived with their food, and they sat at a table near the fire. Janet found the meal more pleasant than she had expected. Jemmy Whiskers curled up next to her right foot, and conversation remained general. Buccleuch and Sir Quinton spoke of kinsmen and general family matters, frequently making her laugh at the tales they told about certain kinsmen. Her thoughts kept returning to the decision she was to make, though, and at last, unable to contain her curiosity, she said bluntly, ''What will you do with me?''

Buccleuch regarded her with amusement. ''That must depend upon what you decide to do, mistress.''

''It seems to me,'' she said thoughtfully, ''that even if I

refuse to marry Sir Quinton, you are honor-bound to protect me, sir. He is your kinsman, and you are his headsman, are you not?''

"Aye, sure, 'tis true; I am.'' He smiled. "Will you abide by my decisions?''

"I expect I shall have little choice about that.''

Sir Quinton chuckled. "She has taken your measure, Wat.''

"Aye, she has. An it please you, mistress, I'd send you to Branxholme—to my wife, Margaret—till we can safely return you to Brackengill or till you marry.''

Janet nodded. "I would agree to that, sir. Your wife is a Douglas, is she not?''

"Nay, 'tis my mother who is the Douglas,'' Buccleuch said, adding, "She has lived in seclusion at her farm in Whitlaw since my stepfather, Bothwell, fled the country. My wife is also named Margaret, but she is a Kerr.'' He smiled, adding, "It surprises me that you ken aught of my family's origins, mistress.''

"My brother speaks of such matters,'' she explained. "I have a retentive memory, and families interest me, but it is difficult to keep everyone sorted out when so many people bear the same names.''

"Aye, I've noted that myself,'' Buccleuch said. "My Margaret is a fine lass, though, and she'll enjoy your company whilst we unknot this tangle. Quin will take you to her, but first the pair of you must determine what course you mean to take.''

She nodded again, and when he addressed his next remark to Sir Quinton, she returned her attention to her supper.

The two men continued to converse desultorily. She enjoyed listening, wanting to learn more about them.

Sir Quinton's deep voice seemed to reverberate in her mind whenever he spoke, and she remembered how it had stirred her when first she heard it in the dungeon. He was handsome and well connected. She could do worse in a husband.

Her brother would be furious with her no matter what she did. Despite any agreement Buccleuch might arrange, it would be long before Hugh would forgive her, if ever he did. And if the arrangement included her return to Brackengill, he would see to it that she suffered for her defiance. Nothing they made him promise would deter him; and marriage to the reiver certainly seemed preferable to that.

Marriage across the line would carry disadvantages even if Hugh and Scrope—and perhaps even Queen Elizabeth—were to permit it. The Grahams—the English ones, anyway—would view it as betrayal, and the Scottish Grahams would not be inclined to accept her as one of them. They were far more likely to cast her off, just as the English ones would. Would Scots in general accept her if she married Sir Quinton, she wondered, or would they shun her, too?

Only dimly aware of the men's voices, she realized that although she had considered the possible consequences, she had given little thought to the marriage itself. What would Sir Quinton Scott be like as a husband? The thought instantly stirred those increasingly familiar sensations inside her.

Surreptitiously, trying to make it appear that she focused her attention on her plate, she watched him through her lashes while she used her knife to spear a chunk of salted beef. He was a handsome man, to be sure. His eyes fascinated her. They looked hazel now, not really gold, but whenever he turned toward the firelight, orange lights danced in them, giving him a devilish appearance. Nevertheless, he was a handsome man. She could see a family resemblance between the two, but Buccleuch was shorter and slighter, and carried less bulk through his shoulders.

Sir Quinton's gaze shifted from Buccleuch to her, almost as if he had sensed her curiosity. Quickly she lowered her gaze.

"Mistress, will you take some wine?" he asked quietly.

"Aye, sir, thank you," she murmured.

He set a pewter goblet in front of her and filled it from a jug on the table, then turned back to his cousin.

Keeping her gaze fixed on the table, Janet continued to consider her options, but her mind seemed resistant to decision, resistant even to orderly thought. She was too much aware now of Sir Quinton's deep, musical voice.

As Buccleuch scraped his chair back and got to his feet, she realized that he was speaking to her.

Looking up guiltily, she said, "I beg your pardon, sir. I was not attending."

His whimsical smile lit his face. "I said, mistress, that perhaps I should leave the two of you to discuss what choice you will make. Shout down the stairs, Quin, when you want me. With the lass to look after, you'll not make Branxholme by sundown even if you leave within the hour, but I'll send some of my lads along to make sure the pair of you get there safely."

Sir Quinton nodded, and a moment later Janet was alone with him.

She felt more vulnerable than she had felt since leaving Brackengill. She could not think of a single thing to say to him.

The silence lengthened while he poured himself more wine. He looked at her, still holding the jug. "A bit more perhaps?"

"No, thank you, sir. If I drink any more, I shall have difficulty sitting my horse without falling off. How far is it to Branxholme?"

"About nine miles, I reckon, if we could travel in a straight line. Since we cannot, it's nearer being twelve or more. You must be well nigh exhausted, lass."

"I am tired," she admitted. Then, smiling, she said, "That is why I did not argue when Buccleuch said that I would likely slow you down."

"Mayhap we would do better to remain here overnight."

"I think that would be unwise," she said.

"Aye, perhaps," he said. "I am not one who makes a habit of considering proprieties, but I warrant your brother would never take you back if you'd spent a night at Hermitage without a proper hostess."

"No, he would not."

"If, on the other hand, you should decide to accept my

offer of marriage, I would not care a damn if you stayed here overnight with us. Wat and I could sleep here, and you could have the bedchamber above. The door has a bar and bolts, so you'd be perfectly safe."

"I do not want to marry you," she said without thinking.

"Do you not? I own, I do not know how well I shall like marriage either. I've naught against you, lass, barring that sharp tongue of yours, but if I can persuade you to set a guard on it, we might scrape along together well enough."

"Her majesty would never allow it," Janet said.

He shook his head, but more as if he thought her naive than as if he agreed with her. "You do not give Buccleuch the credit he merits," he said. "Recall that he said both Jamie and Elizabeth crave peace in the Borders. It is to their political advantage to settle things, and so far their demands have met with small result because Buccleuch has seen no reason to set their preferences above his own."

Janet raised her chin. "You make it sound as if he has only to decide that there should be peace, and there will be peace. Surely, it is not so simple as that."

"Is it not? You do not know him yet. Still, I do remember your saying that Sir Hugh is impressed that Buccleuch can act as warden of two marches and keeper of Liddesdale as well. Consider that before you dismiss his capabilities."

"But how would our marriage help him achieve peace, assuming that he really does desire such an end?"

"Aye, well, that's the rub, isn't it?" Sir Quinton chuckled. "So far, I'll admit, he hasn't displayed much interest in peace. He believes that his people need purpose in their lives as much as they need to believe that the damned English cannot steal their cows and horses with impunity—meaning no offense to you, of course—so he indulges them. Indeed, he often leads them, although he tends to restrict his leadership to only the largest raids. When Buccleuch sends out a call to arms, he can raise three thousand men in a half-day's time, so he does not lead the darting sorts of raids that Rabbie Redcloak leads."

"Godamercy, so many?"

Sir Quinton shrugged. "I warrant he could get more if he wanted them. My point, however, is not that he will declare peace in the Borders as his part in any bargain for our marriage but that Elizabeth's desire for peace will prevent her from demanding my head if I should express a wish to marry you."

"I still do not care much for the notion," Janet said. She carefully avoided looking at him, however, aware that each time she did she found herself more rather than less intrigued by the idea of marrying him.

"I warrant you could see that I did not like it much either," he said. "I think I reacted out of sheer pique with Buccleuch for commanding it, though. I'll have to marry one day, I expect. Indeed, my mother says that I ought to have married long since. I am in my twenty-sixth year, and she says that before someone kills me it would be prudent to get myself an heir. I've laughed at her before, but your brother did bring me face-to-face with the hereafter. I can understand why she frets."

"What is she like, your mother?"

He shrugged. "Like any mother, I expect."

"Well, I never knew mine," Janet said, "so I do not know what most mothers are like."

"Have you truly lived all these years with only that brother of yours to look after you?" He seemed rather shocked by the notion.

Janet smiled. "It was not so bad as that, sir."

"Well, I would not wish my worst enemy into Sir Hugh Graham's household. Indeed, I begin to think that you should marry me, lass. 'Tis a pity that we cannot have Buccleuch's chaplain do the thing here at Hermitage tonight, in the chapel."

"Has he got his own chapel, even here? Hugh has built much at Brackengill over the past years, but we still must go to the church in the village."

"Hermitage has its own chapel and a graveyard, as well. I suppose we're more likely to be married from Branxholme or

Broadhaugh, though. You would prefer that, I warrant, to being married from a Border stronghold.''

"You make it sound as if we had agreed to marry, sir," Janet said.

"Have we not?"

She thought for a long moment, then said quietly, "I will allow Buccleuch to present the notion to Hugh, but the decision must rest with him. I cannot defy him in such an important matter. If he orders me to return, I shall be obliged to do so."

"We'll see about that," he said. "Shall we inform him of your decision?"

Janet nodded nervously, certain that the master of Hermitage would not agree to her stipulations; but again he surprised her, merely nodding and saying that he would see to the arrangements. His attitude was the same, she decided, as if she had submitted completely to his will. He saw them off shortly afterward, assuring them that he would have all in train for their wedding by the following week's end.

Although they began the journey to Branxholme Castle an hour and a half before sunset, it grew dark long before they reached their destination. There was no track that Janet could discern, but the night was clear, and Sir Quinton assured her that he could find his way even in pitch-blackness. Since there was naught she could do but trust him, she was content to let her pony follow his. So tired was she by then that only the chill kept her sufficiently awake to stay on her saddle, and before they reached Branxholme, she was lying forward, bent over the little cat with her head resting on the pony's neck. She had no awareness of riding into the courtyard, nor did she stir much when Sir Quinton lifted her down, carried her inside with Jemmy Whiskers cradled between them, and laid her down on a bed.

He had gone before she awoke the following morning, but she swiftly found a friend in Margaret Kerr Scott. Buccleuch's wife, despite having been married nearly ten years and being the mother of three energetic offspring, was not much older than Janet. She generously offered extra clothing and advice, and evidently placing great confidence in her husband's ability to bring not just Sir Hugh Graham but also the Queen of England around his finger, she immediately began making preparations for a wedding to be held at Branxholme. To Janet's gratification, Margaret was content to talk for hours about the family into which she had married.

"Buccleuch was nurtured amongst broils and feuds," Margaret said later that first day while they sat in her little parlor for a brief respite after a whirlwind inventory of her wardrobe had produced several useful articles for Janet to wear.

"A volatile life is not unusual for any man raised in the Borders," Janet said.

"Aye, perhaps, but he began taking part in the exploits for which his kinsmen are notorious at quite an early age. He had barely entered his ninth year when his father died, you see. He was the same age then as our Wattie be now."

"Godamercy," Janet said. "It is to be hoped that Buccleuch lives to a grand old age and does not leave his son to a similar fate."

"We all hope for that," Margaret said quietly, "but if Wattie reaches his majority before entering upon his inheritance, he will be the first of the Scotts to do so since 1470. That is why, soon after the wee laddie's birth, Buccleuch decided that in the event of his own premature death, Quin should serve as guardian and hold the property in trust until Wattie reaches his majority."

"Do you mean that Sir Quinton would control Buccleuch's estates?"

"Aye, he would. Buccleuch's father and Quin's were brothers, so unless we have more sons, Quin will inherit anyway if Wattie predeceases Buccleuch."

"I see," Janet said, not sure that she truly did. Most men, with history to guide them, would hesitate to name as their heir's guardian the person who would inherit in the event of the heir's death. Buccleuch's arrangement bore strong witness to his trust in his cousin.

Margaret smiled. "I can see that you wonder at the agreement, but Buccleuch believes it will serve his purpose admirably. He spent his childhood under the guardianship of tutors and curators appointed to him by the last will of his father, you see. James, Earl of Morton, served as his tutor and governor, along with the Earl of Angus, and under them stood other stern and powerful men. Owing to the state of the feudal holding of certain portions of the Buccleuch properties, there was a great deal of legal fuss and bother that finally required royal intervention."

"Poor laddie," Janet said sympathetically. She had heard much about the Earl of Morton, who was now, she believed, mercifully deceased.

"Aye, Morton was a hard man," Margaret said. "Indeed, one reason that Buccleuch has enjoyed the King's favor—most days, at all events—is that they shared a similar upbringing and each had to fight to control his birthright. Jamie is but a year younger than Buccleuch, and he spent his youth at Morton's mercy, too. Buccleuch wants better for his son. Unlike Buccleuch, who fought his tutors every step of the way, Quin enjoyed book learning. He was educated at home and at the university in Edinburgh, and Buccleuch says he is a very knowing man."

Janet had rarely spent much time with other women, and she enjoyed her week at Branxholme, especially the long conversations with its mistress. To her surprise, she found that she did not miss Brackengill nearly as much as she had feared she would. She wondered only two or three times a day about how well her brother was getting on without her.

Had anyone asked Sir Hugh Graham on the morning that he discovered his sister's disappearance if he would miss her, he would have declared categorically that he would not. His fury carried him into the following day, assuaged only by thoughts of what he would do when he finally laid hands on her. Monday morning, however, when he descended to his hall in anticipation of breaking his fast, he discovered that all was not as it had been at Brackengill.

Even from the stairwell he noticed that the place seemed strangely silent. It took him several moments to realize that what he missed was the sound of maidservants singing and laughing as they tended to their chores. He also missed the odors of roasting meat and baking bread, and despite the season, he had expected to be greeted by the savory smell of the two grouse he had shot as they turned on a spit in the kitchen. Perhaps, he told himself, it was still too early to start them.

Entering the hall, he found it empty. No preparations had been made to serve his breakfast. Shouting for a servant, he soon heard clattering footsteps on the stairs leading to the kitchen, and a moment later a lad appeared, looking frightened.

Hugh bellowed, "Where the devil's my food?"

"Beg pardon, master, but Sheila and Matty and them didna come the day. Geordie said their menfolk told them they b'ain't to come here again till Mistress Janet returns. Me da says it isna safe for 'em here without her."

Sir Hugh gaped at the lad in shock, but by the time Buccleuch's envoy arrived at Brackengill that afternoon, he had seen for himself just how much had been stolen from him, and he was ripe for murder.

Buccleuch had schemed well, and his emissary was both smooth of tongue and skilled in the art of diplomacy, but Sir Hugh saw to it that persuading him to agree to any marriage took several days and a good deal of money.

Buccleuch and Sir Quinton arrived at Branxholme late the following Thursday evening, surprising Margaret and her guest. The two women were sitting companionably by a roaring fire in the hall when the men strode in, and Margaret leapt up to hug her husband.

"We can hold the ceremony on Sunday if you like," Buccleuch said matter-of-factly as he welcomed her into his arms, speaking over her shoulder to Janet.

Janet reacted with astonishment. "Hugh agreed?"

"Aye, he did," Buccleuch said, releasing his wife to let a servant take his helmet, gloves, and cloak.

Sir Quinton turned to the fire as he pulled off his gloves. Tucking them inside his doublet, he held his hands out to warm them, apparently deaf to the exchange and not eager to take part in the conversation. Janet had caught one darting look as he entered, but she had been unable to read his expression.

"What did Hugh say?" she demanded.

Buccleuch shrugged. "What can it matter, mistress? He has agreed to permit your marriage and therefore will make no legal objection to it."

"If it please you, sir, I should like to know exactly what he said. Did he not send any message to me?"

"Nay, lass, and as to—"

"He said that I am welcome to you," Sir Quinton said without turning.

"Then he does not suspect that you are Rabbie Redcloak," Janet said.

"He does not," Buccleuch said, adding smugly, "You can thank me for that."

"I am sure that I can, sir," she said, "but how can you be so certain?"

In a near growl, Sir Quinton said, "Because his envoy told your brother that I rescued you from Rabbie Redcloak." His voice took on a hard edge when he added, "His man went so far as to suggest that I am willing to overlook the way you entered Scotland, that because I took a strong liking to you, I would marry you despite the damage done to your reputation."

"Did Hugh believe that?"

"Who can say what he believes?" Buccleuch said, eyeing Sir Quinton with disfavor.

Sir Quinton turned then, and to her surprise she detected a flash of amusement in his eyes. He said, "It doubtless will come as no surprise to you that your brother seems to have decided that both Buccleuch and Buccleuch's idiot cousin are hand in glove with the reivers."

"Never mind that," Buccleuch said. "We've details to arrange now, so listen well, all of you. For the booking, mistress, I'll send my own men to wait on the session clerk in Hawick, to inform him that you and Quin have agreed to a betrothal. My men will likewise inform the parson. I trust that you're not a popish lass, or if you are, that you'll not insist on having a priest. Priests are not in good odor these days, and no priest-spoken marriage would be lawful hereabouts."

"I am not popish," Janet said, feeling overwhelmed and remembering what he had said upon entering. "Surely all this cannot happen by Sunday!"

"There's naught amiss with marrying on a Sunday," he said.

"But what of the banns?"

An impatient gesture dismissed the banns. "A single reading will suffice," he said, "and we've our own chapel here at Branxholme. Parson can marry you directly after the service."

"For a fee," Sir Quinton said.

"Which you'll pay, my lad, and without any fuss over it," Buccleuch told him. "You can afford it better than I can just now. You'll also pay the betrothal fee and give my men ample funds to lay down the pawns in Hawick."

Confused, Janet looked to Sir Quinton for enlightenment.

"Yet another fee," he explained. "Laying down pawns guarantees that our marriage will be solemnized. The session clerk will keep the money until we can show that a proper cleric has married us. Then he'll return it. He will not, however, return the fee that I'll pay for sending others in our stead to attest to our betrothal."

"I don't understand this," Janet said. "Need we not hold a proper betrothal ceremony to sign papers and make all legal?"

Buccleuch said, "Here in Scotland you need only speak the words of the marriage rite before witnesses, mistress, after which you'll each moisten your right thumb with your tongue and press them together. We count the violation of any contract so consecrated tantamount to perjury."

"I see. Did . . . did Hugh happen to mention my dowry?"

"Aye, he did," Buccleuch said, his gaze evading hers.

"Well?" She looked from one man to the other.

Buccleuch grimaced, still refusing to meet her gaze, but Sir Quinton looked sympathetic. "I'll see that you have no need for a dowry, lassie," he said quietly.

" 'Tis just as well," Buccleuch said before she could protest such a ridiculous and humiliating notion. "Your pig-headed megrim of a brother said you could be married in your smock, mistress. He'll do naught to prevent the marriage, he said, but neither will he do aught to make anyone think that he favors it. He also said that no respectable Englishman would take you after such time as you had spent in the reiver's clutches. 'Twas then that he said Quin were welcome to you."

Margaret Scott said indignantly, "Husband, have pity! What a dreadful thing to say to her!"

"Aye, but she wanted to ken the truth," Buccleuch said.

"Nevertheless you need not have flung it at her like a hurling of stones," retorted the wife of his bosom with a look of grave displeasure.

He moved toward her, murmuring coaxingly, "Dinna be wroth with me, sweetling. 'Tis sorely I've missed you."

"I'll wager you have, locked up in that great pile of rocks with naught but a hundred loud, filthy men to bear you company, but you'll soon be thinking their company preferable to mine if you do not treat my guest with kindness."

Stunned by the knowledge that Hugh intended to keep her dowry, Janet paid them little heed. She realized that the laws of both countries would support her brother and that she had no recourse against him. For the first time, she sympathized heartily with the reivers. She would have liked nothing better than to ride to Brackengill with an army to retrieve her rightful property at sword point.

Chapter 10

"Her girdle show'd her middle neat
And gowden glist her hair."

On Friday morning, joining Margaret in her parlor to break her fast, Janet said ruefully as she sat down at the table, "I wish Hugh had at least had the kindness to send some of my clothing to Branxholme. Everything has happened so quickly, and I possess no finery to wear to my own wedding. Were it not for your generosity, madam, I would have naught but the clothes I wore when I arrived. I thank you most sincerely for the clean smock your woman provided me this morning."

"You need not thank me," Margaret said with a smile as she poured ale into a goblet for her guest. " 'Tis my pleasure to help. You will soon have gowns of your own. Quinton is a generous man, despite his complaints about money."

"Nevertheless—"

"Do not bother your head about such things now," Margaret interjected. "We've much that we must think about. Trust Buccleuch to declare that all can be arranged in a twink, and then leave me to arrange it."

"Indeed, I do not know how you will manage."

"It will all sort itself out," Margaret said placidly. "He will invite everyone for miles, and gentry from as far as a day's ride away, I shouldn't wonder."

"I do not understand how he contrived any of this," Janet said. "He cannot have got the Queen's permission in so short a time. I doubt that he had time even to obtain Lord Scrope's."

"As he explained it to me, he required only your brother's. Doubtless the merchet will be high, though."

"Pray, madam, what is the merchet?"

" 'Tis yet another marriage tax," Margaret said. "When I married Buccleuch, my father explained that the merchet dates from the Scottish feudal system. It is a tax that a superior exacts from a vassal on the marriage of the vassal's daughter. Proceeding on the principle that giving a daughter in wedlock deprives the overlord of her services, a knight or baron levies merchet from his bondsman, then pays it to his sovereign."

"But how can that affect me? Neither I nor my brother are vassals of your King, and Hugh will certainly refuse to pay any such tax to Queen Elizabeth."

"Buccleuch kens that fine, but someone will expect to receive his due. Presently, the King grants such merchet from persons of opulence to individuals in reward of service. In my view, since Buccleuch or Quinton will pay the King, they do it more to persuade Jamie to side with Quinton if Elizabeth makes a fuss over your marriage. But you need not tell Buccleuch that I suggested as much."

"No, of course not. Do you think the Queen will bother her head about me?"

"Buccleuch says 'tis ever better to be safe than sorry, since one cannot know which way any sovereign may hop. She may dislike your leaving England, he said, but he said also that she cannot express too much rancor when she still insists that after her death we will all be citizens of one country."

"She does not believe that day is near, however," Janet pointed out.

"Nay, of course she does not, but she is aging and has little eagerness to quarrel with Jamie, or so Buccleuch told me."

Janet had noted shortly after her arrival at Branxholme that her hostess had a habit of quoting her husband frequently, and of believing that he knew best about most things. She had noted a similar tendency among Englishwomen she had met, and wondered if it was customary with Scottish wives. She hoped that it was not, for she could not imagine herself assuming that Sir Quinton was the only one whose opinion mattered in her life. She had not allowed Hugh to reduce her to a mere cipher. She certainly would not allow Sir Quinton to do so.

Janet's wedding day dawned in a gloom of heavy fog, but the walls of Branxholme Castle fairly vibrated with its many guests. The bridegroom's feast, which Buccleuch had informed Sir Quinton the latter would pay for, had lasted well into the small hours of the morning, and when the maidservant woke her, Janet was by no means certain that she wanted to arise.

"It cannot be morning already," she muttered into her pillow as she burrowed deeper into the cozy featherbed.

"Aye, but it is, Mistress Janet," the maid said in her soft voice. "I've brung ye hot water, and the mistress will come along shortly t' help ye dress."

When Margaret arrived, a number of other ladies accompanied her, and Janet's dressing ceremony proceeded with pomp and circumstance. To her astonishment, Margaret produced a lovely gown that she declared was brand new.

"But how—?"

Margaret silenced her with a laugh. " 'Tis Quinton's doing, of course. I told him that my woman could easily rework one of my gowns, and that since it would be new to you, it would satisfy tradition, but he would have none of that."

"It is beautiful," Janet said, touching the soft, creamy velvet skirt when Lady Gaudilands, a plump, graying gentlewoman with some forty-five years to her credit, held it out for her inspection. "I do not understand, though. How could he contrive this in such a short time?"

"He bullied Francis, the tailor in Hawick, of course. Francis had finished cutting this gown for Lady Roxburgh who had ordered three dresses from him, and when Quinton told him he required a wedding dress, Francis told him—eventually and doubtless after much argument and persuasion—that he could have this one. He kept his seamstresses up two whole nights to get it finished."

"But how could the tailor know my size?"

"He did not, but Quinton said he told Francis that you were so high and that his—Quinton's—hands could nearly span your waist. That, he said, was enough for Francis to say this gown would suit you. You may ask him to alter it after the wedding if it does not fit perfectly, but tradition forbids any alteration today. Everything you wear to your wedding should be new, so we'll have no argument. Quinton even thought of corsets." She held up a pair of ivory silk bodies with matching ribbon laces and trim.

" 'Tis a good thing ye be slender, Mistress Janet," said Lady Gaudilands. "The dress wouldna fit if ye had to depend on the corset to make you slim enough, for we canna make any knots the day."

"Nor will Quinton be allowed to knot his laces," Margaret said with a grin. " 'Tis a tradition that's led to many a merry moment, I can tell you, for I've known folks who have nigh lost their clothing during the ceremony or afterward."

Dismayed, Janet said, "I'd swoon if such a thing happened to me. Surely, we can pin things together so I need not fear baring myself to the company."

"Ye need ha' no fear, my dear," Lady Gaudilands said. "I ken a few tricks to prevent disaster. The rule says no knots. It says nowt about twisting ribbons round one another. Here, I'll show ye. Slip out o' that smock and into the new one that Margaret be holding for ye."

Before long, Janet stood ready to don her gown, and Lady

Gaudilands had made good her promise. Even the corset felt as if it would stay in place, for she had twisted the ties round each other and tucked in the ends. Despite the lack of knots or pins, Janet no longer feared that she could lose her clothes if she dared to move.

The rich, ivory velvet, open-skirted gown boasted a train and hanging sleeves of ivory velvet over a petticoat of matching silk taffeta. The velvet bodice had narrow crossbands of gold and silver bobbin lace, and the golden satin undersleeves were slashed and trimmed with bands of the same metallic lace. The hems of both petticoat and dress, and the hanging sleeves, were also trimmed with lace and lined with scored and pinked gold satin.

When she was dressed, all the ladies except Margaret and her personal servant left, and the three of them waited patiently until they heard firelocks discharging outside the castle walls to announce the parson's arrival.

" 'Tis the *feu de joie*," Margaret said, looking out a window. "Come and see."

Janet obeyed, feeling a thrill of pride at the huge procession that accompanied the parson. She felt sad that her family could not be present, but it warmed her heart to see that the people of Liddesdale and Teviotdale intended to show Sir Quinton's bride great honor. The procession was a merry one, and that amazed her, too. A number of guests had arrived the previous night and had enjoyed the groom's feast with its attendant imbibing, so she had expected many of the men who had attended those festivities still to be lying abed, nursing the effects of too much drink. Evidently, however, the Scots had heads of steel.

"Do I not wear a headdress?" she said.

Margaret smiled. "Would you do so at home?"

" 'Tis the first time you have asked me what customs would pertain at home, and they are somewhat different," Janet said with a smile. "For one thing, I doubt that Hugh would have allowed me to have a new gown. The cost of fine cloth and trimmings is too great, and fashionable dresses take vast amounts of both.'' She looked down, fingering the luxurious velvet with delight. Then, meeting Margaret's gaze, she said, ''As to what I would wear on my head, I have heard of brides who wore golden coifs or even floor-length veils. In spring, I should doubtless wear a chaplet of roses. However, since there are none blooming yet, I suppose any wreath would have been woven of dried rosemary or gilded wheat-straws.''

''Well, there will be plenty of myrtle and rosemary scenting the rushes in the hall, and dried rose petals to strew at your feet, but a Scottish bride goes bare-headed to her wedding unless she is of the blood royal, and afterward she dons the cap of the married lady. However, in Scotland even the poorest bride is expected to have a new gown for her wedding. Oftentimes the clan or the townspeople will help with the cost as a bride gift. Look now,'' she added. ''It is nearly time.''

The procession below was disappearing into the castle. Janet, observing this, said, ''Should we go down?''

''Not just yet. I have a wee gift for you first, from Buccleuch and me.'' From her sleeve, Margaret extracted a flat, narrow, gray-velvet covered box and handed it to Janet, watching with anticipation as she fingered it.

Janet said ruefully, ''You have done so much, madam. You overwhelm me.''

''Take it, my dear. You be about to become a member of the family. 'Twould be unseemly were we not to do this for you—or for Quinton, come to that.''

''You leave me with naught to say, save thank you.''

''Open it.''

Janet did so and gave a gasp of delight upon seeing the exquisitely wrought gold chain the box contained. ''It is beautiful,'' she murmured, taking it out. ''My hands are shaking. Will you help me put it on?''

''Aye, it will suit you well, I think.'' Margaret unfastened the clasp and then fastened it around Janet's neck inside the high stiff collar of the gown. The chain was long enough to hang just to the swell of her breasts. "That's lovely. Look in the glass, my dear."

Janet did so, and while she was admiring the chain, a scratching sound at the door sent the maidservant hurrying to open it. Lady Gaudilands stepped in, saying cheerfully, "Ye're wanted in the chapel now to begin the service."

It was time. Repressing a surge of panic, Janet obeyed the summons.

Even before entering the chapel, Janet noted the scent of rosemary that filled the stone chamber. The first thing she noticed upon entering was Sir Quinton Scott, who stood at one side near the front between two banks of wooden pews. Wearing a short black velvet cloak over a quilted white satin doublet with large pearl buttons and a narrow white ruff, and black-embroidered white trunk hose of velvet and wool, he made a fine figure. With his shaggy beard trimmed close in the fashionable style, he was even more handsome than she remembered. When his gaze met hers, he smiled, and smiling back at him, Janet felt a rush of welcome warmth.

The chamber was simple, but the window above the altar was shaped like a rose, and she had no doubt that once it had been filled with colored glass. Many Borderers, particularly on the Scottish side, still harbored connections to the Church of Rome. Knowing that the fifth Earl of Bothwell had changed his religious affiliation nearly as often as he had changed his doublet, she wondered if Buccleuch might prove as fickle. At the moment, he just looked impatient.

There was no grand ceremony about the Sunday service, for the parson had also taken note of his host's impatience and sped through it in what Janet thought must have been record time. He called the banns at the appropriate point, then began speaking faster than ever to get to the end so he could begin the nuptial rite.

Janet made the mistake of looking at Sir Quinton just after

the parson called the banns, and found him already looking at her. The amused twinkle in his eyes nearly proved too much for her composure. Quickly she looked down at the parson's neatly shod feet, forcing herself to breathe slowly and deeply, hoping to stifle her incipient giggles in time to repeat her vows without choking on them.

The nuptial rite began at last, and she discovered that it, too, was different in Scotland. Solemn enough, it began with a prayer, just as it would have in England. After that the parson launched himself into an exhortation, calling on the two about to be joined in holy matrimony to consider their duties to each other and to think solemnly on all that their new relationship would demand of them. Since this part seemed overburdened with duties that the wife owed to the husband, Janet began to think he made marriage sound more akin to slavery than to the heaven-blessed union he kept calling it. She dared another glance at the bridegroom and found that although his head was properly bent and his eyes appropriately downcast, he was watching her from the corner of one eye, his mouth quirked in what could only be impudent amusement.

Nettled, she looked back at the floor, and when the time came for her to repeat her vows, she did so in a voice clipped with irritation, scarcely heeding her words. When Sir Quinton recited his vows, she listened more carefully, but other than his vows to protect her, to clothe her and shelter her, she did not think that his end of the bargain would overtax him much.

The parson began another prayer, but when Buccleuch cleared his throat noisily, the prayer rapidly came to an end, and the parson solemnly pronounced them husband and wife. It was done. She was a married lady.

Afterward, men clapped Sir Quinton on the back, and more than one suggested that with such a bonny bride he ought to excuse himself from the wedding feast and carry her straight home to Broadhaugh. Buccleuch put an end to the rowdiness before it gained much support, announcing that any man who

wanted to prove his agility and speed could enter for the winning
of the broose.

"It is to be a foot race from Branxholme to Hawick and
back," he declared, "the winner to have a shilling, the broose
cup, and a kiss from the bride. He can spend the shilling and
keep the cup till the next wedding. Runners will begin in half
an hour and to get the kiss must be back before the bridal pair
leaves, so don't fill your stomachs with drink or you won't be
able to put one foot in front of the other."

Laughter greeted his warning, and everyone trooped into the
hall, where pipers greeted them with lively music. Janet felt
renewed amazement at all that Margaret had done in such a
short time. Long trestle tables accommodated the guests, and
the laird's table sat at one end on a dais. As the first of the
company entered, servants were already bringing in the food.

Taking her seat at the laird's table, Janet said to Margaret,
standing nearby, "You have worked magic, madam."

"Aye, well, I believe you'd manage as neatly in your own
home," Margaret replied, laughing. "Branxholme seems
always to be crowded from cellar to keep with company.
'Twould have taxed us more sorely to provide such a feast in
midwinter, but fewer would have come to it. Now that the thaw
has begun, we can provide fresh lamb and beef, and I've had
a deal of help, as you know. Many of our guests have brought
food and supplies, too, to share."

"It would be the same at home," Janet said, realizing that
she had felt amazement that a Scot could organize such events
as quickly and efficiently as an Englishwoman could. She had
underestimated her hosts. She wondered if she had underestimated her new husband, as well.

The thought did not sit comfortably, and she was suddenly
reluctant to look at him, lest he appear to be different somehow
from the man who had knelt beside her to recite his vows.

He sat at her left, and she could feel his presence in waves
of energy. Her body tingled with awareness of his, and when
she heard some wag shout out a ribald hope that Sir Quinton

would find his bed as warm a hundred years hence as he
would find it on this night of nights, she realized that she was
trembling.

As everyone else found places to sit, a servant set a silver
plate in front of her with a thump that attested to its weight.
Other bowls and platters plunked down on the table one after
the other. A carver stood beside Buccleuch, and when the laird
gestured for him to begin the carving, Janet watched with an
intensity that might have led onlookers to wonder if she were
studying the man's technique.

"Art tired, lassie?"

Starting at the sound of her husband's deep voice inches
from her left ear, she wrenched her gaze from the carver to
meet Sir Quinton's twinkling eyes.

"I believe that I must be," she said, swallowing with effort.

"I, too," he admitted. "To think that only days ago, I was
enjoying the solitude of my own company, pondering such
weighty matters as destiny and death. Yet here I am today,
anticipating my wedding night. 'Tis likewise a weighty matter,
of course, but I own that I look forward to it much more than
I did to the fate your brother intended to provide me."

She felt warmth flooding her cheeks but managed not to look
away. Although she tried to fix her thoughts on Hugh, even
managed briefly to wonder what he had been doing while she
had been getting married, her thoughts quickly shifted back to
the wedding night that lay ahead. It made her knees weak to
think of it, but she was determined to show her husband that
he had not married a weakling.

At that very moment, in Brackengill's great hall, Sir Hugh
Graham was thinking about his sister as he attempted to sort
out his accounts. He had been thinking about her almost constantly since her departure and had been aware since waking
that morning that it was her wedding day.

It had not taken him long to realize that, although Janet had certainly gone off with the reiver, the villain had not abducted her from her bedchamber. By keeping his ear to the ground, he had learned about the toddies served to the guards, and from that point he had managed to sort out much of the truth. Thus far, he had shared the fullness of his knowledge with no one.

Tempted at first to order Yaro's Wat flogged for letting the reiver escape, he realized that he would have to order Geordie flogged as well, since he had no proof of what had occurred and had discovered the reiver's absence during Geordie's watch. Hugh was as certain as he could be that Janet and her reiver had fled before his return from Bewcastle, and he knew that if he interrogated everyone who had remained at the castle that night, he would soon get the whole tale. But that would mean openly admitting that his sister had released the prisoner. He believed that she had, and everything he knew about the events that had taken place that night reinforced that belief. Still, he did not think that she had gone with the villain voluntarily. He knew her well. She would have stayed to fight with him over what she had done. She would not have run away.

Despite that belief, however, he did not believe that Sir Quinton Scott had rescued her from the reiver. Had he done so, the reiver would be in custody at Hermitage, yet Buccleuch insisted that Rabbie Redcloak did not exist. Doubtless the Scotts were hand in glove with Redcloak. He was said to hail from Teviotdale, after all, and that was Scott country. For Quinton Scott to marry Janet meant that Buccleuch had commanded him to do so. Hugh could think of no other reason for any man to marry a woman who had spent a night alone with a reiver.

"What ha' ye done wi' Mistress Janet?"

The indignant voice startled him from his reverie. Looking up from his ledger, Hugh beheld a wiry little boy in a knitted cap over a shock of brown curls, who glowered at him with his feet apart, his hands fisted, and his chin jutted out.

"Is that how you customarily speak to your betters?"

The boy reached up and yanked the cap from his head,

saying, "Me mam needs her. Where is she ... if ye please, sir," he added with obvious afterthought.

"She's gone," Hugh said curtly. "There are no women here."

"Aye, so they tellt me, but I didna believe 'em. What ha' ye done with 'em?"

"I did not do anything with them," Hugh snapped. Then, seeing the boy blink and realizing that he was fighting back tears, he said, "You're Jock and Meggie's Andrew, are you not?"

"Not Jock's no more. He's been dead since afore Christmas."

"Meggie's Andrew, then. Why does your mam need someone?"

"Not someone! She said to fetch Mistress Janet. She's having her bairn, our Nancy says, and there b'ain't no one to help her save Nan and me."

Pushing back his chair, Hugh got up. "We'll find you someone to help your mam. We must all learn to shift for ourselves now that Mistress Janet has gone."

"Ye shouldna ha' sent her awa'! We need her."

Goaded, Hugh said, "I did not send her away. A Scots reiver stole her."

"Then we mun get her back," declared Andrew fiercely.

"She's not coming back," Hugh said, standing over the lad and looking sternly down at him. "What's more, my lad, the only thing that's keeping me from giving you the skelping you deserve for the way you've spoken to me is that helping your mam is more important just now. Still, you keep that impudent tongue behind your teeth, or you'll soon feel the flat o' my hand on your skinny backside."

Glowering back at him, Andrew had the good sense to keep silent, but his expression made it clear that he thought Hugh had served Mistress Janet poorly.

* * *

Quin had never lain with a virgin before, and although Janet had received his comments with a steady intensity, her blushes had warned him that he might have frightened her. She had not spoken to him in nearly a quarter hour—not since he had said he looked forward to their coupling—and although he hoped the constant din of the feasting accounted for her silence, he did not think it the sole reason.

What sexual experience he had came from brief liaisons with knowledgeable women, and seeing her color up like a spring rose reminded him of her innocence. He saw, too, how she reacted to the ribald remarks shouted at them from the crowd of merrymakers, and mentally rebuked himself. He had, after all, sworn not an hour since to cherish and protect her.

Her continued silence made him uneasy. "Have you lost your tongue, lass?"

"I do not know what to say to you."

He was glad his question had not disconcerted her, for he had not meant to speak so abruptly. His glib tongue apparently had deserted him on the night of the Haggbeck raid and did not mean to return anytime soon. First he had stood before Buccleuch, feeling more like an errant schoolboy facing an irate master than the man who, if the Scott history continued as it had begun, might eventually control all that Buccleuch possessed. Now here he was, teasing his bride of less than an hour and unable to think of anything sensible to say to her.

Although her silvery blonde hair, blue eyes, and clear skin had pleased him from the moment he first laid eyes on them, he had not realized how beautiful she was. The creamy velvet gown complemented her skin, and her long, fine hair looked like silvery moonlight spilling down her back. She had not yet donned the cap of a married lady, and he wanted to reach out and stroke her hair to see if it was as smooth and silky as it looked.

"Are many of your Bairns here today?"

Her tone was matter-of-fact, taking him off guard.

"Bairns? Surely, you do not think I have a litter of them running about."

She smiled, raising her chin. "You need not pretend with me, Sir Quinton. If you will but recall, we discussed—"

Suddenly realizing what she meant, he cut her off, saying, "We'll not discuss such things at present, madam." He had collected his wits, and realizing that she had not thought before speaking, he added sternly, "Jenny, lass, with regard to certain matters, you must learn when to speak and when to keep silent."

"My name is Janet, sir."

Her little chin jutted at him, making him want to catch and stroke it to soothe her. He had not had time to consider all that marrying her could mean, because his impatient cousin had left him no time for thinking. What time he'd had he had spent trying to organize his affairs, arranging for funds to pay the merchet, and getting his bride a dress. She had not even thanked him for it, and God knew he had worked a miracle to procure it for her. Francis Tailor had not wanted to part with it, and no wonder, for it was an exquisite creation and suited her well. Francis himself had doubtless seen that for himself, since he numbered amongst the guests. So did Lady Roxburgh, who had been tactful enough to compliment Janet's appearance.

Just then, Buccleuch, who sat at her right, offered to serve her from a platter of sliced lamb. She turned her attention to him and then to her plate. She was dainty with her food.

Hearing masculine laughter to his left, he turned and saw some of his men watching him with broad, knowing grins on their faces. He had no difficulty interpreting their laughter and decided that if he wanted to spare his bride a surfeit of ribaldry, he would do well to devote the same concentration to his meal that she was devoting to hers.

* * *

Janet also heard the laughter, but she ignored it with practiced ease. Had she been oversensitive to the teasing of men in their cups, life in her brother's home would have been a misery. She had long since managed to curb his men's worst behavior, and she had been satisfied with the victories she had won without fretting over ones she had lost. If the men and women sharing her wedding feast wanted to make merry, she had no wish to stop them.

She had quickly realized that she would soon become a target for ribaldry if she sat blushing through the meal. That meant, however, that she had to force her thoughts away from what lay ahead. The whole marriage-bed business was a mystery, anyway. She knew the basics of human coupling, as anyone must who assumed that it bore some resemblance to similar activities in the world of farm animals. But from that point her imagination failed her. She had twice helped at birthings, despite her maiden state, so she knew where the baby came from. She also knew that she owed Sir Quinton some undefined duty, because her brother had spoken often enough of how he longed to see the day when she would have to submit to a husband. But beyond those vague bits of knowledge lay vast unexplored territory that did not bear thinking about in a roomful of watchful people.

Resolutely, she turned her thoughts to Broadhaugh. From Buccleuch's description, she thought the place must be more refined than Brackengill if not as fine as Branxholme. Buccleuch's seat was magnificent compared to any she had seen before. She had not visited often among the gentry, but she had seen the homes of several English notables, and Brackengill in its present state was the finest she had seen before Branxholme—except for Alnwick, of course. She had visited that magnificent residence some years before, when Hugh's guardian had hoped that he could arrange a marriage for her with the powerful Percy family.

Branxholme was beyond anything else in splendor, though. Experts had woven the arras cloths on the walls of its hall. The stone chambers and corridors were immaculate, their furnishings polished, their fireplaces swept daily. The food was so good that she had already requested several of Margaret's recipes.

"How far is Broadhaugh from here?" she asked Sir Quinton.

He smiled, and again she noted the warmth of his smile—and an increasing hunger in his look, which suggested that rather than being a man who had been eating steadily for more than a quarter hour, he had not eaten in a sennight. "Not far," he said, and his voice seemed deeper than ever.

His intense look shot tingling sensations through the core of her body. She felt warmer and wished that someone would open a door to let in cooler air. She swallowed carefully, hoping she looked merely interested in what he would say.

"Are you in such a hurry to get home, madam?"

"I . . . I just wondered how long it would take us to ride there." She wished that he would look back at his food. The way he was gazing at her made her skin feel hot, as if she had a fever.

"There will be dancing first," he said.

"Aye, Margaret told me. Shall we have to ride home in the dark?"

"So you *are* in a hurry," he said with satisfaction.

"Nay, I would not be so impolite as to want to hurry from hosts who have been so kind to me, but I would like to see my new home in daylight," she said.

"Then you shall," he agreed. "We will depart as soon as we can do so without offending anyone. We'll have to wait for the runners to return, though."

"I should think that such a race over rough terrain would be dangerous for them after eating and drinking so much."

"Aye, perhaps, but Border lads thrive on danger."

She looked steadily at him then. "Do you thrive on danger, sir?"

"You must know that I do."

"Well, I have thought about that, you know, and I'm afraid that it must stop."

He blinked. "What do you mean, lass?"

"I generally mean exactly what I say, sir. Now that we are married, you must stop raiding my friends and kinsmen. They'd never forgive me if I let you steal their livestock or burn their houses. It simply must stop."

Sir Quinton stared at her, apparently rendered speechless.

Determined to be sure that she had made her point, Janet said evenly, "I would like you to give me your word, sir—your word as a Borderer."

"Now see here, Jenny lass—" He broke off when the tempo of the music abruptly increased, and it grew louder.

Buccleuch stood up, waving a goblet. "A toast to the bridal pair," he shouted.

Roaring, the men leapt to their feet, raising their mugs and goblets high.

Perforce, Sir Quinton rose to reply with his own toast to the company. Next he toasted his bride.

A myriad of other toasts followed until Janet was certain that everyone in the hall must be tipsy. Then the music changed again, and her husband held out a hand to her. "We must lead the dancing, lass. We'll finish our talk anon."

His voice was stern and his demeanor no longer that of the merry reiver of legend. Suddenly she was not so certain that she wanted to cross swords with him.

Chapter 11

"High on a hill his castle stood,
With halls and tow'rs a height . . ."

Outlined against the setting sun, Broadhaugh Tower's crenellated battlements rose out of thick forestland near the village of Teviotdale, darkly crowning a craggy knoll atop a long, sloping ridge. Despite natural defenses provided by its setting, Janet thought the castle did not look particularly formidable.

She was riding for once like a proper lady on a sidesaddle borrowed from Margaret. Lined with sheepskin and possessing a high cantle, it was comfortable enough but not as stable as the Italian saddle Hugh had given her for her eighteenth birthday in the forlorn hope that she would put away her cross-saddle for good. She still wore her wedding dress beneath the warm cloak that she had worn from Brackengill. Both the cloak and her train draped over the pony's haunches. Sir Quinton, riding beside her, also wore his wedding clothes beneath his thick cloak.

Behind them, a score of armed riders followed, but although their party had started out cheerfully with much laughter and ribaldry, they were mostly silent now except for the jingle of harness and the dull thudding of ponies' hooves.

Janet had scarcely spoken to Sir Quinton since leaving Branx-holme, for she was conscious of their escorts' sharp ears. He had made no attempt to reawaken the conversation about his raiding, and both were tired after the long day. True to his word, he had brought her to Broadhaugh in time to see it by daylight, but the sun had already slipped below the horizon.

"It looks much smaller than Branxholme," she said.

With a touch of amusement, Sir Quinton replied, "If Broad-haugh were larger than Branxholme, it would belong to Buc-cleuch instead of to me. Still, 'tis a proud house, lass, and one of the oldest in Scotland."

"Margaret told me that once Queen Mary stayed here," Janet said.

"Aye, she did. Before the middle of the thirteenth century Broadhaugh was a plain wooden pele tower overlooking vast stretches of Craik and Ettrick forests, but when the richer lords began changing to stone, our ancestor rebuilt Broadhaugh in the French fashion that was popular then. The original tower, the one nearest us on the crag, served as a royal hunting lodge for Alexander I."

"When did the Queen of Scots stay here?"

"Thirty-one years ago, in the spring of 1565," he said. "'Twas when she was involved with the fourth Earl of Both well. That old tower contains some of her embroidery," he added. "I ken little about such things, but my mother always said that the queen produced fine work."

"You have not said much about your mother before," Janet said. "Margaret told me that your father is deceased, but she did not mention your mother. I assumed that both she and Buccleuch's mother would be at our wedding, but neither was there. Are you at outs with her, sir?"

"Nay, but she lives with Lady Bothwell, and since, by royal command, the countess has lived in seclusion since Bothwell went into exile, my mother does not stir from her side. I visit them from time to time, but we are not close. I scarcely ever saw her when I was small. Do you enjoy needlework?'' he asked abruptly.

''I enjoy fancywork when I can find time for it,'' Janet said, adding frankly, ''I have never thought my work above average, however. I did not have a mother to teach me as most young girls do, since mine died when I was quite small. Hugh likes my work, but I do not think him a judge of such things either.''

''Well, you needn't fear that I shall be critical. You can have a free hand with the household, lass. I tidied up some in preparation of your coming, but Broadhaugh needs a woman's touch.''

''Now I know why you did not fight harder to avoid marrying me,'' she said, giving him a direct look from under her lashes. ''You needed a housekeeper.''

He returned the look, and for a moment she thought that she had disconcerted him, but then he grinned. ''Aye, that would be the reason,'' he said.

Without thinking, she stuck out her tongue, then quickly faced forward, astonished at herself for having given in to such a childish impulse. Hearing him chuckle, she felt heat flood her cheeks and did not look at him again.

As they drew nearer the castle, she realized that although at first it had seemed to rise right out of the surrounding forest, anyone approaching had to cross either an expanse of barren land or the River Teviot. In the river's present state of early-spring turbulence, it formed a formidable barrier, made even more so where it met a merry, tumbling burn at the foot of the castle's craggy knoll.

''That's Broadhaugh Water,'' Sir Quinton said, raising his voice to be heard above the roiling water as he gestured toward the burn. ''There's a place on the Teviot not far above where they meet that is fine for swimming when it's warmer.''

''It is beautiful here,'' Janet said. Although she was accustomed to the bleak vistas of Bewcastle Waste and the Cumberland fells, she loved the lush greenery that served as cushion and backdrop to the harsh stone walls of Broadhaugh.

They crossed a gray-stone arched bridge and followed a narrow dirt track up to the main gates, which swung open before they reached them. Inside the bailey, she noted at once that it was smaller than even Brackengill's, but someone with an artist's eye had laid its cobblestones in a patchwork of color that she found pleasing even in the gray light of dusk. She wished that Hugh might have seen it before his laborers had collected the stones for Brackengill's bailey.

It appeared to her that many of Sir Quinton's men must have left the festivities at Branxholme before she and their master had, for besides the dozen or so who stood lined up to greet them, shouts brought others running from the two towers and from several outbuildings, as well.

"There are so many," she said. "I did not know anyone left before we did."

"They did not go to Branxholme," he replied. "Surely you do not think that I would leave Broadhaugh unguarded on a day when everyone in two countries knew that I would be away."

"I did not think about that," she admitted. "Do you really think anyone would have dared attack your home on our wedding day?"

"What better day, lass?" His smile was sardonic. "I'd do such a thing myself, did I want to teach someone a lesson and could be certain that he and most of his company would be from home."

"Are you suggesting that Hugh would do such a dastardly thing?"

"I meant nothing so particular. I have learned to be prepared for the worst, that's all. You will learn to do the same. The English have made it a practice over the past two hundred years to sweep into Scotland with armies of two to ten thousand for the sheer enjoyment of wreaking havoc. They loot and destroy for no purpose other than destruction, and have done so since the days of Edward I.''

''I thought Buccleuch said that Elizabeth and James want peace.''

''Oh, aye, so they say when it pleases them to say it. Nonetheless, the English manage to invent a reason for doing whatever they choose to do.''

''And the Scots do not?''

His grin flashed again as he said, ''I see that being married to you is going to test my wits, lass, but we will not fratch on our wedding day. Welcome to your new home. As I said, I told the lads to tidy up, but I hold no great hope for the result. Neither they nor I are skilled in the art.''

''The bailey looks tidy. I see no horse droppings on the cobbles.''

''Nay, I'd not allow that. The outbuildings are clean, too. We do not live in squalor, lass. We just lack a female's skill for creating a comfortable nest.''

He dismounted and reached for her. As his hands clasped her around the waist beneath her cloak, she slipped her feet from the stirrups and caught up skirts and train in her left hand so they would not remain hanging embarrassingly high over the horse when he lifted her down.

Sir Quinton's strength was evident in the ease and gentleness with which he lifted her to the ground, and as she looked up to thank him, her gaze met his and her body warmed in response to the renewed hunger she saw in his eyes. She wished then that she had thought to ask Margaret to explain certain matters to her. Although the opportunity to do so had arisen more than once, she had resisted revealing her ignorance. Now, recognizing his lust, she wished that she had thrown pride to the wind and had begged Margaret to describe every detail of what lay ahead.

''Your gown is soft, lassie,'' he said quietly without taking his hands from her waist. ''My fingers delight in touching it.''

Feeling uncharacteristically tongue-tied, and uncomfortably

aware of the stares of his men, she wanted to pull away and run for the shelter of the castle. But she did not know where to go, and her feet did not seem to belong to her, in any case. The moment lengthened, and still she stared into his eyes. Her lips had parted, and she seemed to be breathing through her mouth, for her lips felt dry. She licked them and felt his hands tighten. Her right hand, still resting on his shoulder, slipped a little. The material of his cloak felt rough against her palm.

" 'Tis chilly out here," he said. "We'd best get you inside, lass, and warm you up." Looking away, apparently unaware of how warm she felt already, he said to one of his followers, "Get the lads in and tell someone they'll want food."

"What o' yourself, laird?"

He hesitated, then said, "Tell someone to send food and wine up to my chamber."

Feeling as if the exchange had released her from a spell, Janet looked around, searching the teeming throng of men and horses to find the tall man who had carried her cat for her. Sir Quinton had insisted that she would be safer if she could keep her mind on her pony, and she had not argued. "Where is Jemmy Whiskers?"

"Yonder," he said, gesturing. "Hob the Mouse has got him. He'll carry him to the kitchen, and someone there will feed him."

"I want him," Janet said firmly. "He always stays with me."

"Not tonight, lassie. I do not want to share you with your cat."

"You need not share me, sir, but he does not know this place. If he cannot find me, he may try to return to Branxholme or even to Brackengill. He is accustomed to follow wherever I go."

He looked annoyed, and for a moment she feared that he would forbid her to keep the cat with her. If he did, she would resist obeying, but she knew that his will would prevail. He was the master of Broadhaugh. She did not even have a servant of her own. Indeed, it began to look as if she were the only female there.

On the thought, she said, "Have you no maidservants?"

His eyebrows shot upward, and encountering a flinty look, she knew that he thought she was trying to divert him from the subject of her cat and decided that perhaps she was, at that. Then she saw him relax, and the moment passed.

He said, "It would not have been seemly to keep maids here before now, lass. No man wants his daughter serving in a castle full of men, particularly the sort of men who collect at Broadhaugh to follow me."

"Well, I shall require maidservants, sir."

"Aye, I know, and I've made arrangements for several to begin working tomorrow. You may choose one to serve as your personal maid. You won't require one tonight, I promise you, and I'll protect you from my men."

She was not afraid of his men, but she began to wonder who would protect her from him.

"Let's go in," he said again, pressing a hand against her back to guide her.

She dug in her heels. "Jemmy Whiskers," she said again. "I want him."

He sighed. "Very well." Then he shouted, "Hob, where the devil are you?"

"Here, laird," a voice shouted back.

"Bring the damned cat. Her ladyship wants him."

Her ladyship. Janet savored the words. No doubt others had called her so after the wedding or during the subsequent feasting and dancing, but she had gone through those festivities in a fog as dense as any blinding Border mist. In any case, she was certain that Sir Quinton had not called her so before.

The huge, shaggy-headed man so astonishingly called Hob the Mouse came quickly to hand her a closed wicker basket containing a loudly protesting Jemmy.

"He wants oot," Hob said with a grin.

"I can hear that," she said, smiling. "Thank you for taking such care of him. I am very grateful."

"Nae need, m'lady," he said, touching his cap. "He didna fratch wi' me."

She opened one side of the basket, stroked the little cat's head, and murmured soothing words. At the sound of her voice, Jemmy settled down, and raising the basket close to her ear, she heard his rumbling purr.

A nudge from the hand touching her back recalled her to her duty, and she went with her husband up a flight of stone steps into the castle, seeing at once that its layout was similar to Brackengill. The entry was not at ground level but at the floor above, and at one time, she knew, the stairs probably had been wood, so that during an attack the inhabitants could burn them to prevent the enemy's entry.

The heavy wooden main door was ironbound, so that if an enemy tried to burn it, the iron strapping would keep them out. Instead of directly entering the stairwell, however, as one did at Brackengill, one entered Broadhaugh's hall. Though not as large or grand as the hall at Branxholme, its appointments were nearly as modern and it was comfortably furnished with benches and tables. Its walls were bare above the wainscoting, but at some time, someone had expended effort on the place. Despite its masculine residents, it looked generally more civilized than Hermitage.

"I'll take you over the place in the morning," Sir Quinton said. "The lads will be wanting their supper now, though, so we'll go on upstairs."

"The kitchens are downstairs, I expect."

"Aye, there is a kitchen and a bakehouse below the great hall, as well as a scullery and a few rooms that can serve as quarters for your maidservants when they come. We go this way," he added, guiding her toward a circular stairway set into the back left corner of the hall. "I'll carry that basket for you now," he added. "You'll fall if you try to manage it along with your skirts on the stairs."

Without protest, she handed him the basket containing the cat.

As they made their way up the stairs, Janet saw that an arched window in the wall overlooked the hall below. One could easily see who was there without being seen in return. From there, the hall looked warmly inviting. A number of men had entered and were eagerly taking their places at a long table. Seeing servants already passing platters of food, she realized that she was hungry.

An arched doorway with its door ajar revealed another, smaller hall at the next level, and she realized that, like Hermitage, Broadhaugh boasted a master's hall. It was not as colorful, however, and its furnishings looked dull. Here, then, was where Sir Quinton hoped to benefit from a woman's touch. She had no time to examine the chamber, however, for he said quietly, "We go to the next level, lass."

Aware of his presence behind her as she had been aware of no man before, she hurried on, holding up her skirts, watching where she set her feet, and making use of the rope banister looped into iron brackets on the outer wall. The last thing she wanted was to miss a step and fall. As tired as she was, she might easily do so, and she did not want the most lasting memory of her wedding day to be an image of herself falling against him and tumbling the pair of them to the bottom of the stairs.

The image produced by that thought made her chuckle, and behind her, he said, "What's so funny?"

"Only a foolish thought," she said, wondering if he would expect her to share it. She did not know much about what men expected from their wives. Indeed, other than what she had gleaned from a few short, formal visits to households other than her own, she had little knowledge whatever of married folks' habits or customs.

Whenever she had asked questions about such things, the common response had been that once Hugh married, his wife would tell her all she needed to know. But Hugh, having successfully evaded his guardian's numerous attempts to arrange a marriage for him before his majority, had found no one to suit him since then. She wondered if he would be more likely to do so now that he no longer had a competent sister to run his household for him.

That thought had not occurred to her before, but before she could consider it at any length, she reached the next floor. The door there was shut.

"It is not locked," he said. "Just turn the ring, and it will open."

She obeyed, pushed the door open, and stood still on the threshold to gaze at the room beyond.

The first thing she noted was that some thoughtful soul had lighted a fire in the fireplace. The scent of burning wood, and the merry crackling of the fire did more to make her feel welcome than had any of the men's polite comments. She entered, stripping off her gloves and gazing around with interest.

Even in the dim light, she could see that the arras cloth covering two-thirds of the long wall needed a good shaking and sweeping. But the Turkey carpet near the bed looked as if someone had recently brushed it, and the embroidered blue bed curtains looked as if they had been shaken if not taken down and thoroughly cleaned. The plain blue counterpane was smooth, and the room was as tidy and warm as anyone could expect it to be.

"No window curtains?"

He smiled as he set the cat's basket on the floor just inside the door. "It is not as if anyone can look in at us."

"Perhaps not," she said, "but they would keep in the warmth from the fire."

"Also the smoke," he pointed out. "That chimney is temperamental."

"Doubtless it needs cleaning," she said.

He raised his eyebrows. "Cleaning? Do you know where that chimney sits?"

"Do not concern yourself, sir. I will see that someone attends to it."

"Without sending them crashing to the stones below?"

"Aye, I know how it can be done safely." She watched warily as he turned and shut the door, noisily throwing the bolt into place.

He turned back, saw her watching, and said with a smile, "Tip, the lad who serves my personal needs, thinks this room is as much his as mine. Until he learns to recall your presence, we will throw the bolt when we want privacy."

"What of the food you ordered?"

"I'll let them in, never fear. Art hungry, Jenny?" He stepped toward her.

"Aye," she said, stepping back. "It has been some time since our wedding feast, and I . . . I do not even remember what, if anything, I ate."

"You ate enough for three women," he told her, chuckling. "Stand still."

Although it took effort to obey, she did. She liked the way his eyes twinkled when he was happy. His smile was irresistible, drawing one from her in return, but hers faded when he reached for the clasp on her cloak. "I can undo it," she said.

"I am sure that you can, but I want to do it," he said, catching her hand with his. He still wore his leather gloves, and her bare hand felt swallowed up in them. He drew it closer till her fingertips touched the rough material covering his chest. With his free hand, he reached again for the clasp and flipped it open. Releasing her hand, he lifted her cloak from her shoulders. "I do like that dress," he said.

"It is beautiful," she said. "I do not know that it was proper for you to have bought it for me, however. My brother should have paid for my wedding dress."

"We won't think about your brother," he said softly. "I did not mind buying the dress, for I rather like knowing that I own every stitch and bone of you, Jenny."

Stiffening at the thought of being owned like a mare, yet

knowing that in truth that was the way of things, she said, "I told you before, sir, my name is Janet. No one calls me Jenny."

"Now someone does," he said. "I like the sound of Jenny better than Janet."

"Well, I do not," she said evenly. "Jenny sounds like a little girl."

"Nay, then. Jenny sounds like ... like a soft and gentle lassie, one who wants above all things to please her husband." As he talked, he touched her shoulder lightly. Then, slightly frowning again, he paused to take off his gloves.

Stepping away while he was thus occupied, she turned to face him. "I know that it is my duty to please my husband, sir, but you should know that I have not been raised like other girls. I have run a household that is perhaps even larger than this one, and although I have lived with a temperamental man—"

"I said that I don't want to talk about your brother," he said. He unfastened his cloak, flinging it aside and moving toward her again.

Janet stepped back, saying firmly, "This is not about Hugh, Sir Quinton. This is about me. You must not enter this marriage thinking that I will be like other women, for I am not. I am sorry if that disappoints you, but I cannot alter the fact."

His smile vanished and a stern look took its place. "From what I know about Sir Hugh Graham, you did not run everything at Brackengill, Jenny, my lass. For that matter, I doubt that you won many battles with him. Did you not tell me once that he affords rough treatment to anyone who displeases him?"

"Aye, and so he does," she admitted, "but he rarely paid heed to what I did with regard to the household. It was only when I interfered in realms that he considered his own that we crossed swords."

"Crossed swords?"

" 'Tis purely a figure of speech," she said, adding with a sigh, "Not that I shouldn't like to learn how to wield one. It is most unfair that only men can have weapons. I nearly always carry my—"

"Females are not suited to bearing weapons," he said. "Not that lasses don't wield certain weapons of their own, mind you. Some of those are harmless enough, like a smile or the twitch of a fine pair of hips, but I have seen fingernails long enough and sharp enough to claw a man's eyes out. Come to think of it, I have not examined yours to see if they require trimming. Mayhap I should."

She put her hands behind her. "Please, sir, I do not jest."

"Let me see your hands, little wife."

Keeping them safely behind her back, she retreated another step, saying with frustration, "Why do men never listen?"

Gently he said, "Jenny, lass, if one of my men ignored a command the way you are ignoring mine now, I would swiftly teach him never to do so again."

Cocking her head, she said, "What would you do to him?"

He grimaced. "The point has not arisen in years, but I would do whatever I thought best. In any event, what I would do to a man who owes me allegiance and what I'll do to a wife who owes me obedience are scarcely one and the same."

"Are you threatening to beat me if I refuse to show you my hands?"

"Jenny, this is our wedding day. I do not want to quarrel with you. Why do you keep backing away from me?"

"Because I do not know you," she said. "Because I want to know you better, and I do not want you to believe that by changing the name you call me, you can change my nature. If you do not want me as I am, you ought to have said so from the start. If you enter upon our marriage believing that you can mold me to suit some image you've got of a Jenny, I would remind you, sir, that she is as like to be a jenny-ass as to be a jenny-wren."

"Very pretty speaking," he said. "Do you mean to defy me at every turn?"

"I do not want to defy you at all," she said. "I want only

to make matters clear between us. I want to know what you expect of me, and I want you to know that I am not likely to change my nature merely because you want me to.''

A thumping noise diverted both of them, and they turned to see Jemmy Whiskers' head sticking out from under the lid at one end of the basket. A moment later, the little cat emerged altogether and immediately sat down to groom itself.

With a wry smile, Sir Quinton said, ''Now there's a lad that knows how to look after what's important. I shall take a lesson from him just to show you that I am not set upon always getting my way. Do you intend to stand against that wall all night, little wife?''

Glancing over her shoulder, Janet saw that she had nearly backed into the wall near a window embrasure. Outside it was nearly dark, but looking out, she saw that the view encompassed acres of upper-Teviotdale woodland. The Teviot joined Broadhaugh Water far below, and she could hear its merry chuckling.

''It is beautiful, is it not?'' he said, moving to stand beside her. Pride and the love he felt for his home colored every word.

''Aye,'' she said, ''though I'll see it better by daylight. What town is nearest?''

''The only real one for miles is Hawick,'' he said. '' 'Tis where I bought your gown.'' He put an arm around her shoulders and drew her closer. '' 'Tis a soft gown, and gey lovely, but 'tis time to take it off, lass. I would look upon you without it.''

Rivers of heat washed through her, making it difficult to breathe. She did not know what to do with her hands, or what to say. Surely, she should say something intelligent, something wifely, but her imagination failed her. She had no experience upon which to draw. Her lips felt dry, and her breath rasped in her throat. She could feel her heartbeat. Indeed, she could hear it, like a dull thudding in her ears.

Sir Quinton's palm cupped the side of her face. ''I promise that you have no need to fear me, Jenny. I have never beaten a woman in my life.''

"It is not that," she murmured.

"Then what?"

"I do not know what I am supposed to do."

"You need do nothing yet. First, I shall act as your hand-maiden. Just imagine me, if you can, in a maidservant's cap and apron."

The absurdity of the suggestion made her smile.

"That's better. If I had been thinking clearly at the time, I would have asked Francis Tailor to reveal the fastenings on this gown. Where the devil are they?"

"I thought you were the one with experience, sir," she said demurely.

"My experience is not so vast as to include all manner of buttons and laces, madam. Will you show me, or must I devise my own way into this dress?"

"No, don't! You will tear it, and then I shall have nothing to wear."

"Then show me."

Reluctantly, she showed him Lady Gaudilands' clever fasten-ings. He proved an apt student, and when he reached her corset, she stepped away from the window, unable to believe that no one could see them standing there. He chuckled at her modesty but took the opportunity to close the shutters against the night's chill. Next he lit candles at the fire and set them in their holders; then he removed his doublet and shirt before returning his full attention to her.

"Next time I will show you how my clothing must be removed," he said, slipping her gown from her shoulders. It fell, a velvet puddle at her feet.

Although she knew she was blushing, she felt more comfort-able with him. She had feared that a husband might simply demand that she undress herself and let him do what needed to be done to get a child upon her, but clearly that would not be the case. He seemed to want her to enjoy their coupling.

His touch continued to stir new and exciting feelings in her body, fascinating and delighting her, and making her wonder what caused them. Could she stir similar feelings in him? Was it wanton to wonder such things?

Her corset, petticoat, and underpinnings came off next, and she shivered in her thin smock.

"Jump into bed, lass," he said. "I'll stir up the fire."

A knock at the door startled her and sent her flying for the bed. He laughed when she snatched back the blue counterpane and dove beneath it.

Still chuckling, he said, "Shall I let them in?"

"No! Oh, pray, sir, do not!"

He was still chuckling when he went to open the door.

Wondering if she could pull the bed curtain closed from where she lay, she decided in favor of yanking the counterpane to her chin instead.

"I'll take that," Sir Quinton said at the doorway. "You can take yourself off to bed now, Tip. I won't require anything more tonight."

She heard a murmured response, and then her husband's contagious chuckle. When he kicked the door shut and turned, he was holding a large, well-laden tray.

"Now here's a dilemma," he said, grinning. "Shall we satisfy the hunger in our stomachs first, or that of our lust?"

Her stomach growled in reply. "I believe I am famished, sir," she said.

"Tip did not bring us anything as grand as what Margaret provided at Branxholme," he said. "Just bread and meat, and I think that pot has soup in it." He bent his head and sniffed. "Beef broth with bits of something floating in it, and mugs to drink it from, but they forgot to send a ladle."

"We can dip it out with the mugs," she said. "Put the pot near the fire to keep it warm, and we can have the soup later if we want it. All I want now is a slice of bread and beef. Did your Tip bring us aught else to drink besides the soup?"

"Aye, ale and wine both. Which would you like?"

"Wine, please."

He poured some from the jug into a pewter goblet and handed it to her.

She sipped, feeling the warmth of it seep through her as she watched him dispose of the soup pot by putting it almost into the embers at the edge of the fire. Then he set the jug of wine within arm's reach on a side table near the bed. She liked watching the play of muscles in his arms and back as he moved. He was a well-built man.

At last he carried the tray to the bed, and she shifted her legs so that he could set it on the counterpane, which was something she never would have allowed at Brackengill. What civilized person ate in bed? But she said not a word until he handed her a thick slab of bread with a warm slice of rare beef atop it. Then, with deep sincerity, she said, "Thank you."

While she nibbled, trying to keep crumbs from falling into the bed, she watched him cut another slice of beef into strips. He popped these into his mouth, one at a time, chewing while he swabbed up beef drippings from the platter with a slice of bread as thick as the one he had given her. Plainly, he was hungry, too.

When she had finished her bread and beef, he took the tray away and set it on a chest near the fireplace. Snuffing the candles, he came back to bed. Already it was dark outside, but the fire cast a flickering orange-gold glow over the bedchamber, and when he climbed into bed, he left the curtains open.

"I want to see you," he murmured, sliding under the coverlets beside her. "Take off your smock."

Daringly, she said, "I thought you were to act the handmaiden, sir."

"Does your maid take off your smock?"

"If I tell her that she must, she does."

He chuckled again, pleasing her, for she had meant to make him laugh. She was coming to know him better, and that pleased her, too. When he reached for her smock, though, she found it awkward to keep changing position to let him take it off, and so she helped, sitting up while he pulled it off over her head. When she moved to lie back again, however, he stopped her with a hand on her upper arm.

"Don't move. I want to feast my eyes. Jenny lass, you have beautiful breasts. I begin to think that I have won a great prize in you." Bending his head, he kissed the soft rise of her left breast, making her gasp.

While her attention was focused on his moving lips, his right hand cupped her breast, startling her again, but when his thumb brushed across its nipple, she inhaled sharply, amazed by sensations stronger than any she had felt before. She wanted to touch him. Tentatively she moved her hand to stroke his bare shoulder, surprised at how warm it felt. Curious now, she stroked his arm, feeling its muscles tense beneath her fingers.

"Your hands are soft and warm," he said. "Mine are not too cold, are they?"

"No." The whispered word was barely audible.

"Ah, lassie, I think that I am going to enjoy marriage after all. Lie back now, and let me pleasure you."

Inhaling deeply, hoping to calm her fluttering nerves, she obeyed.

Chapter 12

"If foes but kenn'd the hand it bare,
They soon had fled for fear."

Quin marveled at the softness of her skin. Her breasts were firm, high, and plump, her waist so tiny, yet her hips wide and womanly. She would bear children well, and he had a yearning to see those children. They would have sons—a dozen sons—and all strong, fine men of whom a father and mother could be proud. It was easy to imagine this bonny lass a mother of strong sons and beautiful daughters.

She lay naked beneath him, the glow from the firelight dancing on her skin. Her eyes were wide, and he knew that she remained wary of what lay ahead. It was a pity that she'd had no mother to prepare her for marriage, that she had not thought to ask Margaret, or that Margaret had not realized she needed teaching. At the same time, he was glad that he would teach her, that she would learn from no one else.

His body ached for her. The temptation to make her his at once was almost overwhelming, but he feared hurting her. He admired her pride, the way she held her head high and looked men in the eye. Most Englishwomen of his acquaintance behaved more submissively. They kept their eyes downcast, their words soft and gentle. They seemed obedient. They were not all alike, though, for people were different everywhere, and a man who behaved gently one day could be anything but gentle the next. Surely, it was the same with women.

Still and all, Scotswomen of his acquaintance seemed different from Englishwomen. Their tongues were sharper, and they seemed more likely to speak their minds. Shrewdly, he realized that he was thinking of women in his family, and he knew that Margaret Scott spoke more sharply to Buccleuch when they were amidst kinsmen than she did when others were about. Perhaps that was all it was.

Yet Janet Graham had spoken sharply to him from the first. Was it because she had seen him as a captive and thus an inferior? Surely her manner toward him would mend now that she was his wife. Perhaps, like Margaret, she would speak frankly now only when they were alone or with close kinsmen, and would behave with proper, dutiful submission when others were about.

Impulsively, he said, "You sometimes remind me of my mother."

"Do I?" Her eyes seemed wider, larger than ever. "How so, sir?"

"When my father was still alive, she often spoke her mind to him. He told me that once when she thought there would not be enough food to last the household through the winter, she served his spurs to him on a platter."

"Godamercy, she cannot have expected him to eat them!"

"Nay, she expected him to put them on and go a-raiding. For years, our meat was nearly all English bred. In those days, our wealth, like Buccleuch's, lay not in gold so much as in the livestock we owned. That is a common state of affairs in the Scottish Borders, because men fear to plant or even cultivate their land. They believe the English have only to learn of a plowed field to raise an army of raiders."

"Well, you have outwitted the English, sir, for you have taken one to wife, but if you think that I shall ever serve your spurs to you for supper, you are mistaken. As I said before, your raiding days must stop. Surely, if both King James and Queen Elizabeth want peace, and if the two countries will become one when Elizabeth dies, you can begin to cultivate crops without fearing destruction."

"Can I, lass? Do you think your brother means to leave me in peace?"

She frowned.

"Your silence is answer enough," he said. "Sir Hugh will not forgive me for marrying you, or you for marrying me."

"Perhaps he will not."

Her sad tone surprised him. "I thought you did not like him," he said.

"Whatever gave you such a notion? Hugh is my brother, my only close kin, and I love him. We do not always agree, certainly, but we are siblings, sir, and it is human nature for siblings to disagree. I shall miss him fiercely."

"Then we must see if we can mend matters sufficiently to put you on speaking terms again," he said with a smile. "We will think about that tomorrow."

She smiled. "Tomorrow?"

"Aye, because now I want to think only about making you mine."

"You keep making me sound like property," she complained.

"Aye, well, perhaps it is so. How else would you describe a man's wife?"

"She is more important than his cows, I hope!"

Smiling, he touched a finger to the tip of one breast, making her gasp again. Wanting to demonstrate how easily he could stir her, he bent his head and took the nipple in his mouth.

She seemed to have stopped breathing.

He moved one hand, palm down, over her belly and lower to touch the soft curls at the juncture of her thighs. Tickling first the curls and then the opening they concealed, he inserted a finger and felt her stiffen, then relax when her body began to respond to his caresses.

She was ready for him, but he teased her a little more, until he heard her moan with pleasure. Then, shifting so that he could touch his lips to hers, he kissed her gently, then more possessively, exploring her mouth with his tongue while his fingers remained busy below. She stirred, stretched, and moaned more. Her hands clutched him, uncertainly at first and then with more confidence.

When at last he believed that she was aching for him almost as fiercely as he ached for her, he took her swiftly, knowing there was little he could do to protect her from the pain of that first time. He was sorry when she cried out but stifled the sound quickly with more kisses while he reached his own climax. Then, sated, he relaxed and held her close. Kissing her gently, he murmured, "It will not always hurt, lassie, I promise. Next time will be more pleasant for you."

"Will it?" The lazy, contented look in her eyes surprised him. She stretched a little, and when he shifted so that her head lay against his shoulder, she turned her face toward him and smiled. "I thought it would be dreadful," she said softly, "but it was not. I think I might grow to like marriage, a bit."

He chuckled, kissing her lightly. "Do you, indeed?"

"Aye," she said.

He shut his eyes, and the next thing he knew, it was morning. When he awoke, she was curled like a kitten beside him, and he thought he could even hear her purring. It took a moment to realize that the purring came from behind him, and a moment longer to realize that a warm, furry body was stretched alongside his bare back, underneath the coverlet.

Kissing his wife's bare shoulder, he murmured, "Please do not tell me that your cat always sleeps under the covers with you."

"Of course not," she said, turning to look at him. "He sleeps at the foot of my bed at home but never under the coverlet."

"Well, he is under it now," he said. "His fur is tickling my backside."

She chuckled and turned over to face him, discovering as he had hoped she would that he was hungry for her again. Without another thought for the cat, he moved over her, taking care to move gently. Her lips tightened, telling him that she still ached a bit from the night before, but then they relaxed and her body welcomed his. He took his time, enjoying her increasing pleasure as much as his own, and when it was over, they both lay back, feeling pleasantly drained, and slept again.

A rap at the door accompanied by a plaintive meow from Jemmy Whiskers awoke them sometime later.

When Quinton got up and strode naked to the door, Janet said with amusement, "Do you plan to help me dress, sir, or will one of those maidservants have arrived by now?"

"I'll ask," he said, opening the door to his man. "Do not disturb her ladyship, Tip," he said, as if it were necessary to warn the man that he was not alone. "And watch out for the damned cat!"

As he spoke, however, Jemmy Whiskers shot through the doorway, accepting the opportunity to make good his escape.

Quin said ruefully to Janet, "I'll get the lads to catch him. He'll not get far."

"He won't run away now," she said. "Let him explore. They would only frighten him."

He nodded, then turned back to his man. "Forget my things for the moment, Tip, and see if one of the maids you found for her ladyship has turned up yet."

"Aye, laird, Ardith is here. I thought I'd just see first if she were wanted, knowing the state o' dress ye'd likely be in when ye opened yon door of a mornin'. Ye'd ha' sent the poor lassie screechin' for her mam."

Quin looked down at his naked body and sighed. "I expect I'll have to change some of my habits now that we've got women in the place," he said.

"You will, sir," Janet agreed from the bed, "and not just

with regard to your dress. You have not yet given me your word on that other matter, you know, and I fear that I must insist. It is of the utmost importance to me that you forgo your raiding ways now that you have married me. I would never forgive you, you know, if you were to kill one of my kinsmen in a raid, or destroy his home.''

He gave her a stern look. "We will speak more of that anon. Get you gone now, Tip, and send Ardith to her ladyship straightaway.''

"But what about your clothes, laird?''

"I'll dress before you fetch her. Breeks and a jack will do me.''

Tip slipped past him and hurried from coffer to wardrobe, flinging articles of clothing over an arm, taking care not to look in Janet's direction.

"I should have my own bedchamber, should I not?'' she said when Tip pushed a pair of netherstocks and a pair of linen drawers into Quin's hands.

"I expect you should at that,'' Quin said. As he sat on a coffer to pull on the netherstocks, he added with a teasing grin, "For dressing in.''

"I see ye enjoyed a good bit o' the soup,'' Tip said, pausing beside the hearth. "Why did ye no use the mugs?''

"We did not touch the soup,'' Quin said, moving to join him. Small paw prints in the ashes told him at once who the culprit was. He looked at Jenny.

She smiled but then fell silent while he dressed. When he shut the door at last behind Tip, she watched warily, and he realized that she had noted his annoyance earlier. Thus, he chose his words with care, although he would have preferred to issue a flat order, just as he would with any of his men who dared to make impertinent and untimely demands of him.

"You may speak your mind to me privately,'' he said, "but you must not do so when others are about. I'll warrant Sir Hugh does not encourage such candor.''

"He doesn't,'' she admitted, "but I care deeply about this,

sir. I should not have spoken so plainly in front of your man, but I must insist nonetheless that you promise henceforth not to attack my kinsmen or friends.''

His temper stirred, but he said evenly, "My men will expect me to lead them, lass. It is what I do."

"Then you should lead them in the path of peace, sir," she said, her tone matching his.

"Peace requires that both sides cooperate."

"Aye, but one side must begin. Why not yours?"

"Do you think that my people should sit meekly whilst the English raid their homes, burn them out, kill their wives and bairns, and steal their livestock?''

"Surely they will not kill people who do not oppose them."

"If you believe that, you do not know your countrymen," he retorted.

"The men I know would not kill innocent women and bairns.''

"Then the men you know have not taken part in raids against Scotland," he said. "Not long since, in burning out half of Tarrasdale, men from Bewcastle Waste burned a score of cottages, killed six men, eight women, and seven children. Those were your brothers' men, lass. They did it, knowing that my Bairns would avenge the raid and hoping to trap me. As you know, that plan succeeded.''

She frowned. "I did not know about the killing or burning, but many English women and children have died in raids, too.''

"Aye, they have. I don't deny that. My Bairns do not kill innocents, though, unless they want to answer to me. They ken fine that I'll hang them for it."

He heard her gasp and pressed his point. "Life in the Borders is hard, Jenny, and men must be hard enough to match it. Mayhap one day we will all enjoy peace, but that day has not yet come. Until it does, I cannot and will not abandon my men, no matter how winsomely you plead with me. 'Tis my guidance that holds them in check. Without it, there would be more killing.''

She shook her head. "That argument won't serve. You have the power to stop your own men from raiding. Perhaps we cannot end all the killing, sir, but you must prevent your men— our men—from attacking others. Defending their homes is another matter. I would not ask you to deny them your help in such a case."

"I would not listen if you did," he said with a thin smile. "What you do not seem to understand, however, is that attack *is* defense of their homes. If we did not respond in kind, eventually the English would wipe us out."

"That does not make sense. If you would stop attacking them, they would stop attacking you. What would be the point?"

"The point," he replied, forcing patience, "is that before the English would stop, they would beggar every Scotsman in the Borders. I cannot allow that, and even if I were foolish enough to sit by and let it happen, Buccleuch would not."

She sighed. "I cannot stop Buccleuch."

He nearly told her that she could not stop him either, but he decided to hold his peace.

She remained silent for a long moment, still watching him. Then, abruptly, she said, "I cannot blame you for refusing to listen. You did not want to marry me."

" 'Tis true that marriage was not a notion that entered my head," he admitted. Then, with a smile, he added, "But after last night, I believe I will adjust to it without undue difficulty."

Color leapt to her cheeks, and for the first time she avoided his gaze. Wetting her lips with her tongue, she said, "I . . . I, too, believe we may come to an understanding, sir. Nevertheless, it will be much more difficult for me if I have to worry about attacks on those whom I love and care for."

"You must learn to love and care for your new family," he said.

"Aye, and I will. That does not alter my feelings about the raids, though. Is there not some compromise that we might come to?"

He hesitated. It was a fair question. "I'll do what I can,"

he said at last. "I can promise no more than that. If Buccleuch orders a raid, I must go. He is my liege lord and will expect and demand my obedience. Moreover, if my land or that of any of my followers falls under attack, I will do what must be done."

"Still, you need not initiate any raid or attack," she said. "You might also encourage your people—our people—to try the ways of peace. You would thus be obeying a royal command, after all."

"Jamie's commands and Jamie's wishes are often at odds with themselves," he said. "He says one thing—often for no more reason than to be able to tell the English Queen that he has done so—yet he desires another. He is entirely capable of ordering Buccleuch to wipe out an English village on the same day that he publicly deplores the violence in the Borders. Here is your maidservant," he added unnecessarily when a rap on the door announced Tip's return. "Come in," he commanded. "Bring my razor, Tip. You may shave me whilst my lady dresses."

Janet watched Sir Quinton leave, feeling frustration and wondering if he would respond to any of her wishes with anything other than argument. At least he had seemed to listen to her, which was an improvement over Hugh. Still, listening did not mean he would comply with her requests.

She had no more time just then to think about the matter, for plump, redheaded Ardith waited to assist her and another rap heralded the arrival of a lackey carrying a jug of hot water for her ablutions.

She did not look forward with much pleasure to dressing, for there was little choice available as to what she could wear. She had the two skirts and the bodice she had worn when she left Brackengill, a dress that Margaret's woman had altered to fit her, and her wedding dress. She had alternated the two day dresses during her stay at Branxholme, and she was thoroughly tired of both. She knew women who owned far less, however, and if Margaret was typical, Scotswomen paid less heed to their attire than Englishwomen of the same station did.

When visiting Bewcastle or other such residences, she had always taken a sensible variety of clothing, and her hostess had frequently expected her to change her attire several times a day. At Branxholme, however, she and Margaret had dressed in the morning and had not changed all day, even to dine.

It occurred to her that Margaret might have altered her usual practice to accommodate a guest who had brought little with her to wear. Still, the fact that Margaret had given her only the one dress argued that Margaret had not thought she would require more.

"I shall wear the blue bodice and overskirt, Ardith," she said as she moved to perform her ablutions at the washstand, where the young maid was pouring water from the ewer into the basin.

"The laird's man—that Tip—he said the laird would doubtless like ye t' wear one of the new dresses, m'lady."

"What new dresses?"

"He said I'd find 'em in the press," Ardith said, looking around and pointing to the wardrobe. "I trow we'll find them there. Shall I see, then?"

"Yes, please," Janet said, her interest stirring.

She watched with growing delight while Ardith opened the press and took out a loose gown of shimmering golden-brown silk edged with richly embroidered braid. A second gown followed of grass-green satin trimmed with white velvet.

"There be shoes, too, mistress," Ardith said. "Did ye no ken they was here?"

"No," Janet said. "Sir Quinton must have meant to surprise me. I came away from home rather quickly, you see, and—" She broke off, seeing awareness in Ardith's eyes. "But you know all about me, do you not?"

The girl smiled. "Nay then, not all, m'lady, but some. Ye helped the laird escape, and that be all we need ken o' ye—

that and that ye're mistress the noo o' Broadhaugh. Which will ye wear, then?''

Janet's first impulse was to wear her own old dress, since she wanted to explore Broadhaugh from towers to cellars and would likely soil whatever she wore. When she hesitated, looking at the worn dresses, the maid's disappointed expression made the decision for her. It would be her first appearance as Broadhaugh's mistress. She would accomplish no good by appearing in worn-out clothing.

"I shall wear the green," she said.

Ardith nodded her approval. "It will suit you fine, that dress. The master chose well.''

"Aye." As she said the word, Janet thought of Lady Roxburgh and wondered if the poor woman had got any of the new dresses she had ordered from Francis Tailor. She wondered, too, how many other women Sir Quinton had bought clothing for. Feeling her fingers curl into claws, she quickly composed herself.

"I'll wear my hair in a net," she said as Ardith fastened the tiny hooks and eyes on the tight bodice. "I will show you later how I like to arrange it, but I want to inspect the household today, and it will look tidy enough in the net.''

" 'Tis gey beautiful," Ardith murmured, her attention focused on the lacing at the back of the bodice. As she drew the laces tighter, she added, "I ha' never seen hair as pale as what yours is. Almost silver it is, like moonlight.''

"Aye, and it is gey fine, too," Janet told her with a chuckle. "You will find that it does not plait well, or curl. I like to twist it in a knot at the back of my neck, to keep it out of the way, but when we must bow to fashion, there are ways.''

" 'Twould be a pity and all to crimp it, I'm thinking," Ardith said with a speculative look.

"And useless," Janet told her. Twenty minutes later, she stood before the looking glass, pleased with what she saw. Her hair was smoothed back from her brow and confined in a ribbon-trimmed net. The green satin dress made her eyes look green and gave her skin a soft, creamy look. Pinching her cheeks to force more color into them, she announced herself ready to inspect the household.

"Ye'll be wanting to break your fast first," Ardith said.

Janet agreed, and allowed the young maidservant to guide her to the master's hall, where she found Sir Quinton discussing a meal rather larger and more varied than what was customary at Brackengill. Joining him, she contented herself with a freshly baked roll and a mug of milk.

"I like that dress," he said. "It becomes you well."

"Thank you," she said. "It was kind of you to buy me more clothes."

"You'll need more than those," he said. "We'll ride into Hawick one day soon, so you can meet Francis Tailor."

"I am almost afraid to face him," she said. "I shudder to think what you must have done to make him provide such a fine wardrobe for me."

He chuckled. "He was glad he could please me—and please Buccleuch, too, for that matter. If you are worried that Lady Roxburgh is running around naked, you need not. Her husband will thank me for saving him the expense."

"Let me write to Hugh before you commission any more," she said. "Doubtless once he's got over his anger, he will send my things to Broadhaugh."

"Don't count on that, lass," Sir Quinton warned. "He said he'd see you married in your smock, and he meant it. I doubt that he will give in easily. At all events, we won't ask him for favors yet a while. I can provide all that you need."

"You should not have to do that," she protested. "I am entitled to a dowry."

"Nevertheless, we will not trouble your brother. I am not Croesus, Jenny, but I can look after my wife."

She opened her mouth to object again to the nickname, then shut it when she saw that he was gazing at her with amused anticipation.

Gently, he added, "You will want things for the household, too, I don't doubt. Make a list."

Glad that he was proving to be reasonable, Janet turned her attention with pleasure to the household, soon finding her feet in familiar tasks and problems. She had feared at first that Sir Quinton's people might look upon her as an interloper, but she quickly learned that everyone at Broadhaugh shared Ardith's delight. Not only had word spread that Janet had rescued their master but his people seemed to take pride in having a mistress at Broadhaugh again.

The next week passed in a flurry of housework. At Janet's insistence, Sir Quinton hired more maidservants. The kitchen buzzed with activity. Mops and brooms found their way into areas that had not seen the effects of either in two years, and the flagstones in the hall gleamed after a good scrubbing. Wood shone with new polish. Bed curtains and window curtains came down to be shaken, even laundered, and then went up again. Arras cloths, too, came down to be cleaned. Glass windows glistened again, and men dusted and painted every shutter.

Janet discovered with delight that smoke-blackened beams in the hall and bedchamber ceilings, when cleaned, revealed brightly painted scenes, some illustrating familiar Biblical texts, others well-known ballads. Linen presses were turned out, chimneys cleaned, and every pot was scrubbed. Indeed, in less than a fortnight every corner of Broadhaugh showed signs of her energy and competence. No longer did chimney soot fall into pots to flavor everything cooked over the kitchen fire. Maidservants sang as they set to their work; delightful odors emanated from the kitchens, putting smiles on the men's faces as they attended to their chores; and laughter frequently rang through the castle.

Sir Quinton's man, Tip, became Janet's willing slave and, whenever his master did not require his services, could be found harrying lackeys to do her bidding more quickly, or doing small favors for her himself. Janet had arranged for Tip's elderly mother and numerous other tenants in similar circumstances to receive fresh-baked bread from the castle bakehouse once a week, just as she had done at Brackengill, and Tip was almost puppy-like in his gratitude. She supposed that once the cheerful little man grew accustomed to her ways, his close attendance would ease, but for the present she welcomed help from any quarter.

At the end of the fortnight, Sir Quinton made good his promise to take her to Hawick, and despite the awkwardness of the sidesaddle Margaret had lent her—which he insisted she use—both the excursion and the bustling little town delighted her. They entered through the west port at the top of a row of houses that divided two streets, and followed the one on their right until they came to an intersection.

Sir Quinton said, "We'll follow the Howegate down to the Auld Brig, which connects the western portion of the town to the High Street."

"Hawick is larger than I expected," Janet said.

"Aye, well, it's the only proper town south of Jedburgh. Its biggest claim to fame is that when the English attacked thirty years ago, the townsfolk threw all their thatch into the streets and set it afire. The smoke was so strong and smelled so bad that the raiders could not enter the town till they had put out the fires. It was ironic, too, because before then the English had spent the day setting all of Teviotdale afire and had come to Hawick expecting to find food and shelter. Instead, the townsfolk, knowing their purpose, took all their goods to Drumlanrig Tower yonder." He pointed toward the tall stone pele tower on the east bank of the Teviot.

"What did the English do then?"

He shrugged. "They burned the rest of the town. Most of these buildings are new since then, although they spared Drumlanrig. Although Douglas is kin to us, he was friendly to Elizabeth then, and they did not want to alienate him by burning his tower. We'll cross here," he added. "Francis Tailor's shop is by the Market Cross."

Janet nodded, content to follow where he led, and when they

reached the tailor shop, she found Francis and his wife helpful and her new husband generous. Not only did he buy her clothing but also a new sidesaddle similar to the Italian saddle Hugh had given her. By the time they returned to Broadhaugh she was in full charity with him. She looked forward to showing off her new wardrobe and felt confident that they would deal well together. Thanks to his delight in her as a bed partner and housewife, and her determination to bring Broadhaugh swiftly to her high standard, this happy state of affairs continued for some time.

That Sir Quinton still showed little interest in preparing ground for crops Janet attributed to continuing gloomy weather. Although the air had warmed enough to bring sleet or rain rather than snow, she knew that spring might not reveal the effects of its gentling hand on the landscape for several more weeks. He had mentioned having business to tend in Edinburgh, but he did not think it safe to leave her or Broadhaugh just yet. Still, she could tell that he was growing bored with lack of real action, and restless. The only thing he seemed to talk about with much interest was the forthcoming horse races at Langholm.

When word reached them of a raid carried out by the men of Eskdale against a hamlet in the English west march, she could almost feel his yearning. Wisely, she said nothing, but when Buccleuch and Margaret paid a visit nearly a month after the wedding, not an hour had passed before she spoke to Margaret of her concern.

"He's like a hen on a hot griddle," Janet said after a tour to show off the changes she had wrought. The two women had settled in a small sitting room near the room she had taken for her bedchamber, just above Sir Quinton's.

"I know what Quin can be like," Margaret said with a chuckle. "Let me see if I can help remedy the situation."

When they sat down to eat their supper that evening, Buccleuch said abruptly, "I've been thinking, Quin. I ought to have a deputy, and you ought to learn what duties I bear as march warden and as keeper of Hermitage and Liddesdale."

Looking interested, Sir Quinton said, "What would you want me to do?"

Buccleuch shrugged. "As to that, who can say? You could go along as my aide to the Truce Day if that want-wit Scrope ever makes up his mind where to hold the blessed thing. Perhaps I could also leave upper Teviotdale in your care whilst I'm fixed at Hermitage. The title of deputy will give you more power, and perhaps I can arrange for a small stipend from Jamie, as well. What say you?"

To Janet's surprise, Sir Quinton did not point out that Buccleuch had never before required the services of a deputy, or to enumerate duties that would make serving difficult—the sort of casual argument that she had learned was characteristic of him. He just nodded and said, "I am yours to command, Cousin, as always."

"Good, that's settled then." Buccleuch looked at his wife and grinned.

Margaret quickly asked Sir Quinton a question about one of his tenants, and Janet hoped that he had suspected nothing untoward in Buccleuch's sudden offer.

If Sir Quinton suspected her hand or Margaret's in his new position, he said nothing about it. Indeed, he seemed to take the new duties seriously, even to enjoy them, and she began to hope that his raiding days truly were over. She indulged this hope for no more than five days, however, before she discovered its futility.

On the evening of that fifth day, she and Sir Quinton were walking together in the bailey, chatting with lads who were tidying up at the end of the day, when the guard at the postern gate suddenly flung it wide to admit Hob the Mouse. The big man leapt from the saddle before his pony had come to a stop.

"Master," he cried, "raiders from Kielbeck have raided Cotrigg village! They forced everyone outside, then fired the cots and killed Ally the Bastard's wife, his cousin Jock o' Tev, and Jock's three bairns!"

Shocked, Janet gasped, "They killed children? They cannot have done that!"

Sir Quinton's hand clamped onto her arm, silencing her. "Gather the lads," he ordered. "We'll meet at the usual place in an hour." As Hob ran back to his pony, Sir Quinton said grimly, "You go inside, lass, and stay inside. I'll leave lads to guard you, but take no chances. Don't even stand near a window until I return."

"But who can have done this? And where are you going? We've enjoyed weeks of peace, sir. Don't you see that if you retaliate it will all start again?"

"What I see is a disobedient wife," he retorted. "Get inside and upstairs now, where I know you will be safe from harm. I must go."

"But—"

The rest of the sentence stopped in her throat when he grabbed her arm and pushed her ahead of him into the castle. Inside, he released her, but when she turned angrily to face him, he snapped, "Get up those stairs, and don't argue with me. This is not a matter of countries or kinsmen, or one that lies just betwixt you and me. They have attacked my people and my land. You cannot expect me to let them get away with it. Now, not another word unless you want to make me really angry, and I promise you, you don't want that. Go on now." He pointed, and she went.

Chapter 13

" *'Go saddle for me the brown,'* says Janet,
'Go saddle for me the black . . .' "

Furious and frightened, Janet went to the master's hall. An hour later she still sat staring into the fire there, listening to it crackle while her fear warred with her anger. She remembered her threat to young Andrew—long ago now—to skelp him if he dared wave a weapon again before he reached adulthood, and wished she could make the same threat to Quinton and make him believe her as Andrew had.

Just the thought of confronting her large husband and threatening to raise a hand to him brought a reluctant smile. The threat would be as useless with him as it would be with Hugh. She did not think that Quinton would knock her against the nearest wall or drag her by her hair to her bedchamber and lock her in—both of which remedies Hugh had employed in the past. But neither would Sir Quinton Scott, Laird of Broadhaugh, stand for being ordered about or scolded by his wife.

The fire crackled again, and sparks shot into the air. As she watched, her agile imagination began presenting her with

pictures of the Bairns riding into England to avenge the murder
of Jock o' Tev, whoever he was—or Ally the Bastard, for that
matter. Had she been at Brackengill, she would have known
everyone involved. Thinking about home, she understood Sir
Quinton's fury.

He would be leading them now, his cloak flying behind him
as he rode. The memory of his heavy frown and his anger when
he had walked away made her sad, because she did not want
to fight with him. They were bound together for life, and to
face a future filled with such strife was unthinkable. Somehow
they had to reach a reckoning that they both could live with.
First, however, both of them had to survive the night ahead.

More pictures filled her mind. To reach Kielbeck, Sir Quinton
and his men would most likely cross the Liddel south of Hermitage and the Border somewhere in the Larriston Fells, where
she knew that armed guards made their rounds in plump patrols
of as many as forty riders. Several of the men—and Sir Quinton
himself—had assured her that he knew the Cheviot Hills and
the fells between them and Bewcastle Waste better than any
other man alive. Still, she knew that he had nearly met his end
on those fells before, and she could not believe that he and the
others could ever again slip through that heavily guarded area
with impunity. What if this turned out to be yet another of
Hugh's traps to catch Rabbie Redcloak?

Getting up, she paced back and forth, her full skirts swaying
in her agitation. Her thoughts tumbled like the turbulent waters
of the Teviot through her mind. One moment she felt as if she
were drowning in fear that Sir Quinton would be taken, the
next she seethed at his refusal to discuss his decisions or inten-
tions with her.

Jemmy Whiskers, curled by the fire, opened his eyes and laid
back his ears in disapproval of her unpredictable movements.

"He should talk to me about what he means to do," Janet
informed the little cat. "He should allow me to have at least
a part in his decisions if for no other reason than my knowledge
of the English. I was one of them for two decades, was I not?

I have heard Hugh and his men talk about tactics and strategies. I know how they think, so I could help if only that stubborn dolthead would let me."

A more important reason, she told herself, was that a man should treat his wife like a part of himself. He should look not only to his henchmen for help but to her, as well. Women often saw things in a different but nonetheless useful light.

"I hate being left out of important matters," she informed the cat, which now, except for the occasional flick of an ear, studiously ignored her striding agitation. "All my life men have told me that what they do is none of my affair, that it does not concern me," Janet went on, "and that is just plain foolishness. Men *are* fools. One has only to see how they manage events like this one to see that. They think with their swords and their cocks and naught else." Biting her lip, she looked sharply about to see if anyone else could have overheard her. Except for Jemmy Whiskers and herself, the room was empty. Feeling guilty nonetheless, she muttered, "I should not have said that about cocks, Jemmy."

The cat blinked, then shut its eyes and did not open them again.

Janet sighed and walked to the window near the chimney. It was drafty there, and the fire's warmth did not reach her. Lifting her skirts, she climbed onto the bench and looked out, recalling only after she had pushed the shutter wide that Sir Quinton had warned her to stay away from the windows.

The prospect might have delighted her on another, less tension-filled occasion, for moonlight gleamed on the Teviot as it wound its way past the foot of the crag, turning the river into a glittering dark ribbon. Pale, silvery light cast shadows where trees dotted the landscape beyond it and revealed gently rolling undulations. She was looking the wrong way, though, and she felt frustrated. From the ramparts beyond Sir Quinton's bedchamber, she could look toward Hermitage and England, but even from there, mere looking would avail her naught.

An idea stirred. She gazed thoughtfully at the cat, measuring the idea's merit in her mind. If Sir Quinton caught her, he would surely be tempted to use her as Hugh had so often used her, and no one would blame him if he did.

"But if I stay here, Jemmy, he will come home to a demented wife. I will be happier doing something—anything. And perhaps, if aught goes amiss, I can help."

On the thought she jumped down from the settle, snatched up her skirts, and hurried from the room. Growing excitement banished lingering concerns about what her husband might say, and she sped up the stone steps to her bedchamber, only to stop on the threshold when a disconcerting thought struck her. "Why, I have no clothes here suitable for—"

Looking around, she bit off the words before saying anything else aloud. She would do her purpose no good if some well-meaning lackey overheard her muttered scheming. Thinking swiftly, she went down to Sir Quinton's room instead and stood looking around in growing frustration. He was too big. Nothing he owned would fit well enough to do her any good. She had to find someone to help her.

Tip's small, wiry image leapt to her mind. He had been kind to her from the start, and thanks to the fresh-baked bread she sent each week to his mam, he now seemed to worship her nearly as much as he worshipped Sir Quinton.

"Perhaps he will help," she said to the cat when it wandered in, looking for her. "Even if he will not, I do not think he will betray me."

She could not shout for him, however, so she went in search of him, finding him in the kitchen, flirting with the new cook's daughter.

"Tip, I want a word with you."

"Aye, mistress?" He regarded her expectantly.

Janet did not speak.

He got up, grinned saucily at the cook's daughter, and excused himself.

In the dimly lit stone corridor, he said, "What will I do for ye, mistress?"

Drawing him away from the kitchen doorway, she said, "I need clothes, Tip."

"Aye, then I'll fetch Ardith, mistress. I warrant she's no gone far. Likely, I'll find her in the great hall wi' the other lassies, since the master said they was all t' stay safe within the walls this night."

"I do not want Ardith, Tip. I want you. Come away from the kitchen, though, lest someone overhear us."

His expression changed, and he glanced anxiously around as if he expected to see the very stones of the corridor walls begin to grow ears.

When they reached the stairway, Janet said, "I want boy's clothing, Tip, or some from a small man—shirt, jerkin, breeks, and trunk hose." She had been measuring him with her eyes, and he was not slow to catch her meaning.

His mobile eyebrows shot upward. "Ye want lad's clothing?"

"Aye, or that of a small man."

"What for?" His tone now was decidedly suspicious.

Janet grimaced. "I mean to follow the master, Tip. He is riding into danger, and he owes as much duty now to me as he does to Buccleuch and to his men."

"But them Kielbeck bastards raided and burned Cotrigg and murdered Ally the Bastard's wife and cousin and his cousin's three wee bairns," Tip protested.

"I know they did, but if our men raid them in return, the enmity will grow and grow until none of us remains alive and no building remains standing. Who will look after the livestock or the bairns then? Oh, don't you see, Tip, someone has to take the lead. Both King James and Elizabeth of England have demanded peace, and neither is known for patience or for expending compassion on those who defy them. Already Elizabeth has ordered plump patrols set in place of the two-man patrols that used to guard the most common crossing places. What will happen to us all when she sends armies?"

"We'll beat them down," the little man said stoutly.

"Aye, perhaps, but what if we cannot? And what will we do when Jamie takes the English throne after she dies? Do you think the fighting will just stop?"

He frowned, but she did not have time to debate the matter further. "I am going after them, Tip. If anything does happen, perhaps I can help, because I know many of the men who fight on the English side. At least, I know their commanders and most of the English landowners in the area. In any event, if I cannot help, at least I will know what became of them and can ride to Buccleuch for help."

"Aye, that's true," he said thoughtfully, "but ye ken, mistress, the master will ha' left lads behind to prevent ambush on their return. 'Tis ever his way."

"He is taking only twenty men, Tip."

The manservant shrugged.

Janet glared at him. "See here, I am going after them whether you help me or not, but I shall be much safer with your help than without it, shall I not?"

"Aye." He said no more but hurried along the corridor to the service stair, and she followed him up the several flights to his master's bedchamber.

"Why have we come here?" she demanded when he opened the door. "I cannot wear Sir Quinton's clothes. They are miles too big for me."

"Aye, but neither can ye accompany me to my wee chamber, mistress. If anyone should see ye ..." He grimaced expressively.

She did not want to let him out of her sight. "I do not want to stand here waiting whilst you go in search of clothing, Tip. I must leave at once. If I do not, I will never catch up with them."

"Dinna fash yerself," he said calmly. "I ha' clothing here that ye can wear." He disappeared into the tiny closet where he awaited his master when Sir Quinton was out late and would want help undressing on his return. In moments, he returned with garments draped over one arm.

"Do ye ken how t' put these on?" he asked. "Because if ye dinna ken—"

"I do," she said, blushing at the thought of Tip trying to help her. "I've worn my brother's breeks, and I've helped dress small boys. It cannot be so different."

"Nay," he said doubtfully.

"Go away, Tip."

He fled to the corridor, carefully shutting the door behind him.

As she pulled on the netherstocks, Janet wrinkled her nose. They clearly had been well worn since their last cleaning, and she was fastidious, but she could not think of that now. Noting that Tip had brought everything but boots, she decided that she would be better off wearing the fur-lined ones that she had put on earlier to stroll in the bailey with her husband. Pulling them back on, she stood and tucked into her belt the small, sheathed dagger she always carried.

At last, regarding her reflection as well as she could and using Sir Quinton's polished metal shaving mirror to view the hind bits, she hid a smile. No one would recognize her. She was all the wrong shape, for one thing. Her boots looked odd, because there was too much space between their tops and the bottom edges of the breeks, and Tip's netherstocks were baggy on her slender legs. Not that anyone would notice that once she was safely on horseback. Until then, she would just have to take care that she did not attract anyone's particular notice.

A floppy knitted cap concealed her hair, and over her shoulders she draped a plain black cloak that she found in one of Sir Quinton's chests. Though the cloak would be short on him, it was long enough on her to conceal nearly everything, and all the clothing she wore was dark. Even Tip's shirt had been dyed a soft dark brown, which was just as well. Moonlight, however pale, would reflect from a white shirt and quickly betray her presence to any watcher.

She needed her gloves, but then she would be as ready as she could be. Fastening the cloak's clasp, she left the room and found Tip awaiting her just outside. He had changed his attire and was dressed now in much the same sort of clothing that she wore.

"I must get my gloves," Janet told him, "but you need not come out to the stable with me," she said. "I can manage, and the less you have to do with this the better it will be for you."

"I be goin' wi' ye, mistress."

"No, Tip, you are not."

" 'Tis of nae use to argue," he said calmly. "I'll ride wi' ye or I'll follow. I'd prefer t' ride wi' ye, for I ken the ground. I've fetched your gloves, and ye'll be needin' this, as well," he added, handing her the gloves and a riding whip.

Taking them, she grimaced. Knowing the ground was a point that she had not considered as carefully as she should have. Assuming that she had only to follow the track toward Hermitage, she had believed that she would find her way easily by moonlight and that, thanks to Quinton's instructions when they had ridden to Hermitage together, she would be able to read the signal he would leave for laggards at the gathering place. Still, she wished that she knew the Scottish landscape as well as she knew the landscape near Brackengill.

"I do not like putting you in danger," she said, tucking the whip under her arm to pull on her gloves.

Tip's eyes twinkled. "Any danger we might encounter, mistress, would be as nothing to the danger in which I'd find m'self if I let ye ride after them alone. I warrant the master will say that I should ha' locked ye in your bedchamber or sat on ye to keep ye here."

"If you dared to try that—"

"Nay, I would not!" Tip chuckled. "I took your measure long since, mistress, and I'm nae such a fool as to get wrong o' ye. But I'm goin' wi' ye nanetheless. Ye'd best make up your mind to that."

She smiled. "I confess, Tip, that I shall be glad of your company, but I fear that you will pay heavily for helping me."

"Aye, I will. Mayhap ye should give up this daft notion," he said hopefully.

"I cannot. I keep feeling that this must be another trap, that my brother will catch Sir Quinton and this time there will be no one at hand to help him escape. I must prevent that if I can."

"Aye, sure, and d'ye think the master doesna take such risks into his mind each time he leads a raid? Mayhap ye dinna ken his grand reputation, mistress."

"Mayhap you forget that I first made his acquaintance in a dungeon cell," Janet reminded him tartly.

"Aye, well, there is that."

"We are wasting time," she said. "If you are coming with me, make haste." With that, she passed him and hurried down the stairs, delighting in the freedom the breeks gave her to do so. Skirts were a nuisance.

"I'm thinking," Tip said as he clattered down behind her, "that we'd best slip out through the kitchen. We can whisk round to the stable, and they'll no pay us much heed." As they reached the entrance to the kitchen, he added thoughtfully, "Ye might ha' met wi' trouble tryin' to tak' a horse on your own, ye ken."

She glanced at him over her shoulder. "Do you really think anyone would dare try to stop me?"

"If ye come over the mistress, and if the master ha' failed to leave orders forbidding it, ye might win through—if the lads be no so shocked at seeing ye in netherstocks that they fall down dead in their tracks."

"In that event, they would not stop me," she pointed out. Realizing from his set expression that he meant to continue an argument he found promising, she added evenly, "You win, Tip. You have convinced me that I need your help. Tell them whatever you must in the stable, but hurry!"

"Aye, sure." He obeyed but not before muttering, apparently to himself, "They'll be long gone and back afore we catch them up, any road."

Ignoring him, and using the glow emanating from the banked
kitchen fires to see her way, Janet hurried to the door leading
out to the bailey. Opening it and peering out, she said, "I doubt
that anything bad will happen before the Bairns reach Kielbeck
village, Tip, because ambushers are bound to want to catch
them with the goods in hand. It is their safe return that concerns
me most."

They fell silent while they crossed the cobblestones.

Inside the dark stable, Janet helped saddle two horses that
Tip selected, and they rode out through the postern gate, where
the single guard barely glanced at the "lad" with Tip.

"You see," she said when they reached the rough track
leading south along the ridge between the Teviot and Broadhaugh Water. "He scarcely looked at me."

"Aye," Tip said, "because ye rode wi' me, and because
doubtless he thinks we ride to join the raid or to meet them on
their return."

Knowing better than to continue the argument, or indeed, to
continue speaking while they rode, Janet turned her attention
to following him along the rough track. They had not reached
the pass into Liddesdale before she realized that she had gravely
underestimated her ability to follow a narrow, nearly invisible
track in the dark. Often she had no idea what Tip saw that led
him to take one way instead of another. When she realized that
the misty moon, which had hovered to the left for most of the
way, had apparently drifted ahead of them, she called a halt.

"Where are we?" she demanded as she drew her horse
alongside his. "I vow, Tip, if you are leading me in circles to
keep me from finding them, at the first opportunity I will run
you through with a sword myself."

"I wouldna lead ye astray, mistress," he said.

She heard injury in his voice, but she had not lived with a
Border lord all her life only to accept what might be no more
than a serviceable lie. "Why is the moon ahead of us then? It
has stayed to our left until now."

"We've turned a bit is all," he said. "D'ye see them two hills yonder, the ones that look like a lass's soft bubbies?"

Following his gesture, she saw the twin dark mounds ahead. "Aye, so?"

"We were headed straight toward the one on the right. That be Cauldcleuch Head. Two thousand foot, at least, it be. Same as Greatmoor Hill yonder on the left. We aim to go betwixt the two, through the pass. Then we'll follow the burn there till it meets wi' Hermitage Water."

She nodded, knowing now where they were going. "When we can see the castle, it will become easier to see the track, will it not?"

"Aye, well, that depends on if ye want them at Hermitage to see us or no."

Janet sighed. "I had no notion how many pitfalls I should encounter in this venture, Tip. You are right to be exasperated with me. I certainly do not want to have to explain myself to Buccleuch. Not before we find the others, at all events."

"Now, that's just what I were thinking myself," he said. "Himself wouldna appreciate the need we ha' to look out for the master."

Detecting irony in his tone, she chose to ignore it. "Exactly so," she said.

Reaching the top of the pass did not take as long as she had feared, and by crossing Hermitage Water as soon as they reached it, they managed to pass near the castle without having to pass within sight of its great walls. The shrubbery on the banks of the rushing burn shielded them, but Janet was grateful when the moon chose the few minutes of their passing to slip behind a cloud. By the time the cloud drifted on, they had reached the northwest bank of the Liddel.

With satisfaction she saw that she could easily have found the ford, but she made no objection when Tip slipped from his saddle to search for Sir Quinton's mark. He found it quickly.

"They've made for Larriston and Saughtree," he said. " 'Tis just as I expected. They'll be wantin' to cross over the line betwixt Saughtree and Deadwater—on the Larriston Fells, ye ken, the far side o' Foulmire Heights.''

"Why?"

" 'Tis the easiest route into Tynedale, that's why.''

"But won't the English be watching the easiest route the most carefully?''

"Aye, they will, but Foulmire Heights be well named, mistress. I doubt they ken them as well as the master does. And, too, because he kens fine that they'll be somewhere about, he'll spy them easily and avoid their lookouts. We'll do the same if ye'll trust to my lead.''

"They will have mounted patrols, Tip.''

"Do I no ken that? Does not the master? Mistress, ye've ventured into a business best managed by them who've managed it these hundred years and more.''

"I warrant you are right,'' Janet said with a sigh, resisting the impulse to point out that neither Tip nor his beloved master had been doing anything for a hundred years. "I cannot get it out of my head that they will need help tonight. How could I live with myself if I ignored that voice and something dreadful happened to them?''

"Aye, that'd be gey hard, that would,'' Tip agreed.

"So you see, then.''

He did not speak for some moments. Then he said, "I see, mistress, but I dinna think that either of us will persuade the master of such a need.''

She sighed again. "What will he do, Tip—to you, I mean?''

"Best if we dinna think about that,'' he muttered.

Guilt nearly sank her determination then, for it was as clear as if he had spoken the words aloud that he had resigned himself to a dire fate.

"I'll not let him flog you,'' she said fiercely.

"If ye can stop him, ye're mightier than I think ye be,'' Tip said.

Janet swallowed hard. "Should we go back, then? I do not want you hurt.''

Silence. Then Tip said, "Nay, then, we've come this far. We might as well go a bit farther and see what's o'clock." He gave spur to his pony.

Relieved, Janet followed, hoping hers would have sense enough to avoid stepping into a hole.

They passed through Larriston village without seeing so much as a dog or a cat. If any people remained in the cottages, they were keeping sensibly out of sight. Shortly afterward, Janet discerned the shadowy outline of Saughtree atop the next rise, but before they reached the village, Tip turned south. They rode uphill for a time after that, keeping to the darkest shadows and listening carefully as they rode.

The ponies' hooves made little sound on the grass-covered ground, but Janet knew that sound carried far in the night and that the two of them had to be making more noise than one. Still, she was increasingly grateful for Tip's company. She would not have wanted to be alone in the wavering dark shadows.

Sounds of a bubbling burn reached her ears, and she was glad to hear it. They were approaching the pass, the most likely place for watchers, but surely the noise of the burn would cover any sound she and Tip or their ponies made.

She barely saw movement when Tip put one hand in the air, but she had been watching and drew rein at once. They were in deep shadow on a shrub-clad hillside.

Tip slid from his saddle, tied his reins to a handy branch, and moved silently back to her.

Leaning down, she murmured, "What is it? What do you hear?"

"Naught," he replied. "But we'd be fools to ride farther without first making certain the way ahead be clear. We'll no follow the track, any road, but keep well to the right of it. There be another way—along that hillside yonder—and I dinna think the English ken that the wee track exists. A deer would ha' trouble seeing it, the master says, and he kens it fine."

"Will you leave me here, then, whilst you look?"

"Ye can come along if ye like, but ye'd be safer here. 'Tis dark and 'tis off the usual track and not easily stumbled on by them wha' dinna ken it fine.''

What he was thinking, she knew, was that he would fare better without her. He was more accustomed than she was to moving quietly when an enemy was at hand. She was rapidly coming to a new assessment of her prowess, and she did not much like it. Suppressing an unexpected shiver of fear at being left, she said, ''Go then, Tip. I'll stay with the horses. What do I do if I see someone?''

''Ye'll no stay wi' the ponies,'' he said. ''We'll draw them well into the brush, and ye'll keep low under cover a wee distance awa'. That road, if someone should stumble over them, they willna find ye as weel.''

His tone was matter-of-fact, but his words shot another shiver up Janet's spine. Her courage had fled, and she was not certain that she would recover it. Moments later, she was alone in the dark. The mist had thickened, casting a veil across the moon. Its pale glow still shimmered through, barely illuminating objects on the ground, but she could not see as well as she had earlier.

Telling herself that she was safer in the dimmer light did not help, for she could no longer see Tip. She had lost sight of him almost immediately, and she could discern no stirring of shrubbery or other movement or sound that betrayed his whereabouts. He might as well have been a ghost that had vanished. If he were captured or had already been captured, she would not know until he failed to return.

Just the thought gave her new shivers. What would she do? She could not be certain that Quinton would return the way he had gone. He was as likely to make for the Kershopefoot crossing. Indeed, that was the very reason that her anxieties had stirred, because she feared that Hugh would capture him again and hang him before anyone even knew that Hugh had taken him.

Gritting her teeth, she told herself to stop being such a fool.

Her instincts had told her to follow, and she had. She would be at hand when she was needed. She knew it—or so she assured herself.

Minutes dragged into longer minutes, till it seemed as if hours had passed. Common sense told her it had not been as long as that, that time simply had slowed to a crawl. She must not let impatience stir her to do anything foolish. Still, each minute dragged until twenty of them seemed like a year.

Listening, all she could hear was the nearby burn bubbling and sloshing over rocks and boulders as it tumbled downhill to join the Tyne at Kielbeck. What was happening there, she did not know, nor could she. If only, she thought, she could turn off her thinking, could just sleep with her eyes open, so that she would see any danger that came but would not imagine any that would not come.

Movement in nearby brush startled her. She nearly scrambled up to see what it was, then told herself firmly that it was naught but one of the horses moving. Logic told her, however, that the horses were too far away. She might hear a whicker if one were so forgetful of its training as to make that much noise, but she would not hear it if it simply moved a little. The noise came again.

Janet flattened herself to the ground, willing the bushes around her to cover her completely.

"They've been this way, rot their devilish hides, and not long ago, neither."

Stifling a gasp at the sound of the man's voice only paces away, she flattened more and tried to inch her way under the nearest bush.

At that very moment, a large foot came down upon her calf, and she failed to stifle a cry of pain.

"Well, well, well, what have we got here?"

Chapter 14

"The English rogues may hear, and drie
The weight o' their braid swords to feel."

Though Janet wished she could disappear into the earth, she sat up and brushed off her hands, then nearly held one out for the man to help her up before she recalled her disguise. Remembering, she got slowly to her feet, fearing that if she got up too quickly he might knock her down again.

"Ye frighted me, sir," she said, trying to make her voice sound low and common, and succeeding only in making it sound gruff.

"What the devil are ye doin' here, lad? I might as easily have spit ye through as stepped on ye."

"I thank ye for doing nowt o' the sort," she said. Though it was her nature to stand straight and look directly at people, she kept her eyes lowered and let her shoulders slump, knowing that it would make her look smaller and less threatening.

"What ha' ye found there, Gibby?"

A second man approached, and the one called Gibby said,

"Just a lad out on the prowl, Lem. Tell me, lad, ha' ye seen any raiders the night?"

"Nay, sir," Janet said. "I'm shamed to tell ye something spooked my pony when I were riding half asleep. Might ha' been raiders, though I think 'twas naught but a night bird's call."

The newcomer came nearer, leading two ponies by their reins, and Janet watched him warily from the corner of one eye, sizing him up. She did not think Gibby would notice her interest in his companion. The light was not strong enough for him to perceive that she was not still looking at the ground.

The one called Lem looked taller and much thinner than Gibby, for Gibby's shadowy figure seemed almost square. There was not enough light to see their faces clearly, but Lem sported a pointy beard and Gibby looked clean-shaven, albeit a trifle scruffy.

A rustle in nearby shrubbery made both men jump, but when no other sound rose above the bubbling of the burn, they returned their attention to Janet.

She wondered where Tip had gone and hoped that he would not make his presence known if he came back while the two were still with her. He was unarmed, just as she was, but for her dagger, and he would be of little help to her.

"Where d'ye hail from, lad?" It was the second man, Lem, who asked.

"Brackengill," she said instantly. "What of ye? Be ye land sergeant's men?"

"Aye, from Bewcastle," Lem said. "Brackengill, eh? Who's your master?"

"Sir Hugh Graham," she said, as if surprised that he would ask. "D'ye no ken the man?"

Gibby said, "I saw him once. He's a big man, Sir Hugh is, wi' a fearsome temper to match his size."

"Aye," Janet agreed. The two clearly were not Grahams then. She had thought they could not be, but with a clan so large, and with members living on both sides of the line, she did not know them all.

"Let's ha' a closer look at ye, lad," Lem said, and before Janet realized his intent, he snatched the knitted cap from her head. "Christ's foot," he exclaimed when her long, silvery-blond hair spilled free, "he's a wench!"

Grabbing for the cap, she cried, "Give that back!"

"Oh, aye, sure," Lem said, laughing and twitching the cap up out of her reach. "What the devil is a wee lass like yourself doing out in the night like this?"

"I . . . I came to meet someone," she said, hoping that he would leave her be if he believed that another man was coming. "He's as large as Sir Hugh," she added.

"Is he now? I warrant he'll share his good fortune though, or will he not?"

"No!" She tried to run, but Gibby caught her arm.

His grip was tight, but he said, "We should let her go, Lem. The sergeant willna like it an we dawdle wi' her."

"He won't mind if we take him the wee lass as a gift," Lem said.

"How dare you!" Janet exclaimed. "I'll have you know that I am—"

About to identify herself as sister to Sir Hugh Graham, she bit off the words. The likelihood of Hugh's hearing about the incident was too great if she proclaimed their relationship, and that would do her no good. Moreover, it occurred to her that they might take her straight to him in hopes of a reward, and that was the last thing she wanted. Hugh would not hesitate to hold her for ransom if he thought it would embarrass Sir Quinton or Buccleuch. Indeed, he would relish the chance.

"Well, lass, who are ye then?" Lem's tone was matter-of-fact, even kindly, but when she did not answer, he said, "I thought as much. If ye'll no tell us your name, we must assume that ye dinna hail from Brackengill as ye claim but are one wi' them thievin' Scots. Who did ye ride with?"

"No one," she said miserably. "I came here on my own

and lost my horse just as I told you. No one else knows that I am here.''

Lem chuckled. ''Ye followed your man, did ye? Ye ha' more courage than sense, lassie. I think ye'll make our sergeant a fine gift, but mayhap we should just test that to see if ye'll be worth his sport.''

Appalled at his obvious intent, she jerked away and tried to free herself from Gibby, but Lem caught her free wrist and yanked her toward him.

Gibby let go before she was stretched between the two of them. ''Lem,'' he said anxiously, ''I dinna think—''

''Hush your gob, lad. A chance like this does not come to a man every day. She's a wee winsome one in breeks, is she not? I've a mind to see her without them, though, and I'll warrant ye won't mind taking your turn when I'm done wi' her.''

Janet tried to scream, but the sound caught in her throat, and before she could force it free, Lem had clapped a filthy hand over her mouth, stifling any second attempt. His other hand grabbed the front of her jerkin. She grabbed for her dagger.

''Mind her feet, Gib,'' Lem warned when she struggled, ''and get them breeks off her. Quick now!''

Quin and the others, having struck swiftly and without warning, had successfully taught the citizenry of Kielbeck a lesson in raiding. Hob the Mouse and Willie Bell swept the livestock from the green in a trice and were driving them swiftly toward the Larriston Fells. They had taken no sheep, but they had taken every horse and cow in the village, many of which they recognized as their own from earlier raids on Liddesdale and Upper Teviotdale.

Quin rode ahead of the livestock with half of his men. The other half followed to protect them against an attack from the rear. With such a small party, he had not left anyone to guard their route, trusting to his instincts and knowledge of the land to get them home safely.

As they approached forestland at the foot of the fells, he slowed and turned to Curst Eckie Crosier, who rode beside him. "Fall back and tell the others that you and I will ride ahead. They are to proceed carefully, listening for warning from us. If we encounter a patrol, I'll fire a shot to draw its members after us, and you and I will lead them away. If our lads see anyone, tell Jed to sound his horn, and we'll return at once."

"Aye, I'll tell them," Curst Eckie said. Wheeling his pony, he rode off, returning minutes later. "They'll listen and watch well, master," he said.

"Then let's ride." Urging his horse to a faster pace, he led the way into the woods, knowing from experience that English patrols generally did not ride without light. They carried torches that threatened to set fire to any woodland through which they passed, and they rode without giving much thought to the noise their passing created. So long as he could hear night birds calling to each other from the trees, he knew that he and his men were safe from all but the more silent, generally well-hidden two-man patrols. Tonight, though, he thought he could count on the English to mount only plump watches. Against those, a small group like his would remain safe if they stayed alert.

He slowed to let his eyes adjust to the deeper darkness of the forest, and soon he could pick his path easily by the pale glow of mist-veiled moonlight where it filtered through the canopy. His pony's hooves made but slight noise on the soft forest floor, and although he could hear Curst Eckie's pony behind him, he doubted that the noise carried more than a dozen feet, if that far.

The burn flowing through the forest on its way to join the Tyne made a hushing sound like the rustling of a lady's silk skirts. As they made their way toward the heights, he kept his ears attuned to the forest sounds, particularly for any alteration in them. He knew that when they reached the heights, the route would grow more perilous, for recent rains had made boggy areas more treacherous than usual. At the same time, though, those rains were responsible for the soft footing beneath them, so he could not complain.

So certain was he that no one lurked nearby that the figure that sprang out of the shrubbery just ahead startled him into a hastily choked cry as he snatched his sword from its scabbard.

"Nay, master, hold!" The muttered words carried easily to his sharp ears, and possibly to Curst Eckie's, although they would not have carried farther.

"Tip! What the devil are you doing out here? You frightened the liver out of me. What's amiss?"

"The mistress," Tip said. "English louts ha' captured her, and they dinna sound like gentlemen."

"Where? Never tell me you've come afoot all the way from Broadhaugh!"

"Nay, master. They be yonder, on the heights."

"How did you escape?"

"I left her and the ponies for a few wee moments to look for watchers. She were well away from the ponies, though, and well concealed," he added hastily. "I thought she'd be gey safe, master, truly! But when I crept back, I heard voices. There be but two of them wi' her, I think, but they mean her nae good."

"I won't ask what the devil you meant by bringing her here. There is no time for that now, but tell me this. Did you follow our tracks?"

"Aye, sir, as near as I could."

"Then I know where to go. I'll take Curst Eckie, for he'll be more use in a fight than you would be. You wait for the others here and ride with one of them. You and I will talk later."

"Aye," Tip said miserably. "I dinna doubt it."

Signing to Eckie to follow, Quin urged his pony to greater speed, no longer caring if there were patrols about.

* * *

When Janet tried to grab her dagger, Lem stopped her and tossed it aside. She fought like a netted wildcat then, kicking and scratching whatever part of either man she could reach, and she had the satisfaction of feeling her foot connect hard with a soft part of Gibby's anatomy just as she sank her teeth into someone's hand. Her sole reward was a double bellow of pain that told her the hand belonged to Lem. In moments, though, her breeks were down around her calves and the jerkin she wore had been ripped open and shoved halfway down her arms, pinning them back as tightly as any ropes could have done.

No sooner had she bitten Lem than he slapped her hard across her face. The next thing she knew she was on her back with her legs tangled in the breeks, her arms twisted painfully beneath her, and nasty-tasting cloth jammed into her mouth, threatening to choke her.

Lem's big hands clutched her breasts, his long, skinny fingers squeezing and pinching till she groaned with pain, gaining little protection from the shirt she wore.

Gibby muttered, "Make haste, Lem! What if someone comes?"

"Shut yer gob! I thought I told ye to get them breeks off her."

"She kicked me in the bollocks!"

"She won't do it again. Yank them off!" He put his face inches from Janet's, adding, "If ye kick, lass, I'll use my fist to knock your teeth down your throat."

His breath stank, and she turned her face away, still working her tongue to push the horrible gag from her mouth. He pawed at her shirt lacing, then grabbed a handful of the material and tried to rip it off her, but the coarse cloth did not yield. Finally, putting a leg across her body to pin her to the ground, he used both hands and ripped the shirt down the middle, baring her breasts to the cold air. At the same time, Gibby yanked hard on her breeks, jerking them to her ankles.

"Get off her now," a stern voice said grimly, "and I'll grant you each one more minute of life before I send you to the devil."

Janet felt Lem stiffen atop her and heard Gibby gasp. She did not instantly recognize the disembodied voice in the darkness. Only as the two men scrambled away from her did she hear its echo in her mind and know that it was Quinton. Relief surged through her, and she grabbed the torn bits of shirt and clutched them together, concealing her breasts as she struggled to sit.

"Godamercy, 'tis Rabbie Redcloak," Gibby gasped. "We're sped!"

Lem snarled, "Shut ycr gob, ye blazing fool. D'ye want him to shoot us down like dogs?"

"I have considerably more regard for dogs," Quinton said gently.

"Ye'd best be gone from here whilst ye can," Lem muttered. "Ye're a murdering thief, and half the Border's aroused the night, searching for ye."

"Aye, but they are not here now, my lad."

"If ye fire that pistol, we'll soon see how far away they be."

"A point to you," Sir Quinton admitted. "Moreover, despite what you may have heard to the contrary, I am no murderer. Have you got a sword, lout, or must we wrestle like bairns?"

"Master, no!"

Janet heard the second voice, but she was not certain that either Lem or Gibby had. She did not recognize it, so she knew that it was not Tip or Hob the Mouse. She wondered where Tip had gone. Was it he who had fetched Sir Quinton, or had Sir Quinton and the second man stumbled onto them just as Gibby had stumbled onto her? And where were Hob and the rest of Rabbie Redcloak's Bairns?

She managed to sit up and to shrug the leather jerkin up where it belonged, but pulling up the breeks would require extreme finesse if she were not to bare her nether parts again. Where the devil had her cloak gone?

Quinton had not said a word to her. Another thought followed that one, and the profound relief she had felt evaporated. She dared not speak to him either—not as a wife to her husband in front of Lem and Gibby. Her eyes pricked with tears, and her throat ached, but she dared not cry. Even if Quinton forgave her for the rest, she would not soon forgive herself. She realized that her cloak lay beneath her. Using it to cover herself, she struggled back into the breeks.

For the few short moments that had passed since Quinton's demand to know if Lem carried a sword, she had watched their dark shapes and Gibby's. Quinton had slipped from his saddle, ignoring his companion's warning. Neither Lem nor Gibby had said another word.

"Well," Quinton said, "have you got a sword or do you patrol unarmed?"

"I've got a sword," Lem growled. " 'Tis yonder where I set it whilst I—"

"Whilst you raped a defenseless lass, or did you think her a lad you could—"

"I never!" Lem seemed more upset by the suggestion of buggery than by the imminence of his death.

"What of you?" Sir Quinton said to Gibby, ignoring Lem's indignation. "Have you got a sword? I'll fight you both at once, if you like. I warn you, though, if you do not fight fair, my man will shoot you down where you stand."

"I do not want to fight you at all," Gibby said, sounding close to tears.

Choosing her words and accent with care, Janet said, "He did try to stop the other one, sir. I dinna think he would ha' troubled me on his own."

Sir Quinton did not glance her way, but he said to Gibby, "Stand aside then, lad, but heed my warning. If you interfere, you'll soon meet the devil in Hell."

Scrambling back out of the way, Gibby held his hands out

at his sides as if to assure him that he carried no weapon. Janet also moved aside, not wanting to watch, yet terrified that somehow Lem would gain the upper hand and Sir Quinton might die. If that happened, it would be no one's fault but her own, and she did not think that she could live with such knowledge about herself.

Quinton raised his sword but made no attack, waiting for the other man to come to him. Lem, watching him, feinted slightly, but when Quinton did not leap to the bait, he lunged forward with more confidence, thrusting directly at his heart. Quinton parried the cut easily on the outside of his blade and returned a thrust to Lem's face, holding short.

Janet, who had often watched Hugh practice his swordsmanship, needed only a short time to recognize that her husband was by far the better swordsman, that he was merely toying with Lem. To behave so in such poor light when he might easily misjudge the other man's movement seemed foolhardy. Also, she noted, he had failed to remove his cloak, which was another gesture of foolhardiness, since it could only encumber his movement. It was as if he mocked Lem. He seemed to encourage Lem's thrusting and parrying, giving him a false sense of confidence.

Lem threatened with a series of sham moves and false attacks, feints that Hugh called "fluttering," but Sir Quinton parried each with a gentle twist of the wrist, deftly keeping his blade where he could deflect Lem's point.

Janet saw that Lem was tiring, that his footwork had grown less sure. He slipped, and Sir Quinton quickly pulled back his sword, waiting for him to recover.

"Be damned to ye, Redcloak! Make an end of it."

"Did he hurt you, lass?" Sir Quinton asked matter-of-factly as he parried another thrust.

"Only my pride," she answered. "You arrived in time to prevent the rest."

"I do not need a female's protection," Lem snarled, leaping

forward again, his sword aimed straight at Sir Quinton's mid-section. ''By God, 'tis not me who will see the devil in Hell!''

With another deft parry, Sir Quinton picked up the tempo, lunging forward, catching Lem's blade and disengaging only to attack again. Leaping forward, he forced the other man back and back, then eased, letting Lem come to him again.

When Lem did, cutting and thrusting more recklessly, Janet's chest tightened. She could feel her heartbeat and hardly dared to breathe, for the two men looked like shades from Hades flitting about in the moonlight. The only sounds were their breathing, the faint noises of their feet on the ground, and the metallic clashing of the swords. Even the hushing sound of the burn had faded away. Sir Quinton's cloak flapped around him, making him look like a giant black moth.

''Yield,'' he snapped suddenly, harshly. ''I'll grant your life if you'll yield.''

''Never! You shall yield to me, Rabbie Redcloak,'' Lem cried. ''They'll sing ballads to me from this night on.'' He leapt forward, sword flashing.

Instead of parrying the straight thrust, Sir Quinton whipped out his left arm and caught the blade with his cloak, at the same time thrusting hard and true with his sword at full length, deeply piercing Lem's exposed right armpit.

With a gasp of dismay, the Englishman collapsed. Horrid sounds followed, and Janet turned away, feeling sick.

A moment later, she felt strong hands on her shoulders. They turned her and she looked up into her husband's grim face.

''You killed him,'' she said.

''Did you think I would not?''

''I did not know.''

''He left me no choice, but I am sorry that you had to see it. Say no more now,'' he added in a tone that brooked no argument. Then, turning away, he said to Gibby, ''You, lad, tell me this. Do you want to claim his body and return it to his people, or shall we bury him here and leave a cairn to mark the spot?''

"Would ye dispatch me an I say I want to take him back?"

"Nay, then, I offered a free choice," Sir Quinton said. "The lass said you tried to protect her, so you may choose to remain with the body or ride on with us."

"With ye? Ye'd take me wi' ye?"

"Aye, if you want to come. What is your name?"

"They call me Gibby—Gibby Potts."

"A Redesdale man, then. I've a few Pottses amongst my followers."

"Aye, there be Pottses on both sides, I ken."

"Choose, then."

"I'll stay wi' Lem, an it's all the same to ye, sir."

"Good lad. Shall we help you bury him, or will your people tend to him?"

"We'll do it, but I do think the better of ye that ye'd help me."

"We are not barbarians," Sir Quinton said gruffly.

New sounds in the night heralded the arrival of the rest of his men, and for a moment, Gibby looked terrified, but Sir Quinton reassured him with a gesture.

Janet, seeing pale moonlight glint on metal and recognizing her dagger, swiftly took the opportunity to pick it up and put it back in her sheath.

Ten minutes later, Tip had recovered his horse and Janet's, and their party mounted and rode away, leaving Gibby in forlorn attendance on his dead comrade.

Janet rode behind Sir Quinton and the man she learned was Curst Eckie, with Tip beside her. Hob the Mouse and others followed. Sir Quinton had not invited her to ride beside him, nor did she want to do so. She did not think that he would scold her in front of his men, but she could not be certain that he would not.

That he was angry with her was plain. None of his men spoke to her either. At first she told herself that they rode quietly because they still risked meeting a patrol, but once they were safely back in Scotland, she knew that was not the case.

They remained quiet because they did not want to risk angering either their leader or his lady.

As they descended toward the Liddel, the ramparts of Hermitage loomed on the horizon like a great black shadow in the moonlight. She was surprised, though, after they crossed, when Sir Quinton drew rein before their party could stir interest from guards on the castle ramparts.

Quietly he said to Curst Eckie, "You take some of these lads and help drive the livestock north along the water past Sandy Edge, till you reach Stirling Water. Follow that to Broadhaugh. Send the others home by the most expeditious route."

"Aye, master."

Hob the Mouse, riding just behind Janet and Tip, murmured, "Master, how many of us d'ye mean to keep with ye?"

"Just you and three others, Hob. Choose men with fast ponies. I'm for home straightaway, and my own bed. Tip," he added, "you'll ride with Hob and the others. You and I will talk in the morning. My lass will ride with me now."

Janet half expected him to snatch her from her saddle to ride pillion with him, and braced herself to resist, but he did not even speak to her. When he gave spur to his pony and rode ahead, leaving her to decide for herself whether to obey his implicit command or stay with his men, his action caught her by surprise.

Half tempted to linger behind, she decided that would only make him angrier and just delay the inevitable confrontation. Reminding herself that she was no coward, and pushing the contradicting memory of Lem and Gibby out of her mind, she rode after him, hoping her pony could see better than she could.

Chapter 15

"Who stood unmov'd at his approach
His fury to repel."

Sir Quinton slowed when they reached the woodland at the foot of Cauldcleuch Head, allowing her to catch up. Hob and the other three remained a discreet distance behind.

Janet urged her mount nearer to Quinton's but was glad to find that the track was too narrow there to let them ride abreast. It widened on the downward side of the pass, but she stayed where she was, waiting to see what he would do.

He did not say a word to her, and they rode the entire ten miles from Hermitage to Broadhaugh in silence. When they entered the bailey, he dismounted and turned away, and for a moment she thought that he meant to leave her to face his men alone in her breeks and boots.

He shouted, "Ferdie, come take the ponies in, will you?"

"Aye, laird." A groom came running from the stable, looking bright-eyed and alert, despite clearly having waited up for his master's return.

Sir Quinton looked at her. "Can you get down by yourself?"

"Aye," she said, suiting action to words but feeling the last of her courage desert her. When her feet hit the cobblestones, her knees nearly betrayed her. She straightened, hoping she had her clothing all in place and that nothing revealed her struggle with Gibby and Lem. Drawing Quinton's cloak more closely around her, she turned to follow him, still avoiding his eye and those of the others.

Apparently deciding that she would follow him, Sir Quinton turned and strode toward the main entrance.

Hesitating long enough to decide that she would gain nothing by dawdling, Janet hurried after him, knowing that every man who saw her must be wondering at her odd appearance and at their master's unusual behavior toward her.

Inside, she followed him upstairs, past the great hall and the master's hall.

"Please, sir, where—?"

"Not now," he said curtly, silencing her again.

When they reached his bedchamber, he pushed the door open, letting it bang back against the wall, then crossed to the far side of the room, where he stopped.

She eyed him warily from the threshold, her tension increasing considerably when he did not turn at once to face her.

The silence lengthened till she said, "Please, I know that you are angry—"

He turned sharply then, saying, "Hold your tongue, and shut that door unless you want every man-jack in the place to hear what I am going to say to you."

Her throat threatened to close, making it difficult to breathe. She had never before seen such a look of fury on anyone's face. His anger made Hugh's on any occasion that she could call to mind pale by comparison. Her knees had felt weak before, but now they shook. Though her instinct was to flee, not only did she suspect that her legs would not support her but she knew that Quinton would easily catch her and that she would have succeeded only in angering him more.

Gathering what courage she could, she shut the door, trying

to do so with dignity to show that she would obey him but that she did not fear him. Although she felt warm and would have liked to take off the cloak, she did not think it wise to display her breeks again so soon. She forced herself to breathe deeply, hoping to calm her nerves so that she could hold her own in the confrontation ahead. He did not rush her, and for that she was grateful. By the time she turned from shutting the door to face him again, she felt more like her normal, competent self.

One look into his blazing eyes, however, and her resolve evaporated. She opened her mouth to speak, but he kept her silent with a slight gesture.

"Not one word," he said grimly. "Stay right where you are, too. I have not dared to touch you, because I fear what I might do to you if I do. I am no bully, Jenny, but neither will I allow you to make me look like a fool or a felon. Tonight I killed a man out of nothing more than plain fury."

"I know that I should not have—"

"No, you should not," he snapped, "but you did, and the consequences may be much more than you bargained for. You did not spare a thought for consequence, though. That much is plain. You did not think about how your actions would affect others—not just me, but the men who rode with me. Supposing that instead of those two louts you met, you had met your brother with a hundred men? Do you think he would simply have sent you back to Broadhaugh?"

"But I did think of Hugh. Not at once," she amended hastily, "but later, when I nearly told those two that I was his sister. I realized before I spoke the words that they might turn me over to him and that he would be as likely to hold me for ransom as to return me to you."

"Much more likely, I'd say, but that is not all." His tone was calmer now, as if he had regained some control over his temper, but he still sounded grim when he said, "Have you considered yet what will be the most likely consequence of my killing the scoundrel who tried to rape you?"

She had not, but she did, and the possibilities chilled her.

"Surely anyone would understand that you were protecting me," she said.

"Oh, aye, I'm sure of it," he said, and she could not mistake the sarcasm in his tone. "I have only to explain to the wardens at Truce Day that two men attacked my wife on the English side of the line some moments after a Scottish raid on Kielbeck. I would, of course, explain that the raid had naught to do with it, that she merely tripped over two English watchers during an evening stroll—"

"Quinton, stop! First of all, *they* tripped over me. I lay completely concealed from them, for I did not stir a step from where Tip left me. Had that lad, Gibby, not left his companion and come afoot—"

"He was most likely looking for a place to relieve himself," Quinton retorted. "What would you have done if, instead of stepping on you, he had pissed on you?"

She winced, feeling flames leap to her cheeks.

He said, "What you might have done then does not matter, nor would such a tale influence the wardens or a jury. No one would believe it."

"But your Bairns would back any tale you told!"

"Would they? Perhaps they would if I were such a rogue as to ask that of them. Have you stopped to think how they would explain their presence on the English side of the line? Beyond that, have you stopped to think that perhaps Scrope and his jury would believe only that my men were supporting a tale made up to excuse cold-blooded murder?"

"But—"

"No, Jenny, don't try to excuse your behavior. There is no excuse. You defied my orders, and I won't tolerate that from anyone at Broadhaugh. I am master here, not you, and the sooner you learn that, the better it will be."

"What are you going to do?"

"You deserve that I should put you across my knee and teach you to submit to my commands. I may yet do that, but

I am too angry with you to chance it now when my inclination
is to use my riding whip rather than the flat of my hand."

She shut her eyes to the image his words stirred. He had
every right to punish her as he chose, but even Hugh had never
taken a whip to her.

"You will keep to your bedchamber until I am in a better
frame of mind to deal with you," he said. "If you are wise,
you will exert yourself to please me for some days to come.
Go up now, and do not come down again until I send for you."

Fearing that if she tried to speak, she would lose her temper
and shout at him—at which point he would most likely make
good his threat to whip her—she turned on her heel and left
the room. She could not resist shutting the door with a bang,
however, and by the time she reached her bedchamber, her
fury had taken fire. He was wrong to be angry, and she had
been right to go.

Her instincts had not misled her. Had she not followed him,
Lem and Gibby would have lain in wait for the Bairns. They
could easily have summoned a larger patrol, and Quinton and
the Bairns would have been captured. She knew it would be
useless now to debate the point with him, though. Like Hugh,
he would refuse to listen and would simply react, most likely
with violence. She would not allow him to cow her, however,
nor would she try to coax him into a better frame of mind. By
morning she would be well away from Broadhaugh.

Quin stood staring into the flames in the fireplace, fighting
to control his anger and other, less familiar emotions that warred
with it. He had hated sending her away. He had wanted to hold
her. Just thinking of what she must have felt when the English
lout ripped her shirt off made him feel sick. Even now, he
wanted to go to her bedchamber, to hold her tight and make
sure she really was all right.

He could not do it, though. She had to learn to obey him.
Anything else was too dangerous, and she seemed constitution-

ally incapable of understanding that. He admired her courage as much as he admired her beauty, but he did not admire her stubborn nature or her defiance. Clearly, she was too accustomed to getting her own way, to doing exactly as she pleased. She thought she had lived under Sir Hugh's thumb, but Quin knew that it could have been no such thing. Had she lived so, she would never have dared to defy his orders and follow him from Broadhaugh as she had. She would have learned to show proper submission to masculine authority.

Since Sir Hugh had failed, he would have to teach her himself, but at the moment he did not know how he would do so.

He did not know what he was going to do about Tip either. The man had done all that anyone could have expected short of calling for others to help him lock their mistress in her bedchamber. Quin's lips twitched at the thought, but he quickly grew sober again, knowing what he would have done to any man—even one of his own—who had dared to lay hands on his Jenny.

The fact was that he did not think any of them would have dared. Tip would have been the most likely, and only to the extent that Quin believed the little man would have locked his mistress in her room could he have but thought of a way to do so without carrying her there. There was no such way, however, none that Tip could have achieved without Jenny's cooperation.

Tip expected a flogging, and for disobeying his master's command to remain within the walls of Broadhaugh he deserved one. Certainly the other lads would expect him to suffer for helping Jenny in her mad venture. That argument no sooner occurred to Quin, however, than another voice piped up in the back of his mind, reminding him that Tip had fairly flown through the boggy darkness to find him. The little man had kept his head and had put aside any fear of consequence to himself to save Jenny. For that, he deserved a substantial reward.

Quin was accustomed to the conflicting voices in his head,

for he had heard them all his life. He had only to decide to do a thing to hear a quite reasonable voice in his mind telling him that a better way existed. Over the years he had learned to make decisions, even difficult ones, despite the ceaseless mental debates; and he believed that the constant questioning and rethinking made him a wiser leader than he would have been without it. Nonetheless, there were times when he wished that he were not always so conscious of the fact that questions generally seemed to invite more than one reasonable answer.

It occurred to him then to wonder what, exactly, Jenny had thought she could accomplish by following him, and this time his fertile imagination swiftly produced an answer. She had not trusted him to see his Bairns or himself safely home again. Knowing that he had failed once, she had expected him to fail again.

His anger was stirring anew when a soft meow startled him. Glancing over his shoulder, he saw Jemmy Whiskers emerging from behind the bed curtain, where apparently he had been curled up on a favored pillow.

"What do you want?" Quin demanded, even as he realized that Jenny had probably already missed the little cat and was wondering where it was.

Jemmy Whiskers stretched, then sat and scratched an ear.

"Here," Quin said curtly, striding to open the bedchamber door. "Go and find Jenny. Go on now. Scat!"

Jemmy Whiskers cocked his head, blinked, then casually raised a forepaw and began to clean his face.

Quin strode back to the bed, picked the cat up, and carried it to the threshold. Setting it down outside the bedchamber, he firmly shut the door and returned to his contemplation of the fire.

Moments later a soft scratching announced Jemmy Whiskers' desire to return. Quin resisted a strong temptation to let him in, and with difficulty forced himself to ignore the persistent, rhythmic sound until it stopped.

* * *

Janet paced the floor of her bedchamber, trying to concentrate, determined this time to make a plan that would not instantly fail. Recalling the details that Tip had pointed out to her before, she realized that as much as she wanted to do so, it would not be possible to escape from Broadhaugh during the night. She would be wiser to wait until morning and hope that her husband had not issued strict orders that would prevent her from leaving.

He had no cause to do so, she told herself. Doubtless he would expect her to obey an order he had so sternly given her. She would not be so meek, however. Even with Hugh she had established her own way of accomplishing things, of getting her way in matters that were important to her, and of taking part in any significant event at Brackengill. In truth, she had never succeeded in bending Hugh to her will, nor had she ever really tried to do that.

With the world ruled by men, as it generally was (Elizabeth of England notwithstanding), it was practically impossible for any woman to rule any man. It was certainly not as easy as it was for men to rule women. But there were ways, nonetheless, of avoiding total subjugation, of standing up for things in which one believed, of persuading men to do right. If Hugh had not succeeded in crushing her spirit, no Scotsman would do so.

She was grateful to Sir Quinton for his protection, and she admired the love and respect that his men conferred upon him, but she also saw much of Hugh in his domineering ways. Both men demanded respect but did not seem to respect her. She had not expected Quinton to pay her compliments after the night's disastrous events, but she did think he might at least have considered the possibility that events could have transpired differently. Only the fact that she had met Lem and Gibby had prevented them from ambushing the Bairns. If that had happened, she could easily imagine ways in which her proximity to the scene might have proved helpful.

As her husband, Quinton had every legal right to demand her obedience, and she knew that each time she defied his authority he would seek to reestablish it. Still, she could not let him shut her out of things that affected her, things that would affect their people at Broadhaugh, things that would affect their children when they had children. As his wife, she wanted the right at least to express her opinions before he plunged them all into danger.

She understood his loyalty to his men and theirs to him, but she believed that it was time he began to grow into his new duties as a husband and deputy warden, and prepared for the much greater ones he would shoulder when the two countries became one. Whether he found himself guardian to Buccleuch's heir or merely served as landowner and laird in his own right, he would have great responsibilities when the Union at last brought peace to the Borders.

She continued her pacing while these thoughts and others of their ilk paraded through her mind, until at last she pulled off her garments, shoved them into the bottom of the wardrobe, and crawled naked under the counterpane. Although she was certain that her thoughts would keep her awake until she had thought of a plan to escape from Broadhaugh—at least long enough for Quinton to understand the difference she had made there—her scheming lasted only until her head settled into the pillow. Within minutes, she was fast asleep.

When Ardith woke Janet soon after sunrise, she opened her eyes and shut them again with a groan of protest.

" 'Tis already light outside, mistress," Ardith said. "The days do be growing longer each sennight, ye ken. Ye can see sun through the mist, and I'm thinking 'twill be clear long before the morning be gone, although they do be saying we'll see rain again soon. Did ye no sleep well the nicht?"

Realizing from the maid's cheerful greeting that the men had kept silent about her part in the previous night's activities, she called silent blessings upon them and upon her husband, as well. Clearly, he had not informed the servants that she was to stay in her bedchamber. Relieved, she tugged the quilt up a little so that Ardith would not realize that she was naked beneath it.

"I was up rather late," she admitted.

Ardith grinned, and her eyes twinkled. "I'll warrant ye stayed up till the master returned, and then some."

"Aye, I was awake then," Janet said, ignoring her fluttering conscience.

"Ye mun be fair trauchled, m'lady," Ardith said. "Mayhap ye'd prefer to lie abed for another hour yet."

"I'll get up," Janet said. "I am famished, Ardith, but I think I will break my fast here, rather than go downstairs. Perhaps whilst I wash, you could fetch me a bowl of porridge and some bread to toast over the fire."

"Aye, mistress, I'll see to it in a trice. I've already set out a clean smock and bodice for ye, and I stirred up the fire afore I woke ye."

"Thank you." Janet waited until the maid had gone before she got out of bed. Since she had taken off every stitch and had gone to bed in her skin, she knew that Ardith might assume certain things, and she did not want to deceive her more than she already had.

Scrambling into the clean smock and the first of her underpetticoats, she had tied the latter's ribbons and was reaching for her underbodice when she remembered that she had shoved the clothing she had taken off the night before into the bottom of the wardrobe. Telling herself it was a wonder that Ardith had not seen it there when she took out her clothes for the day, and certainly would later when she tidied the room, Janet went at once to put them away more carefully.

Folding the garments, she put them on the wardrobe's high shelf, where Ardith would be less likely to notice them. She would give the things back to Tip at the first opportunity.

Remembering her decision to leave, she looked thoughtfully

at her dresses. She had nearly decided to forego wearing a formal stiffened bodice, to make do with her underbodice alone; however, there was only one place she could go if she left Broadhaugh, and she did not want to arrive looking like a beggar.

Thus it was that when Ardith returned, carrying a tray, she found her mistress attired in her best silk underbodice and wearing a green satin petticoat over her everyday red flannel one. Janet had managed to tie the underbodice ribbons, but the busk-stiffened "pair of bodies" she would wear over it lay ready on the bed.

"I am going to wear the green velvet," she said calmly.

Ardith's eyes widened. "Do ye expect visitors, mistress?"

"No, but I mean to ride out to enjoy the day, and I want to keep warm."

"The sun will be shining bright afore noon."

"Perhaps," Janet said, relaxing at this further indication that Quinton had left no orders that would keep her in her bedchamber. " 'Tis still March nonetheless," she added smoothly. "I shall not smother in velvet. Is that my porridge?"

"Aye, mistress. I'll put it on the wee table yonder, shall I, whilst I help ye wi' your lacing?"

Janet nodded, and minutes later, the bodice firmly laced, she slipped a loose gown on to protect her from drafts while she broke her fast. Drawing a chair to the little table, she sat down and poured fresh cream over the hot porridge.

Ardith hung a small pot of milk to warm on the hob, saying over her shoulder, "I brought ye an apple, too, mistress."

"Excellent. I shall take it with me when I ride out."

"Ye'll be taking one o' the lads along. Mayhap I should tell Cook to put up some food for the pair o' ye, and some bits for them wha' ye visit? It isna baking day, but she will ha' buns or bread that she'll be gey happy to send wi' ye."

Janet hesitated. To say that she would take nothing would surely stir Ardith's curiosity, but she did not want to burden herself, nor did she want to visit tenants along the way.

Casually, she said, "Is Sir Quinton at home?"

"Nay, then, mistress. The master rode out quite early. Said he were going to Cotrigg village to see what needed doing. He willna return afore suppertime."

Janet began eating her porridge to give herself time to think. If Quinton was away, most likely no other barrier stood in her path. She did not believe that he would have given orders to prevent her leaving. He was a fair man, and he would assume that she would obey him. Moreover, he would not want to betray their quarrel to his men. The notion of his fairness stopped her train of thought for a moment, and niggling guilt made it difficult to continue.

She saw Ardith eyeing her curiously and quickly collected her wits, saying, " 'Tis good that he is looking after the people of Cotrigg. I should have known that he would be, of course. I am trying to think of anyone else who might need anything that I could take them today."

"Ye went to Tip's mam and the others but two days ago," Ardith said.

"Yes, I did, and the men will be dividing up the stock taken last night, I expect. Perhaps it would be wiser to wait until they have finished with that."

"Aye, sure, they'll ken fine then who might need summat else."

"I'll ride north along the Teviot then," Janet said with a smile. "I'm finished now, so you can help me with my dress."

As Ardith fetched the green velvet skirt from the wardrobe, Janet watched to see if she would notice Tip's clothing. It occurred to her then that Ardith might have smelled it the moment she opened the wardrobe, but she quickly realized that the strong scents of herbs and other sweeteners that customarily filled it ought to prevent that. In any event, the maid did not seem to notice anything amiss. Nor did she question her further about her plans, as any maidservant who had served her at Brackengill since childhood would have done as a matter of course. It was good, Janet decided, occasionally to have servants who did not believe that her every move was as much their business as her own.

Taking her whip and gloves from the table where she had laid them the night before, she let Ardith drape her cloak over her shoulders and declared herself ready. If the maid thought she looked too fine merely to be taking the air on a pleasant morning, she kept that opinion to herself.

By the time Janet reached the bailey, she had decided that she could not refuse an escort. If Quinton had said anything to the men it would be that she must not ride out alone. Indeed, knowing the ways of the Borders, his men were as likely to object to her riding out alone in broad daylight as Tip had been to object to her going alone the previous night. Thinking again of Tip, she wondered what his fate had been, and hoped that Quinton had not been too harsh.

She did not see the little man about, nor did she inquire after him. To have done so would have raised eyebrows unless she could think of a reason for wanting him. He was Sir Quinton's personal servant, and although he frequently offered to do her bidding, it was not her habit to send for him.

No more than the usual number of men attended to duties in the bailey or stable, and the lad she asked to saddle her horse simply gave a polite nod and shouted, "Ferdie, bring out her ladyship's pony and one for yourself. And dinna be wastin' time about it!"

Just as well, Janet decided, that she had decided to take someone with her.

Guilt stirred again when she saw the sidesaddle that Quinton had bought for her in Hawick, but she remained resolute. He had his good points, but if they were to live together for the rest of their lives, he had to learn to respect her opinions and her decisions. Putting her foot into Ferdie's cupped hands, she mounted quickly.

The guard at the postern gate grinned at her as he opened it. " 'Tis a fine soft mornin' for ridin', m'lady. Ye'll see the mist gone in less than an hour, I'm thinkin'." Then, stepping closer, as if he would speak without Ferdie's overhearing him, he added in a low tone, "Ye'll no be riding south now, will ye?"

"Just up along the dale," Janet said.

"Aye, that's good, that is. Ye'll be safe in the dale, but after last night I'm thinkin' the master wouldna like it an ye rode toward the Border. Them thievin' Kielbeck men be like to cross over, can they but find ponies to carry them." He chuckled, clearly believing they would find no horses left in Kielbeck.

"I'm sure I shall be safe," Janet said.

"Aye, she will," Ferdie said, drawing aside his short cloak to reveal a pistol underneath. "I've me bow along as well," he said, gesturing toward the longbow slung across his back.

"Aye, then," the guard said, "ye'll be as safe as a wee chick in its nest wi' Ferdie, mistress."

Smiling warmly at each of them, Janet rode through the gate and down the hill, giving spur to her mount when she reached the narrow track along the river. The increased speed exhilarated her, and she breathed deeply of the cool, damp morning air. Shreds of mist clung to tree branches, but she could see that new leaves were forming where none had been only two days before. Spring was stirring.

Ferdie was a taciturn man, but the noise of the fast-moving river would have precluded casual conversation in any case. Thus, Janet was alone with her thoughts, and they soon proved discomfiting. Despite the easy pace they settled into, she was well aware that she was leaving Broadhaugh behind. A sense of guilt began to nibble at her conscience. What would result from this latest impulse of hers?

Quinton would be angry. That much was plain. What he would do about it, however, was not plain at all. She did not think he would beat her. He did not seem like a man who ever employed violence against those who could not fight back. His servants and his men showed deep respect for his temper, but they did not treat him with the same profound awe as Buccleuch.

It occurred to her only then that Buccleuch might be at Branxholme when she arrived.

For a few shaky moments, she hovered on the brink of turning back. Then she told herself that there was nothing wrong with visiting Margaret. Branxholme was less than eight miles away, after all, and she had traveled farther than that when she had visited tenants, both with Quinton and without him. To this reasoning, her conscience rudely replied by reminding her that her husband had confined her to her bedchamber and would expect to find her there upon his return from Cotrigg.

It was nearing noon and her stomach had begun to growl when Branxholme's ramparts appeared at last on the horizon.

"I didna ken ye was coming so far, mistress," Ferdie said doubtfully. "I warrant the master would say we should ha' brought more o' the lads wi' us."

"We scarcely saw so much as a rabbit," Janet said. Since they had passed through several small villages along the river, that was not precisely true, but she did not care. Her gaze was fixed on the ramparts above the castle entrance. "Buccleuch's banner would be flying if he were at Branxholme, would it not?"

"Aye, it would," Ferdie growled. Glancing at him, she saw that he was staring straight ahead. His jaw was set.

Persisting, she said, "He is not here then."

"Nay, he is not. Did ye want him to be, mistress?"

"I came to pay my respects to his lady," she said airily. "I did not think one thing or another about him, but I expect he is likely to be at Hermitage."

"Aye, he should be."

Janet managed to conceal her relief. She was in no mood to confront Buccleuch. Yet, had he been at Branxholme, she would have had no choice. The guards had noted their approach by now, and had they tried to turn back, doubtless a heavily armed party would have ridden after them to inquire into their business. She would have had to brazen it out and face the consequences later. It was far better if Buccleuch was still fixed at Hermitage.

Fifteen minutes later, when she was shown into Margaret's parlor, Margaret leapt to her feet, exclaiming, "My dear, how providential! You can have no notion how glad I am to see you, but where is Quinton? Did he not accompany you?"

"No, I came alone," Janet said. "I came to—"

"How vexing," Margaret cut with a distracted frown. "His being here would have saved us a good deal of time. I was just going to send someone with a message for him, you see, because Buccleuch will arrive within the hour."

"Here?" Janet knew that she sounded dismayed, but Margaret did not notice. Her own thoughts seemed to consume her attention.

"He will want to see Quin at once," she said worriedly. "At least, he will if he is in any case to speak with anyone."

"In any case . . ." Janet stared at her then, her fears forgotten. "What has happened, madam? Is aught amiss with Buccleuch?"

"They say he fell from his horse," Margaret said, wringing her hands. "Such clumsiness is most unlike him, but one of his men rode in not a quarter hour before you to say that they are carrying him here on a gate. Branxholme was nearer than Hermitage, he said, but that makes sense only if one knows where they were when Buccleuch fell, of course."

"Don't you know where it was, madam?"

Margaret shrugged. "He may have told me, but I did not heed it if he did, because he also said that apparently Lord Scrope has at last decided to hold the next wardens' meeting in ten days' time. Forgive me, my dear, but I must not stand talking," she added. "I simply must send someone to fetch Quinton at once."

Chapter 16

*"High was their fame, high was their might
And high was their command."*

Buccleuch did not arrive on a gate, for he would not allow his men to carry him into the castle. He rode in on his horse, but he swayed dangerously in the saddle, and when he tried to dismount, only the swift action of two of the men saved him from collapsing.

Margaret stood stoically in the doorway, watching.

Beside her, Janet said, "At least he is not bleeding."

"Not that we can see," Margaret muttered. "His father died when he was only five-and-twenty, you will recall."

"He is not going to die," Janet said firmly. "Look at him."

Buccleuch had an arm around the shoulders of two of his men, and just then he grinned at the one on his left, saying something that made the man laugh.

"He wants us to look at them," Margaret said. "If we stare at his ape-grin, we might not notice that his face is scraped and bleeding or that he is not putting any weight on his left foot. Doubtless it refuses to bear weight, and it may well be broken. At least his horse looks healthy. He would hate to have to put that one down, and if he had to do so because it had stepped into a rabbit hole through some carelessness of his, he would behave like a surly bear for weeks.''

Turning, she raised her voice to say to a hovering maidservant, ''Mary, tell them to fetch hot water and clean cloths to the great hall. They must tear strips of linen if they have none ready to hand. His leg will need binding, and I shall want compresses, too, both hot and cold. Oh, and send someone to fetch Alys the herbwoman from her cottage straightaway.''

''Aye, m'lady.''

As Buccleuch hopped up the steps toward them, leaning heavily on his aides he said, ''Take that grim look off your face, Mag. They'll be hearing rumors of my death as far away as London town if anyone sees you looking so dour.''

''Take him into the hall,'' Margaret said quietly to the men, ''and settle him in his own chair. Set a stool for his leg. How bad is it, sir?''

'' 'Tis naught but a curst nuisance,'' he said, but Janet noted that he did not meet his wife's steady gaze. ''The only pain is that it was my own fault,'' he added. ''Everything seems to work well enough, but I'm seeing two of everything.''

Janet drew breath to speak, but before she could, Margaret said calmly, ''You hit your head then, I expect.''

''Aye, I did,'' he admitted. ''I've got a fair-sized knot above my right ear. I don't know what I hit, but it put me right out, and how the devil I managed to hurt a leg and my head all in one toss, I do not know.''

''Ye should ha' seen him, m'lady,'' the man on his left said. ''The pony stepped wrong, and Himself flew through the air as if he'd growed wings. Had he no kept ahold o' the reins, he'd be flyin' yet, I'm thinkin'.''

'' 'Twas the pony stepping on his leg when he landed at the puir beast's feet that did the damage,'' the second man added, ''but if it's broke, we canna tell.''

They had reached the hall, and Margaret gestured toward

Buccleuch's armchair. "Fetch pillows," she said to a lackey who peered in through a doorway at the far end of the hall.

"And ale, lad," Buccleuch called as the lackey turned to do her bidding.

"Bring him water," Margaret commanded. "I'll not have you fuddling your brain more than you already have, sir," she added with a winsome smile.

He frowned, but when he met her gaze at last, his expression softened. "You'll enjoy this more than I will, lass," he said, grimacing. "Did the lads I sent ahead tell you that that damnable snake Scrope's agreed at last to meet at Dayholm on the seventeenth?"

"Aye, they did, and before you ask, I've sent someone to fetch Quinton."

He looked sharply at Janet. "Do you mean to say that he's not here?"

"No, sir," Janet said. "I . . . I came alone."

"What the devil for? Not that you are not welcome," he added hastily with a guilty look at his wife. "Still, the Borders are grumbling more than usual. It is not safe for anyone traveling alone, particularly a bonny wee lass like yourself."

"I had Ferdie with me," Janet said. When he frowned, she added quickly, "It was perhaps not wise to bring only a lackey, sir, but it was such a fine day that I could not resist riding along the river. We just rode on, and . . ." Spreading her hands, she left the rest of the sentence unspoken, leaving him to draw his own conclusion. Although she had planned to be frank with Margaret and beg for her support, she felt unable to tell Buccleuch that she had left Broadhaugh.

He seemed to accept the implication that she had simply ridden farther than she had intended, for he said, "It is just as well then that Mag's sent for Quin. He'll not be pleased to find you here, though, lass. Don't think he will."

"I know he will not," Janet said truthfully.

Margaret's attempt to remove Buccleuch's boot snapped his attention back to his injuries and showed that he had understated the pain they caused him. His wife soon provided compresses for both the swollen leg and the knot on his head, and managed to persuade him to sip barley water in place of the ale he would have preferred. He quickly grew impatient, however, with his inability to move freely or to see clearly, and by the time the elderly herbwoman arrived at last, Janet knew that everyone in the hall felt the same relief that she did to see her.

Margaret said warmly, "Thank you for coming so swiftly, Alys. As you see, the laird has injured himself. He complains that he sees two of everything, and his injured leg has swollen considerably despite my compresses."

"Aye, well, it would," the old woman said, peering at the offending limb for a long moment, then setting the compress aside to examine the injury through his knitted netherstocks with swift, practiced movements. At last, she looked at Margaret and said in a tone of deep disapproval, "Summat fell on it."

Buccleuch said, "They tell me my horse stepped on it after I took a toss and landed on my head."

Janet thought his tone seemed surprisingly respectful. Hugh had no use for herbwomen or apothecaries and tended to dismiss any advice either might give him. Clearly Buccleuch was not so intolerant.

"Likely it's cracked then, and ye'll do well to keep to your bed and keep it rested," the old woman told him. "D'ye walk on it, ye'll do it more hurt—your pate, as well. I've seen them wha' took such a knock feelin' well one minute and fall over dead the next. Ye should stay abed till ye can see clearly again."

"His injuries will result in no lasting harm then," Margaret said, making a statement of fact rather than asking a question.

The herbwoman smiled, revealing wide gaps between her yellowed teeth. "Not an he keeps his head still and looks after himself," she said.

"Then he will do as he is bid," Margaret said, giving her spouse the same look that she might have given a recalcitrant child.

Buccleuch grinned at her.

Sternly, she said, "I need you whole and healthy, sir. Will you allow these lads to take you quietly up to your bed now, or shall I leave you here alone to look after yourself?"

"Aye, and she'd do it, too," Buccleuch said. "I'll let them take me upstairs but only to your cozy parlor, sweetling. Someone can set up a bed there if you insist on me being in one, but unlike the days when a gentleman attended to his daily business in his bedchamber, mine is a far less comfortable place to receive visitors than your parlor is, and I've much to do."

Margaret pressed her lips together in such a way that Janet knew she would have liked to say more, but instead she just signed to the men to take Buccleuch upstairs. That she worried about him was clear, but he looked healthy enough to Janet. A blow to the head could be worrisome, she knew, but she did not think he looked softheaded. More than likely he had dented whatever stone he had hit.

She had more to worry about, in any case, and long before anyone could reasonably have expected Sir Quinton to arrive, she found herself looking out onto the bailey to see if he had. She had retired to a small sitting room so that her hostess could tend Buccleuch with privacy in her parlor, and the sitting room window overlooked the bailey. As she watched, Janet told herself more than once that she was not afraid of her husband.

Unfortunately for her peace of mind, she could not recall exactly what she had expected to accomplish by leaving Broadhaugh. Somehow, in her earlier thinking, she had decided that her husband would learn a lesson, that he had only to realize that she had left him to understand that he had overstepped the mark of what she would accept in his behavior toward her. She had expected him to see that, in following the raiders, she had wanted only to help. He should recognize that she had been brave to follow them, and could have proved useful in an emergency. The more she tried to persuade herself, however, the guiltier she felt. As a result, she was in no case to deal with her hostess, let alone with Sir Quinton.

Margaret soon joined her in the sitting room, saying with a

sigh, "I finally persuaded him to try sleeping. His vision has not improved, however, and he expected it to do so at once. I do not know how long I can bring him to coddle himself. Truly, Quinton cannot get here too soon."

Janet grimaced.

Margaret said gently, "What is it, my dear? It occurred to me whilst I was sitting with Buccleuch, and praying for him to recover quickly, that I never thought to ask why you came here alone as you did. You are not a fool, although Buccleuch would have it that you behaved foolishly, and doubtless Quin will say the same."

"I ran away from home," Janet said baldly.

For the first time since Buccleuch's arrival, the worry vanished from Margaret's expression, and she chuckled. "Let me get my needlework and something for you to do, and you can tell me all about it."

By the time Janet had finished relating her tale, Margaret was no longer smiling. "You were not wise to leave as you did," she said.

"No, I can see that quite clearly now. You know Sir Quinton better than I do, madam. What will he do?"

"Godamercy, you might just well ask me if it will rain on Tuesday next, or snow tomorrow. His temper is more predictable than Buccleuch's, to be sure, but that is true of every man in Scotland save the king. Quin will be angry. I cannot doubt it, but I do not think he will do anything horrid whilst you are here with us."

"Then perhaps I should stay until Christmas," Janet said with a sigh.

"Do not anticipate trouble," Margaret recommended. "It is difficult enough to deal with it when it finds you without facing the possibility of its doing so a hundred times beforehand. You set a very fine stitch," she added. "Did I chance to show you Queen Mary's embroidery when last you were here?"

"No," Janet said, recognizing and accepting the diversion.

"Then this would be an excellent time to do so. Come along,

and leave your worries here for a wee bit. Likely, they'll wear themselves out.''

It was nearly suppertime before Sir Quinton arrived at Branxholme, and if he was in a fury, Janet could not discern it. He gave her one cool, appraising look that turned her innards to jelly, but then he demanded to know what was amiss with Buccleuch, and Margaret took him upstairs.

She returned minutes later to tell Janet that Buccleuch had wakened and was insisting that they take their supper with him. ''He says he is starving and will not eat pap, which is what Alys said he should eat, of course. I cannot prevent him from doing as he pleases in that respect, however, nor do I mean to try.''

''In my experience,'' Janet said quietly, ''men eat what and when they want to eat. I have rarely seen that it does them harm. Indeed, it would be worse for him to feel weak, I think.''

''Well, I do not know whose advice is best in such a case, but I will take yours because it will keep my husband from flinging boots or whatever else he can lay a hand to. I'll tell them in the kitchen to serve us upstairs, and then you and I can go right up. You and Quin will stay the night, of course—longer if you like.''

Janet swallowed. Branxholme was large enough for Margaret to offer her a private bedchamber, but since she had not done so already, she most likely would not. The thought of spending the coming night alone with Quinton set her nerves dancing. Whether they danced from fear or more anticipation, she could not tell.

He and Buccleuch were talking in low voices when she and Margaret entered the parlor. A bed had been set up against the inside wall near the fireplace at the far end, and Quinton had drawn a chair up near the bed. He stood politely when they entered, and Buccleuch said, ''I have just been explaining what must be done.''

"About what, sir?" Margaret asked.

"The wardens' meeting, of course. Thanks to this devilish leg and my damnable vision, I cannot do it all, and Quin may as well learn what duties I bear. We'll be sending word out and about at once, of course, so we must tell everyone that any grievances against the other side that have not yet been filed with a warden should go either to Quin at Broadhaugh or come here to me."

"Must we look into them all beforehand?" Quinton asked.

"Nay, what we think about them does not matter, though we'll want to know their nature, of course, since such knowledge will aid us in selecting jurors. We'll simply forward the complaints as a lot to that want-wit Scrope, and he will forward to us any complaints that he receives betwixt now and the day. Our responsibility is to see that all men the English name in their grievances attend the proceedings."

Raising his eyebrows, Quinton said, "Have you received many from them?"

"Aye, of course."

"Any against Rabbie Redcloak?"

"Nay, and that troubles me some. There are nearly always several, as you know, and except for the time that chap from Hawick told them Rabbie was English, someone consistently has stepped up to claim that he does not exist. Mayhap they have simply given up trying to identify him."

"I doubt that," Quinton said.

Buccleuch's eyes narrowed. "I heard about last night," he said.

Janet's breath stopped in her throat. She dared not look at Quinton.

He said calmly, "What did you hear?"

"That you were out and about again, over Kielbeck way."

Janet looked at her shoes, waiting for him to continue.

He remained silent.

Quinton said, "Anything else?"

"Is that not enough? Christ, Quin, you're a married man

now, and my deputy. You should know better than to go flitting around the countryside with naught but a score of men to look after you.''

''I was under the impression that I was looking after them and rightfully defending what is mine,'' Quinton said.

''Aye, perhaps you were at that. How did you fare?''

''Forty head of kine, about half that in horses. Half went to Ally the Bastard.''

''He'd rather have his wife back, I expect.''

''Aye.''

Janet darted a glance at Quinton and saw that he was looking at her. She looked hastily away again.

Buccleuch said, ''If you are going to serve as my deputy, you'll have to put the raiding behind you. I thought I had made that clear before, but I do understand your reaction to the raid on Cotrigg. I'd have done the same, albeit with more than twenty men.''

''Aye, I know that,'' Quinton said. ''Last time you led a raid, as I recall the matter, you led two thousand.''

''I do not dabble; I control,'' Buccleuch said grimly. ''I want your word on this now, Quin. It would have been bad enough to have to ransom you when that blasted Hugh Graham got his hands on you. But now . . . Christ, I do not want to find my deputy's name on the grievance list.''

''I'll willingly pledge my word to take care,'' Quinton said evenly. ''I cannot promise, however, to do naught that might require your ransoming me. That would mean letting the thieving English burn my people out, and I won't do that.''

Janet looked at Buccleuch and saw his face redden ominously.

The ensuing silence held menace, but the danger evaporated when he shrugged and said, ''I'd say the same, I expect. Just watch well then, and know that you'll be inviting disaster if you don't take care.''

''Aye,'' Quinton said, then added in a different tone, ''Do we wait till the day to decide everything? It seems to me that on previous occasions, you managed to settle some of the disputes beforehand.''

"Aye, that's true. They will make some offers, and we will make some. But in any case not settled beforehand, we are bound to summon the accused to the day of truce, and also to deliver any persons previously convicted to answer for their crimes. I've got a list, and you will see to all that. Indeed, I'm thinking that you may have to attend the meeting in my stead. I'll be damned if I'll let that dunderclunk Scrope see me hobbling about.''

"I've attended Truce Days before, of course," Quinton said, "but I cannot say that I've ever paid heed to the procedures. You'll have to tell me how to go on.''

"You'll not be alone," Buccleuch said, grinning at him. "Gaudilands and Todrigg and others of their ilk will be along to keep you from putting a foot wrong. Still, I'll tell you a bit now, and more as the time draws near. We've still ten days to plan, after all, and mayhap I'll be recovered by then. You'll attend, in any event.''

"Here's our supper," Margaret said, when first one servant and then several others entered and began putting food on a table. "Shall I prepare you a tray, sir?''

"Nay, lass, I'll sit at the table like a Christian," her husband said.

"But—" She broke off when he glared at her, then said lightly, "If you must.''

"I must. Quin, give me a hand.''

It took Quinton, a manservant, and a period of awkwardness that tried Buccleuch's temper, but they got him seated at last at the head of the table. When the platters were in place, he sent the servants away, saying, "We'll talk more comfortably without them. I can trust them to keep silent on most subjects, but we want no tongues repeating aught that I say about Scrope or his deputies.''

Janet said stiffly, "Perhaps I should remind you, sir, that my brother is one of Lord Scrope's deputies.''

"I know that, mistress, but you are one of us now. A fine thing it would be an I sent you away whenever I wanted to talk about the English. I believe I can trust you not to repeat what you hear between these walls."

"Yes, sir, you can. I thank you for honoring me with your trust."

"Bah, there is no honor in that. I'd be a fine kinsman an I failed to do it."

She liked him better in that moment than in all the moments she had hitherto spent in his presence. Shooting a look at her husband, she saw that his attention was firmly fixed on Buccleuch. She wished she could tell what Quinton was thinking. Her sphincter muscle twitched at the thought of facing him later, alone.

Buccleuch said, "You will have an important role to play, Quin, and you must never forget that."

"You know," Margaret said, "it occurs to me that Sir Hugh Graham is likely to be present at Dayholm. Will he not recognize Quin and cause a stir?"

"If he is there, he will not be at the wardens' table, for only the wardens and their clerk sit there," Buccleuch said. "Moreover, he knows Quin only in one guise. They have not met otherwise, as far as I know." He shot a look at Quinton.

"I suspect that we may both have attended the same functions at Jamie's court, but no one has ever introduced us," Quinton said. "I certainly did not recognize him as anyone to whom I had spoken before. In any event, I should think that someone would have to look after Cumberland and Carlisle in Scrope's absence. That would most likely be Graham, would it not?"

"Aye, perhaps," Buccleuch agreed.

"Even if he should attend, I will look much different as Sir Quinton Scott than as Rabbie Redcloak, and he saw me only in the gloom, never in a clear light. I took good care not to get close to him, I promise you."

"Excellent," Buccleuch said. "You were full-bearded then, too, as I recall. If you shave off your beard altogether, we should have no cause for alarm.'' Ignoring Quinton's look of dismay, he added, ''Once we settle what grievances we can settle beforehand, you will need to make certain that any one of our lads who is supposed to be at Dayholm shows up. I do not want to stand surety to anyone if we can avoid it,'' he added. ''That can prove damnably costly.''

''Perhaps I should round up all the felons and lock them up at Hermitage until the day,'' Quinton said with a wry smile.

''Nay, do not even think such a thing,'' Buccleuch said. ''Keeping prisoners is a devilish expensive nuisance. Just get each man to swear on his honor that he will be there.''

''Aye, I know,'' Quinton said with a chuckle, giving Janet to realize that he had been teasing his cousin in retaliation for the order to shave.

Buccleuch shot him a speaking look and said bluntly, ''You'll shave it off, my lad. You may look a bit boyish without it, but you will have Gaudilands and Todrigg to add to your consequence. Gaudilands is widely known to be my natural brother and to carry the weight of my name, just as you do. And Todrigg commands a large number of men-at-arms. That draws respect in any forum.''

They talked more about Quinton's duties as Buccleuch's deputy, and Janet listened carefully, wanting to understand the procedures and the reasoning that lay behind them. She had attended several wardens' meetings and had thought them much like town fairs. Although she knew that at times in the past some such meetings had proved dangerous, she had never seen anything to warrant concern. In her experience, they were exciting and fun, and provided a rare chance to socialize.

Evidently, however, Buccleuch did not share her opinion. ''I cannot warn you often enough, Quin, to guard your back. Scrope did not want this meeting. When I pressed him, he answered me with delays. Remember that, and tread warily.''

''Aye, I'll take precautions.''

''Hold rigidly to the traditions,'' Buccleuch advised. ''Where strict procedure is followed, fatal misunderstandings are less likely to occur."

"Aye," Quinton replied solemnly. "That makes sense."

"Weigh the whole emotional state of affairs before you approach the other side. Examine their lines for troublemakers, count their men-at-arms, and note their demeanor. Watch the English country folk, the vendors, and others who attend in hope of increasing their wealth. Such folk will not take absurd chances. If they seem genuinely merry and boisterous, they expect no trouble. You still must take care, of course, but they have ways and means of sensing danger in the wind."

"Once we have picked the juries, is there aught else that I must do?"

"They will be sworn in by the clerk, and when grievances are presented, whether a trial is necessary or not, you will be expected to help decide penalties for those against whom a grievance is proved. If the jury decides to impose a death penalty, there is naught else to decide, but if they demand the payment of a fine, you and Scrope must decide the amount, and it must be carefully calculated."

Quinton nodded.

"One thing more," Buccleuch said. "Do not let yourself be drawn into declaring on your honor that any Scottish defendant is an honest, law-abiding man. The temptation may be great, but weigh carefully your knowledge of the man, because if he is caught red-handed at the same offense soon afterward, you will pay his fines, not I."

"What of those who do not show up to respond to grievances against them?"

"They will be found guilty," Buccleuch said flatly. "You will doubtless learn afterward that many have sought leg-bail."

Bewildered, Janet said, "Leg-bail?"

Buccleuch smiled. "It means that they have crossed into another jurisdiction—either into the next march or over the line—seeking refuge." Turning back to Quinton, he said, "It is important wherever possible to strike an even balance between

English and Scottish penalties, even if it means letting bills of grievance stand over till the next meeting. The two sides can occasionally wipe the slate clean by agreeing to use one bill to cancel out another.''

"Is that fair?''

"It is expedient,'' Buccleuch said. "If we were to pursue every complaint to a finish, we would soon fall years behind in handling them all.''

"I doubt that such a tit-for-tat method recommends itself much to those whose cattle were stolen, though,'' Quinton said.

"They will do as they are told,'' Buccleuch said.

Quinton chuckled. "Aye, perhaps. They can simply await the next full moon, can they not, and take compensation the hard way.''

Buccleuch shrugged. " 'Tis often quicker than depending upon legal action.''

"And far more satisfying,'' Quinton said, shooting an oblique look at Janet.

She saw it and knew that he was teasing her. She did not let herself be drawn into the conversation, though, knowing she would learn more by remaining silent.

The men continued talking, and the platters of food soon were empty, but no one stirred from the table. Sipping wine from her goblet, Janet realized that it was nearly empty and reached for the jug to pour a bit more for herself.

Quinton's hand closed over hers, warm and startling. She met his gaze.

"I'll pour it for you, lass,'' he said.

They were the first words he had spoken to her since his arrival. Buccleuch had fallen silent, and in that moment it was as if he and Margaret had vanished. She could not seem to look away from Quinton. Only when he lifted the jug did the spell shatter. She put her hand back in her lap and watched him pour.

As if the interlude had never happened, Buccleuch said,

"And for the love of heaven, do not offer yourself as hostage for anyone."

Looking astonished, Quinton turned back to say, "I wouldn't!"

"Good. Others may offer. If an offer is good, and the English accept it, you can agree to it. However, you must take particular care when you hand over any hostage, especially if it is the prisoner and he cannot pay his fine. The process of handing him over can be delicate, because there have been instances in the past of prisoners breaking loose at the moment of transfer."

"Is that not punishable by death?"

"Aye, it is, and it has been for years now, but still it can happen."

"That seems overly harsh," Janet said. "One cannot blame someone for trying to escape, especially if he is to be imprisoned by his enemy."

"The law is just," Buccleuch said to her. "You must remember that an attempted escape from a Truce Day would almost certainly start a fight between the two sides. Such a fight could result in mass slaughter."

The thought of such a scene made Janet's stomach churn. What if Quinton acted impulsively and such a thing occurred? What if someone else caused it to happen and Quinton were killed?

Without thinking, she said, "I shall attend the meeting, too, shall I not?"

The two men replied together in a tangle of words.

"Aye, lass, of course, if you like."

"You will not!"

Looking at Quinton, she said quietly, "Would you have my kinsmen conclude that you married me against my will, sir, or that you have locked me up at Broadhaugh to keep me in Scotland? Or would you prefer to show them how happy I am in our marriage and how firmly I support you and your kinsmen?"

"You'll go with him, lass," Buccleuch said, his tone and the look he shot Quinton making it clear that he would tolerate no further debate. "Send for my man now," he said to his wife. "I'm for bed."

"We will bid you good night then, Wat," Quinton said. "Come, Jenny. We have some matters to discuss privately, I believe."

Her spirits sinking, she rose to go with him, knowing that she would have been wiser not to announce her desire to attend the Truce Day. He had nearly smiled at her only moments before, but now he looked like thunder again.

Quinton did not like to be challenged when others were at hand, she recalled belatedly. She still did not know him as well as she knew Hugh, but in that regard both men were the same, and she ought to have remembered.

Chapter 17

"His looks grew keen, as they were wont,
In dangers great to do."

Wrapped in her thoughts—in truth, trying to ignore the images they suggested about her immediate future—Janet paid no heed to where Quinton was taking her. It seemed as if scarcely a minute had passed, though, when he opened a door and, with a firm hand on her back, urged her into a cozy chamber where a small fire crackling cheerfully on the hearth set shadows dancing on the walls.

Barely aware of anything but the flames ahead of her and her large husband's intimidating presence behind her, she experienced a brief, disorienting sense of having stumbled into the lair of the devil. The thought startled her, and she gave herself a shake and tried to collect her wits.

The sound of the door latch snapping into place behind her nearly destroyed her careful composure, but she had not dealt with Hugh for most of her life without learning to conceal discomfiture. She turned to face her husband.

His expression was not hard to read. His eyes had narrowed,

and they glittered dangerously. Logic told her they were only reflecting the firelight, but logic did little to quell her fluttering nerves. Impulse urged her to defend herself; instinct recommended silence. The two warred in her mind while she strove to present an image of calm. At least his face did not grow red as Hugh's did when he was angry. She tried to tell herself that was a good sign, but his failure to burst into speech the minute he shut the door was more disconcerting than she might have expected it to be. Apparently he expected her to speak first.

The silence lengthened uncomfortably until she could stand it no longer. No sooner did she open her mouth to speak, however, than he said quietly, "You have disappointed me, Jenny."

The five words hit her like physical blows. Her throat closed painfully, and she could not find words to reply. Indeed, she did not understand him, but when she tried to tell him so, she could not force the words past the terrible ache in her throat. Unexpected tears welled into her eyes.

As she fought her emotions and tried to speak, he added, "I did not think you were such a coward as to run away."

The tears evaporated, and she said indignantly, "I did no such thing!"

"How else would you describe this impulsive flight to Branxholme?"

Belatedly, she remembered telling Margaret that she had run away from home. She had not meant what he meant, however, and Margaret had known that. Quinton should know it, too.

Raising her chin and straightening her shoulders, she tried to match his even tone when she said, "You sent me away, sir."

"I did not send you to Branxholme."

"No, but you sent me away like a child to my room without so much as a discussion of what had transpired. You never asked why I followed you and your men. You merely assumed that I had acted stupidly."

"I assumed nothing. I would not have been so unkind as to

call your action stupid. But you acted impulsively and without using good sense, you defied my orders, and you deserved my anger, Jenny. You deserve more now.''

She knew what she deserved, but she would not give him the satisfaction of admitting it. Still striving for calm, she said, ''I might well have acted impulsively, Quinton, but you must understand that I am not accustomed to seeking advice before I act. For years, I've had no one to advise me but Hugh, and I generally knew what he would say. And for that matter, you did not expect me to seek your advice before I purchased things for Broadhaugh or hired new servants, even a new cook.''

''That is different, but even so, had you hired anyone I did not like, I would have told you so and expected you to get someone else. Moreover, in matters concerning the household, I know that you are capable. Most women are.''

Having no interest in discussing most women with him, she said firmly, ''I am also competent to express opinions and to make decisions for myself.''

''Not decisions that go against my orders, lass. You will meet grief every time, taking that road. Surely, you are not going to try to tell me that your decision to follow us was a sensible one. You do recall what nearly happened to you as a result, do you not?''

''That was unfortunate,'' she said, adding hastily, ''and I will admit that in my haste I did not think carefully enough about my own safety, but—''

''Or Tip's,'' he interjected.

''What did you do to him?'' she demanded.

He was silent.

''If you—''

''We are not going to discuss Tip,'' he said. ''You have admitted that you did not think before you followed us. We need not discuss that, either. In future, you will control your impulses and do as I bid you.''

Fighting frustration and anger, she nibbled her lower lip.

Quinton said evenly, ''I do not want to be a harsh husband,

Jenny, but I would be failing in my duty toward you if I did not take steps to prevent you from flinging yourself into danger.''

"I did not fling myself. I feared for your safety, and as it happened, you'd have run into an ambush if those louts had not stumbled over me!''

"I know that you have little faith in my ability to look after myself or my men," he said.

"That is not true!''

"It *is* true," he snapped. The sharp tone silenced her. He said more calmly, "I cannot blame you for harboring such feelings, considering how we met. Nevertheless, even if I had somehow been unable to look after my lads, you could have done nothing to help the situation.''

Much as she wanted to argue the point, she knew that she could not win it. Worse, she suspected that he was right, that in thinking she might have been of help in any situation, she had been harboring a delusion. What had seemed logical while she sat by herself worrying about what might become of him seemed anything but logical now. And without logic firmly on her side, it would be particularly difficult to make him understand her point of view.

The ache returned to her throat. That, added to her frustration, kept her silent.

He said, "Why did you run away from me?''

The first thought that leapt to her mind was, "So you would discover how much you would miss me." Suppressing it, she muttered instead, "I was angry, sir, as angry as you were." The ache eased enough for her to add, "I know that much of your anger was stirred by fear. You said as much, and I understand that kind of anger. I wish you would try to understand that my need to follow, to help if I could, was born of a like fear.''

"I do understand that," he said.

"I don't think you do. It was not what you think.''

"It does not matter," he said with an impatient gesture. "I

swear, lass, you would try even Job's patience.'' He drew a deep breath, clearly finding it difficult to keep his temper. ''We are not going to debate this further.''

The note of finality in his voice irritated her, but her irritation turned to wariness when he turned away and began to unfasten his belt.

Defensively, she said, ''You should not treat me like a child, sir. At home, I have dealt with many responsibilities much like yours over the years, and I am capable of dealing with them competently. Even Hugh does not ignore my advice or opinions out of hand. I just think you should—''

''Take off your clothes, Jenny.''

She froze. ''What . . . what are you going to do?''

''We are going to bed, lass. I am too tired to fratch, and if you press me too hard, I am like to do something we will both be sorry for. Now, can you manage by yourself or do you need help?''

''I . . . I'll need help,'' she admitted. ''This dress has too many laces and hooks in the back for me to do it myself.''

Quin watched the play of emotions on her expressive face and hoped that he had made his position clear to her. He understood her difficulty. Living with a man like Hugh Graham and lacking the guidance of a mother or any other responsible female, she had grown up in a most haphazard way. He would not quickly teach her to submit to his authority unless he were willing to treat her as he believed her brother would. He did not want to be harsh, but his hands fairly itched to shake her for what she had done. She could ignite his temper more rapidly than anyone he had ever known before.

He had taken off his belt and his doublet and pulled his shirt free of his breeks before he could trust himself to touch her. He was glad that she did not speak. She just watched him, and her expression remained wary.

He was glad, too, that she showed the good sense to be a

little frightened of him. He would never have another peaceful moment if he could not trust her to rein in her impulses and behave sensibly. The Borders were too dangerous, and the Scotts had far too many enemies. Not all of those enemies lived across the line, either. Jenny did not know whom she could trust and whom she could not.

She trembled when he put his hand on her shoulder and turned her away so that he could unhook her gown.

His body stirred, just being near her, and he wanted to take her in his arms and make love to her, to force her complete surrender to his will. Gently, resisting the temptation, he helped her take off her dress, then loosened the lacing of her underbodice. A few minutes later, standing in her smock, with her fine, silvery-blond hair unbound and pushed back behind her ears, she looked like the child she insisted that he believed she was. She was no child, though. The soft, inviting breasts beneath her smock were plain testimony of that. Her nipples thrust hard against the linen. She was getting chilled.

"Get into bed, Jenny," he said gruffly.

"Quinton, I want to—"

The words ended in a gasp when he grasped her shoulder and turned her toward the bed with one hand and gave her a smack on the backside with the other.

"Go," he said, knowing from her reaction that he had smacked harder than he had intended. Watching her scramble into the bed, he felt an impulse of his own to apologize, but ruthlessly he quashed it. He knew that any apology would be spurious. So, too, was the thought that he had smacked her harder than he had intended. He had not. In truth, he had wanted to punish her, to put her across his knee and skelp her until she promised never to give him such a fright again.

He was not sure even now if his failure to do it sprang from nobility or fear that he might do her an injury.

She had terrified him, not once but twice. First she had nearly got herself raped, maybe even murdered, and then, only a few hours later, she had defiantly left Broadhaugh with only a single lad to protect her.

He paused to put two more logs on the fire before divesting himself of the rest of his clothing and moving to join her in the bed. She had not asked again about Tip, and that was just as well. He knew her well enough to believe that, as punishment, her worry about the little man's fate would serve as well if not better than any beating.

She wriggled away to the other side of the bed when he got in. Plumping the pillows behind him, he leaned against them, extended an arm, and said, "Come here, lass. I have some few things left to say to you. I want you to pay attention."

Though her reluctance was plain, she obeyed, shifting herself to lie stiffly in the curve of his arm with her head against his shoulder.

This would not do, he decided. He wanted to watch her expression while he spoke to her. With the fire dancing high again and the bed curtains open, there was enough light, but the angle was wrong. He was looking at the top of her head.

Shifting onto his side, he felt her stiffen more and knew that she was still afraid of what he might do. "Relax, Jenny," he said. "We're in bed because you were getting cold and because I did not want to chance becoming so angry with you that I'd do something I do not want to do."

"You just want to give me orders," she muttered. "All men are the same."

"I'll warrant we all have traits in common," he said, "but we are not all the same. Would Hugh react to what you did in the same way that I have reacted?"

She was silent, but when he saw her nibble her lower lip, he knew she realized that Hugh would have been just as angry with her, if not much more so.

"More to the point, lass, you say you followed us because you were afraid that something would happen. You have told me that you care about your brother, too. Would you have followed him and his men on a raid?"

He felt her shudder.

"Answer me, Jenny. Would you have done that?"

Her gaze flicked toward him resentfully. "You know that I would not, but neither did I allow Hugh to dictate my every move and opinion."

"I have not attempted to do that either," he pointed out. His anger had dissipated the moment he had climbed into bed with her. The stirring in his loins had not. It took every ounce of his will to lie quietly beside her without touching her. This matter was too important to both of them to let his baser instincts guide his actions, however. He just wished the lower half of his body understood that as easily as his mind did, or that his mind could control his lower half more easily.

She moved, and he suppressed a groan at the sensations that radiated through him. Then she said quietly, "It's true that you do not try to order my every breath, sir, and you have been generous about the household and . . . and my clothes. You have also exerted yourself to be patient with me, perhaps more patient than I deserve. I do know that. But you also dismiss my feelings and my opinions as if they held no merit. Had you not simply sent me away when word came of the raid on Cotrigg, had you allowed me to take part in the discussion, at least, and to know more about your plan, perhaps I would not have felt as fearful."

"It is not the business of men to discuss their battle plans with womenfolk, lass, and raiding is much like going into battle. I have told you that I will protect you, and I will. Truly, you can trust me on that head."

"It is not that I do not trust you," she said. Then, catching his eye, she grimaced. "You may be partly right about that. Perhaps I would not have reacted so impulsively to my feeling of unease if I had not met you in a dungeon. I cannot be certain one way or another about that, but your point is reasonable. I can see that now. Why can you not see that my feelings of unease were likewise reasonable? Had those men not stumbled across me, you would have run right into them."

''Most likely they would have run into Tip first,'' he said. She met his steady gaze, and kept silent.

He realized then that he had made her point for her. ''Very well, they might have surprised us,'' he admitted. ''They might even have succeeded in calling down a large patrol around our ears. I will grant that your instinct for trouble was a good one, but what you did in response to it was not, Jenny. You know it was not.''

''Aye, I can see that now,'' she said. ''Indeed, if I must speak honestly, I knew it when Tip and I reached the bailey and I realized that on my own I would not have been able to order a horse to ride out, that anyone I asked would most likely have refused to do my bidding.'' She paused, and he knew as if she had spoken the words that she wanted to ask him again about Tip's fate.

''I do not know that anyone would have dared defy your direct order,'' he said, deciding that her honesty demanded a like frankness on his part. ''What I hope would have happened is that you would have found it necessary to explain yourself, and that someone would have ridden after us to warn . . .'' He fell silent, realizing that the point was no good.

''You know that no one would have paid my instincts any more heed beforehand than you did afterward,'' she said.

''Including myself,'' he admitted. ''I do see that. I did not even heed my own custom last night, and I've been thanking the fates that Buccleuch did not learn about that when he learned the rest. The only place I left anyone to watch our back was near Kielbeck, so we would know that our route out of the dale was safe. I did not take enough men with me to leave lads at points all along the way.''

''Thank you for admitting as much,'' she said. ''Now, if you would just call me Janet, instead of Jenny . . .''

He shook his head. ''I don't do it to annoy you,'' he said. ''I just like Jenny, for it has a softer sound in my mind than Janet does, and it's the way I think of you in my mind. Mayhap, Jenny just sounds more obedient,'' he added with a sigh.

Shifting so that she looked directly at him, she said, "I know that I've made mistakes, Quinton. I acted without thinking things through both in following you last night and in riding to Branxholme this morning. In fact, I suppose Hugh would say that I acted impulsively when I freed you from your cell at Brackengill."

"I have not objected to that impulse, however," he said with a little smile.

"That's not really true," she said. "You were angry when you first saw me that night, because you had told me to stay away. Then you abducted me because you did not think I could deal with my brother's anger. I do see now that I cannot leap to action here in the same manner that I might have at home, because I do not know the way of things here as well. Still, I will learn, sir. My being a woman does not make me a fool."

About to reassure her that he had never thought her a fool, he realized that he *had* dismissed her, that he had sent her away whenever something important arose, and that he had done so the night before knowing that she opposed the raiding. Not only had she feared for his safety and that of his men but also for the people of Kielbeck, who were her countrymen.

She moved and her hand inadvertently touched his bare thigh. Inhaling sharply, he forced himself to focus on their discussion, saying, "We both have been thoughtless, Jenny. If I try to do better, will you do likewise?"

"Aye," she said, but her expression looked wary again.

"What?"

"Will you expect me to obey your every command without question?"

"I should be able to expect that," he said, but the amusement her words stirred revealed itself in his tone, and he knew she heard it.

Her eyebrows shot upward. "I do not believe that even the Scottish marriage rite made me your slave, sir."

"You promised to obey me."

"Aye, and I will when your commands are reasonable."

He sighed. "Jenny, lass, I have admitted being thoughtless. I know that in fairness I ought to have taken time to hear what you had to say before sending you away, both before I left for Kielbeck and later, before I sent you to your room. But do not take that to mean that I will debate my every command with you, for I will not. If you insist on defying me, you will invite grief, so from now on, if you decide to ignore an order of my giving, be prepared to suffer the consequences. I promise you, I am not always as understanding as I am trying to be now. Our marriage is young, and I want it to grow strong. Thus, I am willing to compromise, but only a bit, lass. You will not usurp my position as master of Broadhaugh."

This time, when her hand touched his thigh, he knew she did it deliberately. His body did not know the difference, though. It leapt in response.

She said softly, "Hold me close, Quinton. I want you to make love to me."

He did not hesitate, and if there was any question about who won the final point, he did not care.

Janet lay awake for some time after her husband had fallen asleep. The fire had died to embers, and she could no longer make out his features, but she liked to listen to his breathing and to feel his body close beside her while he slept.

Their lovemaking had taken on a new dimension. He had taken her as if he had meant to conquer her, to force her to abject surrender, and it seemed curious that she had not minded. Indeed, when he had teased her body, taking her to heights of sensation beyond any she had experienced before, she had responded in a way that surprised her. Learning from his actions, she tried many of the same tactics with him, and learned that she could enjoy tormenting him and making him beg for more. In the end she was not certain who had conquered whom, but the encounter had been more than satisfactory. She looked forward to repeating it.

During the next ten days, she gave him full marks for keeping his word. She noted on more than one occasion that before issuing a command he took a moment to explain to her what he was about to do. Instead of simply disappearing from the castle with a party of men, he told her where he was going. And twice, when he went elsewhere, he even sent someone back with a message. It was far more than Hugh had ever done.

She kept busy, too, preparing to go with him to the wardens' meeting; and she kept her end of the bargain. She did not even attempt to leave the castle without an armed escort of at least two men, and once, when Quinton said that he did not think it safe for her to go out, she submitted gracefully to his decision.

They remained at Branxholme for two days, so that Buccleuch could prepare his deputy as much as possible for the meeting. Before they left, he had accepted the fact that his leg would not mend in time for him to make the journey to Dayholm and made it plain that Quinton would act in his stead.

" 'Tis a good thing that the horse races at Langholm are still more than a month away," he added, "or 'tis likely I'd have to miss them, too."

Proud as she was to know the important role her husband would play at Dayholm, Janet greeted the news with mixed emotions. She saw little of Quinton after they returned to Broadhaugh, for his duties took him away from home nearly every day, and often he was gone overnight.

As soon as they returned, she tried to discover what Tip's fate had been, but although the little man answered her summons, he refused to answer her questions.

"I'm no to speak of it," he said flatly. "The master did say he would make me gey sorry did I tell ye what transpired betwixt us, and I ken fine that he would. Pray, mistress, dinna command me to speak of it."

Since Tip displayed no visible signs of rough treatment, Janet was willing to drop the matter, recognizing her husband's devious intent immediately.

She told herself that he had not flogged the little man, that he had merely scolded him the same way that he had scolded her. Even so, she could not help wondering about it and knew that Sir Quinton had taught her a lesson.

For the moment, things remained good between them, but she believed that was due as much to his frequent absences as to anything else, and she was not so foolish as to believe they would remain so indefinitely. In any event, she resolved never to involve others in any future escapade.

Chapter 18

"O were there war between the lands,
As well I wot that there is none . . ."

Truce Day arrived at last, and Sir Quinton and his lady rode at the head of a respectable entourage to Dayholm, where narrow Kershopefoot Burn divided the two countries. They had dressed with particular care—Sir Quinton because he wanted to look as grand as Buccleuch would look on such an occasion, and Janet because her pride was at stake. She expected to see old friends and did not want them to think that she had made a dreadful mistake in marrying across the line.

"You look grand, sweetheart," Quinton said with a smile, raising his voice to be heard over the jingle and thud of harness and hooves, punctuated by bursts of conversation and laughter. "You'll have every man slavering with lust and every woman spitting in envy."

"I don't look for such vulgar reactions," she said, lifting her chin but struggling not to smile back. "I just want to do my part to lend you consequence, sir. Scrope will be less likely to make outrageous demands if you surround yourself with the trappings of Buccleuch's power, and that includes a richly garbed wife.''

"And a dutiful one," he replied dryly. "Doubtless I shall test that trait before the day is done, lass. Just see if I do not."

"You may try," she said, but she laughed at the threat. The day was filled with sunshine, her pony wore trappings rich enough for King Jamie, and she knew that she looked her best. Ardith had arranged her hair more elaborately than usual, and if the pins tended to pull, the small discomfort did nothing to spoil the day.

The men and women behind them laughed and chatted gaily. The entourage was not excessively large, but it included many members of the Scottish Border nobility, their men-at-arms, and a few of their wives.

Even the more somber aspects of the day would not detract much from the merriment and feasting, Janet thought. Certainty that both sides would honor the truce would give everyone a sense of unfettered release. The feeling was welcome, for it was one that rarely visited the Borders. Janet heard men singing as they rode, and someone was playing the pipes. The lively music made her smile again.

Riding south by way of Hermitage Water till it met the Liddel, they crossed the river at Whithaugh and continued toward Kershope, keeping to higher ground once they could see the merrily tumbling little burn and follow its course. They rode in a more westerly direction now, toward the meeting site at Dayholm on the flat bit of ground where the Liddel met Kershopefoot Burn.

Janet glanced at Quinton, remembering that it was not far away, across that burn, that Hugh's men had trapped him. Thinking of Hugh reminded her that her brother might attend the meeting, but she did not think he would recognize Rabbie Redcloak in the richly garbed, clean-shaven gentleman who rode at her side.

If Scrope followed the pattern that Buccleuch had described, he would lead a cavalcade from Carlisle comprising Cumberland and Northumberland gentry and nobility, which certainly included Sir Hugh Graham. However, someone would have to act as Scrope's deputy while he was away. As Buccleuch had suggested, that someone was likely to be Hugh, but Scrope did have other deputies.

It was as much to bolster her courage as for any other reason that she had taken such care with her dress. She would need courage if she did have to face Hugh. Having not seen or directly heard from him since the night Quinton had taken her away from Brackengill, she had no idea how he would behave. She had missed him, but her emotions were mixed. Perhaps he would not come.

Deciding that he would not, she dismissed all but a lingering tickle of worry and settled to enjoy herself, looking forward to seeing the first recognizable Graham face. If her kinsmen were not delighted by her marriage, at least no one would be in any hurry today to express his or her displeasure to her face. She had missed her family and friends and looked forward to seeing them again.

Half an hour later they topped a rise and looked down on the flat plain near the hamlet of Dayholm, which snuggled into the V-shaped area where Liddel Water met the little burn. Sir Quinton raised his hand to call a halt.

"Why have we stopped?" Janet asked.

"We'll wait here for Scrope and his men to show themselves," he said.

"Should they not already be within sight?"

He smiled. "Buccleuch warned me how it would be. Scrope will want to know that we are here so that it will not look as if he let us keep him waiting. It is all part of the little dance we do," he added. "Doubtless someone is watching from that hilltop across the way, and Scrope is below the crest awaiting his signal."

The singing and laughter had stopped, and now the chatter died away to muttered comments. It was, Janet thought, as if a cloud had slipped across the sun.

Five minutes later, across the way, a flutter of colorful banners preceded the appearance of a wide array of horsemen lining the crest of the hill.

"We'll wait a bit longer," Quinton said. "See how many they are."

Hearing an unfamiliar note in his voice, Janet glanced at him again, but there was nothing to read in his stony expression.

As trumpets sounded on both sides, Quin tried to remember everything that Buccleuch had told him during the past ten days. All he could recall just then, however, was his cousin's admission—astonishing at the time—that he always felt nervous in the moments just before a wardens' meeting. That had been, Quin realized now, a vast understatement of the reality. The awesome appearance of the armed horsemen across the valley, heralded by the martial notes of the trumpets, stirred tingling up and down his spine and tightened every muscle, making him wish that his followers numbered a thousand more.

The distance between the two forces being less than a quarter mile, he recognized a host of familiar banners, even a few familiar faces. Many of those lined up on the other side were enemies who in times past, when not in the actual heat of battle, had proved more friendly than hostile. He had probably drunk ale or wine with half of them in the taverns of Carlisle and Kelso.

Instinctively he estimated the number of lance points, considered the bearing of the riders, the weight and deadliness of their arms.

"I'd guess they be five hundred or so," Hob the Mouse muttered beside him.

Quin glanced at him. "Buccleuch said we could expect that many. Scrope likes to make a grand display, and we have nearly as many ourselves, after all."

"Aye, counting our lasses, but them yonder ha' none," Hob pointed out.

" 'Tis likely their women wait behind the hill,'' Quin said. "Only a few of the men carry themselves as if they were here for anything but common ritual, and I'll warrant they do that out of habit.'' He glanced again at the big man beside him.

Hob was still scanning the opposition force, but within moments he visibly relaxed. "It is so,'' he said. Looking over his shoulder as if to take stock of the men behind them, he added, "Our lot looks much the same, and none here seeks war. Still and all, master, Truce Days ha' been known to end in blood.''

"Aye,'' Quin agreed. Both sides had been guilty of transgressions. Only ten years before at Cocklaw, Scots had murdered the English Lord Russell. On that occasion, Buccleuch had said, the English had made the mistake of taking assurance before they had seen the Scottish force, which they later claimed was unusually strong and drawn up in battle array. Quin would not make that mistake.

"Hob, tell the women and other unarmed folk to stay back till we have met for the embrace and taken our seats at the wardens' table,'' he said, still scanning for known troublemakers in the group across the way.

"Aye,'' the big man said, wheeling his mount to carry out the order.

"That is not Scrope's banner,'' Jenny exclaimed suddenly, drawing his attention. Leaning forward on her saddle, she muttered, "Godamercy, it's—''

"There are many banners, lass,'' he interjected, trying to follow the direction of her gaze.

"The central one,'' she said impatiently. "That is Brackengill's banner, sir, or I am much mistaken. May heaven help us—it is Hugh leading them, not Scrope!''

Suppressing his own dismay, he forced calm into his tone as he said, "Scrope must have learned that Buccleuch was sending a deputy and decided that it was beneath him to meet with an inferior, so he has sent his own. You may stay at my side until they have demanded assurance, Jenny, but then I want you to withdraw and wait here with the other women until we know they mean no mischief.''

"Look, he's sending his men now.''

Indeed, two riders had separated themselves from the others and were cantering down the hill toward the burn. The Scots watched as they splashed to the Scottish side. Moments later they drew rein in front of Quin.

The elder of the two said formally, ''In the name of Thomas, Lord Scrope, England's warden of the west march, Sir Hugh Graham requests assurance that you and yours vow to keep the peace until sunrise tomorrow.''

"In the name of Sir Walter Scott of Buccleuch, warden of the Scottish west and middle marches, and Keeper of Liddesdale, I vow and declare that there shall be peace until sunrise tomorrow,'' Quin said loudly enough for his followers to hear.

The two visitors nodded, then wheeled their ponies and trotted away.

When they had reached the hurrying little burn, Quin said, "Hob, tell Gaudilands and Todrigg to ride across now and demand Graham's assurances.''

"Why did you wait for Hugh to request the truce first?'' Jenny asked.

"It is the tradition,'' he said. "Buccleuch said that generally the meetings take place on the Scottish side and the English request first assurances. When any war betwixt us ends, he says, the Scots must first demand peace, but during peacetime, at meetings like this, the English make their demand first.''

"But why?''

"He said that long ago a Scottish warden, one Robert Kerr, was murdered at a meeting on the English side. After that we Scots swore we would never again seek justice on English ground.'' His men had reached Sir Hugh. "Go now, Jenny, and join the other women until we know that all is safe.''

"I believed before that Hugh would not recognize you, but do you not fear that he might if the pair of you sit cheek by jowl all day?''

"I doubt that he will know me without a beard and in these trappings," Quin said, hoping he was right. "I will take every care nonetheless, lass, I promise."

The two Scottish riders were taking longer than he had expected. Recalling Buccleuch's strict instructions, Quin resisted his natural inclination to watch them and continued to scan instead for signs of trouble among Sir Hugh's followers. He could see nothing amiss.

"Here they come," Jenny said on a note of relief.

"I told you to get back, lass. Now, go!"

Obedient for once, she backed her pony and began to turn away.

Satisfied, he turned his attention again to the opposite side.

Minutes later, Gaudilands and Todrigg cantered up to him, and before they drew rein, Quin knew by their expressions that a hitch had occurred.

"What is it?" he demanded.

Sardonically Gaudilands said, "Sir Hugh Graham, leading an easy five hundred armed horsemen, presents his compliments to Sir Quinton Scott and requests that your 'embrace' with him take place midstream."

"It seems," Todrigg said, adding his grim mite, "that Sir Hugh Graham demands such a meeting so as not to have it thought that an English warden is under any obligation to go into Scotland but crosses over of his own volition."

"He said," Gaudilands added, "that when you raise your hand, he will accept the gesture as your agreement to make the embrace of peace midstream."

Jenny said anxiously, "What does he mean? Is this some sort of trick?"

"You know your brother better than I do," Quin said, smiling to give her reassurance that he did not feel. In the presence of the others, he refrained from demanding to know what the devil she meant by defying his orders again.

"It is not the normal way," Gaudilands said curtly. "Buccleuch would not accept such terms, nor would Scrope be such a jackanapes as to demand them.''

Although his preference was to tell Sir Hugh Graham to take his notions of an embrace and fly away with them, Quin knew that his cousin would demand his head on a platter if he did any such thing. Stifling annoyance, he backed his horse enough so that he could see his men without looking away from those on the other side. Raising his hand, he said clearly, ''I hope I need not remind any man here of his oath to keep the truce. Anyone who creates trouble or attacks without the unavoidable provocation of a breach by the other side will answer to me and then to the Laird of Buccleuch. Do you all hear and understand me?''

A chorus of ayes answered him.

''On your word as Borderers?''

''Aye!''

''Then we ride. I shall meet the English deputy midstream. You will all remain on the bank, but keep a path clear for us to the wardens' table.''

His attention was focused so sharply on the approaching English that he did not realize until they had nearly reached the river that Jenny rode beside him again.

''Damnation, lass,'' he muttered. ''Fall back as I told you to do.''

''He is my brother, sir,'' she said firmly. ''I will remain at your side, and no one will harm me. My position as your wife protects me from the Scots, and my close kinship to Hugh and many others protects me from the English.''

''And do you think it protects me from them as well?'' he growled.

''Aye, it should.''

''And that your kinship to them will protect you from me?''

She looked sharply at him then, and he gave her look for look, but it was too late now to insist that she fall back, and he could see that she knew it. Moreover, he knew that, at this point, her sudden departure to the rear would look as if he feared an attack, which would considerably undermine the peace before it had begun. Resigned, he faced forward, reining in his temper and fixing his full attention on Sir Hugh Graham.

Beside him, Hob said, "Ye willna really embrace that scoundrel, will ye?"

Surprised by a bubble of laughter, Quin glanced at him. "Buccleuch said that on rare occasions the wardens actually do embrace, but I think we will not."

Despite what he had told Jenny, it seemed impossible that Graham would not instantly recognize him as Rabbie Redcloak, which left him nothing to do but to take a high hand. After all, he told himself with increasing amusement, it was what Rabbie would do. Straightening and haughtily raising his newly bared chin, he reminded himself that Sir Hugh had never seen him in bright daylight or without his beard. Nor had the man seen him in attire that befitted his station. The man had seen him only in darkness and by torchlight in a dark stable. He tried to recall the faces of the men who had surrounded him, and found to his relief that he could not.

His cloak had covered his figure then, and he had made no attempt to stand upright or to look his captors in the eye. Indeed, and most uncharacteristically, he had kept his eyes downcast. At least, he hoped he had. He had a niggling suspicion that he was unlikely to have submitted to his fate as completely as it seemed now that he had. He knew himself well enough to suspect that he had taunted Sir Hugh at least a little, perhaps even laughed at him. Moreover, even if he could maintain the demeanor of a stranger who knew Sir Hugh only as his opposite deputy, he would still have to take care that his voice did not betray him. As Rabbie, he generally affected the broadest of Border accents, but knowing that occasionally he was apt to forget, he could only hope that such a lapse had not occurred at Brackengill.

The most nerve-racking detail, of course, was that many on the Scottish side knew exactly who Rabbie Redcloak was, and Grahams lived on both sides of the line. Indeed, many Grahams had followed him on occasion, because the Scottish ones were broken men—abandoned or evicted by their clan—who had taken up residence in the Debatable Land and would serve any master who could keep them in order. He did not readily reveal his true identity to such men, and he doubted that his more faithful henchmen had given him away intentionally. Still, far too many people on the Scottish side knew his dual identity for him to remain comfortable as he watched Sir Hugh's approach. Face to face with the man, discerning no sign of recognition, Quin felt a surge of welcome confidence.

He reminded himself that many of the men with Graham were acquaintances, even friends, of Sir Quinton Scott and that those who were not would respect the power of his present position. Awareness of that power settled over him like a familiar, magical garment, increasing his confidence so that it nearly matched the zestful delight he experienced when leading a raid. Power was heady stuff.

Reaching the stream, he signaled his men to wait and rode without pause to meet Graham.

Sir Hugh rode forward alone, too.

When Quin met his stern gaze, his confidence ebbed a bit. His breathing felt labored, but he ignored the tension, keeping his gaze fixed warily on the other man. The relief he felt when Sir Hugh extended his right hand exhilarated him, renewing his confidence.

"We meet at last," Quin said heartily, emphasizing his university English as he gripped the outstretched hand.

Sir Hugh said evenly, "I did not learn until yesterday that Buccleuch's deputy was my new brother-in-law." He did not seem particularly gratified by the fact, but neither did he show any sign of recognizing his erstwhile captive.

"Nor did we realize until minutes ago that Scrope was sending a deputy," Quin replied. "I should not have known your identity until your men named you had Jenny not expressed her delight at seeing you."

"How is Janet?"

The gentle emphasis on Jenny's preferred manner of address made Quin's lips twitch, but he repressed the smile, saying in a manner haughty enough to befit Jamie's own minister of state, "You must ask her yourself, Sir Hugh. As you see, she awaits us with the others. I warrant that she will be pleased to speak to you."

"I heard about Buccleuch's accident," Sir Hugh said. "I hope he is mending."

"He is," Quin replied. "Forgive me for pressing the point, and pray believe that I mean no offense, but I did expect to deal with Scrope."

"He thought the experience would benefit me," Sir Hugh said blandly.

"Ah, indeed. Shall we take our places then? This water is rather too cold to keep the horses standing in it long."

Sir Hugh gave him a challenging look. "I hope that my request to meet midway did not offend you."

"Not in the least," Quin replied, returning the look. "Where strict procedures rule the day, fatal misunderstandings are less likely to occur. Do you not agree?"

"Aye," the other man said curtly. Gesturing to his followers and spurring his mount, he splashed to the Scottish bank.

Turning deftly with him, Quin rode beside him up the pathway formed by his own men to the table where the two deputies would sit to hear grievances.

In moments, men from both sides had mingled to erect tents and trestle tables, and to tap enormous casks of ale. Women spilled down the hillside on the English side of the line, carrying baskets and cloths which they spread on the tables before helping the Scottish women set out the food. Dogs barked and tried to steal morsels of food. Traveling merchants appeared with their packhorses, quickly unloaded them, and set out their wares to attract buyers. Vendors of wine, spirits, and other creature comforts set up, as well. There were even sideshows, with spokesmen crying out for all and sundry to see such delights as a two-headed lamb and a woman who could tie herself in knots.

Although some folks wandered off to see the sights, most stayed near the wardens' table to keep an eye, for a time at least, on the business of the day. Complainers and defenders crowded around with friends and families to support them, not in solitary groups but in teeming hundreds. Laughter and the cries of vendors punctuated a din of conversation against a musical background of skirling pipes, blaring horns, the clinking of bridles and other gear, and the stamping and snorting of horses. There were even children, running after each other, shouting and laughing, made merry by the grand freedom of the day.

The clerk proved to be a short, thin, middle-aged man from Carlisle who had been approved by both sides. He spread a gilt-fringed, red-velvet cloth on the wardens' table, and Quin and Sir Hugh set their brass-bound grievance boxes upon it. Following normal procedure, Lord Scrope had forwarded the English complaints to Buccleuch and had received the Scottish ones in return.

The clerk took his place between the two deputies, set down his log, carefully extracted two quills and his inkwell from a leather pouch, and set them out neatly between the brass-bound coffers. Then he straightened, looked at the two deputies, and said in solemn but stentorian tones, "Sir Quinton Scott of Broadhaugh, and Sir Hugh Graham of Brackengill, are you both prepared to swear the oath?"

"Aye," they said as one.

The crowd grew quiet.

The clerk continued, "Then, if you please, Sir Quinton, repeat after me . . . 'I, Sir Quinton Scott of Broadhaugh . . .' "

"I, Sir Quinton Scott of Broadhaugh . . ."

" '. . . do swear by the High God that reigneth above all kings and realms, and to whom all Christians owe obedience . . .' "

When Quin finished, Sir Hugh swore the same oath, and

then they took their seats—the wardens in armchairs, their clerk on a stool.

The clerk said, "If it please you, Sir Hugh, you may call your first juror."

Sir Hugh nodded and gazed out upon the multitude. The murmur of conversation that had begun as the three men took their seats died away in anticipation of hearing the first name called. Sir Hugh would choose the six Scottish jurors and Quin the six English ones. Quin appreciated the subtle suggestion that they would make their choices on the spot and at random, for despite Sir Hugh's casual pretense of searching the crowd, Quin knew that just as much calculation had gone into the Englishman's selections as had gone into his own.

Wardens could not simply pluck jurors like flowers from the field. They had to weigh personality, circumstance, and family relationships against the grievances with which they had to deal. At times, as he had learned from his surly mentor, the calculation required the craftiness and wisdom of a sage. Moreover, they were supposed to impanel only respectable men on their juries. Since the law forbade naming traitors, murderers, fugitives, betrayers, and other infamous persons from sitting, life being what it was in the Borders, wardens from both sides often had to overlook the rules in order to find twelve men to serve.

Impaneling the two juries took little time, however, and the clerk had them all swear their oaths as one. They were ready to begin the day's business.

The clerk selected the most recent bill of complaint first and read it aloud to the company for consideration. The complaint being against an Englishman, the six Englishmen whom Quin had selected would hear it.

In a solemn, carrying voice, louder than anyone might expect from so slight a man, the clerk intoned, "Jed Elliot and Wat Tailor, step forward and be heard!"

Two burly men emerged from the throng, urged on by shouts

from their cohorts. Glowering at wardens and jurors alike, both looked very determined.

The clerk said, "Jed Elliot, you have filed grievance before this body. Have you honestly declared the truth of what your goods were worth at the time of their taking had they been bought and sold in a market all at one time, and do you also declare that you know no other recovery but this, so help you God?"

The burly Scotsman rolled his eyes heavenward, then muttered, "Well, as to knowin' no other recourse—"

Quin cleared his throat loudly, drawing Elliot's startled attention.

The Scotsman sighed, looked at the jury, then declared hoarsely, "I do, then, by God and by Christ Almighty, as weel."

The clerk, expressionless, turned next to the Englishman. "Do you, Wat Tailor, swear by heaven above you, hell beneath you, by your part of Paradise, by all that God made in six days and seven nights, and by God himself, that you are sackless of art, part, way, witting, ridd, kenning, having, or resetting of any of the goods and cattle named in this bill, so help you God?"

"Aye, I do swear," the Englishman muttered.

The clerk turned to the two wardens. "This bill is cleared by the defendant's own oath of innocence," he declared.

"Here now," Elliot protested. He fell silent when Quin looked at him, but the expression on his face made it plain that at best his silence would be momentary.

Quin understood Buccleuch's warning about fairness. When one man held the fate of another in his hands, he could easily lose sight of all but the awesome power he wielded. At Broadhaugh he possessed great power, including the authority to order men drowned in the pit or hanged from the gallows, but the consequences that could result from Broadhaugh justice were small compared to this. At Dayholm a misstep could start a war between two countries. The thought sobered him.

To Sir Hugh, he said, "Can Tailor call others to swear to his innocence?"

Sir Hugh bellowed the question to the crowd, then waited a few moments. When no one stepped forward, he said, "Apparently, no man speaks for him."

"Then let the jury decide," Quin said, nodding to the six Englishmen he had chosen for his assize court.

They returned their verdict after a brief muttering conference: "Guilty."

Glancing at the bill of grievance, Quin said, "The charge declares forty head of kine and three oxen. At thirty shillings apiece for the kine and forty for the oxen, the amount . . ."

". . . would be sixty-six pounds, sir," the clerk said quickly.

"Sterling," Quin added. "Can Tailor pay such an amount?"

"He can and he will," Sir Hugh said, exchanging a look with the burly Tailor. "I will stand good for it myself."

The clerk called the next case, and business proceeded in a generally orderly fashion until noon, when the acting wardens declared a recess for dinner.

Chapter 19

*"And have they e'en ta'en him . . .
Against the truce of border tide?"*

Janet had watched the proceedings for only a few minutes
before she had seen a kinswoman helping to set out food.
Dismounting with Hob the Mouse's help, she left her horse
with another man-at-arms to look after it and went to join the
other women. She thought her old friends and family members
looked pleased to see her, but they did seem reticent at first
and less friendly than in the past. Not until she noticed that
each woman she spoke to looked beyond her rather than at
her did she realize that she had brought along a somewhat
intimidating escort.

Since she had walked away after seeing her horse safely in
the care of Quinton's man, she had not seen Hob signal two
others to follow her. Seeing them now and knowing she could
do nothing about them, she shrugged, grinned at the woman
with whom she was speaking, and said, "My husband frets
about my safety, I'm afraid. He does not seem to realize that
with kinsmen on both sides of the line, I am most likely safer
than most folks."

"It does not do to be too sure of such things," the woman said wisely.

Janet agreed with her, but she was glad to see old acquaintances again and felt certain that because of the truce, nothing untoward would happen. Enjoying the company of women from both sides of the line, she paid little heed to the trials as they proceeded. Just as one of the older women was suggesting that the men would soon call a halt so they could eat their dinner, she saw another old friend.

"Andrew, is that you?"

The boy was with several men, and when she called to him he glanced at her, then glanced away again.

She recognized one of the men with whom the boy stood as a friend of Hugh's. The man took a step toward her, then seemed to change his mind, and she remembered her ubiquitous escort. When she looked over her shoulder to see Quinton's two men frowning, their hands on their daggers, she sighed. It explained, however, why Hugh's friend was walking away without speaking to her.

Andrew, too, had turned away.

"Andrew, come here. I want to talk to you."

Hesitating only a moment, the boy strode to meet her. Touching his cap, he bade her good day, his dignified manner telling her that he wanted people to think him older than his years.

Concealing her amusement, she said, "What are you doing here, my lad?"

"I come to see them bluidy Scotch reivers, is what," he replied grimly.

"And what else have you seen?"

He looked directly at her, and his eyes lit with pleasure more in keeping with his age. He said, "I seen a lamb with two heads, Mistress Janet. Did ye see it?"

"I did," she acknowledged. "How fares your mam? Is she here today?"

"Nay, she's wi' the bairns. We got a new one since ye left.

It's nobbut a lass, though, and a puling one at that. Sir Hugh himself helped wi' her birthin', though.''

"Hugh did?" Janet was amazed.

"Aye, there were none else to help, so I fetched 'im, and then he sent Ned Rowan to look after the place, 'cause he said we needed a man about. I could ha' taken care of 'em,'' he added resentfully. "I dinna like Ned Rowan. He's sweet on me mam, but she doesna want him.''

"Then she need not have him,'' Janet said kindly.

"Sir Hugh says she will, though, unless she wants to go to Brackengill and look after him instead. All them women at the castle left when ye did, Mistress Janet, and their men willna let them go back.''

"Oh, dear,'' Janet said, knowing that if her departure alone had not infuriated her brother, the circumstances that resulted from it must have done so.

"Aye,'' Andrew said. "Be it true, then, that the reiver carried ye off, like they say he did?''

"Aye, true enough,'' she said.

"They do say it were Rabbie Redcloak that took ye and that ye married wi' him. Be that true, as well?''

Janet's breath caught in her throat. Before she could think of something sensible to say, she was startled to hear her brother's grim voice behind her.

"Janet, I want to speak to you.''

Turning to see Hugh striding toward her, she noted with relief that he could not have heard Andrew's remark. She bent quickly to say in a low voice, "Andrew, what you heard is not true, and you must not tell anyone that it is. Promise me!''

"But I—''

"Run along, lad,'' Hugh said curtly. "I want to speak to Lady Scott.''

Andrew looked puzzled, and Janet said, "That is my name now, Andrew. Go now, and remember to tell your mam that I think of her often.''

As the boy took to his heels, disappearing into the crowd, Hugh said, "What were you talking to him about?"

"He told me that you helped Jock's Meggie when her time came," she said calmly. "That was kind of you, Hugh."

"Aye, it was," he agreed. "It was a damned nuisance, as well."

"He also said that you sent Ned Rowan to look after the place. Meggie does not like Ned, however, and won't marry him. You will have to find someone else."

"That is not for you to say, Janet. I'll do what I think best. Are you well?"

"You can see that I am," she replied, accepting the change of subject. "Thank you for agreeing to the marriage. It was the best course, I think."

"It was the only course," he said bluntly. "One day we'll talk about your part in the reiver's escape, lass. I know well that you are not blameless, but this is no place to talk." His tone promised that the future conversation would not be pleasant.

Before she could reply, one of his men shouted that the clerk was ready to call the proceedings to order again, and Janet felt only relief at having the conversation curtailed. Clearly, it was no time to mention her dowry to him.

She was sorry, however, that she would not have time to speak to Quinton before he had to resume his duties. She would have liked to tell him what Andrew had said. There was no hurry, though. The truce would keep him safe long enough to return to the safety of Hermitage or Broadhaugh. She would tell him then.

Quin and Sir Hugh had no sooner taken seats again than the clerk called the next bill: "Sir Edward Nixon accuses Arch and Will Crosier of taking eight head of kine and six horses from Bewcastle. Accused and accuser, step forth and be heard!"

Sir Edward Nixon, a richly attired gentleman known to everyone there, was the first to obey. The clerk recited the accuser's oath, to which Sir Edward declared loudly, "I do so swear it, by God."

The two accused strode forward next, and when the clerk had recited the oath, they looked at each other and muttered gruffly in unison, "Aye."

The clerk turned to the wardens. "The accused are quit by their own oaths."

Silence blanketed the crowd, and Quin could not wonder at it. The two Crosier brothers, kin to Curst Eckie of that ilk, were a pair of thieving scoundrels known the length and breadth of the Borders on both sides of the line. He was not surprised when Sir Hugh, with a glint of amusement in his eyes, said, "Can any other man avow the innocence of this worthy pair?"

Concealing his own amusement, Quin was about to shout the question to all and sundry when Will Crosier known fondly to his friends as Ill Wild Will—said, "There be two wha' will speak for us. Rob and Martin Armstrong will."

Chuckles rippled through the crowd, and seeing the two men whom Ill Wild Will had named standing near the front, Quin beckoned to them.

"Will the pair of you avow the innocence of these two men?"

"Aye, I will," Martin Armstrong declared, jutting forth his bearded chin as if to defy anyone to question his sworn word. "By Christ's wounds, I will."

Meeting that defiant gaze, Quin held it for a long moment, then turned to Robert Armstrong. "Rob, will you avow the innocence of these two?"

Rob looked at the ground and scratched his chin whiskers for a long moment while the crowd seemed to hold its collective breath. Then he looked at Quin.

Quin returned the look steadily.

Rob's gaze slithered away and inched back. He drew a deep breath, avoided looking at anyone but Quin, and said quietly, "Nay then, I'll no forswear m'self before God Almighty to summat I dinna ken to be true."

Quin said, "Then under the truce this bill will be declared proven."

"Christ's blood," Ill Wild Will swore. "We've our three oaths against one!"

Quin glanced at Sir Hugh, then back at the accused. His voice carrying easily, he said, "We have weighed your three oaths against Sir Edward's, Will, and we find yours the weaker." To Sir Edward, he said, "Will you accept payment, sir?"

"I will for the cattle," Sir Edward said. "I want the horses back if you can get them. As you have seen by my declaration, they are particularly valuable beasts."

"We will see what can be done," Quin promised. "You have my word."

The Crosiers looked unhappy, but they did not debate the decision, and business continued until the last grievance against the Scots had been decided. A number of bills remained unsettled against the English, but when Quin suggested calling an end, Sir Hugh nodded in agreement.

"These others will hold till next time," he said, "and Scrope will be glad that you suggested it. He reminded me that even though the law says we should deal with all the grievances that have been filed, it is wiser to settle bill-for-bill. As to the imbalance in amounts favoring England today, that need not concern us. Our side always pays up promptly, after all, and will doubtless do so this time long before your Liddesdale lot pays a jot of its share."

Quin recognized the comment as provocation and ignored the temptation to remind him that more grievances had been filed against the English. That could change by the next wardens' meeting, and besides, he knew that what Sir Hugh had said was true. It was not only that Liddesdale did not like to pay, though. Generally speaking, the Liddesdale men were less able to pay than their English counterparts were. Keeping these thoughts to himself, he began to put away his papers.

Little remained to do beyond allowing the clerk to read their

joint proclamation of what the day had accomplished and to
name a date for the next meeting. Having achieved the first
task easily and the second with less conviction—surprising no
one, since everyone knew there would be much haggling over
that date or any other—the clerk declared the day's business
at an end.

The acting wardens charged their followers to keep the peace
until the next Truce Day, then made their farewells to the
assembly. As trumpets sounded and the crowd began moving
away to collect belongings and prepare to depart, the clerk said
to Quin and Sir Hugh, "I shall make fair copies of the order
of business for each of you. And since neither of your principals
was here, I shall make copies for them, too, and will send them
all as soon as I have completed them."

Thanking him, the two deputies stepped away from the table,
still keeping a watchful eye on each other as they moved to
join their separate companies.

It took Quin a few moments to find Jenny, but he spotted
her at last, talking with a lad he assumed was a kinsman.
Managing to catch her eye, he waved, then shouted to Hob the
Mouse to collect their people and prepare to depart.

The sun was nearing the western horizon and soon would
set. He wanted to be well away from Dayholm before it did.

His party was soon mounted and ready. Lifting Jenny to her
saddle, he swung into his, signed to the others, and spurred his
horse to a canter, turning away from Kershopefoot Burn to
follow Liddel Water to the nearest fording place. The group
following him was smaller and quieter than at the beginning
of the day. Many had already departed for their homes, and
everyone was tired,

Looking back, Quin saw that a significant number of riders
from the English cavalcade lingered on the Scottish side of the
burn, and although they rode near the burn, they seemed to be
keeping pace with his party. When he and his men rode over
the rise into Liddesdale, he lost sight of them briefly but saw
them again soon afterward, riding along the crest. He recognized

some of the men but not their leader's banner. As he and his men neared the ford, two of the English riders shouted taunts at Ill Wild Will and Arch Crosier. The Crosiers shouted back.

Quin glanced at Hob the Mouse, who growled at the Crosiers, "Hold your whisst, ye fashious bairns."

Quin saw Jenny frown at the riders following them, but he was not unduly concerned. Each person attending the truce was, by law, inviolate to his enemies until the next day's sunrise. Therefore, even with hostile riders on the hillside above keeping step with him, he and his company should be safe. Nevertheless, instincts honed by years of raiding and battle set the hairs on the back of his neck to tingling.

At a point where the landscape to the east soared up through forestland to the Larriston Fells and the Cheviots, as Quin and his party neared the ford, the group above them suddenly spurred their horses.

"Ride, master," Hob shouted. "They be breaking truce!"

Even before Quin heard the warning and saw the well-practiced battlefield maneuver with the horses, he had feared an attack. The signs had been undeniable, for the other party was heavily armed and had watched him and his people more closely than mere taunting would account for. More than once he had seen one man lean near another to talk without looking away from the Scots.

"Hold where you are, everyone," he shouted before his men could spur their ponies. "They outnumber us, and I'll not risk my Jenny or any of the other women by encouraging them to chase us or make battle. We'll face them down."

"They'd never dare harm me," Jenny said stoutly. "I know that banner, sir. It is my cousin, Francis Musgrave. I cannot believe he would dare to break the truce."

Moments later, the leader of the English party, closely followed by his men, rode up to Quin and declared loudly, "You are under arrest, Rabbie Redcloak, for theft and for murder. You are to come with us."

Stunned by the unexpected identification, Quin fought to collect his wits.

Jenny said angrily, "You are mad, Francis Musgrave. This is Sir Quinton Scott, Laird of Broadhaugh, close cousin to the Laird of Buccleuch, and my husband! You cannot arrest him. He is deputy warden of the Scottish middle and west marches, as you know right well!"

"He is under arrest nonetheless," Musgrave said firmly, adding with a flinty look at Quin, "We outnumber you, Broadhaugh, two to one."

Quin saw other riders coming over the rise and realized that Musgrave had planned his attack well. "I'll go peacefully," he said. "Jenny, ride to Buccleuch with Hob and our other men and tell him about this. Do not, under any circumstance, put yourself in danger, but do exactly what Buccleuch tells you to do. Now, go, lass."

Tears glittered in her eyes, but she raised her chin. "Recall that I know you well, Francis Musgrave," she said angrily. "Moreover, if I find out that Hugh had aught to do with this outrage, I'll . . ."

"Do not blame Sir Hugh, cousin," Musgrave said. "We learned only a short time ago that Broadhaugh is the notorious reiver, Rabbie Redcloak. I will do you the courtesy to pretend you did not know of his past. However, you should know that we mean to make a gift of him to your brother, and Hugh may not be so credulous. We mean you and the others no harm, though. You may depart in peace."

"Peace!" she snapped. "What do you know of peace, to break a solemn truce like this? You should be ashamed of yourself. God will punish you, Francis, and by heaven, if I can help him send you all to perdition, I will!"

"That's enough now, Jenny; go to Buccleuch," Quin said calmly. Turning to Hob, he added, "Stay with her. I depend upon you to guard her well."

"Aye, master," Hob replied. "And, mind, we'll have moonlight again."

Chapter 20

"Now word is gane to the bauld keeper,
In Branksome Ha', where that he lay . . ."

Ignoring tears that streamed down her cheeks, Janet watched as they constrained Quinton like a common felon with his arms tied behind him and his feet bound beneath his horse's belly. He held himself erect throughout the humiliating process, and his dignity reminded her of her position as his wife. She did not raise a hand to dry her tears, but they continued to flow.

Beside her, Hob murmured, "We should go, mistress, whilst we can."

"We will wait until they have ridden away," she said, not bothering to lower her voice to match his. "They must see that we are outraged, Hob, and not think for a minute's time that we fear them. We will sit quietly and watch, so as to make them constantly aware that we can serve as witnesses to this unlawful act."

"By God, madam," Gaudilands said behind her. "Were it not for you and the other women, we'd soon teach them a lesson. I can promise you that."

"Then you would give them grounds to declare later that you caused the trouble instead of them," Janet said without turning her head. "This way, they can never say that we initiated any of this. They are wholly in the wrong, and we shall be able to say so without fear of hearing any action of ours condemned in turn."

The Scots sat silently after that until the English band had disappeared over the rise with their prisoner.

Hob said quietly, "Now, mistress?"

"Now," Janet agreed.

Leaving half of their men to escort the other women, she rode ahead with Hob, Gaudilands, and Todrigg to Branxholme, where Buccleuch had remained to let his leg mend itself. Darkness fell some hours before the big gates swung open to admit them to the torchlit bailey.

Leaving their horses with lackeys, Janet hurried into the hall with Hob and the two gentlemen following. She found Buccleuch alone, sitting at his ease in a cushioned armchair with his leg propped on a bench set lengthwise before him. A goblet of wine rested companionably on a small table at his elbow.

He frowned at her hasty entrance, but made no move to stand. "What's amiss, lass?" he demanded. "And why the devil have you brought Todrigg and Gaudilands with you? Where's Quin?"

"They've seized him, sir. They've broken the truce, and I am ashamed to say that those who took him are Musgraves, members of my mother's family and hitherto men for whom I held both respect and affection."

His startled reaction sent the goblet at his elbow flying, but he paid no heed to the resulting clatter or mess. "The devil you say!" he exclaimed, sitting bolt upright now. "They've broken the truce?"

"Aye, Wat," Gaudilands said angrily. "We'd scarce left the ground when Francis Musgrave and about a hundred others swooped down upon us."

Todrigg said, "They arrested him as Rabbie Redcloak."

"Damnation," Buccleuch exclaimed, adding as an obvious afterthought, "I beg your pardon, lass."

"Quinton said to ride straight to you, sir," she said. "What can we do?"

"We will protest, of course, for they have broken the law. You are certain that none of you crossed to their side of the line?"

Gaudilands snapped, "Of course no one did! Christ, Wat, we were about to cross the Liddel near Whithaugh. We could scarcely have wandered the opposite way, across the Kershope into England, without noticing."

"I'll send a protest to that blasted Scrope at once."

Todrigg said, "Ye'd best send it to Sir Hugh Graham at Brackengill. Them what took Quin did say they mean to make Sir Hugh a gift of him."

Buccleuch frowned thoughtfully at Janet. "Did they, indeed?"

"Yes," she said, "they did. They also said that Hugh did not know of their intent. In point of fact, they said that they had just learned that Quinton is Rabbie Redcloak. Someone must have told them—someone who attended Truce Day."

Buccleuch nodded. "I see what you are thinking, lass, and I own, I ought to have considered that possibility sooner. Who on our side might have had reason today to feel anger or resentment toward Quin?"

"Those devilish Crosier brothers," Gaudilands said instantly.

"Aye, Arch and Ill Wild Will," Todrigg agreed.

The two men, speaking in turn, described the events of the day. Before they had finished, servants brought wine and ale, and afterward Buccleuch invited them to linger and take a late supper with him.

"For that matter," he added, "you may as well stay the night, all of you. I cannot send Quin's lady back to Broadhaugh without an armed escort, and my lads will accomplish that with greater safety in the morning." Turning to Janet, he added, "Margaret has taken the bairns and gone to Ferniehurst to visit with her kinsmen, lass, but you can stay the night in your old room. Just send for one of the maidservants to stay with you."

"Thank you, sir; I will gladly accept your kind offer," Janet said. "Pray, will you send someone at once to Brackengill? I do not think Hugh would dare hang Quinton when so many know exactly what occurred. Indeed, I believe that Hugh will be shocked to learn what Francis Musgrave dared to do in his name. Still . . ." She let her words trail to silence and sent him a beseeching look.

"I take leave to doubt Hugh's shock," Buccleuch said grimly. "However, if he dares to lay a hand on Quin, he'll answer to me. That I promise you before God."

His tone chilled her, but she could not find it in herself to defend Hugh—not while Quinton remained at risk.

"Todrigg," Buccleuch went on, "you'll take my message to Brackengill as soon as you have supped. Christ, but I resent this outrage, for it touches my honor. 'Tis an insult to Scotland and a defiance of my authority as warden. I shall complain fiercely about this breach of the truce and demand Quin's immediate release."

"Good," Todrigg said grimly.

"Take a score of my men to augment your own—ten from here and ten from Hermitage, for you'll pass it on your way. And be prepared to go on to Carlisle," he added thoughtfully. "Under the circumstances, Sir Hugh may think it wiser to let Scrope deal with the matter this time."

"Aye, Buccleuch, I'll see to it all," Todrigg said, nodding. "An God wills it, we'll ha' Quin safe home again by tomorrow sunset."

"I'd like to stay here until we know that he is safe," Janet said evenly to Buccleuch, hoping that her firm, matter-of-fact tone would persuade him despite Margaret's absence.

He shook his head. "That would not be suitable, lass. Although my leg is mending, I am in no case to look after you, and most of the womenfolk have taken advantage of my lady's absence to visit their own families. If you do not want to remain alone at Broadhaugh, I'll have my lads take you to Margaret at Ferniehurst, but in any event, you must leave here at first light. I'll command Hob the Mouse to look after you till Quin returns. None will plague you with Hob at your side."

She bit her lip but did not attempt to argue with him, knowing that it would be useless. It was enough for the moment that he did not send her home at once. While they supped, the three men discussed all that might lie ahead, and she listened with interest. She was not surprised, however, when Buccleuch dismissed her as soon as lackeys began to clear away the platters from the table.

"You go along now," he said absently. "We've important matters to discuss."

Hiding her resentment, she obeyed him, realizing only when she reached her old bedchamber how tired she was. By the time she had shouted for water, and a maidservant had found an old smock of Margaret's for her to wear to bed, she could hardly keep her eyes open. Sending the maid away, she promised to bolt the door. Doing so, she climbed into bed, fell asleep at once, and did not stir till the same maidservant pounded on the door late the next morning.

"My lady, Himself said to tell ye to get dressed and go down to break your fast, for Hob and them will leave within the hour," the maid shouted. "D'ye hear?"

"I hear," Janet muttered, wishing she could tell the woman to go away and leave her alone. The maid pounded again, at which she shouted, "I'm coming!"

"Aye, good," the maid shouted back. "I ha' hot water for ye!"

Admitting her, Janet quickly splashed water on her face and got dressed. Rejecting further assistance, she dragged a comb through her hair and confined it in the net she wore when she rode. Then, smoothing her wrinkled skirts as well as she could, she hurried down to the hall.

The table was laden with food again, and Buccleuch was eating. He glanced up at her entrance and said without preamble, "Todrigg's messenger arrived only minutes ago. He was well nigh asleep in his saddle, and I've sent him off to bed."

"I did not expect any news yet," she said, knowing it could not be good if the man had ridden through the night at what must have been reckless speed to bring it.

"They've taken Quin to Carlisle," Buccleuch said grimly. "Your brother sent me a damned officious message, but I have decided to ignore it."

"What said he, sir?"

"He insists that he knows naught of the arrest of Sir Quinton Scott," Buccleuch said. "However, he admits having received word that his cousin Musgrave did capture a notorious reiver engaged in a raid on Bewcastle."

"*What?* Bewcastle?"

"Aye, Bewcastle. Musgrave's men had to chase the reiver, he said, and when the villain crossed over into Scotland and tried to raise the country against them, they were forced—in self-defense, your brother says—to take him into custody and deliver him to Carlisle."

"Is it possible that Hugh does not know the truth?"

Buccleuch looked at her, his derision clear.

"No, that is not possible," Janet admitted with a sigh. "Francis Musgrave would never lie to Hugh about such a matter—or anything else. He wouldn't dare."

"That is what I think, too," Buccleuch said. "Todrigg sent his lad to me to report all that he had learned and to tell me that he has ridden on to Carlisle. Pray to God that that villain Scrope possesses more sense than Musgrave or your dolthead brother. Now eat. Hob and the others are ready to leave for Broadhaugh or Ferniehurst. They wait only for you to decide which it is to be."

"Broadhaugh an it please you, sir. I should be at home."

"Aye, that's what I thought, too, lass. I am sending Gaudilands home, as well. He will provide part of your escort, and since his tower house is but a few miles from Broadhaugh, he will be close at hand if you need him for anything.''

"Thank you," Janet said. "You will keep me apprised of the situation as it develops, will you not?"

"I will," he promised. "You can depend on that."

She doubted that he would do any such thing, and later that day, when Gaudilands and his men left her at Broadhaugh with none but Hob the Mouse or her maid, Ardith, to confide in, she felt abandoned and more resentful than ever. Had she been a man, she told herself, Buccleuch would not have dismissed her so easily.

Two days later, however, she learned that she had misjudged him. She was speaking with a dairymaid in the buttery when a lackey ran in to tell her that Buccleuch had sent a messenger. Hurrying to greet the man, she recognized him at once from Branxholme.

"What news have you?" she demanded.

"It isna good, my lady," the man said warily.

"I shan't snap your head off," she said, "but do not keep me on tenterhooks. Tell me at once."

"The Laird o' Todrigg came to Branxholme this morning," he said. "Himself said t' tell ye that Scrope—'that scoundrel, Scrope,' is what he said."

"Aye, I know what he thinks of his lordship," Janet said. "Todrigg did not have Sir Quinton with him, then. What else did Buccleuch say?"

Rolling his eyes upward and contorting his face, the man exerted himself to recall his master's exact words. At last, just as Janet was ready to scream, he said carefully, "Himself said he would first exhaust the resources of civilization so that none can complain that he's as barbaric as them thievin' English. Therefore, he said, he'll be sending a formal letter to Lord Scrope, declaring that Sir Quinton ha' been unlawfully captured and detained in direct violation of Border law. Himself be feelin' right quarrelsome, my lady," he added in his natural voice.

"I'll warrant he is," Janet said. "Does he think that Lord Scrope will heed a second demand when he ignored the first?"

"Nay, then, he did call Scrope a devilish fool, near as great an apehead as what Sir Hugh Graham is. Beggin' your pardon," he added hastily.

"You need not do so," Janet said. "I agree that Sir Hugh behaved badly, and the Musgraves behaved worse. I am ashamed of my own kinsmen, and that is the plain fact of the matter."

Three fretful days passed before she heard more, and it was all she could do to contain her soul in patience. Then it was Margaret who came to her, braving a light shower of rain and accompanied by a score of Buccleuch's men.

"Don't look so shaken, my dear," she said when, despite the rain, Janet ran into the bailey to receive her. "I bring bad news, but it could be much worse."

"They have not hanged him then," Janet said, trying to sound confident and sounding only wary. She barely noticed the raindrops.

"No, of course they have not," Margaret said, accepting the help of one of her escorts to dismount. " 'Twould be enough to start a war, with Buccleuch as furious as he is. He received a message from Scrope, though, and it has put him into a worse temper than ever. I returned from Ferniehurst to find him packing to leave for Hermitage. He left at once, despite the weather and his bad leg, and he asked me to bring you word myself, because he knew you would want to know."

"What did Scrope say?"

"The villain chooses to pretend that Quin is no one but Rabbie Redcloak," Margaret said indignantly. "He wrote that Rabbie was such a notorious offender that he dared not release him without authority from Elizabeth herself."

"Godamercy!"

"Aye, Buccleuch is in a towering rage," Margaret said, gently grasping Janet's arm and urging her back inside. "He says it is as if they had captured him, for Quin is his deputy, and thus it is by way of being the same thing. He would like to raise all of Liddesdale and Teviotdale and bring Carlisle Castle down around Scrope's ears, but until his leg mends he can do little more than swear.''

''I hope he does not do it more injury, riding to Hermitage,'' Janet said.

''Well, whether he does or not, I could not stop him,'' Margaret replied. ''He had clearly been fretting at Branxholme, feeling too far away from things. I would not have left him, but he commanded it, saying one of us would murder the other if I stayed.'' Grinning, she said, ''Order us food, my dear, and I will tell you all I know. I do not mean to linger, but perhaps your people could see to providing mine with something warm to drink and a bite to eat.''

''Forgive me, madam, I forget my duties,'' Janet exclaimed with embarrassment, looking around for a lackey.

Hob the Mouse, never far from her side, nodded reassuringly and turned away to deal with the matter.

''Your people serve you well, my dear,'' Margaret said cheerfully. ''Hob will see to everything, and you and I can talk quietly upstairs by ourselves.''

By the time they reached the master's hall, Janet had her emotions under control again. Gesturing for Margaret to take Quinton's comfortably padded Italian armchair, she said, ''Surely, if Buccleuch has ridden to Hermitage, his leg must be mending more swiftly than anyone expected.''

''He is roaring,'' Margaret said, ''so I presume that he is as fit as he can be at the moment. Nonetheless, he required assistance to mount his horse, and it was clearly a painful ordeal for him. I doubt, from what Alys the herbwoman and others tell me, that he will be himself again for yet another month or longer.''

''Godamercy,'' Janet said. ''Then what can he do about this?''

''He has sent word to the English ambassador in Edinburgh

and to King Jamie," Margaret said. "He is certain that Jamie will write to Elizabeth himself."

"London," Janet said, frowning. "They must send all the way to London."

"Aye, but Buccleuch says they will make all speed. We should know the queen's answer in a fortnight or mayhap even less time than that, he said."

"A fortnight." Janet sighed, adding, "That is very fast, I know, but it seems like a lifetime. And for Quinton, it may be just that."

"I know that you must miss him dreadfully, for 'tis clear that you love him," Margaret said. "I tell you, though, they will not dare to harm him."

Janet did not believe her, much as she wanted to, but she could hardly say so, and thus she made no objection when the older woman changed the subject. However, as the days passed, her worries increased until she could scarcely concentrate on anything. The weather continued to produce as much rain as sunshine, which did nothing to lift her spirits, and things now ran so smoothly at Broadhaugh that she did not have to give much thought to daily chores. At times she found herself wishing that she had more to do.

It was not that she missed Quinton particularly, or so she told herself at least once a day. She was merely fearful for his safety, as anyone would be who had a grain of compassion. And she was angry, too, of course, as anyone with a sense of justice must be. But for Margaret or anyone else to suggest that she had fallen in love with her husband was nonsense.

Even to suggest that she missed him was putting the matter too strongly. She was not lonely. How could anyone be lonely who was surrounded by loyal followers and who had grown up in the manner that she had? Even men known to number among Rabbie's Bairns frequently appeared at Broadhaugh to ask her for news, and they all promised to do whatever they could to help. No one should be lonely with support like theirs.

She had often longed for Hugh to go away just so that she

could have solitude and the freedom to do as she pleased without facing censure or carping—or worse. And just as it had been with Hugh, with Quinton around, no one could ever wonder who was in charge. Even though the people at Broadhaugh showed her respect, and even though Quinton had given her free rein to run the household, she knew that oftentimes his people went to him to make sure that they should carry out her orders. He had never countermanded one, to be sure; but still, there it was.

She felt the lack of his presence more than she had felt Hugh's, though, for Quinton had seemed larger than life from that very first meeting. Even as a prisoner in a dungeon he had made his presence more strongly felt than any other man had. She always knew when he was within the walls of Broadhaugh, too. The place fairly crackled with his presence and felt lifeless by comparison with him gone.

She had slept in his bed every night that she had spent at home since they had taken him, but who would not do the same if they had the right? His bed was more comfortable than hers was. When she recalled waking with lustful intent from a dream in which Quinton's arms were wrapped around her to find herself alone in his bed, a tear trickled down her cheek. She brushed it away. She did not miss him and could not imagine why she felt like weeping. In any event, he would be home soon, or the good Lord would be hearing some straight talk during her daily prayers.

Since she knew from a tale that one of Hugh's tutors had told her that the gods only helped them who helped themselves, she decided to do her part without bothering to consult anyone else. Accordingly, she sent a message to Lord Scrope, formally requesting permission to visit her husband.

Scrope's reply came swiftly, informing her that to the best of his knowledge her husband was not residing at Carlisle. *In any event,* the message went on, *Sir Hugh Graham has informed us that he objects strenuously to his sister's penchant for fraternizing with felons.*

It was not a reassuring missive, but she could not complain to anyone, since she was fairly certain that Buccleuch would not approve of her having written to Scrope without first applying to him for permission to do so. Although Hob the Mouse knew where her messenger had gone, she told no one else what she had done, but when ten more days had passed without word from Buccleuch, she could stand it no longer. Sending for Hob, she said, "Order out an escort for me. I mean to ride for Hermitage within the hour. Get word to Rabbie's Bairns, too, to hold themselves ready in the event that I shall require their help."

"Mistress, ye canna—"

"Do not tell me what I cannot do," she snapped. "Arrange for that escort and arm them well. Then send word out to the others. If Buccleuch refuses to do anything more to help Quinton, I must ride to Carlisle myself and confront Lord Scrope, and I will need the Bairns as well as our own men to protect me."

"But, mistress—"

"Not another word, Hob. You would not dare to argue with me if the master were here."

"But if he were here . . ." His words trailed to silence in the face of her increasing anger. Abruptly, he nodded and went out.

Calling to Ardith, Janet told her to pack clothes to take to Hermitage. "Tell Tip that I want the clothing that he provided for me before, which I returned to him, and a suit of clothes for the master in case Buccleuch should succeed in getting him released. You will have to come with me," she added. "There will be the devil to pay over my doing this, but at least if I have another female with me and ride there properly on a sidesaddle, Buccleuch cannot simply order me to ride home again."

He could, of course, and she knew it. She could think of little else during the maddeningly slow ride south to Hermitage, but she told herself over and over that she would not let him send her home. By the time her little company passed through the gates, she had nearly convinced herself that he would not.

Quin thought the prison accommodations at Carlisle vastly superior to those at Brackengill if only because, thanks to a small barred window set high in one wall, his cell enjoyed regular daylight. Its furnishing left much to be desired, for there was no bed or even a bench to sit on. However, there was also no muck on the floor, merely a pile of rags, their origin impossible to guess, to ease its hardness.

Unlike Sir Hugh Graham, Scrope did not starve him, but the single meal he got each day consisted only of bread and water, and occasionally some soup. He had suffered a few bruises at the hands of Francis Musgrave's men before his arrival at Carlisle, but he had recovered from them and had suffered none since, although his guards delighted in entertaining him with speculation about whether Scrope would hang him, drown him in a pit, or simply send him to the queen as a gift. He knew that he had lost weight, and the lack of food made him weak, but he would not give in to that. He worked daily to maintain what strength he had.

Worst of all was the boredom. The window was too high to look out unless he pulled himself up, which he forced himself to do daily for the exercise. He could not hold himself there for long, however, and he took good care whenever a guard entered to present the image of a rapidly weakening prisoner. The window faced east, and knowing that he was looking homeward gave him a sense of peace.

To ease the boredom and occupy his mind, he often thought of Jenny. Seeing her cry when they took him away had hurt him more than the beating they gave him later. It had also stirred his temper, though, to know that she had witnessed his humiliation. Had they given him any chance to fight back, he did not doubt that he would have given a good account of himself.

He spent a good portion of each slowly passing day sitting on the floor, leaning against the wall opposite the cell door, with his eyes closed, imagining Jenny at Broadhaugh. Doubtless she was making life miserable for Buccleuch, he thought, but perhaps Buccleuch could handle her.

The thought made him smile. He doubted that anyone could handle his Jenny. She was probably wishing right now that she had been born a man—a very powerful man—so that she could lead an army of ten thousand to free him. She also was probably wishing that she had not promised to curb her impulses. She was gey impulsive, was Jenny.

Over the long, lonely hours, various images presented themselves: Jenny with her long, silvery hair hanging free to her waist; Jenny with her hands on her hips, spitting fury at him; Jenny laughing; and Jenny in bed beside him, moaning with pleasure as he stroked her soft and supple body and made love to her. That thought stirred memories of another body, a furry one, stretched along his backside, purring.

"Damnation," he muttered, "I even miss her blasted cat."

Chapter 21

"Now Christ's curse on my head," he said,
"But avenged of Lord Scrope I'll be!"

When Janet entered the master's hall at Hermitage, Buccleuch was sitting at his table with his estate books spread out before him and his leg propped up just as it had been the last time she had seen him. Lines of pain and worry etched his face, making him look older. "What is it, lass?" he demanded. "What's amiss now?"

"What is amiss, sir, is that I have heard not a word for nigh onto a fortnight, and I could not sit still at Broadhaugh for one minute longer."

"There be naught else for you to do, come what may," he said, scowling.

"Then I will wait here at Hermitage until someone brings news," she said, striving to sound implacable.

His eyes narrowed. "Send your lass upstairs," he said. "Hob, you go down to the great hall with the lads. I'll send for you when I want you."

Hob left without comment, and swallowing hard, Janet nodded to Ardith. When the maid had gone, she braced herself, certain that she was about to experience the full force of Buccleuch's famous temper. Before he spoke, however, the door opened again, and the Laird of Gaudilands strode in.

He nodded at Janet, then said to Buccleuch, "Ha' ye no told her yet?"

Buccleuch's scowl grew even fiercer. "Shut your gob, you fool!"

"Told me what?" Janet demanded, then answered her own question. "You've heard from Queen Elizabeth!"

"I have not," Buccleuch retorted. "Her guts-griped pigeon of an ambassador refuses to write to her, and although our Jamie persuaded the fen-sucked dogfish to write to Scrope, that letter got us no more than my own. Scrope still insists that he's got no one but a notorious reiver locked up at Carlisle. Even were that so, it still touches my honor," he added in a near growl. "The spleeny English have flagrantly violated Border laws upon which we all rely. Worse, they've infringed on *my* powers and they seem to think that there is naught I can do about it."

Janet bit her lip, forcing herself to keep silent.

A gleam of appreciation lit Buccleuch's eyes. "Speak up, lass," he said. "You've shown courage till now. Don't keep your thoughts to yourself."

Raising her chin, she said frankly, "I was just thinking, sir, that of all those Border laws, inviolability of the truce seems to be the only one to which you and your Borderers pay any heed whatsoever. Yet here you are, behaving much as you would if the sky had fallen."

"Aye, and what if I am?" he retorted. "The whole object of declaring a day of truce is to ensure that those who attend— particularly the witnesses, of course—can travel in peace without risking intimidation, assault, or battery on the way. Moreover, that scrofulous bastard Scrope informed the queen's ambassador that our truce lasts only from sunset the day before to sunset on the meeting day."

"Well, I know that is not what they agreed to at Dayholm, but if there is some question about that in other—"

"There is no question," he roared, adding more mildly, "You have only to think on it, lass. What good would be a truce that ended before most folks had got well away from the ground? 'Tis naught but that distempered malt-worm Scrope spitting lies again through his rotting yellow teeth! He had no business to seize Quin or any other man within my jurisdiction."

Agreeing, she said bluntly, "What do you mean to do about it?"

"I can tell you what I'd do if I had all my limbs about me," he snapped. "I'd raise two thousand angry Borderers and bring the walls of Carlisle down on that bat-fouling miscreant Scrope's head."

"But you do not have all your limbs about you, sir," she said. "Nor can you ride so far with your bad leg. Have you any deputy who could lead your men?"

"No one with my genius," he replied. "That is not conceit," he added when she raised her eyebrows. "It is plain fact. Our Borderers will not follow just anyone. The only man they might follow as easily as they follow me is Quin. Neither Todrigg nor Gaudilands, nor any other man hereabouts, has our ability or my power. I'll have to think long and hard about this, but I *will* think of something."

Though she was dying to make a suggestion, Janet held her tongue, and this time he did not command her to speak.

Gaudilands, having stood silently through the exchange, reddened when Buccleuch glowered at him and snarled, "What did you want then, besides to stir coals wi' the lass?"

Visibly gathering dignity, Gaudilands said, "I had no such intent, Wat. I merely came to see if ye'd decided what ye mean to do. We canna leave Quin moldering in a cell at Scrope's convenience."

Buccleuch grimaced. Turning to Janet, he said, "You'll be wanting to have a wash, lass. You may stay to dine, but then you must take yourself and that young woman of yours back to Broadhaugh and leave this business to us.''

Drawing a deep breath to steady her nerves, she said quietly, ''I mean you no disrespect, sir, but Quinton is my husband. I would like to hear your answer to the question that the Laird of Gaudilands just put to you.''

''You will not like it,'' he said. ''I made this leg of mine worse by riding here, and they tell me that I must not ride again for at least another fortnight unless I want to risk crippling myself permanently. I don't, so we're forced to wait a bit longer before we can do anything more to help Quin. Still, Scrope will not dare to harm him, and something may happen in the meantime to—''

''What will most likely happen is his untimely demise!'' Janet retorted. ''You cannot simply leave him there to rot! With respect, sir,'' she added belatedly.

''Your 'respect' leaves much to be desired, lass.''

''I am a trifle overwrought, perhaps,'' she admitted.

He cocked his head to one side. ''I did not think you even liked Quin much. As I recall, you married him only because I left you little choice.''

Feeling a surge of heat in her cheeks, she had all she could do to keep her countenance. ''I care for my husband as any wife should, sir. In any event, my feelings are irrelevant to the matter at hand. It would be a dreadful mistake to wait, sir. Surely, you can call upon his Bairns to help. They have offered to do what they can, and they are loyal. I warrant they would not fail you, or him.''

''So you care only as any wife should, eh?'' He eyed her shrewdly for a long moment, and she found herself wondering if Margaret had confided to him her thoughts on that particular subject.

She did not reply, and after a moment, he said, ''The Bairns would certainly follow me, lass. Moreover, lest you fear that I have put my leg above Quin's safety, let me assure you that is not the case. I must consider the injury when I judge the likelihood of a raid's proving successful, however. I dislike feeling helpless, believe me, but under the present circumstances I'd prove more liability than asset, and my Borderers, like Quin's, have better sense than to follow a weak leader.''

She could see that it had cost him to admit as much, but she said stubbornly, ''I think you could persuade them to follow someone else, sir. If you were to name someone like Gaudilands or Todrigg as your deputy—''

''I told you, lass, neither has my skill,'' Buccleuch said.

''Unfortunately, that is true,'' Gaudilands told her. ''Neither of us has a knack for keeping rogues like Rabbie's Bairns in order. Recall that many are broken men who are as like to lend their loyalty to an English leader as to a Scot. A successful raid—especially one of the magnitude that you want—would depend on such men agreeing to follow our orders without constantly debating their worth.''

''If it please you, sir,'' Janet said to Buccleuch, ''I think I can persuade them. They . . . they have shown considerable loyalty to me, as well as to Quinton. I think that, for us, they would agree to do whatever you commanded of them, even were you not present to enforce your commands.'' Realizing belatedly that her words might give offense, she added hastily, ''I did not mean to imply that you require my support, or Quinton's, to see your commands obeyed, sir, but—''

''I take your meaning well enough,'' Buccleuch said dryly. '' 'Tis fortunate for you that I do. When I am not at hand to knock heads together, my own Borderers forget any sense of discipline. Few leaders have managed to engage the loyalty of the Liddesdale men, let alone those who live in the Debatable Lands, and no one has ever done so from a distance—not without sending an equally fearsome deputy.''

''Will you at least let me talk to Hob the Mouse, sir? I trust his instincts, and if he thinks he can lead the Bairns to rescue their master, he will tell me so. If he cannot, he will admit that, too, but if he can, would you perhaps provide some of your own men under the direction of either Todrigg or Gaudilands to assist them?''

Buccleuch hesitated, and she could not tell if he wanted to reject the idea out of hand or if he actually was considering Hob as a suitable leader. She knew that it would be difficult for any gentleman to leave to a minion the direction of a raid sizeable enough to take Carlisle Castle, but she hoped that he would want her to believe him willing to try anything to free Quinton.

He said lightly, ''We can at least try it, I suppose.'' He cast a speaking look at Gaudilands, and she knew that he was merely humoring her.

She did not care about his reason, though. It was enough that he had agreed. ''Thank you, sir,'' she said. ''I will talk to Hob the Mouse at once. If he is willing, we can quickly get word to the Bairns. We must rely on you for a good plan of attack, though. Quinton said no one is better than you are at planning a big raid.''

He looked amused. ''You flatter me, lass. Do not think that you can twist me round your thumb, though. There will be no raid unless you can deliver the broken men and Rabbie's Bairns and guarantee their absolute, unquestioning obedience to Todrigg and Gaudilands, as well as to Hob the Mouse.''

''Well, I do think that I can do that—or that Hob can by enlisting their loyalty to me and to Quinton—but what shall I have Hob tell them, exactly? How will we arrange to gather everyone together in the event that he succeeds?''

''There will be plenty of time to discuss that after you have persuaded them to accept Hob as their leader and to obey orders from the others,'' Buccleuch said.

''But that is just it! The only way any plan can succeed with them is if it is put swiftly into action. We all know the Bairns will not just sit quietly awaiting those orders, and you said that you cannot ride for at least another fortnight—''

''Perhaps longer,'' he interjected with a grunt.

''We cannot wait! Quinton could have an accident, or they

could hang him for march treason as Rabbie and say afterward that they are sorry to have mistaken your deputy for a reiver.''

"They won't—"

"Please, sir, at least make a plan so that if all the men do agree, we can provide them with a simple way to know when and where to meet. Otherwise, we'll have to waste more time sending messengers out and about to explain the details.''

When Buccleuch hesitated, Gaudilands said tentatively, "There be the races at Langholm on the twelfth, Wat. Ye ken fine that everyone will be there.''

"Aye,'' Buccleuch agreed. "Tell Hob that he can tell the lads we'll pass final word on the matter along to them then. Mayhap my leg will surprise me, and I'll be there to lead them.'' Smiling, he added, "Your heart led you right, lass, however it ends. Now, run along and wash your face. They'll soon be bringing in the food.''

Janet bobbed a curtsy and obeyed without another word. If he looked a little surprised by her ready acquiescence, she knew it was nothing compared to what he would feel if he could hear the thoughts tumbling through her head.

Ardith waited to help her change her dress for dinner, but Janet declined to do so. "Pack my things again,'' she said. "We will be off again after I dine.''

"Away so soon? But whither, mistress?''

"You are going home to Broadhaugh,'' Janet said.

"But what of ye?''

"Never mind me,'' Janet said, shaking out her skirts while Ardith attempted to tidy her hair. As fine as the silvery blond tresses were, they resisted every effort to keep them confined. "You may attend me whilst I dine,'' Janet added. "It would not be suitable for you to go alone to the hall to dine with the men-at-arms.''

Ardith did not argue, and Buccleuch welcomed her to the table, clearly relieved to have succeeded in calming Janet so easily. She knew that he believed her mission would fail, and she was content to let him enjoy that belief as long as it served her purpose. When they finished their meal, he offered to escort her to her horse. Clearly he had already sent word to her men, ordering their preparation to return to Broadhaugh with their mistress.

Janet did not countermand the second part of those orders until they were safely beyond sight of the men-at-arms on Hermitage's ramparts. Once over the first rise, however, she said, "Call a halt, Hob. I want to speak to you."

"We can talk as we ride, mistress. Himself said we're no to dawdle more than we must wi' ye on that sidesaddle. The weather be no so certain these days, ye ken, and them clouds yonder be boiling up some." He gestured toward the west, where puffy white clouds were gathering just as they had nearly every afternoon or evening for weeks. Admittedly, they did frequently spit showers, if not by afternoon then sometime during the night, but Janet had no wish to discuss the weather.

"I see the clouds," she said, "but we are not returning to Broadhaugh, whatever they bring. At least, you and I are not going to Broadhaugh—not just yet."

He reined in. "What are ye saying, mistress? We must return."

"Come away from the others," she said. When he had obeyed, she said quietly, "What would you think if I were to tell you that Buccleuch has agreed to let you lead Rabbie's Bairns to Carlisle?"

"I'd think ye'd gone mad, mistress," the big man said frankly. "Himself wouldna try to put me in the master's place, come what may. There be any number o' men in Liddesdale—aye, and in Teviotdale, too—that he'd think on afore he'd choose the likes o' me."

"Well, to be truthful, he did not choose you," Janet admitted. "I did. Moreover, I am certain that he believes he was merely humoring me when he agreed to let you try to persuade the Bairns. He demands their utter obedience to his commands and to those of Todrigg and Gaudilands, since he will not be present to lead them. He does not think they will agree to that, or that they will follow you.''

''I dinna think so either.''

''They do want to rescue the master, do they not?''

''Aye, but without a proper leader . . .''

''The master told me when he was held prisoner at Brackengill that I had only to get word of his whereabouts to his Bairns and they would set him free. Was that not true?''

''Aye, it were true,'' Hob said, but his tone was hesitant. ''It were different then, though,'' he added.

''You listen to me now,'' Janet said sternly. ''Although Buccleuch's injury precludes his leading a raid of any kind, let alone one on a castle as well fortified as Carlisle, he has promised to devise a scheme to take it. The lairds of Todrigg and Gaudilands will lead as many men as they can call together. We need only persuade the Bairns to join them and to follow Buccleuch's orders.''

''We'll need tongues as glib as Rabbie's own to do that, mistress. Neither Todrigg nor Gaudilands kens much about raiding. They just follow Himself.''

''The Bairns might do it for Rabbie Redcloak,'' Janet said. ''And for me, Hob. Many have offered help, after all. Who amongst them could persuade the others?''

''Aye, well, they might listen to me,'' Hob said after a moment's thought.

''I believe they would, but I need you with me.''

''I'd no leave ye in any case, mistress. Both the master and Himself expect me to keep ye under me eye.''

''I know that,'' Janet said gently, ''and no one could keep me safer. Who else might persuade them?''

''Ally the Bastard might, if I could persuade him.''

''Then we will persuade him together,'' Janet said.

''But, mistress—''

''It is useless to argue with me, Hob. We have already wasted nearly three weeks since he was taken. Heaven alone knows what they have done to him or what state he is in. Sir Hugh did not even feed him, you will recall, and I doubt that Scrope will be more hospitable. I must do something. In any event, you cannot go to Ally the Bastard and also watch over me—not unless I go with you."

"He could come to Broadhaugh, could he not?"

"We will go to him," Janet said firmly. "Choose one of the other men to go with us, and choose one with a good horse in case we have to travel any distance to find Ally the Bastard."

"I ken fine where to find him," Hob the Mouse said indignantly.

"Do not quibble. Just do as I bid you."

"Aye, sure." Giving spur to his pony, he approached one of the other men.

Janet took the opportunity to catch Ardith's eye and gestured to her. When the maidservant rode nearer, she said, "That large bundle tied to your saddle contains my extra clothing, does it not?"

"Aye, mistress, and the master's things that Tip sent. I'd never entrust your garments to these witless men."

"Good," Janet said. "Dismount and follow me—and bring that bundle."

"But, mistress—"

"I do wish everyone would stop saying 'but, mistress,' " Janet snapped. "I did not ask for your opinion, Ardith. Just do as I say."

"Yes, my lady."

The men, clearly believing that the two women were seeking the privacy of nearby shrubbery for the usual reason, did not question them and discreetly looked away. As soon as they were out of sight, Janet said, "You got those other clothes from Tip as I bade you, did you not?"

"Aye, mistress." Ardith hefted the bundle. "They be here, as well."

"Get them out, and be quick about it. I want to get changed before Hob the Mouse wonders what is taking us so long."

Ardith's lips pursed, then pressed firmly together while she hastily opened the bundle and took out the requested garments. Janet's riding dress came off with uncustomary speed, and she sent silent thanks heavenward for the fact that male clothing was more speedily donned than female attire.

"I shall keep my cloak," she said. "I'll need it for warmth, and 'tis plain enough to pass for a man's. Moreover, it may keep the lads from noticing at once that I have changed my clothing."

"They'll surely see that you have lost your petticoats, mistress."

"Mayhap they will," Janet agreed, noting, too, that Ardith's already unwieldy bundle had grown even greater in size. As she knelt to help tie it, she added, "It does not matter if they do notice."

With the bundle securely retied, they hurried back to join the men.

Janet said, "You and I will trade horses, Ardith. Yours is a sturdy, well-built little horse, and it is easier for us to trade horses than saddles. I want to travel faster than my sidesaddle will allow."

"Pray, mistress, tell me what ye mean to do."

"Do not look so fearful," Janet told her. "I am merely going to help Hob raise an army to free Sir Quinton."

"I'll warrant ye've more in your mind than just talking," Ardith said shrewdly. "I ha' seen that look before. What's more, I'll warrant that Hob the Mouse doesna ken all ye've got in store for him."

Avoiding her keen look, Janet said, "You would do well to hold your tongue, Ardith, if that is what you think."

"Aye, sure, but take care. If ye fling yourself into a scrap, 'tis likely that the master will ha' summat to say about it after, and that willna be so good."

"So long as he is free, he can be as angry as he likes," Janet said.

"Aye, well, first we'll see what Hob the Mouse has to say about this."

Hob had much to say, both then and in the hours that followed, but none of it availed him much.

Nearly twenty-four hours later, when the solid ramparts of Carlisle Castle hove into view on the horizon before them, Hob the Mouse viewed them with disfavor. "I dinna ken how I let ye talk me into this," he said dourly.

The third member of their party chuckled, then fell silent when Hob glowered at him. He was younger and much slighter of build and went by the interesting name of Wee Toad Bell.

"Coming to Carlisle was the natural thing to do," Janet replied. "Once we had talked to the men and learned how eager they were to rescue their master, we quite naturally realized that we would all need to know more about the place. Having come so far last night, it was but a step more for us to look the castle over."

"Aye, sure, so ye say," he said, "but we had no business to ride all the way into the Debatable Lands. It isna suitable for ye to be with just the two of us."

"It took much less time with you persuading half the men whilst Ally the Bastard persuaded the others," Janet reminded him. "As to riding so far, we did so to meet with Jess Armstrong because of my meeting him before with the master and our both knowing him to be loyal. We have discussed all this, Hob."

"Aye, but I ken fine what the master will say about it. He didna like it afore when ye wore lad's garments and fell into a scrape, and he—"

"I am no longer wearing those," Janet pointed out, cutting him off without compunction. "These skirts are perhaps not what he would wish to see me wear, but it was kind of Jess Armstrong's sister to lend them *and* for them to shelter us for the night. Whilst it was safer for me to ride in Tip's clothes to persuade the Bairns, there are many Grahams living in Carlisle who might know my face. It would not do for any of them to see me in men's clothes, so these will serve me better today.''

She was riding astride, as she had since leaving Ardith and the others the previous day, albeit now with her skirts kilted up to reveal her bare calves. She wore her drab cloak and her leather boots, and she fancied she looked like any ordinary female in town on a market day. In a covered basket tied to her saddle, she carried minced lamb pies that Jess's sister had baked for her to sell. Anyone who did not recognize her at once would see only a common street vendor.

Hob and Wee Toad wore their usual accouterments, including steel bonnets and leather jacks, but neither carried the usual number of weapons. Hob's crossbow was strung to his saddle-bow, his sword hung at his side, and his dagger and pistol occupied their customary places. But he carried neither lance nor Jedburgh ax.

"We are going to estimate how high the walls be; that's all," he said.

"Well, we must have some notion of how long the scaling ladders must be," Janet said reasonably. "You told me that yourself."

"I were talking wi' Jess," he said. "Ye was sleeping, or so I thought."

"I have learned the importance of listening," Janet said. "How will you measure them?"

"We canna do more than look and tak' a guess," he said, still frowning. "More oft than not, such ladders prove too short, but we'll give it a try."

Wee Toad Bell looked from one to the other, his head bobbing on his thin neck like an apple on a twig. He said nothing, however, having met with Hob's displeasure nearly every time he had gathered enough courage to speak. Janet knew the younger man had heard only what Hob wanted dearly to say to her, and she was sorry to cause Wee Toad discomfort, but having come so far, she would not leave Carlisle without first learning exactly what she had come to learn.

Occasional thoughts intruded of what would happen when
Buccleuch discovered—as he certainly would—that she had
not gone home as he had thought she had. Quinton would be
angry with her, too. She did not doubt that for a moment, and
just thinking about it sent prickles of ice through her veins, but
she would not let that stop her either. She had meant every
word she said to Ardith. It would be far worse never to hear
him scold her again. She would bear whatever punishment he
chose to mete out if only he were still alive to do so. As to
Buccleuch, she would not think about that until it was unavoidable.

Their view of the great castle was daunting. Its great, square,
red-stone keep squatted solid and strong at the top of a steep
slope behind plain but massive walls. From her position on the
Stanwix Bank, a line of bluffs that reared above the River Eden
on its north side, the huge castle seemed to tower above them.
It was the English Border's greatest stronghold, a fortress not
to be taken easily.

They descended from the bluffs to cross the river at a ford
that the recent rains and runoff from melting snow had made
deeper than usual, and Janet noted that Hob kept a close eye
on her. For all the heed he paid to Wee Toad Bell, the younger
man might have been swept away into Solway Firth without
his noticing.

Casually, as they approached the bustling town nestled round
the base of the castle wall, Janet said, "You will be more easily
recognized than either of us, Hob. Perhaps you should study
the height of the walls whilst we walk a little apart from you
and mingle with the townsfolk. No one will think it odd that
you have come into Carlisle, but if anyone should recognize
you and me together, tongues might flap, and we can gain
nothing good from that."

Knowing that he could dismiss her reasoning as weak, especially since it would be far more dangerous for her than for
him or Wee Toad to be recognized, she did not look at him,
pretending to be fascinated by the bustle in the street.

Wee Toad said cheerfully, " 'Tis true, Hob. Them what ken ye in Carlisle would think only that ye've stepped across the line to ha' a drink in a guid tavern."

Instead of silencing the little man again, Hob said, "Ye willna stray far, mistress. I'll want to keep ye within sight."

"I'll not stray far," Janet said, thinking that "far" was an ambiguous word at best. "Come, Wee Toad. We'll tie our ponies yonder."

"Nay, then," Hob protested, "we'll no be leaving good ponies standing within reach of these thievin' English—begging your pardon, mistress."

She grinned at him. "Then you take them. I can hardly pretend to be selling meat pies from the back of a horse."

" 'Twas a daft notion, that," Hob said.

"It will serve excellently well," she retorted. Without waiting for Wee Toad to offer assistance, she slipped down from her saddle and untied the basket of meat pies. Slinging it over one arm, she began to walk toward the castle. For some moments, feeling Hob's sharp gaze on her, she wandered aimlessly from one side of the street to the other. As the big man strolled nearer the castle wall, she did likewise, hoping that he would think she was just hovering near him. But the moment his back was turned, she slipped into the crowd and hurried toward a postern gate that she had noted as they crossed the Eden.

"Mistress, wait!" Wee Toad broke into a run behind her. She had, perforce, to slow, lest he shout her name or—worse—shout his concern for everyone in the street to hear. "Ye mustna go so far," he scolded breathlessly when he caught up.

"I am going into the castle, Wee Toad," she said calmly. "If you wish to come with me, keep quiet. If you want to tell Hob what I am doing, then go. He cannot stop me, nor will you. I mean to learn exactly where these villains are holding the master."

Chapter 22

"I would slight Carlisle castell high
Though it were builded of marble stone ..."

Comically, Wee Toad Bell's eyebrows flew upward. "D'ye think ye can find him, mistress?"

"Aye, for I know of at least two Grahams who work inside the wall," Janet said. "They are kinsmen of mine, and if either is here today, he will help me."

Wee Toad offered no more argument after that, trailing in her wake as she approached the gate. Casually, she swung her basket and smiled at the gatekeeper and the man-at-arms standing guard beside the gate.

" 'Tis a fine morning, is it not?" she said, speaking in the broad accent of a common English Border woman.

"Aye, it is," the gatekeeper said, grinning back at her. "What's in your basket, lass?"

"Meat pies for my cousin, Neal Graham," she said. "D'ye think one o' ye could be so kind as to fetch him for me?"

"I'm no lackey," the guard said, "but if ye'll give us a pie each, the keeper here will let ye slip in and look for your cousin youself. 'Twill give the lads inside a rare treat to see a bonny wench like yourself struttin' about.''

"Ye're welcome to ha' a pie each," she said, fluttering her lashes. "Neal will not miss them, for I packed plenty and more for him to share."

"I wish I had a cousin like you," the gatekeeper said, chucking her under the chin with one thick, grubby finger.

She tossed her head saucily. "Mayhap ye do," she said. "I'll warrant ye dinna ken all your cousins, me lad."

Laughing, he opened the gate, and she looked at the mechanism as she passed through. The bolts were stout ones though, and the gate heavy and ironbound. Inside, she noted that there were thick iron bars to set across it at night. Doubtless Buccleuch would already know these details, but one never knew. In any case, she decided, it would be foolish to waste such an opportunity.

Finding Neal Graham proved easier than she had expected, when one of the men in the inner bailey offered to fetch him for her.

A few moments later, Matty's burly cousin hurried through a nearby archway. Had he not clearly been searching for someone, Janet would not have known him, for it had been years since she had seen him and he had grown considerably in girth. She had walked right up to him before he paid her any heed, and then he did so only because she said clearly, "Cousin Neal?"

"Who are ye, lass? I be looking for me cousin Matty fra' Brackengill."

"Look at me, Neal."

He did then, and his eyes widened in shock. "Mistress Janet?"

"Aye," she said, "but pray, do not shout my name to everyone here."

"Well, I did hear that Sir Hugh were here, and I thought it odd that Matty would ha' come wi' him, but if she came wi' ye—"

"Hugh is here?" Janet's knees threatened to betray her.

"Aye, did ye no come wi' him, then?"

"No, and he mustn't know that I'm here! Pray, do not tell him, Neal."

"Most likely I willna see him," Neal said with a shrug. "But if ye didna come wi' him, how came ye here at all?"

"I am married now, Neal. I married Sir Quinton Scott of Broadhaugh."

"Och, aye, I did hear summat about that."

"Is he well, Neal? Have they hurt him?"

"Who?"

"Sir Quinton, of course! Don't be an apehead. He is a prisoner here."

"If he be here, mistress, I havena seen him. The only prisoner I ken aught about be the reiver, Rabbie Redcloak."

"They have the wrong man locked up, Neal. That so-called reiver is my husband. I was with him when they broke the truce and seized him."

By the way he opened his mouth, she knew that he wanted to contradict her. Doubtless, in whatever version he had heard, no one had broken truce. He did not speak, and she said quietly, "Please, Neal, tell me at least that he is well."

"Aye, he is that. That be his window yonder, second from the end at the top. Ye'll no see him looking out, though. Yon window's set too high in the wall."

"Have they at least fed him?"

"They take him food now and again. Not that it be what he's accustomed to if he be your husband, mistress. If he is, ye'd think Sir Hugh would ken him."

"He knows right well who he is," she said indignantly, but this second mention of her brother reminded her that she was borrowing time. She would not have any chance to see Quinton, but she had learned what she had come to learn.

"I must go, Neal. It would not do for any of Hugh's people to see me, and you must promise me that you will say naught of this."

"I dinna talk much, mistress. Does no one ask me if I've spoken wi' ye, I'll no mention it on my own."

Thanking him, she remembered to hand him the basket of pies, smiling at his astonishment. Then, signing to Wee Toad to follow her, she hurried back into the outer bailey, and toward the postern gate. At a turning, she stepped aside to let two men-at-arms pass, and when she stepped forward again, a boy carrying a pair of boots darted in front of her, head down, too quickly for her to avoid bumping into him. When he looked up, she exclaimed aloud, for it was Meggie's Andrew.

Her astonishment was nothing compared to his. "Mistress Janet!"

"Andrew, what are you doing here?"

"I came wi' Sir Hugh and Ned Rowan," the boy said. "I didna tell them, Mistress Janet. I swear it. It was Scots what told. I were trying to warn ye."

Understanding that he meant he had not told anyone that he had heard men link Sir Quinton with Rabbie Redcloak, she said, "I never thought for a moment that you had repeated what you heard, Andrew. Wicked men started the rumors, and it was they who caused Sir Quinton to be taken. But where is Sir Hugh?"

"I dinna ken. Ned Rowan sent me to fetch his boots from a cobbler in the High Street." He hefted the pair he was carrying.

"You must not tell anyone that you have seen me," Janet said.

"Nay, then, I won't."

"Will you be going back to Brackengill soon?"

"I think so. Sir Hugh and Ned Rowan be going to the races at Langholm on Saturday," the boy said with a shrug, little realizing the effect his words had on her.

By the time Janet and Wee Toad met Hob the Mouse outside the castle walls, instead of thinking that Hugh's presence at Langholm would ruin everything, she had thought of a way to

turn it to good account. So delighted was she with herself over
this feat that it was a moment before she noted the expression
on her larger protector's face. When she did, she decided that
it was an excellent thing that Hob held no authority over her.

Wee Toad ducked behind her, and when it looked as if Hob
might reach past her to grab the little man by his scrawny neck,
Janet said, "We must not stand here. I have just learned that
my brother is here, and it would not do for him to see me."

"Nay, then, it would not," Hob growled. "I might be
tempted to give ye to Sir Hugh as a wee gift. It is no my place
to be tellin' ye what to do, mistress, but ye should *not* ha'
given me such a fright."

Realizing that she had truly alarmed him, she apologized
sincerely. "I did not think about what you might believe if I
disappeared, Hob, but I knew that you would only argue with
me if I did not. I discovered where they are keeping him."

He sighed, relaxing visibly. "I'll no deny that's a good thing,
mistress, but I dinna want to be near when he learns what ye
did, or when Himself learns of it."

Striving to sound casual, she said as he lifted her to her
saddle, "I do not think we need tell Himself just yet, you know.
That knowledge, or lack of it, will scarcely alter any plan he
makes for breaching the castle wall, and we do not want to
make him so angry that he will command us to forget our
mission altogether."

Hob's awe of his liege lord was such that he proved difficult
to convince, but the ride back to Liddesdale took time, and
Janet was persuasive.

They stopped briefly at Jess Armstrong's and again in Tarrasdale so that Hob could pass along his rough estimate of the
length required for the scaling ladders; but the threatening
weather held off, and they made good time otherwise.

On the ridge above Hermitage, Janet called a halt. "Now,
remember, Hob," she said, "you will tell Buccleuch only that

the Bairns have agreed to his provisions if he will help set their master free. You must also tell him that you visited Carlisle long enough to estimate the height of the walls and have already taken the liberty of ordering men to build the scaling ladders.''

" 'Twas yourself gave that order, as I recall it,'' the big man said sardonically.

She smiled. "They want to please me, I think. Your Scottish Borderers have been extremely kind to me, Hob.''

"They ken fine how the master feels about ye, mistress.''

Feeling heat in her cheeks again, Janet said hastily, "They cannot know what he thinks of me. They merely do honor to their laird's wife.''

"Nay, then,'' Hob said, his harsh features softening. "Ye've been gey kind to many of them and theirs, mistress, and they dinna forget kindness.''

"We've no time for this,'' she replied, feeling unfamiliar tightness in her throat. "Buccleuch will be waiting to hear from you, and Wee Toad can wait here with me. I promise, I will not leave you to face him alone for long.''

"I dinna ken how ye will fool him in that dress, mistress.''

"Only because you know where it came from,'' Janet said. She had kept Jess Armstrong's sister's skirts, not bothering to disguise herself for the return journey except by bundling her distinctive hair into an oversized cap. Quinton's people knew her now, and they would do her no harm.

Hob did not look convinced, but if he had learned anything, he had learned the futility of argument. Touching his cap, he wheeled his pony and rode over the hill to Hermitage.

Twenty minutes later, having edged their way round so as to approach from the direction of Broadhaugh, Janet and Wee Toad Bell followed. A little to her consternation, Buccleuch was in the great hall to greet them. He sat in a large armchair with his bad leg propped up before him on a cushioned bench.

"I've been expecting you, lass,'' he said, giving her a direct look.

"Have you, sir?'' She smiled. "I warrant you have learned

that I do not possess much patience. I thought I would find Hob the Mouse returned to you by now, and so I came to hear his news." Having carefully avoided presenting him with an outright falsehood, she tried to ignore the sense of guilt that stirred within her.

His expression was unreadable. He said evenly, "Apparently the Bairns have agreed to follow him. I own, I did not believe he could be so persuasive."

"But that is excellent," she said.

"Indeed." He turned to Hob and said in the same even tone, "You will have arrangements to make before Saturday, so get yourself some food. Then return to me in an hour and we will discuss exactly what I want you to do. Todrigg is here, and Gaudilands will come later. I'll arrange for an escort to see her ladyship safely back to Broadhaugh. You can follow after we've had our talk."

Tempted though she was to protest being sent away, Janet held her tongue.

"We'll go upstairs," Buccleuch said to her, signing to several of his men. With their help, and despite the logistical difficulties, he made it up the spiral staircase to the master's hall, where they settled him again. Then, at his brusque command, they took themselves off, leaving Janet alone with him.

For the first time since her arrival, instinct warned her of danger. Reminding herself that he was smaller than either Quinton or Hugh, that his injured leg made it unlikely that he could do her harm, she took a deep breath and let it out. It did no good whatsoever. Her nerves fluttered, her skin prickled, and her mouth felt dry.

"So you rode over from Broadhaugh just to speak to Hob the Mouse, did you?" His tone was still matter-of-fact, but she was not fooled. Although she wanted very much to dampen her dry lips, she did not, nor did she reply.

The silence lengthened until it became clear that he would wait for her.

"Quinton is my husband, sir," she said quietly at last.

"You are a strange woman," he replied, shaking his head.

"If you mean that most women would wring their hands and weep, then wait helplessly for men to act, then perhaps I am strange," she said.

"Most women would show the good sense to realize that men are better suited to act," he retorted, not bothering now to conceal his anger. "I will not ask you to tell me all you have done, and for that you may thank my deep affection for your husband. If I should learn the extent to which you persuaded men who owe me fealty to defy my commands, I should be forced to punish them, and I need them at their full strength just now. But I will not remain dependent upon others for long, lass. Remember that, and defy me again at your peril."

"Well, as to that, sir . . ."

"There is no 'as to that!' " he snapped. "You will do as I bid you."

"Forgive me, sir, but truly, I do not act out of defiance."

"Ah, Christ, lassie, I ken fine why you act, but you're nobbut a bit lass. I want Quin free, but I'll no want to face him if I've let you be harmed through failure to force your obedience."

"Please, sir, will you give me but fifteen minutes to explain my thoughts? I vow, if I cannot persuade you, I will do exactly as you bid me."

"You'll do as you're bid, regardless, for there is naught you can tell me that will alter my opinion."

"My brother Hugh will be at Langholm," she said. "Doubtless he will have a number of his followers with him."

"Aye, and so what? 'Tis not unusual for men from both sides of the line to attend the races. How better to judge each other's horseflesh? For all that it's practically march treason to sell horses across the line, men do it all the time."

"Aye, sir, but my point is that my brother's people are as loyal to me as they are to him, and it is not so unusual for women to attend the races. No one would think it odd to find me there, in any case. You see, I wrote to Lord Scrope a fortnight ago, begging his permission to visit Quinton."

"I know you did that, lass. I would not be who I am did I not ken fine how to keep an ear to the ground. I know also that he refused your request."

She wondered what else he knew, but pushed the discomfiting thought aside to say, "Then you must see that people will simply believe that I am still trying to get word of Quinton. I'll have opportunity to talk with many Grahams, sir, and I'll tell them what really happened. I have good cause to believe that many do not know the truth about how he was taken. Moreover, regardless of what you think of them, they will disapprove of breaking the truce. That certainly cannot hurt our cause."

To her surprise, he did not instantly order her to put all thought of attending the races out of her head. She even detected a twinkle in his eyes when he said, "I think I mentioned before that I am no fool, lass. What you say makes sense, but there is more, is there not? You, not Hob the Mouse, are the beacon round which Rabbie's Bairns have gathered. 'Tis for you they will act and for you that they have agreed to obey men whom they consider to be less able leaders. It occurs to me that it will be helpful if they can manage to keep their purpose firmly in mind right up to the moment they gather to depart for Carlisle."

She hardly dared to breathe. It was as if he had read her mind.

"You may attend the races, lass," he said at last. "I own, my worst fear has been that without a strong leader, Rabbie's misfit Bairns may begin fighting amongst themselves, or simply ignore orders and thus bring the whole raid to naught. Your presence at the races will remind them why they are going to Carlisle. Hob the Mouse will pass word at Langholm of the place and time to meet Todrigg and Gaudilands. He'll lead the Liddesdale men who are taking part."

"How many men will you send?" she asked.

"The raiding party will not be large, less than a hundred men, but it will be large enough for the purpose. We want to get across the line without drawing too much notice, and I must see that Broadhaugh remains well guarded, too, you know.''

She nodded, able to breathe easily again. A hundred men did not seem enough, but she knew a larger force would make her scheme less likely to succeed. Getting to the races would be just the beginning. While the plan passed from man to man, she would do her part while studiously ignoring Hugh and any Musgraves who were present. She did not think they would seek her out, and it would underscore for the rest of her kinsmen what she thought of their breaking the truce. After the races were over, wherever the little army gathered, her real work would begin.

If Hob was surprised to learn that she had survived her confrontation with Buccleuch with her dignity intact, she could see no sign of it. When she informed him that she meant to attend the races, he said only, ''Aye, Himself did tell me that.''

Reassured, she said, ''You will be gathering the men after, will you not?''

''Aye.'' He watched her with fascination.

''I mean to be there, as well,'' she said firmly. ''Buccleuch agrees that the Bairns should see me there.'' Buccleuch had not said that exactly, but she was certain that he would not object. Not to that part of her plan, at all events.

She had expected to encounter resistance, and when she did not, her suspicions stirred. Buccleuch was not a man who would brook much defiance. Was it possible that he had taken steps to prevent her from putting her plan into action?

Shortly before daybreak Saturday morning, when she descended to the bailey, despite assurances from Ardith that Hob and an armed escort were waiting to accompany her to Langholm, she half expected to find them already gone. They were there, however, and she saw at once by the number of arms they carried that, as she had expected, they meant to act swiftly after the races.

"I don't want the sidesaddle," she said when she saw it on her pony. "The distance is too great, and we should have to travel too slowly."

Hob nodded to one of the lads, and Janet nearly laughed when the lad immediately led another horse from the stable, already saddled with her favorite cross-saddle. She looked at Hob.

Grinning, he shrugged, then moved to help her mount. "Will I tie this bundle to your saddle, mistress?"

"If you please," she said, hoping he would not ask what it contained.

He did not. Nor did he ask what had become of Ardith, and again her suspicions stirred. Surely he wondered what she thought she was doing, riding nearly twenty miles from home without a female to attend her.

They had traveled nearly five of those miles before the sun peeked over the hills to the east. Janet, riding beside Hob at the head of their entourage, had made no attempt to initiate conversation. The men chatted amongst themselves, but Hob seemed lost in thought.

"There are rather a lot of clouds," she said at last, casting an eye skyward.

"Aye, it rained again in the night," he said. "Likely it will tonight, too."

She looked directly at him. "How many of these men are you expecting to send back with me tonight?"

Returning her look, he said, "As many as ye require, mistress."

Uncertainty flooded through her. Was he daring to threaten her?

"I told you," she said, "I mean to go to the gathering place."

"Aye, Tromble's Tower. That's where we're all to meet."

"You'll not try to stop me?"

"Nay, mistress. Himself said I were no to fratch wi' ye."

"What else did he say?" she demanded suspiciously.

"He said to give ye your head," Hob said.

"He didn't!"

"Aye, then, he did. He said he could order ye locked up, but ye'd most likely just find a way out and get yourself in a worse scrape."

"I'd get out, at all events," Janet agreed.

"Aye, well, he said it's no our job to put ye in a cage. Our job, he said, is to get the master free so that he can deal with ye."

Certain that she heard a note of satisfaction in his tone, Janet did not press the issue further. He would not stop her, and that was enough. If her blood chilled a little at the thought of facing Quinton afterward, she ignored it.

It was an hour before sundown when they gathered, more than a hundred strong. Janet, in the breeks and boots she had carried in her bundle, and wearing a jack of plate like many of the others, draped her heavy cloak over her saddle bow to accept the golden-brown steel bonnet that Ally the Bastard handed her. The helmet gleamed from regular polishing with sheep fat. It was uncomfortable to wear, but she had twisted her long hair into a topknot to serve as a cushion.

Ally the Bastard said curiously, "Why the bonnet, mistress?"

"I am going with you," she said.

As word of her reply spread rapidly through the gathering, she heard gruff protests and swearing.

"Hear me," she cried. "I must go. Carlisle Castle is immense, and I am the only one who knows exactly where they are keeping Sir Quinton prisoner."

"Aye, that's true," Hob the Mouse shouted.

"Just tell us where he is, mistress!"

"I cannot do that unless someone amongst you already knows the interior of the castle well enough to understand my directions. Moreover, I can find my way more easily than I can describe it."

More grumbling greeted her words, but there were no more overt protests.

She fastened the strap of her helmet carefully, then turned to Hob the Mouse. "Will that do?"

"Aye, mistress," he said with a chuckle.

"Sweet Jesu," Wee Toad Bell exclaimed, shaking his head. "The master will have all our heads for this!"

"Only mine," Janet told him.

Hob stood in his stirrups and waved. "Lads, can ye hear me?"

"Aye," they shouted.

Janet surveyed the army she was rapidly coming to think of as her own. Ally the Bastard had assembled his scouts—mostly Armstrongs—a short distance to her right. To her left, men of the fighting party helped Todrigg's assault group tie the long scaling ladders, two to a pony. They also loaded them with crowbars, pickaxes, sledgehammers, shovels, and other tools—anything that might be helpful to break down walls or gates—or to undermine them, if necessary.

"Ye all ken our plan," Hob shouted. "Ally the Bastard will captain the scouts. The fighting party will ride next wi' me, the Laird o' Gaudilands, and the mistress. The Laird o' Todrigg will follow wi' the main body. They'll be carrying the ladders and assault tools, ye ken, so we canna get far from them."

A roar greeted him, and Janet grinned at their increasing enthusiasm. After a moment, she held up a hand for silence. When it grew quiet again, she shouted, "Can you hear me?"

"Aye," they roared.

"Remember, everyone, this is a rescue, not a raid. There must be no plundering tonight."

Exaggerated moans and groans answered her.

She waited until the noise had died to muttering.

"Hear me well, all you Bairns," she shouted then, wanting to be certain that no man among them could claim later that he had not heard her. "No one is to lay violent hands on any townsman or any woman. No man is to take so much as a stone from Carlisle Castle or injure one of its inmates without strong provocation. Anyone who does will answer both to Sir Quinton and to Buccleuch. Put plainly, lads, there must be no murder or mayhem. We are simply reclaiming one of our own who was captured in violation of the truce."

This time the silence continued after she stopped speaking. A moment passed during which she felt tempted to look to Gaudilands or to Hob the Mouse for reassurance, but she did not. Instead she shouted, "Do I have your word on it, lads?"

"Aye," they shouted back.

"Your word as Borderers?"

"Aye!" This time their response was lustier, and cheers followed. Satisfied, she nodded to Ally the Bastard, who spurred his mount and rode off at a gallop, followed by his ten scouts. Even before they had disappeared from sight, Janet saw them begin to spread out, each man taking a separate route.

Flanked by Hob and Gaudilands, she followed Ally at a slower but steady pace, with the others falling in behind. The sun was just touching the western horizon, shooting rays under the ominous-looking cloud bank overhead, setting the billowy clouds afire with orange and red. As the company rode, the sky darkened, and they reached the line at the river Esk as the last colors faded, making it too gloomy to see the famous reddish cast of the Esk sand on its banks.

Not until Janet's horse stepped from damp sand into the water did she look back. Excitement and pride in equal measure filled her when she saw again the host of riders following them. As she crossed from Scotland into England, she understood as she never had before Quinton's powerful enthusiasm for raiding.

Chapter 23

"But 'twas wind and weet, and fire and sleet,
When we came beneath the castle wa'."

Darkness closed around the riders. Black clouds hid the moon, and gusting wind shook trees and shrubbery and sent the temperature plunging, but the gathering storm thrilled Janet nearly as much as the steady drumming of hoofbeats behind her. Buccleuch's plan counted on another dismal night, and the hoped-for bad weather certainly threatened. It would rain soon, and they still had six miles of hostile territory to cross before they reached Carlisle.

Her blood raced, and when the first pellets of sleet stung her cheeks, she felt an impulse to cry, "We'll have moonlight again!" Only her awareness that enemies might be lurking nearby kept her still.

They rode on, pushing with surprising quiet into the southern moss, but their pace soon slowed to a walk. The night winds grew more savage, howling as they swept unchecked across King Moor, and darkness was complete. Without so much as a star, let alone a good Border moon, the pace seemed agonizingly slow, but greater speed would endanger not only the men but their cause as well.

Not long after crossing the Esk, Ally the Bastard sent a man back to tell them that the way was clear, and to warn them not to overrun his scouts, who were also, perforce, moving slowly. After that, a scout reported every half hour and remained with them until the next report came before riding ahead again. The only good thing about the slow pace was that the assault group could easily keep up with them. It would do them no good to arrive hours before the laden ponies did, because they would only have to wait for them.

The dark, rainy night provided excellent cover, Janet knew, and so she did not mind the horrid weather. Even when sleet mixed with the rain pelting down in sheets, and lightning flashed and thunder boomed like cannon fire, her steel bonnet and heavy, silk-lined cloak protected her from the worst of the chill.

Although it was only six miles from the Esk, they took the best part of the night to cover the distance to Stanwix Bank, but thanks to the weather, they did so without meeting anyone. Most sensible people had taken cover from the storm.

At last they reached the line of bluffs rearing above the north bank of the Eden, and in the glare of jagged lightning bolts got their first view of Carlisle. When the sky darkened again, Janet turned to Gaudilands. Over rolling thunder, she shouted, "How long till dawn?"

"Two hours, as near as I can reckon it," he shouted back.

"The river looks dangerously flooded!"

"Aye," he said.

With each flash of lightning, even through the driving, sleet-filled rain, she could see frothing whitecaps on roiling water as they descended the slippery track from the bluffs. The nearer they rode, the more her imagination threatened to undo her. Her pony would never make it across. They could all be swept into Solway Firth and out to sea. Sensible people would turn back. Then she thought of Quinton, imprisoned and miserable inside the great castle, the massive walls of which loomed

darkly on the southern horizon. She could not abandon him,
nor could she let these faithful, determined men know how
frightened she was.

She knew, too, that her fear could communicate itself to her
horse. Already, it felt skittish beneath her. Inhaling deeply, she
fought to steady herself both in mind and body. Quinton's life
and freedom might well depend on her. The men would go on
without her, but they would not find him as quickly. Description
was never as good as seeing the place, or knowing the door
behind which he lay. Her husband would doubtless accuse her
of acting impulsively again, but she had weighed the alterna-
tives, and this time she knew she had done the right thing. At
least, she had believed it before she faced the boiling waters
of the wild, clearly misnamed Eden.

"Lass . . . my lady . . ." Hob's tone was anxious.

Janet turned, managing a smile for the huge man, doubting
that he could see it but sure that he would hear it in her voice.
She said, "I'm here, Hob. Do we just charge straight across?
I confess, I've not crossed wild water like this before."

"Ye'll follow the Laird o' Gaudilands with Ally's man
upriver o' ye to break the flow, and I'll keep below ye on your
right flank. These ponies be bred for tasks like this, so if ye
can but trust yours, ye'll make it safe. And if ye don't," he
added with a chuckle, "I'll snatch ye up afore the water washes
ye awa' into the Firth."

She laughed then, turning her face up to the rain and sleet.
"Let's ride then."

When Gaudilands took the lead, she followed him into the
water. Fifteen minutes later, their entire fighting force was
across and most of the assault party. Knowing the land ahead
was mostly a barren slope, they rode on toward the castle at
speed.

The storm reached its zenith as the assault force reached the
wall, and Janet scanned the battlements anxiously, knowing
everyone else was doing the same. She listened intently for
voices, but neither heard nor saw any sign of life. Evidently

the townsfolk and even Scrope's guards had taken shelter from the storm's fury.

Her relief turned to dismay, however, when the first ladders went up, and she saw that they were too short.

"The men can't get over the walls," she cried. The wind whipped her words away, but she knew she did not need to repeat them. Todrigg and Gaudilands had also seen that the ladders were too short. She saw Todrigg wave his men away from the wall and was startled to see them race toward the ponies. At first, she feared that they meant to turn back. When they began snatching tools from the ponies' backs, she relaxed again and turned her attention back to the battlements. The castle might have been empty for all that she could see.

Gaudilands led part of the fighting force through the town to be sure that no one surprised them from that direction, but the town remained quiet, too. Another glance at Todrigg's men showed them running toward the postern gate with shovels and picks in hand. Others followed Todrigg's men, carrying axes, swords, daggers, lances, and even pitchforks.

Janet glanced at Hob the Mouse, still riding at her side. "What are they doing now, Hob?"

"They'll undermine the gate or break the bolt and bars free," he shouted. Neither of them cared any longer about making noise. Nothing they did or said would carry over the wall. The storm was too loud.

"We must stay with them then," Janet shouted back. "When they break through, we'll go in with them. You'll not try to stop me, will you?"

"Nay, mistress, not unless I see them runnin' into a trap. They'll need me inside, too, ye ken, if the master canna move gey quick on his own."

No one had mentioned this last possibility aloud before, but Janet had thought about it. She had not liked thinking that Quinton might be injured or, worse, incapacitated, but she was grateful that Hob—and doubtless others, as well—had thought

about it and would deal with whatever state he was in when
the time came.

She spurred her pony around the wall to the postern gate
and rode up just as the men broke through. She saw Gaudilands
and Todrigg take the lead, tackling the gatekeeper. Others
grabbed the guard with him, and soon the pair were trussed
like Christmas geese. The raiders tucked them into the guard
house, out of the storm, and then crossed the yard toward the
archway leading to the inner bailey and the keep.

"Follow me, Hob," Janet said as she slipped from her saddle
and pulled her dagger from its sheath.

Hob signaled to Ally the Bastard, who gathered several
Bairns, sending others to help secure the castle proper. The
first group followed Janet to the door in the west wall that Neal
Graham had pointed out to her. Axes and picks quickly reduced
the locked and barred door to rubble, and she picked her way
carefully through it into a stone-walled anteroom. Holding her
dagger in one hand, she seized a torch from a bracket with the
other to light her way.

"Lead on, lass," Hob the Mouse muttered behind her, no
longer considering the proprieties. "We're ahind ye. If ye're
challenged, just step aside quick."

"We must find the stairs," she said.

In that same moment, she saw a guard in the room ahead,
and when he vanished at sight of them, fear leapt within her
that he or someone else might harm Quinton. Running now,
hearing shouts ahead, she found the stairs and darted up them
to the next level, where she found a long, empty corridor.
Running along it, past a number of closed doors, she did not
pause until she reached the second one from the far end.

Stopping, she stood back, pointing. "There," she said. "Oh,
be quick!"

Seizing an ax from one of the men behind him, Hob the
Mouse swung at the door. The second stroke splintered the
wood and broke the door almost in two. It lurched drunkenly
from one iron hinge, and when the bolt slid out of its socket,

that half fell to the floor. Hob the Mouse began shoving wreck-age aside, but impatiently Janet dropped her torch and ran beneath his arm into the shadowy cell.

"Quinton, it's us," she cried. "Oh, my dear, speak to me! Godamercy, but I hate finding you behind bars."

He was slumped in a back corner on what looked like a pile of filthy rags. Though he stirred, she doubted that he had recognized her.

"Quinton, wake up! Speak to me!" Grabbing his face between her hands, she forced him to look at her. "It's Jenny, my love. Oh, look at me!"

"What the devil?" His words were almost undistinguishable. Had she not known him well, she would not have understood them. "You cannot be Jenny."

"Aye, it's me. I disobeyed you again." She straightened, putting her fists on her hips. "What are you going to do about it, eh? You cannot even stand up."

One of the men had carried a torch into the chamber, and she could see Quinton collect himself. His eyes narrowed as he fought to regain his wits. She saw bruises on his face, and he looked thin and haggard.

"I have food, love, and ale," she said coaxingly, adding in a harsher tone when he did not respond, "We are taking you home. Now, damn you, get up! I cannot carry you, you know."

"I'll take him, mistress."

She looked up and saw Hob the Mouse looming over them. Feeling perilously near tears, she muttered, "Aye, you carry him. But mind, he must stand when we reach the courtyard. He'll not want any damned English to see him carried out of here like a sack of laundry."

"You want your mouth washed with strong lye soap," Quinton muttered, grunting when Hob picked him up and slung him over one shoulder.

Janet looked at his upside-down face. "At least you didn't fling my English birth in my teeth, but you just try that soap, my laddie, and see what it gets you. You couldn't wash a babe, as weak as you are.''

''We'll see about that,'' he said, and she noted with relief bordering upon euphoria that his voice sounded stronger. That he did not complain about Hob's carrying him was not a good sign, though.

Following the huge man and his precious burden out of the cell, determined to keep Quinton talking in the hope that it would help him gather strength, she taunted him again when they reached the stairs. ''I suppose you will want to take command when we're outside again,'' she said, ''but this is my army, so don't be thinking that you can just start ordering them about. They answer to me, sir.''

Hob glanced at her over his shoulder, and she was grateful to see the twinkle in his eyes. He knew what she was doing. To her astonishment, none of the other Bairns contradicted her declaration either.

One of them stood at the foot of the stairs. ''Good, ye've got him,'' he said, adding cheerfully, ''We've taken the castle. They sounded an alarm, but our lads outside set up such a clamor that Scrope and his lot think we must be a thousand or more. They ran off when they heard the din, and they've holed up in his keep behind a great barred door.''

''Leave them there,'' Janet said instantly.

''Aye, sure, mistress, but we was thinking 'twould be a good thing to take a captive or two. Their ransom could feed all of Liddesdale for a year or more.''

''No,'' Janet said, and heard her husband echo her reply.

''Set me down, Hob,'' Quinton said.

Without protest, the big man obeyed.

''There will be no plundering,'' Quinton said sternly, his voice sounding steadier than he looked.

''I told them that before,'' Janet said, ''and they promised.'' She looked directly at the man by the doorway. ''You and the others promised as Borderers, Will Elliot. I'll not allow you to go back on your word.''

"We wouldna do that, mistress," the man assured her. "We just thought . . ."

Quinton straightened, looking more like himself. "We will do naught to anger Elizabeth," he said. "Scrope will soil himself over this business, as it is, and that must satisfy us for now. Is that my cloak you're wearing, Jenny?"

"Aye," she said. "It's a bit damp. Do you want it?"

Hob said, "I've an extra cloak and blankets on my saddle, master."

"Keep it then, lass," Quinton said. "It will keep your backside warm until we get home again."

A note in his voice told her that he was angry with her, but she did not care. He was safe. If he decided to beat her for her part in the rescue, she would deal with that when the time came.

Hob the Mouse put a strong hand under Quinton's elbow until they reached the bailey. Then he let go, but Janet was glad to see that he stayed near, ready to catch Quinton if he stumbled.

He didn't. With each step her husband seemed to grow stronger. The cold air clearly stimulated him. She saw him look around alertly, watching for attack, but none came. The castle was theirs for the taking, and she knew that their men must be itching to take it, so that they could tell the world that they had conquered the great English stronghold with fewer than a hundred men.

"Collect our lads, Hob," Quinton said as they approached the postern gate. "They'll be growing impatient, and the temptation is great here to do mischief."

"Aye," Hob said. "I dinna suppose we could take just one or two wee—"

"Not so much as a scrap from Scrope's dining table," Quinton growled. "As it is, he will shriek his woes all the way to London. Get them now before anyone puts a foot wrong. Does Buccleuch know of this?" he added, turning to Janet.

"Aye, he does," she said. "He planned it."

"Don't tell me that he knew you would be here tonight."

"He did not say that I could not be," she said carefully.

Quinton did not look away. His eyes narrowed, making him look fierce.

"He knew that I would see them off, but he did not know that I meant to come with them," she admitted.

"Just as I thought. Well, you can tell him yourself, and maybe you can make *him* understand what demon possessed you to do such a thing."

"I—"

"Not now," he said. "Use what time you've got before we get home to make up a good story. Not that any story will be good enough," he added ominously.

Hob murmured, "We'd no ha' found ye so quick, master, had the mistress stayed at home, for it was herself that learned where Scrope were keeping ye."

A shiver shot up Janet's spine. She knew that he had meant only to help, but by the way that Quinton stiffened, she could tell Hob had only made matters worse.

"We will talk later," Quinton said as they passed through the gate. He waved to Ally the Bastard and the others. Todrigg had already gathered most of them, and in minutes the rest joined them with no sign of resistance from within the castle.

As they mounted, Quinton looked back with a sudden grin. "Makes me feel almost as if we ought to lock up after ourselves," he said, chuckling.

The nearest men laughed and passed his comment on to the others, so that as they rode away, an increasing roar of laughter accompanied the wind's howl and the clarion call of trumpets sounding their retreat.

Looking back, Janet saw beacons fire up in the town, and when the trumpet notes and laughter faded, she could hear bells ringing and drums beating to arms. Day was breaking, the sleet had stopped, and although it still drizzled, she worried that anyone giving chase might see them easily and catch them. A misty fog rose from the ground, however, and to her surprise, when they reached the north side of the Eden, fog seemed to have swallowed the town. Even the castle looked like nothing more daunting than a gloomy gray shadow at the top of the hill.

Able to see more clearly in semi-darkness than they had during the black night, even the assault force could move swiftly, and an hour's ride saw them deep in the Debatable Land, nearing the River Esk. Janet began to think that their venture would end without incident.

Quinton rode beside her, wearing a heavy cloak that Hob the Mouse had given him and chewing bread and meat, with an occasional swig of ale from a flask that Janet had brought. He looked tired, but the triumph in his expression when he looked around at his Bairns and everyone who had supported them gave her hope that his anger with her would ease long before they reached Broadhaugh.

Ten minutes later, without warning, steel-bonneted riders bearing lances and swords galloped out of the misty gloom ahead.

"Ambush! Sound the charge," Quinton shouted.

"Those are Hugh's colors," Janet protested as trumpet notes rang out.

"You fall to the rear, my lass," Quinton retorted. "Now!"

Instead, she reached for the strap on her steel bonnet and ripped it free. Riding by balance alone, she tore off the helmet with one hand and reached for her topknot with the other. With a twist of her hand and a shake of her head, her silvery blond hair flowed free. Spurring her horse, she charged ahead of Quinton and his men before he could realize what she meant to do.

"Fall back, you Grahams," she shouted to the men drawing rein before her. "We have no quarrel with you. We ride for Scotland!"

"It's Mistress Janet!" The words flew from tongue to tongue in a veritable chorus. The heavily armed horsemen quickly turned their mounts aside to let her pass, and as they did, she heard their astonishment echoing from man to man.

Smiling at men she recognized, she rode on, feeling as if she held everyone around her in the palm of her hand. Her smile widened, and she nodded and waved at the others as she passed.

"Mistress Janet," they shouted, waving back.

She was thoroughly enjoying herself, certain when she recognized loyal Graham kinsmen everywhere she looked that the danger had evaporated. As she turned to wave to men on her left, a lone horseman loomed out of the mist ahead, startling her and forcing her to rein in hard.

"Hugh!"

"Aye, it is Hugh, right enough," he snarled. "I will escort Lord Scrope's prisoner back to him now if you will stand aside."

"I won't," she snapped. "Francis Musgrave arrested him in violation of the truce, and we have merely taken him back again. Let us pass, Hugh, or do you mean to run your own sister through with that sword?"

His horse stepped toward her, but he reined it in even before his men began to mutter in protest. Looking around at them, he shouted, "Rabbie Redcloak is our prisoner, lads. Do you mean to let a wench make you let him go?"

"Ye'll no be touching Mistress Janet," a disembodied voice shouted from the crowd, and others shouted, "Let them pass!"

"They can all pass but Redcloak," Sir Hugh said grimly when silence fell again. "We'll be taking him back to Carlisle."

"Not without a fight, Hugh," Janet said. "I'll remind you that the man you call Rabbie Redcloak is my husband, Sir Quinton Scott. Francis Musgrave made a mistake, and he broke an honorable truce to do it. If you press this matter now, you will be as guilty as he is. Now, let us pass in peace."

"Musgrave made no mistake, lass, and well do you know it," Sir Hugh said.

She saw flinty determination in his eyes, but his tone was gentle, not challenging. She thought he sounded almost weary.

Behind her, Quinton said, "I'll fight you if you like."

"No!" Janet cried out without thinking. Looking back at him, she realized that she ought to have kept silent, for all she had gained was an angry look and nothing she could say would stop what was about to happen. She wanted to cry, but men from both sides were shouting for a fight.

Sir Hugh nodded and said grimly, "On horse or afoot?"

"Whatever you like."

"We'll fight afoot then," he said with a slight smile.

Quinton dismounted, sword in hand, and threw his cloak to Hob the Mouse.

Flinging herself to the ground, Janet confronted her husband angrily. "You are too weak, Quinton. He'll kill you!"

"He will not."

"Then you'll kill him." She fought tears. "He is my brother."

"He is my enemy, Jenny. You should have done as I told you and remained safely at Broadhaugh. Now, stand aside, lass."

Looking over her shoulder, she saw that Hugh was as determined as Quinton. A big hand gripped her shoulder, and she looked up through her tears at Hob.

"Ye must stand awa', mistress," he said. "Ye'll no want to get in their way."

Choking back a sob, she let him lead her away. The men from both sides formed a large circle, making way for her to stand near the front.

Quinton and Hugh circled, watching each other intently. The light was gray, for although it was well past dawn, the day remained gloomy and wet. The muddy ground beneath their feet looked slippery. If either one survived, Janet thought, it would be a miracle.

"God have mercy on them," she murmured.

"Aye, and on their immortal souls," a man beside her muttered.

They circled for what seemed an age. Their eyes were narrowed, their mouths hard slits. Their chins jutted stubbornly. Neither intended to give quarter.

Janet knew how heavy Quinton's sword was. She had hefted it herself, and she did not believe that at the moment he was much stronger than she was. He had eaten bread and meat as he rode, and he had drunk ale from her flask, but she knew that he could not be anywhere near his customary physical readiness. The weeks of imprisonment had taken a heavy toll, and Hugh was an able swordsman.

The men remained silent. No one cheered or shouted encouragement. They just waited. Quinton and Hugh kept circling, their booted feet making slurping sounds in the muck. Light drizzle continued, but both men had taken off their cloaks and helmets, and both looked soaked to the skin.

Quinton made a gesture with his sword, and Hugh's weapon flashed to meet it. Quinton parried and Hugh went on the attack at once. Their swords seemed to take fire, but after only a minute or two, Janet realized that Quinton was making no attempt to attack. She had seen him fight before and had watched him practice often enough to know that he was well off his usual pace. He parried every stroke deftly, conserving what strength he had, but Hugh pressed him hard.

She knew that her brother had insisted they fight on foot because it would tire Quinton more quickly than fighting on horseback. The decision was a sensible one for Hugh, who doubtless knew himself outmatched in skill and could hope to beat Quinton only if the weeks in prison had sufficiently worn him down.

Quinton slipped, and she cried out, clapping a hand to her mouth to stop the sound. But others shouted, too, on both sides, and the tense silence vanished in uproar. The audience was caught up in the fight. When Hugh nearly slipped under Quinton's guard, his men cheered, but the other side echoed those cheers when Quinton parried and neatly twitched Hugh's sword out of his hand.

The sword fell into the muck.

Janet could breathe again, thinking Hugh would have to submit, but fear gripped her anew when Quinton lowered his sword and Hugh leapt to snatch his up.

"Wipe it off," Quinton said curtly, and one of the men threw Hugh a cloth.

In moments their fighting was fiercer than ever.

Sweat and raindrops streamed down both men's faces, ignored but for occasional swipes with a free if sodden sleeve. The ground beneath them grew more treacherous by the moment. Their feet dug ruts and pushed up ridges as they leapt and sidestepped in the familiar dance of swordplay.

The fight seemed to have lasted hours, but Janet knew that only minutes had passed. She remembered Quinton's once telling her that even the strongest swordsman could last only ten minutes before mind-numbing exhaustion set in.

As the thought flitted through her mind, she saw that the tempo had changed. Quinton was pressing now. Instead of nimbly sidestepping and moving in circles, he pressed forward, forcing Hugh toward the circle's perimeter. The men backed away, but Quinton moved quickly, his sword flashing in, out, up, and down with such speed that it seemed to have three blades attached to its hilt instead of just one.

A treacherous root caught Hugh's heel and sent him crashing. As he landed, Quinton's sword point touched his throat and he froze where he lay.

Janet tried to scream but no sound came. The roars of the men stopped, too, and in the ensuing silence, she heard only the whispering pit-a-pat of raindrops.

Chapter 24

"If ye like na my visit in merry England
In fair Scotland come visit me!"

Except for his heaving chest, Quinton stood utterly still, his sword point indenting Hugh's throat. Hugh lay with his chin pointing upward, his eyes wide, his chest pumping hard, waiting for the coup de grace.

Janet could not breathe. No one spoke. The only sounds that mingled with the hushing patter of the rain were an occasional whicker or stamp from one of the ponies and the stertorous breathing of the erstwhile combatants.

Then Quinton stepped back, raising his sword.

A general sigh went up, but still no one spoke.

His breath still coming in harsh gasps, Quinton said with detectable amusement, "Do you mean to lie there till the Second Coming?"

"Finish the job, damn you," Hugh growled.

"A fine fellow you must think me if you believe I can spit my wife's only brother without a second thought. Get up now, man, before I change my mind. If you want another fight, come challenge me at Broadhaugh. I'm too tired to accommodate you today.'' With that, he extended a hand to Hugh.

After a moment's pause, Hugh took it. When Quinton tried to heave him up, though, both men faltered, and in the end Hugh had to exert what remained of his own strength before he could rise.

Janet wanted to run up and hug them both, then bang their two stubborn heads together. Since she could do neither, she stayed where she was. Steam rose from both men. They were creating their own clouds of fog.

No one seemed to know what to say next.

Finally, it was Hob the Mouse who said practically, ''We'd best be getting home, master. The mistress is soaked through to her skin.''

Indignantly, Janet turned to him, but before she could speak, Quinton said, ''Aye,'' and then, ''Lads, get yourselves mounted. We'll ha' moonlight again.''

Janet stepped toward him.

''Jenny, you get mounted, too,'' he commanded. ''Do you need assistance?''

''I want to speak to Hugh.''

''Suit yourself, lass, but we'll wait only a moment. You are not the only one who is wet through, you know.''

As if she had complained! As if he really would dare leave without her!

She glowered at him but said nothing, fearing that he would order her to mount her horse at once and knowing that Hugh would support him if he gave such an order. Keeping these thoughts to herself, she nodded and hurried to Hugh.

''Are you hurt?'' she demanded. ''You hit the ground hard.''

''Don't remind me,'' he said, looking rueful.

His attitude amazed her. ''Hugh, you *must* be hurt. Is it your head?''

One of his men, overhearing, stifled a chuckle and turned hastily away.

Janet glanced at him, then turned back to her brother. ''I

didn't mean that the way it sounded, you know. It was just . . .
falling backward like that . . . you know."

"I do know, lass. It was a good fight, a fair fight. He's better
with a sword than I am, even worn to the bone as he must be."

"Aye, he can fight in his sleep, I think."

"Is that what he does in bed then?" Again the odd note of
rueful amusement touched his voice.

"Hugh!"

"Sorry, lass. Mayhap my brain *was* addled by that fall."

"I do not understand you, either of you. Only moments ago,
you wanted to murder each other, and now—"

"Not murder him," Hugh protested, "only take him back
to prison."

"Unfairly back to prison."

"Aye, perhaps. It is a moot point now unless Jamie will give
him back to Elizabeth voluntarily."

"You know that he will not, nor will she ask him to."

"Mayhap she will not, but she'll set up a screech over this,
you know. She could yet demand your husband's head on a
platter, or Buccleuch's. Anyone who cannot detect his fine hand
in this business does not know the man."

Janet bit her lower lip to stop the words of agreement in her
throat. How easy it was nearly to betray someone. Not that Hugh
was wrong, for she knew that he was quite right. Elizabeth, even
King James, would look for someone to blame, and they would
not settle for the Bairns. They would seek a leader, and any
suggestion that a woman had instigated the whole thing they
would reject out of hand.

Even without anyone to point a finger at Buccleuch, James
and Elizabeth would assume that the powerful Border lord had
led the rescuers, and no amount of denial would protect him
if they decided to charge him with the raid. He had known that
when he agreed to plan it, and he would accept the responsibility
because he would know that he could have stopped them. Much
as Janet might have liked to think that she could have rescued
Quinton by herself, she knew she would not have tried. Without

Buccleuch's reluctant agreement, she would have accepted defeat.

Hugh picked up his sword and turned to take his wet cloak and helmet from the henchman who held them.

"Hugh." His name leapt from her lips without thought.

He looked over his shoulder. "Aye, lass?"

"I am glad that you were not hurt."

He turned to face her, opened his mouth as if to speak, then shut it again and moved nearer, his long cloak hanging heavily from his arm. Raindrops glistened in his beard. His expression softened. "I'm glad, too," he said. Then, in a rush, putting a hand on her shoulder, he added, "Jannie, I've missed you. We've all missed you."

Hearing him call her by a name she had not heard since childhood brought tears to her eyes. She had not realized until that moment how much she had missed her own people, even this domineering brother of hers. It was unlikely that she would ever return to Brackengill to live, but she knew now that she did not want to go through life thinking of the people there as enemies.

"I . . . I have missed you, too, Hugh, and everyone at Brackengill. H-how are Matty and Sheila, and the others? And how does Jock's Meggie fare, and her bairns?" She did not want to tell him that she had spoken twice with Andrew, but she relaxed when he smiled.

"Meggie is at Brackengill, and young Andrew and Peter are helping there in the stable. They like the horses and seem to deal well with them."

"And Nancy?"

"Helps her mam. I missed the music, lass," he added. "Everyone grew so dour, you wouldn't know the place. At first, I just took Meggie and them off the farm because I wanted to keep Ned Rowan there and Meggie refused to marry with him. I was going to send her away, order her off to live with her kinfolk, but I knew that ragged lot of Grahams would set up a fearsome howl."

True enough, she thought, but how it must have angered him when Meggie refused to submit to his decree that she marry Ned Rowan. She said, "But why did you keep her at Brackengill?"

Again the rueful twinkle danced in his eyes. "She can bake," he said, "and she's a practical lass when all is said and done. And, too, once she set up as cook, with her bairns running all about the place, some of the others agreed to come back."

"Thank you for being kind to them, Hugh."

He shrugged. "Will ye come home now and again to visit us?"

"I shall have to ask Quinton about that," she said.

"Aye, I can see how you bow to his every wish and decree," he said dryly.

She smiled but said, "He is still my husband."

Hugh looked past her. "Aye, and if you have any respect for his temper, I'd advise you to get back on your horse, lass. He's beginning to look darker than last night's thunderclouds. Come to us when you can," he added. "You'll be welcome."

"Thank you," she said again, smiling warmly at him.

Turning on her heel with a lighter heart than she had felt in some time, she had walked several steps toward Quinton and Hob the Mouse before she realized that the rain had stopped and that Quinton was looking stormy. With a sigh, she quickened her pace. Clearly his victory over Hugh had not banished his anger with her. She would still have to answer for her disobedience, and at the moment he did not look as if he would be in any mood to be merciful.

Janet paid little heed to their route until the clouds broke and the warming rays of the sun peeped through. Then, seeing that they had reached the confluence of the Esk and the Liddel, she realized that Quinton meant to make for Hermitage rather than riding through Teviotdale to Broadhaugh. She did not know whether to be glad or sorry that she would be present when Buccleuch learned that they had succeeded.

Most of the Bairns and many of the men riding with Gaudilands and Todrigg turned off toward their own homes long before they reached Hermitage Water. Their party numbered less than a score when they arrived at the castle.

When they entered the great hall, Buccleuch stood to greet them, clearly forgetting about his leg in his relief at seeing Quinton. Janet thought he looked much better, but he was plainly in no mood to hear her say so. He did not even look at her, nor mention her unfeminine attire.

"Are you fit, then?" he demanded when Quinton approached him.

"Aye, fit enough," Quinton replied.

"He fought with Hugh," Janet said.

"And beat him," Quinton added.

"Did you? Well done. This is going to cause a damnable fuss, you know."

"Aye, Elizabeth won't like having her stronghold breached by fewer than a hundred men."

Buccleuch shrugged. "I'll wager that Scrope's account will number them at two or three thousand, if not more," he said.

Quietly, Janet said, "Hugh mentioned you, sir. He suspects that you were behind the whole thing. Will Scrope suspect the same?"

"Doubtless he will, but it makes no difference. Whether I planned it or not, Elizabeth will blame me, and Jamie will, too. They are my Borderers, lass."

Catching Quinton's eye, Janet said nothing more.

The two men talked for a time about the raid, but neither asked her any questions. Nor did either of them order her to leave, so she sat quietly until Quinton said, "We'll not stay, Wat. I want to get home to Broadhaugh."

Startled, she said, "You should rest! Should we not stay the night here at least, and return tomorrow?"

"I want to sleep in my own bed," Quinton said evenly. "I have thought of little else these past four weeks."

"You'll be safe here," she said.

"I'll be safe at home, too," he said. "Are you ready, or should you visit the necessary before we leave?"

Realizing that it would serve no purpose to argue with him, she prepared to leave. A number of his men were still in the castle, but if they were disappointed to be departing so soon, not one of them said so.

Except for a few white puffball clouds scudding overhead, there was little to remind them of the great storm. The air warmed as they rode, and the miles to Broadhaugh passed swiftly, almost too swiftly to suit Janet. She knew very well that one reason Quinton was in such a hurry to return was that he wanted to deal with her privately. The closer they got to Broadhaugh, the more nervous she became.

When the castle walls loomed into view, she glanced at him, but he did not look angry. His eyes were shining and his lips parted. He gazed at Broadhaugh, which, in the sunlight, looked like a golden crown on the craggy hilltop with the sparkling waters of the Teviot and Broadhaugh Water forming a rippling blue ribbon at the foot. Whatever Quinton had been thinking or feeling before, the only thing in his mind now was his homecoming. She felt herself relax.

In the bailey, he dismissed his men, giving orders only to be certain that some would maintain a normal guard on the ramparts while others got needed rest.

Janet spoke to one of the servants, ordering supper served as soon as the cook could manage to put together a decent meal for them. She turned back to find Quinton still talking with Wee Toad Bell and Hob the Mouse.

"Would you two like to stay and dine with us?" she asked.

Hob's lips twitched, and she saw that he avoided looking at Quinton. Wee Toad was not so tactful. With a glance at Quinton, he said hastily, "I'd best be getting on home to my own lass, mistress. She'll be fretting about me."

"Hob has to go, too," Quinton said. "He needs a good sleep."

"Right . . . that's right," Hob said.

She saw sympathy in his eyes.

Instantly, she straightened, giving him look for look. "Thank you, Hob, for all your help. Our venture would never have succeeded without you. You, too, Wee Toad. My husband is fortunate to have such loyal henchmen.''

Both men nodded gratefully. Then Hob said, '' 'Twas yourself wha' did the thing, mistress. We'd none of us ha' thought of taking Carlisle had ye no stirred us to do it. The master should be grateful to ha' such a brave lass all his own. I'll come in the morning for orders, sir,'' he added. Tucking his steel bonnet under his arm, he bobbed his version of a bow and left, with Wee Toad Bell scurrying after him.

Silence reigned for several moments before Quinton said provocatively, ''I wish I could be certain that I am still the one who claims their loyalty.''

''You know you are!''

''Aye, perhaps. Have you concocted that tale for me yet?''

''I have no need to concoct anything. You know perfectly well all that transpired. You talked the whole business over with Buccleuch, did you not?''

''Aye, and he told me he had no notion that you meant to accompany the lads to Carlisle. If I were not a kind husband, I would let you answer to him for that.''

''He told Hob to let me have my head,'' she said, seeing no reason to tell him that Buccleuch had also said that he would leave it to her husband to deal with her later. ''Moreover,'' she added thoughtfully, ''he did not seem angry.''

''Nay then, he was furious,'' Quinton said. ''I know him better than you do.''

That was true. Still, she did not think Buccleuch had been angry. ''He's got a fearsome temper when he's angry,'' she said.

''Aye, it's an inherited trait.''

There seemed to be nothing beneficial to say to that. ''We should go inside,'' she said at last. ''I told them to prepare your supper as quickly as they can.''

''Good, I'm famished. But first I want to wash the stink of Carlisle off myself.''

"Go on upstairs then. I'll send men up with a tub, water, and some soap."

He smiled, but there was little humor in the smile. "I don't need a tub, lass. The Teviot will serve me well enough. Why don't you walk with me? If you've still got your wee dagger, you can cut me a good switch whilst I'm enjoying my bath."

Prickles stabbed at her spine, but she would not give him the satisfaction of seeing that his words disturbed her in the least. Instead, calmly, she said, "Even in the Teviot, sir, you will want a bit of soap. And I'll warrant you would like some clean clothes to put on after wearing those things all these weeks. They look and smell like something that should be buried."

He shrugged. "I hardly notice the smell anymore."

She wrinkled her nose. "I will tell Tip to fetch clean clothing for you, and I will bring you soap. You go ahead down to the river. I'll find you."

He gave her a stern look. "You had better. If I have to come and find you, you'll be sorry to have put me to the trouble."

She looked right back. "I am not a coward, sir."

He smiled then, a real smile. "No, Jenny, you certainly are not. Go along now, and collect what you will, but bring it all down yourself. I'll be in the river."

She went quickly and soon found Tip, telling him that his master required a change of clothing. "Warm things," she added. "He's like to be chilled after swimming in the river."

"It's no so bad, mistress," the man said as he gathered the required clothes. "It's April now, the chill is off, and the sun is shining. Bairns ha' been swimming a sennight or more now, and them that dinna swim still like splashing about. They'll be in and out of the water near every day now till the snow flies again."

His words stirred an idea. Quickly snatching up the bundle he had prepared for her, she hurried back downstairs and out the postern gate, then down the hill toward the bend in the river, where Quinton had said he liked to bathe.

He was in the river, splashing childishly in a deep pool.

She waved. "I've brought soap. Do you want it?"

"Aye, toss it here. Let me see if you've got a good arm for throwing."

She threw it, and he caught it easily. He ducked his head under and came up shaking it. Drops of water flew everywhere, glittering in the sunlight. He lathered his whole head, then moved to shallow water and stood up, a gleaming wet, muscular god. Janet stared, thinking how much she had missed him. He had lost weight, and his body was pale everywhere. Even his arms, which had been deeply browned from the sun, had faded almost to match the whitest parts of him.

Remembering her plan, she wrenched her gaze from his still splendid body and soon spied the clothing he had shed in a pile near the riverbank. Shrubbery and May trees grew close to the river there, and she carefully tucked her bundle in the fork of one, where it would stay dry and out of sight. Then, strolling to the pile of cast-off clothing she began to gather it into another bundle, boots and all. Leaving only his sword and dagger, she turned away and walked back into the shrubbery to the thicket of trees. Glancing over her shoulder, she saw that he was still scrubbing, clearly enjoying himself, glad to be clean again at last. Smiling, she stepped back into the shrubbery, out of his sight.

Moving cautiously so that he could not tell from waving bushes exactly where she was, she moved upriver from him, listening, aware that he had already taken longer than expected to notice that she had gone. Clearly he felt safe from attack, even though they were out of sight of the castle ramparts. Had he been as alert as usual, he would have noted her movements the minute she turned away.

Insight stirred, and she wondered if he purposely was ignoring her to attend to his own needs. He probably thought that she was worried about whether he really meant to beat her, wondering if he would really make her cut the very switch that he would use. Doubtless he intended to keep her guessing.

By the time he shouted her name, she was far enough up the river to suit her purpose. Quickly she stripped off the male clothing she still wore and folded it in a neat pile on a warm rock, setting her boots and dagger beside it.

"Jenny," he roared, "answer me! Where the devil are my clothes?"

Managing a smile, pretending that she was not frightened half out of her wits, she turned and stepped into the water, instantly realizing that Tip's notion of warmth and her own were many, *many* degrees apart. But she was naked now, and if any of Quinton's men heard him shouting, the two of them would soon have unwanted company. She had to hurry.

Without sparing another thought for Quinton's anger or the temperature of the water, she plunged in and came up sputtering. The icy water took her breath away, and she realized that its temperature might chill her plan before she could put it into action. She could not let that happen. Swimming toward the middle, she let the steady current carry her downriver. The current was not particularly swift, for just there the river flowed wide over shallow sandbars on both sides.

She saw Quinton before he saw her. He stood near the riverbank in calf-deep water, hands on bare hips, glaring at the thicket of shrubbery as if his anger could force her to materialize out of thin air.

She could see that the current quickened not far beyond him, for there were rocks on the Broadhaugh side, and water foamed around them. Thanks to Hugh's teaching years before, she was a strong swimmer and she knew how to work with the current to keep from being swept away, but it would do her purpose no good to let the water sweep her too quickly past Quinton. If he had to chase her down the river, his anger would only increase.

She whistled and had the satisfaction of seeing him start. He looked right and left, then up the river, but his gaze passed over her because he was searching the banks of the Teviot. She whistled again.

"What the devil?" His voice carried easily to her ears. "Jenny?"

She waved.

"What the devil!" He stepped impulsively toward her, and either slipped or stepped into a hole, for he stumbled into the water and came up gasping for air. He quickly found his feet again, however, and dove after her. When his hands closed around her ankles from beneath, she screeched and tried to kick free.

He held her easily, and the next thing she knew, his hands were at her waist, and then he had turned, bringing one arm around her shoulders, so that her head rested against him. With a few strong strokes, he was in water shallow enough to stand again. His body measured itself against hers, and she leaned on him.

"Are you all right?" he growled into her ear.

"Aye, I'm fine."

"Where the devil are my clothes? For that matter, where the devil are yours?"

His hand moved to one bare breast, and she gasped. "Yours are yonder on the bank where those trees are. Mine . . ." She chuckled. "Mine are up the river. I thought only of surprising you, not of how I would get back to them."

"Faith, lass, I ought to beat you here and now. Was there ever before such an impulsive and foolish wench, I wonder."

"We should be in the water or out of it, sir. Did you lose the soap?"

"I did not. It is on that rock in plain sight. Do you want it?"

"Aye, since I'm wet. Those clothes I borrowed are not much sweeter than yours are."

"Then you can leave them where they are."

"Quinton! Would you have me parade through the bailey in my skin?"

"Don't tempt me, Jenny. You deserve whatever I choose to do to you." He moved to fetch the soap as he spoke, and she hunkered down in the water, since it felt warmer now to be in it and out of the breeze.

She hoped he was teasing her. Surely he would not make her walk naked back to the castle. Looking back toward where she had left her clothing, she wondered if the current was gentle enough to let her swim against it.

"Don't even think about swimming back," he warned, wading toward her with the bar of soap in one outstretched hand. "You'd only wear yourself out."

She reached for the soap, but he held it away, out of reach.

"Don't tease me, Quinton. This water is little more than melted ice."

"Then the quicker we get you washed, the quicker you'll get warm again. Stand up, lassie."

Involuntarily, she glanced toward the river bend and the thicket of trees that hid the castle from sight.

"No one will come unless I shout for them," he said. "Now then, you can stand up, or if you'd rather, you can go and cut me that switch."

"I left my dagger with my clothes."

"You can use mine." He waited, arms folded across his chest.

Slowly, grudgingly, she stood.

"Hold out your arms."

Glaring now, she obeyed him, and he soaped her arms, beginning with the fingertips of her left hand and lathering soap to her shoulder. Then he did the same to the right arm.

"You can put your arms down now, and turn around," he said.

Shivering, she obeyed. "Hurry up," she said. "I'll be a block of ice before you're done."

"Then we'll have to think how to thaw you out, won't we?"

The edge in his voice kept her silent while he lathered her back, buttocks, and thighs. Soon, despite the cold water swirling at her feet, the sun began to warm the rest of her.

"Turn again."

She hesitated.

"Now, Jenny. Turn and look at me."

She turned, eyes downcast at first, but when she saw that he was aroused, she looked up in surprise.

He was grinning. "What you do to a man is probably proscribed by the kirk, lass," he said. "Come nearer now."

She forgot the cold water, moving closer so that he could soap her breasts and her belly, thinking now only of the sensations he stirred in her body with the soap. He moved the bar lower, to the juncture between her thighs, and his fingers tickled and penetrated, making her moan softly and lean toward him. His free hand was at her right breast, sliding over the nipple, teasing it, moving to her throat and then down to the left breast. The bar of soap and the fingers of his right hand went on with their busy work, teasing her, making her squirm and arch against his hand.

"We've got to rinse the soap off you, sweetheart," he murmured. "I want to get inside where it's warm to continue this." With that, he picked her up and walked right into the deep pool with her, holding her close while he swirled water over and around them both to rinse away her soap. "Now, show me where my clothes are."

"Mine, too," she said as he helped her from the water. Walking gingerly over loose pebbles, roots, and other debris on the riverbank, she took him to the tree where she had left the bundles of his clothing.

"Here," he said, handing her the shirt that Tip had sent for him. "Put this on."

"But my clothes—"

"We are not going to tramp upriver to wherever you left them just to fetch those filthy clothes," he said.

"But—"

"No," he said flatly. "Tip can find them himself, and you are never to wear them again, Jenny. Do you understand me?"

"Aye, sir, but please don't make me go back naked."

"Then put on that shirt."

Reluctantly, she obeyed him, then chuckled when the hem of the shirt reached her knees and the ruffles on its sleeves hung inches below her fingertips.

"You'll set a new fashion," he said, chuckling, too.

"I am not decently clad, though," she said, "and what will you wear?"

"The doublet, breeks, and jacket will suffice. You can wear my netherstocks to keep your legs warm, and the cloak. No one will see that I am barelegged under my boots and breeks. Tip sent enough clothing for a midwinter's night."

"I told him you would be cold," she said as she sat on a boulder to draw the knitted hose over her legs. When she had tied them, he draped his cloak over her shoulders. Though knee-length on him, it hung respectably to her ankles. "I've got no shoes," she said. "If you'd just be so kind as to fetch my boots and dagger—"

"You won't need them," he said, fastening his breeks.

"I can't walk back in your netherstocks. They don't provide enough protection for my feet. Moreover, I'll snag them on things."

"You'd better not. That pair cost me five shillings!"

"Well, but—" The protest ended in a shriek when he scooped her up and tossed her over his shoulder. "Quinton! Put me down!"

"I cannot have you snagging my hose, sweetheart. Be quiet now. You're making my ears ring."

"I won't be quiet! Put me down, sir!"

In response, he smacked her backside.

Gasping, she fell silent at once.

"That's better," he said amiably. "You'd have had the garrison out with that screeching of yours. Now, see if you can behave yourself until we get back inside. I want to get warm again."

Comforting herself with the knowledge that her predicament could be much worse, Janet held her tongue, but she vowed that one way or another she would get even with him.

She shut her eyes when they entered the bailey through the postern gate, ignoring the shouts and laughter that greeted them. Quinton carried her inside and up the twisting stairs. When they reached the master's hall landing, she opened her eyes when a servant said, "Master, Cook says ye can ha' your supper straightaway."

"Tell Cook to keep it warm," Quinton said without pausing. "I've business with my lass before I eat."

Janet shut her eyes again tightly, fearing that if she did not she would see the lad's look of astonishment or—worse—his amusement at seeing his mistress carried in buttocks foremost like a prize of war.

Up more stairs they went until they reached Quinton's bed-chamber. Opening the door, he stepped inside, still holding her. "Go away, Tip," he said.

Wishing she were the wildcat he had more than once called her, so that she could growl and scratch, Janet scarcely breathed as she felt Tip pass them.

"Welcome home, master," he said politely. "Good evening, mistress."

The sound that issued from Janet's throat in reply sounded more like a growl than any human comment.

Quinton set her down. "I believe those are my clothes, sweetheart," he said. "Let's see now. Shall I watch you take them off, or shall I do it for you?"

Chapter 25

"Come, hold me fast, and fear me not,
The man that you love best."

Janet's knees felt weak, and she watched Quinton warily. "I do not know which you would prefer," she said, striving to sound calm and scarcely able to hear herself over the thunder of her heartbeat.

His eyebrows shot up. "So my preferences are important to you, are they?"

"Quinton, I—"

"Answer me, lass. Tell me how important my will is to you."

She could not follow his moods. Just before they left the river, he had seemed cheerful, but now she was not certain what he seemed. Swallowing, she reminded herself that he had been in prison for weeks. Not only that, but he had fought Hugh, had ridden from Carlisle to Hermitage and then to Broadhaugh, and he had taken a chilly swim before carrying her back to the castle. He could not have much strength left. Even if he were to punish her as he had threatened earlier, she would likely survive the ordeal with only minor bruising. And the plain fact was that he no longer seemed to be thinking about punishment.

Drawing a deep breath, she said, "You are important to me, sir, more than you can know."

She saw his lips twitch, and she could definitely discern a gleam in his eyes, but he shook his head. "I do not hear you saying, however, that my preferences are important to you."

Reassured by the twitch and the gleam, she took a chance. Meeting his gaze, she reached for the clasp that fastened his cloak at her throat, released it, and shrugged the garment off, letting it fall to a pool of dark wool at her feet. Then, holding his gaze, she lifted the hem of the shirt enough to reach the lace points for the baggy netherstocks, which she had simply tied round her thighs. A push sent first one then the other to join the cloak. Stepping out of the pool of clothing, she fingered the shirt lacing, then paused.

The hunger in his eyes was clear. He waited.

She did not move.

"Take it off, lass," he murmured.

"Perhaps." Still watching his eyes, she licked her lips invitingly and moved her hand from the lacing to touch her breast. Brushing one finger against a fold of the material there, she let her hand turn, so the backs of her fingertips brushed the nipple. She heard him inhale. The only other sounds were the movement of a curtain stirred by a breeze through the open window and the distant murmur of the river.

"Come here," Quinton said, his voice sounding lower-pitched than usual, as if it nearly had not made it out of his throat.

"Perhaps," she said again, her fingertips still moving gently as she reached with her other hand to untie the lacing. The opening of the shirt gaped. It was wide enough, she knew, to slip off her shoulders. Idly, she trailed her fingertips up toward her neck, playing with the narrow lace edging. With her other hand, one aglet at a time, she pulled the lacing free, letting the opening gape wider and wider.

Quinton watched, transfixed. She saw the tip of his tongue slip out to dampen his lips, and she saw, too, that he was becoming as aroused as he had been at the river. No longer was he looking into her eyes. He was watching her hands.

Slowly, slowly, she eased the shirt off one shoulder, then the other, letting it slip down her arms till the soft upper portion of her breasts showed above the lacy edge of the opening. Then, without another word, she lowered her arms and let the shirt slide down them and drop to the floor.

Quinton was practically panting. Already he was reaching for the buttons on his doublet. She smiled and stepped forward, naked. "Let me," she said.

His eyes widened, but he did not speak, taking his hands away and letting them relax at his sides. She unbuttoned the first button, taking her time, knowing that the longer she took the more aroused he would become.

He did not wait for her to finish. When she reached for the third button, he grabbed her and pulled her into his arms, hugging her tight and claiming her lips with his. He moaned deep in his throat when she responded, and a moment later, he picked her up and carried her to the bed.

She lay there and watched while he cast off doublet, breeks, and boots. His hunger for her was so plain that she wondered if he would fling himself on her and take her swiftly. Right up to the moment when he stood naked, looking down at her, she thought—even hoped—that he would, and her own desire ignited accordingly.

He climbed onto the bed, but then, with a wry little smile, he hesitated. "You should take care, lassie," he said, "lest you get yourself hanged for witchcraft."

"Art going to talk or make love, sir?"

Chuckling, he licked a finger and touched it to the tip of one breast.

She gasped and reached for him, but he leaned back. "It is my turn," he said.

Grinning, she said, "Do your worst, then. I'll survive it."

His hand left her breast and moved lower to her belly and below. She closed her eyes, letting the sensations flow through her until his lips and then his tongue replaced his fingers, and she could no longer remain still. Following his lead, she began to try things she had never even imagined doing before, and when he claimed her at last, she felt as if they had tempted the flames of hellfire, but she did not seem to care. All she cared about was Quinton and what he could make her feel.

He took her twice before they were sated, and when they lay back against the pillows at last, she felt as if every ounce of energy had drained from her body.

"I'll never move again," she murmured sleepily.

He did not answer for so long that she thought he might have fallen asleep. Then he said lazily, "Don't count on that."

"Again, sir? So soon?"

"Nay, but I've acquired a taste for your favors, lass, and I have missed you sorely. I'll want to savor them again very soon."

"Good." She did not have enough energy to say more, but when rhythmic scratching at the bedchamber door interrupted the silence, she started to sit up.

"Stay where you are," Quinton said. "I'll let him in. I've missed him, too."

He let Jemmy in, then got back into bed and, pulling her closer, drew the covers over them. A soft thump at the foot of the bed and a purr announced that Jemmy had joined them, but Janet barely acknowledged him. Her head had settled into the hollow of Quinton's shoulder, and a moment later she slept.

Janet awoke to a tickling tingle that radiated through her right breast. A teasing finger caressed its nipple, and the tingling flowed through her like a river in spate. As she stirred in response, warm lips touched hers, and she opened her eyes to see her husband's face against the gray light of dawn illuminating the room.

"Good morning," she murmured against his lips. "I don't suppose it matters, but I was sleeping."

"It is time to wake up," he said, as one hand moved over her belly and down, following the flow of the tingling river. His fingers teased for only a few moments before he was inside her and her body was stirring in response. When he relaxed again, he said, "This is a much more satisfactory way to wake up in the morning than Scrope's way. I am very glad to be home."

Deciding that her tactics had worked wondrously well, she said demurely, "Then may I take it, sir, that you have decided not to beat me after all?"

"I shall have to think about that," he said, "but I believe I can collect all you owe me without a switch. I will enjoy growing accustomed to certain of the things you did for my entertainment last night that you had not done before."

Feeling heat in her cheeks at the memory, she said, "Perhaps we can make an agreement then."

"It is not agreement we need, sweetheart, but practice."

Hearing laughter in his voice, she said, "We can do as you like, sir, but take care that you do not overstep your mark. Recall that my temperament is not placid."

"Thank God," he said.

"There is one thing that I should tell you," she said.

"While I am in this exceptionally good mood?"

"Aye. I talked a bit with Hugh yesterday after . . ."

"Aye, and . . . ?"

"And he misses me, he says. He would like me to visit Brackengill. He says that he misses the music and the laughter."

"And you, Jenny lass, do you miss Brackengill?"

"Not enough to want to return and live there, but I would like to visit from time to time, just to see that all is well."

"Do you trust him?"

"I don't know."

"Then we will think on it together and not make a decision straightaway."

She nodded. "That is a good notion, I think."

This accord between them continued; however, ten days after their return from Carlisle, a messenger arrived from Hermitage with a disturbing message from Buccleuch.

Sir Quinton and his lady were sitting companionably in the master's hall, while she mended one of his shirts and he looked over his accounts to decide whether to subject one of his fields to the plow. After hastily reading the missive and dismissing the messenger, he said, "Apparently, Scrope sent his own version of the raid to Elizabeth and she is demanding Buccleuch's head."

"Buccleuch?" Janet exclaimed. "I knew such a thing was possible, of course, and he did plan the raid. Still, it hardly seems fair for her majesty to be angry with him when she cannot know that he did and when he was not even there!"

"According to Scrope, not only was he there but he led the raid himself and did all manner of damage to Carlisle. Scrope told Elizabeth that Buccleuch was the fifth man into the castle, that he was actually heard to cry out threats to the garrison. Furthermore, Scrope wrote that there were five hundred in the raiding party, that they undermined the postern and got in and out before resistance could be made."

"He should be ashamed of writing such lies to his queen," Janet said indignantly. "None of that is really true."

"There's more," Quinton said with a wry smile. "I am said to have given my word not to escape, which certainly is not true, and he blames the Grahams—"

"The Grahams! Does he even blame Hugh?"

"Nay. At least Buccleuch does not say so, and I doubt that Scrope would. He says Scrope called the Grahams caterpillars who gnaw at their own countrymen and a 'viperous generation.' And," he added with a glinting look at her, "he suggests that it was a female Graham who learned the exact whereabouts of his prisoner. We have not yet discussed that particular venture of yours, have we, sweetheart?''

"Did Elizabeth write directly to Buccleuch?" Janet asked hastily.

"Worse," Quinton said with a look that told her he knew she wanted to divert him from the subject of that first visit to Carlisle. "She sent her complaints to Jamie, and apparently Jamie has suggested that Buccleuch should answer them in person."

"In person!"

"Aye. According to Buccleuch, who seems to be treating the entire matter as a jest, Elizabeth called him 'God's curse' and even suspects him of popish plotting. She demands that he be jailed forthwith."

"Godamercy, James will not cast Buccleuch into prison, will he?"

"Buccleuch does not think so. He believes that we can trust Elizabeth's ambassador, who is a shrewd and capable chap, to explain to her that Scrope understandably neglected to mention his own incompetence in representing himself as a mere victim of Buccleuch's villainy. I doubt that anything will placate her, however. A royal fortress was breached, after all. She will not easily forgive that."

"What will she do?"

"Most likely, she and Jamie will enjoy a debate that will occupy them for some months, but in the end his need to give her contentment may well result in his ordering Buccleuch to London to face her."

"Godamercy," Janet said again. "Well, if he goes, I must go with him."

"You will do no such thing!"

"But I must. It was as much my doing as anyone's, and so I must tell her."

"And what about me? Do I accompany you or remain safely at home?"

"You can't go!" In her haste to assume some of Buccleuch's

blame, she had not thought of that. "What if she clapped you into the Tower?"

"I suppose it would be better if she clapped my wife up instead."

His tone was sardonic now, and she knew that he was growing angry again. Swallowing hard, she held her tongue, unable to think of anything to say that would soothe him or make him understand her feelings.

After a long moment, he said, "What would you say to her if you did go?"

"You're teasing me now," she muttered resentfully.

"Perhaps, a little, but you have a habit, sweetheart, of acting first and thinking afterward, and once you get a notion in your head, it isn't easy to get it out again. Imagine yourself in London with Buccleuch. Imagine him facing Elizabeth, telling her that he did not lead the raid, that in fact it was Lady Scott who did."

"But he would not! Indeed, it was Hob the Mouse, and the Laird of Todrigg, and Gaudilands—"

"Just imagine it," he said sternly as he stood up and assumed a royal posture with his arms folded across his chest and his feet apart. "I shall be Elizabeth. What will you say to me after Buccleuch betrays your part in the matter?"

His eyes narrowed, and in that instant he looked as fearsome as any monarch might, and she saw how absurd her suggestion had been. She had never seen the queen, but she had heard much of her temper, and she could not, in her wildest fantasies, imagine the powerful Buccleuch offering his cousin's wife up as a sacrificial lamb.

"Lady Scott," Quinton said in that daunting, royal manner, "is it true that you led the Borderers who attacked my castle at Carlisle?"

"Aye, madam," Janet snapped, deciding to play his silly game and see how far he would take it. " 'Twas all my doing. The men rode because I asked them to."

The gimlet gaze narrowed even more. "Rise, Lady Scott,

and approach. One does not remain seated in the royal presence if one wants to keep one's head.''

Setting her mending aside, Janet got up and made a deep curtsy. What began in a sense of mockery, however, suddenly no longer felt like just a silly game. The Queen of England carried the power of life and death in the flick of a royal finger.

"Approach, Lady Scott," Quinton repeated softly.

Janet obeyed, coming to a halt a few feet away from him and trying to control fluttering nerves by reminding herself that it was just a game.

"You are our subject, are you not?"

Forcing calm, she said, "It is true that I am English by birth and breeding, *madam,* but I married across the line. My husband claims my loyalty."

"Very prettily said. Did your husband command you, then, to lead that impertinent raid against our castle at Carlisle?"

Janet hesitated, worried less about what an imaginary queen might think of her reply than what Quinton would think. She would not prevaricate, however. She said, "My husband commanded me to leave everything to Buccleuch, but when his diplomatic efforts failed, I took matters into my own hands."

"Indeed, madam. We wish to know how you dared to undertake such a presumptuous venture against the queen's peace, particularly when you acted in direct opposition to your husband's will."

Straightening, Janet lifted her chin and said firmly, "What does a woman not dare to do when her honor and all else that matters to her is at stake?"

The harsh look on Quinton's face eased, replaced by a reluctant smile.

"Well said, lass. Such a declaration might well sway Elizabeth. Indeed, Buccleuch could do worse than to say much the same thing to her when our Jamie orders him off to London to face her."

"You do think that will happen, then."

"Aye," he said. "She is a cantankerous old woman who

likes to get her way about things, and Jamie is determined to placate her for the sake of peace.''

"Do you not wish to placate Jamie?''

"I don't care a whit for Jamie's feelings,'' he retorted. ''My loyalty is to Buccleuch and to our Borderers. When Buccleuch wants peace, we will have it.''

"Here, too, Quinton? Will we have peace at Broadhaugh?''

He looked thoughtfully at her, and in that moment she knew that if the English Queen held the power of life and death in the crook of her little finger, Quinton held the power of happiness or misery in the twitch of an eyebrow. Her heart pounded, for she knew that his answer mattered more to her than she had thought it could.

He said, "Is it true that everything that mattered to you was at stake in Carlisle?''

"Aye, sir,'' she said quietly. ''I knew that my going would make you angry, but I could not sit meekly at home and wait for others to decide your fate. Are you still angry with me for taking part in the raid?''

"Lassie, how could I stay angry with you for saving my life? If our Jamie had ten thousand men possessing courage like yours, he could shake the firmest throne in Europe. You should know,'' he added gently, ''that already, whenever my men or Buccleuch's speak of the Carlisle raid, they speak of you as 'Janet the Bold.' Doubtless, they will soon be singing ballads about your exploits.''

"Does that mean,'' she said bluntly, ''that you will pay greater heed to my opinions in future, sir, and not simply issue commands to me?''

"Do you truly want peace, Jenny?''

"Aye,'' she said, sighing, ''I do.''

He pushed a hand through his hair, a boyish gesture of rueful irritation. ''I'll tell you true, lassie, you can make me as angry as I've ever known myself to get, and although the anger I felt when I realized what you had done has passed, I do not know that we will ever live in true peace. We're going to have children eventually, and I cannot imagine us agreeing on everything even without them.

Once we have them, it will be impossible. We're both of us too hardheaded and stubborn, and we both seem to fire up too quick. We're going to fratch, Jenny lass, and when we do, the rafters will quake. But I think we've both learned some things.''

"Aye," she said, "but have we learned enough?"

"We'll see, but I'll tell you this, lass. I love you as I never believed I could love anyone, and I know now that you love me. We have learned a bit about the art of compromise, and we can learn more. I'm willing if you are.''

She was quiet for a moment. He had offered no apology, but neither had he demanded one. Compromise did have its points.

"I'm willing," she said. "Oh, Quinton, I'm more than willing. I do love you so. Who would have thought that an Englishwoman and a Scotsman could care so passionately for each other?''

"Passion is but one way for strong feelings to reveal themselves, sweetheart, and passion can stem as easily from love as from anger. England and Scotland will learn other ways, too, I'll warrant. When Jamie holds the thrones of both countries, there will no longer be any Border, after all.''

"There will always be a Border," Janet insisted.

"Nay, lass, not when they blend us all into one country, but I don't want to talk any more about politics tonight, national or personal. Come here to me.''

"Are you giving me arbitrary orders again, sir?''

"I am, and you will obey them, madam, or pay the penalty.''

"What penalty?''

"You will see if you do not obey me." His eyes twinkled.

She lifted her chin. "I think, sir, that you must learn to put your orders more diplomatically. You should soothe me, and pay me pretty compliments.''

"I've no patience for soothing. I've a glib tongue when I require it—''

"Aye, and nearly talked yourself into a hangman's noose with it before we'd ever met," she reminded him. "What if I had not been at hand to save you?''

"My Bairns would have found me in time."

"As I recall, they were all still at home when we reached Broadhaugh."

He nodded thoughtfully. "That's a fact, right enough."

She grinned, then shrieked when he caught her arm and pulled her into an embrace. The shriek turned to muted chuckles when he kissed her, but she quickly responded to his passion. His lips felt hot against hers, and his hands moved over her body possessively, seeking ties and laces. In moments, her skirt and petticoats fell to the floor in clouds of lace and cotton. Her bodice soon joined them, then her stays. His mouth held hers prisoner until she stood in nothing but her smock. Then he straightened, but his hands moved teasingly over her breasts, making her gasp at the sensations that surged through her body.

"Bedtime, sweetheart," he murmured, scooping her into his arms only to kneel a moment later and lay her gently on the furry hearth rug.

"What if someone comes in?"

"My people know better than to interrupt their lord when he is engaged in important business." Rising, he cast off his doublet, stripped his netherstocks and boots from his legs, then stood a moment in his shirt, gazing down at her. "You are the bonniest lass in the Borders, sweetheart, on either side of the line."

"Aye," she said, smiling lazily up at him, "and you are the luckiest man, sir, to have Janet the Bold for your wife."

Chuckling, he removed his shirt and lay down on the rug beside her. "Show me how bold you are, sweetheart," he said. "I would have you serve me."

"More orders, sir? I would prefer that you serve me."

He raised his eyebrows. "I see that another compromise is in order."

"Compromise? But how can one compromise on such an issue?"

"I'll show you, lass."

And, to her delight, he did.

Dear Reader,

I do hope you enjoyed *Border Fire*. The inspiration for the story came partially from reading a host of Border ballads and partially from the author's interest in her own family's genealogy. The general plot is based on *The Ballad of Kinmont Willie*. The version used is cited in *Scottish & Border Battles & Ballads* by Michael Brander (Charles N. Potter, Inc., New York, 1975) and also in many other sources. Quotes used for chapter headings come from *Kinmont Willie* and also, generally when referring to the heroine, from *Hardyknute or The Battle of Larges* (same source). There is an exception, of course, in that the quote for the first chapter appears in various forms in numerous Border ballads. Apparently, the Liddesdale men ought to have stayed at home on more than one occasion.

Since Kinmont Willie was a real person, and definitely was not the stuff of which heroes are made, I took certain liberties, the greatest of which was letting the heroine do much that, in reality, Buccleuch or others did.

The general details of the raid are as historically accurate as I could make them (if one omits the presence of the prisoner's wife). The information came not only from the ballad, which is more dramatic than accurate in spots, but also from the following: *Border Raids & Reivers* by Robert Borland, *The Steel Bonnets* by George MacDonald Fraser, *Upper Teviotdale & the Scotts of Buccleuch* by Mrs. J. Rutherford Oliver (1887), and *The Border Reivers* by Godfrey Watson. I heartily recommend them all to anyone interested in learning more about the Border reivers.

Generally, I avoid long bouts of historical description, but in the case of Hermitage Castle, I wrote more than usual. I did so for the benefit of readers who, like me, fell in love with the Earls of Bothwell in Jan Westcort's wonderful books, *Border Lord* and *The Hepburn*. Realizing that they might like to know how a castle that figured so powerfully in Bothwell history had fallen into Scott hands gave me the little excuse I needed to include a good deal of its history.

I suspsect some of you might also like to know that young Wattie did achieve his majority before inheriting his father's position. He was 24 when Buccleuth died in 1611. Wattie was, in fact, the first of the Scott heirs to do that since 1470. He was also said to be the first of his line to die during a time of peace in the Borders.

Lastly, lest you think that some of the distances traveled by the Borderers seem too great, either when raiding or just going to the horse races, let me assure you that they are not. According to all sources, men and women of the Borders were intrepid riders and the Border ponies they rode were sturdy, sure-footed and fast! They are known to have traveled amazing distances on many such occasions.

If you enjoyed *Border Fire,* I hope you will read *Border Storm.*

Sincerely,

Amanda Scott

Please turn the page for
an exciting sneak peek
of Hannah Howell's
HIGHLAND VOW
from Zebra Books.

Chapter 1

Scotland—1546

"My fither will hunt ye down. Aye, and my uncles, my cousins, and all of my clansmen. They will set after ye like a pack of starving, rabid wolves, and tear ye into small, bloodied pieces. Aye, and I will spit upon your savaged body ere I walk away and leave ye for the carrion birds."

Sir Cormac Armstrong stopped before the heavy door to Sir Colin MacRae's private chambers so abruptly his muscles briefly knotted. It was not the cold threat of vicious retribution that halted him, but the voice of the one who spoke it. That soft, husky voice, almost too deep for a woman, tore at an old memory—one nearly ten years old, one he had thought he had completely cast from his mind.

Then doubt crept over him. There was no reason for that tiny Murray lass to be in Sir Colin's keep. There was also the fact that he had not had anything to do with the Murrays since they had so graciously aided him, nothing except to send them word that he had cleared his name and a fine mare for a gift. He could not believe the little girl who had saved his life was not still cherished and protected at Donncoill. His memory could be faulty. And how could Sir Colin have gotten his hands on her? And why?

"Weel, we ken that at least one of your wretched cousins willnae be plaguing us again," drawled Sir Colin. "That fair, impertinent lad who rode with you is surely feeding the corbies as we speak."

"Nay, Payton isnae dead."

Such deep pain, mingled with fervent hope, sounded in those

few words that Cormac could almost feel it, and he cursed. It was hard to recall much after so many years, but the name Payton seemed familiar. Placed side by side with that voice, a voice that brought forth a very clear memory of a tiny, well-scrubbed hand thrust out for a kiss made Cormac finally move. He was not sure what he could do, but he needed to know what was going on. This was clearly not a friendly visit and that could mean that the tiny Murray girl was in danger.

In the week since he had brought his young cousin Mary to Duncaillie for her marriage to Sir Colin's nephew John, Cormac had made an effort to learn every shadowed corner of the keep. He did not like Sir Colin, did not trust the man at all. When his cousin's betrothal had been announced, he had been almost the only one to speak out against it. He had not wanted his family connected by marriage to a man he had learned little good about.

After assuring himself that no one could see him, he slipped into the chamber next to Colin's. No guard had been placed at the connecting door between the two rooms. Sir Colin was either too arrogant to think anyone would dare to spy upon him or the man simply did not care. Cormac pressed himself against the wall next to the door and cautiously eased it open. He glanced quickly around the room he was in, carefully noting several places he could hide in the event that someone noticed the door was cracked open. One thing he had learned, and learned well, in two long years of running from the wrath of the Douglas clan was how to hide, how to use the shadows and the most meager of cover to disappear from view. Taking a deep breath to steady himself, he peered into the room.

"That untried lad is of no consequence now," snapped Sir Colin.

"Untried?" The scorn in that husky voice even made Cormac flinch. "Even the beardless amongst my brothers and cousins have had more women than ye e'er will."

When Sir Colin bounded out of his heavy oak chair and strode toward his tormentor, Cormac had to clench his fists tightly to stop himself from doing anything rash. To his relief the man halted his advance directly in front of the woman, raising his hand but not delivering the blow he so obviously ached to. Cormac knew he would have lost all restraint if Sir Colin had struck the tiny, slender woman facing him so calmly.

There was no denying what his eyes told him, although Cormac tried to do just that for several minutes. It was hard to believe that Elspeth Murray was standing in Sir Colin's chambers, alone and far from the loving safety of Donncoill. Cormac was not sure he was pleased to see that he had been right all those years ago. Elspeth had definitely grown into a disarmingly beautiful woman.

Thick, wildly tousled hair tumbled down her slim back in heavy waves to stop teasingly at the top of her slim legs. Her hands were tied behind her back and Cormac had to smile. Those hands did not look all that much bigger than they had on the day she had soothed his brow as he had lain bleeding in her father's dirt. Her figure was almost too slender, too delicate, yet just womanly enough to stir an interest in his loins. The way her arms were pulled back clearly revealed the perfect shape of her small breasts. Her waist was temptingly small and her slim hips gracefully rounded. Elspeth's face still seemed to be swamped by her thick hair and wide, brilliant green eyes. There was a childish innocence to her gentle, heart-shaped face, from the small, straight nose to the faintly pointed chin. The long, thick lashes rimming her big eyes and the soft fullness of her mouth bespoke womanhood, however. She was a blood-stirring bundle of contradictions. She was so close to the door he felt he could easily reach out and touch her. Cormac was a little surprised by how hard he had to fight to resist that urge.

Then she spoke in her rich, deep, husky voice and all hints of the child, all signs of innocence, were torn away. She became a sultry temptress from her wild, unbound hair to her tiny, booted feet. Cormac felt the sharp tug of lust. It struck as hard and fast as a blow to the stomach. Any man who saw her, heard her speak, would have to be restrained from kicking down the heavy gates of Donncoill to reach her. If his heart was not already pledged to another, Cormac knew he would be sorely tempted. He wondered if Sir Colin had simply succumbed to her allure.

"What? Ye hesitate to strike a lass?" she taunted the glowering Sir Colin, her beautiful voice heavily ladened with contempt. "I have long thought that nothing ye could do would e'er surprise me, but mayhap I was wrong."

"Ye do beg to be beaten," Sir Colin said, the faint tremor in his voice all that hinted at his struggle for control.

"Yet ye stand there like a reeking dung heap."

Cormac tensed when Colin wrapped one beefy hand around her long slender throat and, in a cold voice, drawled, "So that is your game, is it? Ye try to prod me into a blind rage? Nay, my bonny, green-eyed bitch. Ye are nay the one who will be doing the prodding here." Three of the five men in the room chuckled.

" 'Tis to be rape then, is it? Ye had best be verra sure when ye stick that sad, wee twig of flesh in me that ye are willing to make it your last rut. The moment it touches me, 'twill be a doomed wee laddie."

Sir Colin's hand tightened on her throat. Cormac could see the veins in the man's thick hand bulge. His own hand went to his sword, although he knew it would be madness to interfere. Elspeth made no sound, did not move at all. She kept her gaze fixed steadily upon Sir Colin's flushed face, but Cormac noticed her hands clench behind her back until her knuckles whitened. Cormac had to admire her bravery, but thought it foolhardy to keep goading the man as she was. He could not understand what she thought to gain from the man, save for a quick death. When Cormac decided he was going to have to interfere, no matter how slim the odds of success, Sir Colin finally released her. Elspeth gasped only once and swayed faintly, yet she had to be in pain and starved for breath.

"Some may try to call it rape, but I mean only to bed my wife," Sir Colin said.

"I have already refused you," she replied, her voice a little weaker, a little raspy. "Further discussion of the matter would just be tedious."

"No one refuses me."

"I did and I will."

"Ye will have no more say in this matter." He signaled to the two men flanking her. "Secure her in the west tower." Sir Colin brushed his blunt fingertips over her full mouth and barely snatched them away, out of her reach, before she snapped at them, her even white teeth clicking loudly in the room. "I have a room prepared especially for you."

"I am humbled by your generosity."

"Humbled? Oh, aye, ye too proud wench. Ye will soon be verra humbled indeed."

Cormac gently pushed the door shut as far as he dared, stopping just before it latched. A moment later he was in the hall again, using the shadows cast by the torchlight to follow Elspeth and her guards. Only once did someone look back, and that was Elspeth. She stared into the shadows that sheltered him, a frown briefly curving her full lips. Then she was tugged along by her guards. Cormac did not think she had seen him, but if she had, she clearly had the wit to say nothing. He followed his prey right to the door of the tower room, all the while struggling to devise some clever plan of escape.